Anthony J. Harrison

i

License Note

REDEMPTION DENIED - A Conor McDermott Novel.

Copyright© April 2019 by Anthony J. Harrison. All rights reserved.

ISBN: 978-1-7324081-4-2 (printed version)

ISBN: 978-0-4636949-2-3 (eBook version)

Cover design by:

Robert Gray of Channel Islands Design

http://www.channelislandsdesign.com

Editing service performed by:

Cecily Tartaglione of Red Pen Editor

http://redpeneditor.weebly.com

This book is dedicated to:

To those who are strong enough to see past the grief of losing a loved one, knowing that they are at peace with their decisions.

Chapter ONE

Aberdeen, Scotland

The echoes of guitars and drums pierced the surrounding neighborhood each time the doors hung open at the impromptu concert arena. A local organizer was subletting the formerly busy business which supplied goods to the oil derricks to showcase the talents of struggling musicians. Small groups who met outside were enjoying a smoke from a distance. The smells gave a keen observer insight between the legitimate-type of cigarettes and those which were not.

In the shadows of a panel van, the bloom from a butane lighter lit the blackness, highlighting the face of two young men huddled together. The conflagration, its blue tongue swaying in the dark, heated the end of the glass orb causing the dark crumb of hashish to boil.

Each of the men took turns hitting the pipe, inhaling the drug into their lungs to experience the high they sought. Across the car park, an angular figure watched their desperation to devour what he'd just sold them. He slipped the 100 pounds they'd given him into his wallet, delighted in the evenings take from the sell. Climbing into his car, he left them to their addiction, getting the red Ford Cosworth on to the pavement to head back to his flat.

As the night carried on, small cliques of people left the locale. One couple shuffled their way along the trail ahead of the group. As they trudged towards the car park, a young woman in the group paused. "Did you hear something?" she challenged her companions.

"My ears are still throbbing; I can't hear a thing," one companion responded.

Off in the shadows, she picked up the gentle whimpers of someone sobbing between faint gasps of breath. "It's coming from over there." She pointed out towards the panel van and grabbed her friend's arm and yanking him towards the noises. "Come on, it might be a wee one needing help," she said, her parental instincts coming to the forefront.

As she got closer, the young woman spun to subdue her partner. She angled her head to one side, straining to once again hear the cry in the shadows. Her curiosity quickly shifted to horror as she walked around the end of a truck and looked at two figures, one prone and one kneeling.

The unusual appearance of the casualty lying on the gravel made her gut twist inside, her limbs becoming soft and limp. The blood-sodden shirt and the pocket knife protruding from the young fellow's chest sent her screaming past her friend as she scrambled back to the warehouse.

"What did I do?" the second youth sobbed, looking at the gathering throng lead to the location by the earlier screams.

"You're truly fucked, fella," a drunken concert patron said, his slurred observation bringing a chorus of rebukes from those more sober.

Off in the distance, they could hear the howling of a siren growing stronger. As the emergency vehicles sped down the country road, the few cars drew to one side to allow them ample room to proceed to their destination.

***

Sergeant McKee stood off to one side while emergency personnel turned to the fatality. Glancing to her left, she looked at the suspect being put into the police van for transporting. A handful of constables were standing off, holding the remaining patrons of the concert at bay. Sergeant McKee glanced down at her notes as she turned back to the couple. "You said he was sobbing when you spotted him?"

"Yeah, as if a wee wane needing changed," the young woman said.

"But before that, what were you doing?"

"We were inside," the young fellow replied. "Our friends had just wrapped up their set, so we were going to the pub for a drink."

"Had either of you noticed the two men before this evening?" the constable asked.

"No."

"And you did nae meet up with them inside?"

"With over two hundred others milling about the concert, it was nae likely," the young man countered. "Besides, we came just for our friends, so we did nae arrive when things started."

Sergeant McKee jotted down the accounts, cussing to herself at the witness's brevity. Looking up from her notebook, she spied one of the forensic technicians from the lab walking towards her. "Fancy having you out and about this evening, Devin?"

Police Constable Devin Eakins ducked under the police tape as he drew closer to the sergeant. "I traded shifts so I could pick up an extra day on holiday next week," he replied. "Where's the casualty?"

"Over by the white panel van," McKee said, pointing to her right.

It took several strides to catch the victim lying in the shadows alongside the van. Turning back to the police van, he cried out to his colleague. "Andy, bring out two torch stands and the small generator, will you? Set them up so we've got one at the bonnet and the other near the boot."

Opening his bag, Devin pulled out a pair of cloth booties and slipped them over his Doc Martin boots. Next, he slit open a pouch containing a mylar coverall and stepped into it, securing the Velcro closure up to his collar. His final step before nearing where the victim lay was donning blue nitrile gloves and a nuisance mask.

"The chief inspector must appreciate your work, you know," McKee commented, watching the technician preparing for his macabre duties. "I've never been to an incident like this where he wasn't near."

Eakins turned to face the sergeant. "He left precise orders to the evening watch this week not to telephone him," the technician answered. "Besides, after the farce at the harbor last month, this is nae too awful." Slipping his mask over his nose, he shifted his scrutiny to the crime scene.

Under the harsh glow of the spotlights, Constable Eakins followed his training, singling out evidence while his colleague wrote what the constable was looking at. As he knelt next to the victim, the blood-stain now a darkening shade of mahogany congealing the texture of the shirt, Devin spied several things under the van.

"Andy, indicate the existence of a glass pipe and a butane torch next to the victim, 45 centimeters to the right," Eakins said. Taking a pair of forceps, he drew up the pipe to study it under the light. "Appears someone was handling it recently." His nose crinkled at the putrid contents as he pulled his mask from his face and sniffed the cylinder. "Probable use was marijuana or hashish," Eakins noted, slipping it into a transparent evidence pouch.

"And the torch?" his companion pointed out.

Eakins picked up the lighter. "Nothing unique about this." He released it into its own pouch, where he wrote in the blocks of information before passing it over to his associate.

Standing up, Eakins looked behind his fellow technician and noticed the absence of a pack. "Did you not consider to bring the camera, Andy? You consistently need to capture the scene, notably how the victim's body is before the para-types move it," Devin explained. "Go on... go fetch it. We've got a few more things to do before we can close up and grab a mug of tea."

Sergeant McKee stepped closer to Eakins. "Being a tad rough on the fellow," she whispered.

Eakins turned in surprise.

"What?"

"You sound a wee bit like the chief," McKee pointed out.

"Better for him to hear my preaching than Chief Inspector McIntyre," Eakins said. "I've still not forgotten my first time in front of him." He could easily recall the rebuke he was subject to by the forensics chief.

With the arrival of his partner, with camera gear in hand, Constable Eakins photographed the body. As he stepped around, he directed his younger partner to pick up the cloak covering the body one last time. "All right then, just one more item to deal with," Eakins said, passing the camera over and pointing to the open pack. "Hand me a large bag from the gear."

"Here you go," Andy said, holding up the clear evidence bag.

Devin pulled the sheet away to reveal the corpse that still displayed the protruding knife. With a solid grip around the handle, he tugged the weapon loose, a slight gurgling sound acknowledging its release from the body as fresh blood oozed from the wound, adding to the already congealed scab.

He used considerable care in sliding the knife into the bag, securing it closed, and annotating the date and time. Looking up, he nodded to the two medical representatives from the hospital who were standing by for him to finish. "All right, lads, he's yours for the taking," Eakins said.

Andy's complexion was even paler under the spotlights, a complexion that always occurred from watching the eventual step of pulling out a knife. Devin knew all too well his partner would seek to lose himself in a pint or two when the shift was over, seeking to expunge the vision. But it wouldn't help. It never did.

"Sergeant, the fella being piled into transport, is he your suspect?" Eakins asked, as he pulled off his gloves.

Sergeant McKee turned to the technician, having done her best not to watch him withdraw the knife. "Aye, it was that poor fella," she answered. "They were friends from what I picked up from the other sergeant," McKee said, walking alongside Eakin.

"I wonder what forces a person to use drugs if they're to become violent?" Eakins asked. "Surely we'll have evidence once someone searches both suspects and the lab conduct its analysis." Glancing back at the crime scene, he spotted his partner grapple with the lights, prompting him to end the exchange. "Looks like Andy forgot the lamps are a wee touch hot," he laughed, nodding at the technician waving his hand.

"Well, you better help him, or you'll be hearing from your chief if your partner shows up with burnt fingers," McKee said as she headed to her patrol car. She paused at the nearest officer speaking with members of a band.

"Is there a problem, Willie?" she asked.

"We need our van," one crew member replied before the constable could respond.

"The van our victim was discovered by is theirs," he explained, nodding to the five men and one woman gathered around him. "Seems they need to bundle up and make their way to Glasgow for an appearance tomorrow… I mean today," the officer corrected himself after a glance at his watch.

"Well, the body is gone and the scene's been documented, so they can move it now," McKee answered. "If you need anything else, I'll be back at the station writing my report," she replied with a wave before getting into the patrol car.

***

The day after the stabbing in North Aberdeen, Blayne Taggert sat on a cross-town bus. As he pulled out his e-tablet from his leather satchel, and began scrolling through the local news feed from the last month. Scanning various pages on the screen, he saw the notices on the recent run of murders associated with the drug trade. "Everyone needs a vice," he murmured reading the story.

Sliding his finger across the screen he stared at the photo of the police investigation. Occupying the center of the image was Chief Inspector McDermott and the forensics chief McIntyre conversing while a corpse was being slid into a van behind them. Taking his fingers, he enlarged the picture of Chief Inspector McDermott. "And what are you going to tell me?"

The driver announced the approaching stop. Looking up, Taggert could see the swaying masts of the service boats in the harbor. Sliding the tablet back into his bag, he hopped off the bus and skipped quickly across the street towards the docks. He recalled the information from the newspaper identifying the berth of the platform support vessel *(PSV)* *Nordic Supplier* being the Regent's Quay. Glancing at the placard affixed to the light post, he saw it showing the berth off to his left.

The few vessels still left in the harbor showed a kaleidoscope of colors, each reflecting itself off the water. As he walked towards a group of vessels, he cautiously sidestepped around a group of dockworkers moving pallets of goods into a container. "Can you point out the *PSV Nordic Supplier?*" he shouted at one.

"Second boat to your left," the roughneck answered.

With a wave he pushed further down the dock until he stood next to the orange and cream-colored service boat. For a minute he stood, closing his eyes trying to envision the last moments of his brother's life. The shrill blast of a boat's horn shook back to the present, when he noticed a young man standing on the deck of the vessel looking him over.

"Is the captain aboard?" Taggert shouted over the din.

"I'm the captain," the young man replied. "What is it you want?"

"May I come aboard?"

Malcolm Spiers looked warily at the man on the dock. Ever since he'd passed his exams in Inverness and was given command of the *Nordic Supplier*, it seemed he was always having to answer someone's questions. This fella didn't appear to be any different than the rest. "Mind your step," waving Taggert forward.

As a former Royal Marine, Taggert was all too familiar with being onboard a ship and it showed. Stepping over the rail, he quickly found his footing and made his way up the ladder to where Malcolm Spiers stood. "Thank you, Captain ...?" he said holding out his hand.

"Spiers, Malcolm Spiers," the Scotsman replied. "And you are?"

"Derek Foote," Taggert answered with the lie. "I'm working on an investigative piece for the Independent out of London," announcing his cover story for being onboard. "Seems the incident from last month quite possibly is linked to another in Liverpool."

Spiers had heard many angles to the shooting death from last month, something he wasn't present to witness. "I'd like to help, but I wasn't involved," he answered. "I was just recently handed command of the Supplier," acknowledging his recent promotion.

"Is there anyone I can talk with?" Taggert asked knowing several crew members were taken hostage by his brother.

"Second Officer Collins and Seaman Carr were both present when the incident took place," Spiers said. "Mister Collins is still recuperating from a spill he took last voyage, but Seaman Carr is onboard," reaching for the shipboard intercom. "Seaman Carr, to the bridge," he announced.

Moments later a spunky diminutive woman, clad in orange coveralls came trotting up the stairway. "You wanted to see me Malcolm?" she asked before noticing Taggert standing off to the side.

"Mister Foote is doing a story on the incident from last month and would like to ask you a few questions," the young captain said.

"There's nae much else I can say," Fiona replied. "I've given my statement to the police on what happened. I mean, I was tied up on the floor and didn't see anything outside the ship. The only thing I'll nae forget was seeing the fella's head explode like cooked haggis," shaking her head recalling Dunbar's death.

"But what prompted the police to shoot the assailant though?" Taggert asked scribbling on a notepad.

"The police did nae take the shot," Fiona said. "I saw a reflection come from the weather office a few moments before hearing the shooting," acknowledging someone other than the police killed Angus Dunbar.

Hearing this first-hand account of his brother's death sharpened Taggert's focus on what Seaman Carr was saying. "But the police reports don't mention an arrest of a shooter from the roof," he said. "Which would lead me to believe they are covering up the events,' scribbling again in his notepad.

"Well, all I can say is what I know," Fiona replied. "But there was a rumor going around about a group of mercenaries tracking this bloke down, but they've never been found."

Taggert spend the next ten minutes asking mundane and routine questions. Even as the seaman talked, he searched his memories of his brother trying to understand who could catch his brother unaware. Just like himself, Angus prided himself on the craft of situational awareness and keeping his enemies at bay.

"That's all I can tell ya 'bout what happened I'm afraid?" Seaman Carr said.

Taggert closed the notepad. "Your version helps in putting together a complete picture Seaman Carr," he replied. "If I have any more questions, I'll be in touch," shaking her hand before offering it to Captain Spiers. "Thank you, Captain," before exiting the bridge.

"God, I hope that's the last time I've got to explain to someone what happened," the young woman said as a tear rolled down her cheek.

As he noticed the emotions well up in his crewman, Malcolm stepped over to her, placing his arm across her shoulders. "I'll do my best to keep them away Fiona, I promise," pulling her close to his side.

Chapter TWO

Belfast, Northern Ireland

Chief Inspector Conor McDermott sat in the back of the patrol car, hardly acknowledging the scenery passing by the window. Rows of newly constructed brownstone tenements were gradually supplanting the earlier homes built before the conflict. Some of those homes remained, boarded up and embellished with graffiti from both Protestant and Catholic parties from previous conflicts. Others, though, sat blackened from being scorched, waiting their time for the wrecking crews.

"Is this your first time in Belfast?" the Police Service of Northern Ireland sergeant asked.

"Yes," McDermott answered from the back seat. He'd already cautioned his partner about speaking out of turn in front of the driver.

Several weeks prior, the chief inspector from Scotland Yard finally caught a break in the drug trafficking case. His partner, Inspector Andrew Fletcher, came across a conversation between a ship operator and a corporation in the Northern Ireland capital. Before he could track down the individual described in the call, protocol dictated he pay a visit to the chief constable.

As they approached the entrance, the sergeant glanced at the inspectors. "You'll need your identification handy when we get to the front gate." He turned the car towards the entrance. The headquarters of the former Royal Ulster Constabulary force looked more like a prison than the headquarters of the third largest police force in the United Kingdom. The guard who exited his station reinforced this perception, an HK sub-machine pistol at the ready.

"Afternoon sergeant," he greeted the driver before bending over to look at both McDermott and Fletcher. "Identification please, gentleman." As each inspector held up their identification, the guard, now joined by another officer outside the car on the opposite side, took their badges and scrutinized them. "Very well, inspectors. Welcome to Belfast." He waved the car through the gate which had slid open. Within moments, the sergeant had parked and was leading them to inside to meet Chief Constable Rooney, the current appointee.

"Where's the loo?" Fletcher asked.

"To your right, just over there… the second door," the sergeant replied, coming to a standstill. "You too?" he asked with a glance at McDermott.

"Aye, better now than later," Conor replied, following his partner through the door.

Even though a direct flight from Aberdeen would have been just over an hour, Miss Sinclair booked the two inspectors through London. This added three and a half hours to their morning of sitting around waiting for flights. And McDermott was not in a mood for being patient.

"Do you think their superintendent will be forthcoming with information on the company?" Fletcher asked as he washed his hands.

"I'm no sure of anything," McDermott replied, tearing the paper towel to wipe his hands with. "But be mindful on what you say; they're a wee bit edgy when dealing with Metro politics." he warned, alluding to London's manner of handling Belfast issues.

As both men exited, the sergeant led McDermott and Fletcher to the office for Chief Constable Darcy, the current head of the PSNI. Walking through the outer office, a secretary stood to greet them as they entered. "Mister Darcy will be with you in a moment."

Fletcher looked at the wall, its surface adorned with names and pictures of former Royal Ulster Constabulary officers that died in the line of duty. He noted with an odd curiosity the dates all preceded the "Good Friday" Agreements, symbolizing the end of the fighting between the Protestants and Catholics.

A chime from the intercom interrupted both inspectors as the secretary announced the senior officer was ready to see them. As she opened the door, McDermott stepped in, followed by Fletcher. "Afternoon, gentlemen," Patrick Darcy greeted them, waving to the chairs positioned in front of the desk. "Please have a seat."

The clutter on the desktop of Northern Ireland's chief constable comprised of two stacks of files, while a spent tear-gas canister held a bevy of pens. Sitting behind him on a credenza were three framed photos, each one a reminder of past events.

"Someone can see this visit as a historic event, don't you think, gentlemen?" Darcy began. "Consider it. I mean, when has Metropolitan Police ever reached out to the PSNI for help in a national matter?"

"Mister Darcy, I'm not one to dwell on the historical significance of the matter," McDermott replied. "I just want to get the bastard responsible for moving drugs that caused the deaths of six individuals to date." His frustration was already starting to show. "Our investigation has identified a firm here in Belfast, and we're keen on getting answers."

Darcy unfolded a letter sitting on his desk. "I understand your desire to close the case, Chief Inspector McDermott," he said. "And Chief Superintendent Collingsworth's letter was clear on the matter of your investigation. But I'm concerned about the lack of detail in which firm you intend to raid."

McDermott shifted in his seat while Fletcher blinked at the term Darcy used to describe their visit. "What do you mean by a raid, sir?" he asked.

The Ulsterman glanced back and forth at each of the Scotland Yard inspectors. "Most of the firms here in Belfast, hell, in Northern Ireland, won't be very welcoming if they feel they're under investigation by an outside entity," he explained, taking a sip of his coffee. "Which firm is it, anyhow?"

Before Fletcher could answer, McDermott spoke ahead of him. "It's identified in the communication as Callaghan and Higgins Limited," he sighed. "And the records show someone answered the call here in Belfast."

"And what sort of business are they involved in?"

"Andrew, your notes," McDermott motioned to his partner.

Fletcher already had his pad out, flipping pages. "The firm is an up-and-coming pharmaceutical supplier with its headquarters in Dublin and production facilities in Limerick." He looked back up when he finished reading his notes.

"And why are you in Belfast then? Shouldn't you be having this conversation with the Garda Síochána at Phoenix Park in Dublin? The last thing I want to see is trouble being created by Metro and then left for me to finish. You understand, don't you, Chief Inspector?" he asked with a stare at McDermott.

"Our investigation in Aberdeen has led to a firm here, not Dublin," McDermott replied.

Stabbing the call button, Darcy waited a few moments for his secretary to answer.

"Yes, sir?" came the woman's response.

"Noreen, please collect all the information you can on Callaghan and Higgins Limited, but just for here in Belfast," he said.

"Yes, sir," she answered before the unit went silent.

"Noreen is efficient, so I don't expect it to take her long. In the meantime, what say you read me in on your case, Chief Inspector McDermott," Darcy said. "It'll help in determining what type of support I need to muster when the time comes around."

Over the next hour, McDermott recalled the events which led he and Fletcher to Belfast. Chief Constable Darcy was a good listener, allowing McDermott to speak on the matter, interrupting only when he wished to jot down a detail or two.

"Just before trial, the captain admitted arranging for a container of hashish to be transported from his boat in Aberdeen to Glasgow," McDermott explained. "And we believe it ended up here in Northern Ireland."

"Hashish? Is that all?" Darcy scoffed. "We've got bigger problems with heroin here than just some refined marijuana." The opioid crisis plaguing the nation wasn't a secret to any of them. "Not to mention Nicaraguan immigrants coming for IRA training who were peddling their cocaine." The Sandinista rebels and their terrorist tactics were coming to learn bomb-making and their terrorist tactics.

Before the conversation could continue, a knock at the door interrupted them. "I've got the information you requested, sir," the secretary said, handing over a single sheet of paper.

"Thank you, Noreen," Darcy replied.

"And you've twenty minutes before evening prayers," she reminded him as she closed the door.

Fletcher tilted his head to one side, raising his eyebrows raising a fraction. "Evening prayers?" he asked.

"Yes, Inspector. I make it a habit to meet with the leaders of each watch section twice a week," Darcy said. "You see, when I was a young constable on patrol, my superintendent always ended the briefing sessions with a prayer." His eyes closed in remembrance. "Not solely for our safe return, but for those before us who didn't. I've never forgotten how dangerous this job is and how comforting a moment of reflection can set a man's mind at ease."

Darcy changed the subject and looked over the printout from his secretary. "Seems there is just one business listed in the downtown district that matches your communique, McDermott." Glancing at his watch, he suspected the patrons of the firm would have left for the day. "You'll have the services of Sergeant Kennedy. He'll see you to your hotel, and then we can prepare for your visit in the morning." Rising from his chair, Darcy motioned to the door. "If you'll excuse me, I've got a briefing to attend."

As both inspectors came to their feet, McDermott held out his hand. "We appreciate your help, Mister Darcy," keeping his eyes fixed on the senior officer.

"Here's to a successful visit then," he replied shaking Conor's hand and then Fletcher before leading them into the hallway before looking at McDermott. "Sergeant, see someone settles these gentlemen in at their hotel and arrange for their transport in the morning, say seven o'clock?"

"Aye, seven is fine with us," the Scotsman answered, following the sergeant out to the car park.

***

Stabbing out his second cigarette of the morning, Sergeant Kennedy stood outside the hotel, his breath creating wisps of condensation in the early morning cold. "You have a pleasant night?" he asked McDermott and Fletcher as they exited the building.

"Aye, it was nae bad," Conor replied, "as long as you can put up with screaming kids and newlyweds humping," he teased, climbing into the front seat of the patrol car.

"I slept like a lamb," Fletcher muttered to himself.

Kennedy held out a folder for McDermott to take. "Mister Darcy had the night watch prepare this for you."

With the folder in hand, he opened it to glance at the contents. Inside was a printout with the address for Callaghan and Higgins

Limited in Belfast, but it further included locations in Dublin and Limerick.

"No names?"

"Guess not," the sergeant answered, maneuvering the car through traffic.

McDermott held the folder over his shoulder for his partner to take. "Andrew, keep ahold of this will you? Make sure it gets filed once we get back to Aberdeen."

"I've got a quick stop at the barracks to pick up Constable Flynn, then we'll be on our way," Kennedy replied, mentioning the police station in Knock.

"Aye that'll be fine," McDermott said, his gaze focused on the road ahead of them.

After a brief drive, they saw Flynn standing outside the gated station, his hand in the air. While the car came to a stop, the officer noticed he'd be relegated to the back seat as McDermott occupied the front next to Sergeant Kennedy.

"Morn' sergeant," Flynn greeted his partner. "Eric Flynn," he announced to Fletcher, holding his hand out to the inspector.

Fletcher reciprocated the greeting in his reply. "Inspector Andrew Fletcher, Scotland Yard."

Flynn tapped McDermott on the shoulder while offering his hand in greeting. "And you're...?"

"Chief Inspector McDermott," he answered with a brief nod to the young officer, keeping his gaze fixated on the road, noticing the buildings growing taller.

"So, what's the drill for this morning?" Flynn asked.

"You and Sergeant Kennedy will assist us as directed," McDermott said matter-of-factly. "Inspector Fletcher and I will conduct our interviews with the staff; you two just need to be visible so your citizens don't get the wrong impression."

The city center of Belfast was a mix of old and new structures. One of the tallest buildings that dominated the skyline was the Lagan Boat structure. Its circular I covered in glass reflected the sun across the waterfront it overlooked.

Sergeant Kennedy pulled up to the entrance, and the valet service stepped aside after noticing the PSNI markings on the car. McDermott took notice of a vintage Jaguar parked a few meters ahead, in a spot of privilege.

"Remember, Andrew, we need to establish a motive for the firm receiving the communique before anything else," McDermott said as they walked through the glass entryway. Approaching the central desk, he saw two uniformed guards watching him stroll through the open door.

"Morning, gentlemen," McDermott said. "Could you tell me which floor Callaghan & Higgins is on?"

"Twenty-first floor," one guard said. "Take the second lift from the right to bypass the first ten floors," he explained, pointing out the express elevator. In less than a minute, the four officers stepped out of the elevator and stood outside the office door.

"No time like the present," Fletcher said, opening the door.

The outer room was furnished like most businesses, with moderate-priced desks and chairs taking center stage. Behind one, an attractive woman sat talking on the phone. Erin Malone noticed the four men enter while engaged in her phone conversation. Before placing her hand over the phone, she asked, "Can I place you on hold for a moment?" to the person on the other end of her call.

Sitting up in her chair, Erin looked up at the disheveled Scotland Yard inspector stepping to the front of her desk. "Can I help you… gentlemen?" she asked, glancing between the other officers.

"My name is Chief Inspector McDermott," Conor said. "I'd like to see your superior if they're in this morning?"

"One moment please," Erin said picking the phone up again. "Ma'am, can I get back to you later this morning? Thank you." She quickly hung up the call before turning back to the men. "Now Inspector, you mentioned wanting to speak with my superior, is that correct?"

With a heavy sigh, McDermott answered the young woman. "Yes, you're correct." Rocking on his feet, he continued. "Are they in?" he asked, clasping his hands behind his back.

Just then, a young Irishman bolted through the office door carrying a paper sack in one hand while balancing two cups in the other. Noticing the two uniformed officers in Kennedy and Flynn, he came to a stop, unsure why the constables were present in the office.

"And who are you?" Sergeant Kennedy asked, surprised by the young man's entry to the office.

"Geoff... Geoff Brennan," he said. "I'm the driver for Mister Higgins, why?"

McDermott and Fletcher shared a glance between them hearing the driver use their suspect's name so openly. This innocent revelation provided the Scotland Yard inspectors with a concrete connection between their drug trafficker and the captain of the Nordic Supplier. Before further questions could be asked or answered, one of the inner office doors swung open.

"Erin, could you see to..." the occupant asked. As he noticed the police officers, he held the rest of his statement. Shifting his gaze from the two officers to McDermott and Fletcher, he asked his next question. "Am I interrupting something?

McDermott stepped towards the man, his slim yet athletic build visible under his Armani dress shirt. "It depends on what your status is with this firm. And your name is...?"

"Mister Connelly. And you are...?"

McDermott pulled out his identification. "Chief Inspector Conor McDermott of Scotland Yard." Tilting his head towards Andrew who stood behind him, he continued. "And this is Inspector Fletcher."

Michael Connelly wasn't surprised on most occasions, but the sudden appearance of Scotland Yard in his office had come close to disproving it. He fought hard to keep his expression neutral in front of the inspectors, though he felt his palms becoming damp from the awkward situation he was in.

"We're hoping to discuss several of your business transactions from the past several months," McDermott said. He was reluctant to say anything of substance in front of the officers with PSNI.

"We can do that in my office," Connelly answered, waving his hand towards the open door. "Erin, hold my calls for the time being, will you? And see to these officers." He nodded to Kennedy and Flynn before following Inspector Fletcher into his office and closing the door.

"Yes sir," the woman said. "Would you like coffee?"

As Connelly showed the inspectors into the private office before closing the door, the three men stood in awkward silence until the Irishman invited them to sit. "Please." He waved his hand at the vacant chairs. "So, what can I do for Metropolitan Police this morning?"

McDermott sank into the wing-backed leather chair, an audible whoosh of air escaping the cushion as his body settled. He shrugged his shoulders before grasping his hands together, placing them on his lap. Clearing his throat, McDermott began his questioning. "What business do you engage in outside of Belfast, Mister Connelly?" he asked, glancing at the artifacts behind the executive.

"Callaghan & Higgins is a growing pharmaceutical company inspector," Connelly recited. "We're working hard to establish clients throughout Britain and Ireland. With global firms like Amgen, Bayer, and Pfizer to compete with, we need to go where the demand for innovative medicine exists," he explained as he reached for his coffee. "How rude of me," he exclaimed. "Would either of you like a cup?"

"No thank you," McDermott replied. Returning to his questioning, Conor continued. "Would part of your business plan also include a venture in Aberdeen?"

Connelly's stomach twisted at the question. He covered his mouth, feigning a cough, before answering. "Like I mentioned, Inspector McDermott, we're working to establish our markets throughout the isles, which includes Scotland."

McDermott sensed this level of questioning would not provide him with the answer to the one eating him inside. Taking in a deep breath, McDermott took a different tactic. "And what of your man Higgins? Is he one of your traveling salesmen?"

Connelly leaned back in his chair and chuckled.

"You find my questions amusing, do you?" McDermott asked.

"I apologize, Inspector," Connelly answered. "You see, we don't have a salesman by that name. However, what you've done is mentioned the name of my deceased grandfather. He and his partner, Rubert Callaghan started as chemists in Dublin before committing themselves to build up the firm." He nodded towards the black-and-white photograph across the room.

"But just a few moments ago in the outer office, your man Geoff said he drove for a Mister Higgins," Fletcher said, interrupting McDermott's questioning of the executive.

Once again, Connelly failed to suppress his amusement.

"You'll excuse me for mentioning this," McDermott said with a touch more force in his tone, "but I'm nae seeing the fun in this," He leaned forward into Connelly's space. "I'm here investigating several capital offenses and in the act of one those, it identified your business."

The cold stare from McDermott caused the Irishman to falter before responding. Collecting himself, Connelly leaned forward against the desk's edge. "You must excuse me for thinking this was a lark, Inspector," Connelly said. "When I was younger, many of the older workers would mistake me for my late grandfather." He pulled a framed photo from the sideboard behind him and pointed out one of the gentlemen. "As you can see, I had a close resemblance to him when he was younger. So, they called me 'Mister Higgins' just as they did with my grandfather," he explained before returning the photo.

"Rather convenient for your sake," McDermott muttered under his breath. "If that is the case; your grandfather passing away, that is, why keep his name on the business?"

"He and Rubert worked very hard to establish what there is today, I'll not shame him by asking for someone to remove it. Besides, I've no say in the business other than to keep production and distribution moving," Connelly said.

"Even being a family member, you've no standing in the business?"

"Oh, I've got a share of the profits when they occur, but I also share in the losses, too," Connelly explained. "But I'm not a voting member of the board if that's your question. Those privileges still belong to my mother."

"And what of your employee, Mister Gilmore?" Conor asked.

Connelly sat, hoping the inspectors couldn't see the muscles in his face tense at the question about his absent barrister. It was going on three weeks since he last heard from Sean and his disappearance was wearing on him.

"Mister Gilmore is not under the employment of the company, per se," Connelly answered. "I call him upon on occasion to review litigation regarding distribution rights, though, since that is his specialty."

Fletcher leaned over and pointed to a name on his notes to his partner: *Alistair Hunt.*

McDermott nodded, planning the questions in his head about the crime syndicate boss being held in the isolation of a cell at HMP-Barlinnie outside Glasgow. Before he could press on with them, a knock on the door interrupted the conversation as Connelly's secretary entered.

"I'm sorry for interrupting, sir," Erin stammered, embarrassed for causing the intrusion. "But Mister VanHoorst is on line 2. He said it was urgent that he speak with you."

Michael Connelly nodded to the young woman. "It's okay Erin; I'll take the call." Looking at the two inspectors, he continued. "If you'll excuse me gentlemen, but I have a business to attend to." He rose from his chair and showed them to the door. It was clear the meeting was over. "I do need to take this call gentlemen, please excuse me."

McDermott and Fletcher walked out of the office, with Conor turning to the Irishman. "We'll be returning," he promised, nodding for the two PSNI officers to follow behind.

The four men rode the elevator in silence to the ground floor. As he stepped out, McDermott pulled his partner aside. "Give us a wee minute, will you, Sergeant?" he asked while he and Andrew walked in the opposite direction. Stepping outside the building, he and Fletcher faced the waterfront.

"Something wrong?" Fletcher asked as he shielded his eyes from the glare of the window.

McDermott glanced down at the murky river below and grasped the handrail along the walkway. "Something does nae seem right with this fella."

"Is this your gut instinct again?"

"You did nae notice the Foreign Legion device on his desk?"

"Having a trinket on your desk doesn't mean you're a former member of an elite fighting force, Conor," Fletcher replied. "You see nothing from my days as a Royal Marine on our desk, do you?"

"Not in Aberdeen, but you've got a few back in London, don't you?"

"So?" Fletcher replied. "What makes Connelly out to be different?"

McDermott scuffed the concrete under his feet while contemplating his partner's question. He couldn't put a finger on what made him consider Connelly an adversary. But this brief encounter with the Irishman gave Conor the impression something wasn't right. And his gut instinct only reinforced the feeling.

"Come on, let's see if we can catch an early flight." He tugged his partner's elbow, turning away from the water and strolling toward the waiting police car as he contemplated the next move in their investigation.

Chapter THREE

Michael Connelly watched the four officers shuffle out of the office before he mentioned anything. The hairs on the back of his neck had stood on end when the haggard-looking inspector with Scotland Yard mentioned his missing barrister, Sean Gilmore. "Erin, could you please start a fresh pot of coffee?" he asked as he as he returned to his office.

"Yes, sir," she replied before heading to the small kitchen area.

Settling in his chair, Connelly picked up the phone while selecting the flashing light on the panel. "Good morning, Kurt," he replied in clipped Afrikaans to the man on the other end of the call. "What a pleasure to be hearing from you, my friend."

The weapons dealer and former mercenary from South Africa sat huddled in a small office within his warehouse. The building, a massive corrugated-metal structure with three large delivery bays, shook from the wind. Along with the gale, rain beat furiously outside as an early spring storm passed over the tip of the continent.

"Michael, there's been a setback," VanHoorst said. "The Turkish police raided one of my suppliers last month. It appears I'll be short fifty trigger mechanisms to complete your order."

Connelly swiveled his chair so he could face the waterfront of Belfast. "I appreciate your honesty, Kurt. As it is, I'm behind schedule myself. Still, I hope to regain it in the next few weeks," he said. Thinking back to the call from his manager Liam, he knew the creation of the drug and anecdote were still months away.

"So, are we in agreement we continue with our transaction?" VanHoorst asked. The agreed price of the weapon supply was one and a half million rand, and he did not want to lose it.

Connelly squinted as a ray of sunshine burst through the morning cloud cover and stabbed at the office building's exterior. Turning away, he blinked several times as he tried to regain his focus from the sudden light. Thinking about the consequences tied to different scenarios, the Irishman returned his focus to the call. "Yes, our agreement is still in place." *It'll give me time to make other arrangements seeing Sean is not around*, he thought. It was the barrister who contacted the Algerian, Nazim Aziz about transporting the assault rifles from Africa to Ireland early in the year.

A sudden gust rattled the overhead windows lining the warehouse perimeter, causing Kurt to jump. Looking out the office window, he watched another gust of wind force a bay door to cave in, its rollers coming off the tracks secured to the walls. "I've got to go, Michael," he said before hanging up.

Connelly looked at the phone, its buzzing the only indication that the call was over. "Au revoir, mon ami," he said, placing the phone back in the cradle. Walking around his desk, he noticed the door open. Erin was bringing in his coffee.

"Sorry for the delay, Mister Higgins," she said as she filled his cup with the fresh brew. The aroma of the Jamaican Blue blend as it rose from the carafe caused her nose to twitch and wrinkle.

"I see you're still not fond of the coffee," Connelly chuckled.

"No, sir," Erin answered, setting the cup in front of her boss. "I'm a tea drinker, just like all the women in my family. Will there be anything else?"

"No, I'll give you a ring if I need anything."

As Erin left the office, Connelly blew across the surface before he took a sip, cautious not to burn his tongue. Closing his eyes for the moment, he savored the simplicity that drinking the coffee provided. Each fresh cup allowed him to calm down and refocus on his business.

"Chief Inspector McDermott," he said aloud while sitting up. "What has he and Scotland Yard found out about the operation, I wonder?" Pulling open his desk drawer, he pushed aside several files until he exposed a folder tied closed. As he opened it, he extracted a notepad with a dozen pages already rolled over the top.

The last entry described the effort to move the container of hashish from Aberdeen to Glasgow. "Sean threw you a morsel with the other boat and you took the bait," he mused as he read the previous page. "But it wasn't enough somehow," drumming his fingers on the desk. "You weren't happy with finding it, so you're not satisfied, are you?"

Connelly pulled open a smaller drawer and grabbed the cell phone that lay inside. As he entered his security code, the screen lit up where he could select a list of contacts. Connelly knew he needed Taggert, but he wasn't sure on what he wanted him to do at the moment. Reaching his name, he pushed the small icon resembling a phone and listened to the tone.

The Hotel Café situated in central Aberdeen was noisy as several university students acting as busboys and wait staff carried bins of dishes cleared from now vacant tables. Sitting by himself, Blayne Taggert was busy reading the Press-Journal article on the local fishermen facing quotas on their mackerel when his cell phone rang.

As he picked up the phone, the waitress stepped alongside his table. The fragrant steam rushing up from the hot platter of his breakfast greeted him. Nodding his thanks to the waitress, he answered the call. "Hello?"

Connelly heard the young man answer after the fourth ring. "Good morning Mister Taggert. I hope I didn't catch you indisposed, did I?"

The lilt of the Irishman's accent gave Taggert a clue who the caller was. As he cleared his throat, he answered him. "I was just settling in for breakfast, Mister Connelly," came his reply. "I assume this isn't a social call; so, what task am I doing for you today?"

Connelly was surprised at the directness the Scotsman answered. Hearing it almost aggravated him to the point he wanted to lash out. Mentally ordering himself to calm down and relax for the moment, he continued. "Earlier this morning, someone visited me. They identified themselves as inspectors from Scotland Yard," he said. "They asked about an incident in Aberdeen, so I'd like you to find out how much they know about the situation."

"What are their names?" Taggert asked, stacking portions of egg on top of some blood sausage. As he stabbed the fork through his food, Taggert listened to Connelly. His head leaned to one side, cradling the phone between his shoulder and ear and allowing him to tear his biscuit in half.

"The senior man is McDermott," Connelly replied. "His partner goes by the name Fletcher. This McDermott character seemed to be out of his element. He relied on the partner for his information, which leads me to think he'd be the easier mark of the two. I'd look into his affairs first." Conor's weathered field-jacket that seemed to match his scuffed dress shoes made Connelly suspicious.

26

Taggert took a sip of tea, washing down the bit of biscuit he'd just bitten into. "You said the other was Fletcher? What about first names?"

"I don't recall them mentioning their first names, and given the situation, I didn't press them on the formalities," Connelly said. "But they mentioned my barrister who is missing, so they've something which links me to him. Seeing they were just here in Belfast, I wouldn't expect them back in Aberdeen till tomorrow."

"All right, give me till the end of the week; I'll see if I can find something about them," Taggert said. He sat in silence for a moment, wondering if he should tell the Irishman what he learned regarding how his brother died. Not by the police as reported, but by another gunman.

"I'll look forward to your call then, Mister Taggert," Connelly replied before hanging up. Spinning his chair to face the city, he looked out across rooftops. The Irishman stared into the emptiness, pondering his ability to see his plan to correct the errors surrounding his families name during the struggles his great-grandfather endured to unite the divided nation.

***

As he strolled up the steps leading to Aberdeen's Police-Scotland headquarters, Blayne Taggert made sure his notepad and pen were ready. Using the same plan when questioning the seaman from the Nordic Supplier, he'd try to bluff his way to gain information on the inspectors for Connelly. As he neared the door, he saw an older woman preparing to exit. "I'll get that, mum," he exclaimed with some enthusiasm.

"Bless your heart, young man," Miss McLeish replied as she shuffled past.

Glancing down, Taggert noticed the light-blue slippers contrasting the rest of her civil constables' uniform. A smile came to his face as she grasped the handrail. "My pleasure ma'am," he replied, watching her take slow, methodical steps towards the street.

As he strolled into the station, he spied the information kiosk where two, fresh-faced constables sat waiting behind the glass partition one spoke through to gain entrance. Even with the flow of officers and the public milling about, they never fixated on one person. Instead, they scanned the room, using a technique they had learned just a few months ago.

27

"Can we help you, sir?" a constable asked over the speaker, watching Taggert approach.

As Taggert noticed his reflection in the glass, he leaned over to place his mouth near the louvered opening. "I'm here to speak with an... Inspector McDermott," he explained, glancing at his notes before noticing the CCTV camera over the constable's shoulder.

"Your name, sir?" the officer asked.

"Foote. Derek Foote of the Independent in London," he answered using the alias he offered at the *Nordic Supplier*.

"If you'll just have a seat, we'll see if he's available," the constable said, motioning to several chairs underneath a map of the city.

"Thank you." Taggert shuffled over to the chairs. As he took a seat, he glanced down the main corridor, noticing a scuffle break out between a suspect and two constables. Several voices came over the intercom system announcing a need for additional officers. In short order, three more uniformed constables appeared, subduing the suspect and leading him to a nearby cell.

Moments after the melee began, it was over, but not without making its presence known. Taggert's nose twitched before his eyes felt the slight burn of the pepper spray used to subdue the suspect in the corridor.

While both officers and patrons moved about the front lobby of the station, Taggert noted the officers' demeanor. Many were relaxed, almost jovial, while a few others exhibited the telltale signs of fatigue. Their haggard looks were clear not only in the face but their uniforms too. "Rather a sloppy bunch," he muttered under his breath as a mother, her young child reluctant to follow, sat down next to him.

"Are you waiting to be called?" the woman asked.

"Ah... not exactly," Taggert replied. "I'm meeting with one officer for a news story," he explained, holding up his notepad.

"They caught my son with a bunch of hooligans last night," she said as she dabbed a tear from her eye. "I told him to leave them be... but no, he had to try to prove himself."

Mrs. Appleby perched on the edge of her plastic seat. With one hand holding her small child close to her side, she was pinching her pocketbook in a death grip in the other. It had been three hours since the constable had called about her Brian. After arriving at the station, she'd spent another ninety minutes jostled between the constable's office and the holding cells. Now, she was back sitting in this chair under photos of constables receiving department citations.

"Mister Foote," came a crackling voice over the speaker.

"Excuse me, ma'am," he said as he stepped past the woman and child, striding up to the constable behind the kiosk. "I'm Foote," he answered once again through the portal.

"The sergeant will meet you at the entrance," the constable replied while pointing to his left.

Sergeant Giles appeared through one of the locked doorways leading to the Administrative office. Looking over the gentleman, the sergeant wasn't especially impressed with the reporter Taggert was impersonating. "I'm sorry, but Chief Inspector McDermott is away on assignment. Is there something one of the other officers can help you with?"

Taggert opened his notepad before addressing the constable. "I'm following up on the incident from last month," he started. "There appears to be a similar incident in Liverpool with a killing of a crewman on a workboat, just like the one here," he lied. "I'm working on a follow-on piece for the Independent and my editor believes there might be a criminal element making its way into the worker's union and setting a precedent."

Giles listened to Taggert, but he knew the truth about what happened on the docks last month. It had to do with a kidnapping attempt and subsequent murder of their suspect by an unknown gunman. He likewise knew McDermott left strict instruction not to discuss the case without his permission.

"I'm sorry, sir, but Police-Scotland is not able to discuss the details of any investigations still underway," Giles said, reciting the standard pitch on divulging information. "I recommend you contact the Sheriff's office and discuss your request of the counselor of record."

"Sergeant, I was hoping to avoid using conventional channels," Taggert sighed. "And I didn't want to enact Her Majesty's Freedom of Information statue if I could help it." He closed his notepad. "I've come all the way from London; isn't there some information you can provide?" he asked, trying a softer approach.

Over the last three weeks since the shooting, the news types, both locals and the ones from Edinburgh had come and gone with their requests. But eventually, their pace had slowed to the odd phone call asking for any additional information, never in person.

Giles contemplated the question for a few moments, but noticed Taggert fidget with his pen and pad in nervous anticipation. He seemed eager to hear something, almost too eager for the sergeant. "As I said, nothing can be released," the sergeant replied. "If you'll excuse me, I've other errands which need attention. I'm sorry." Entering the secure corridor and leaving Taggert behind signaled the end of their conversation.

Before he could raise a question in protest, Taggert was alone by the door. A sense of resignation swept through him momentarily as he tilted his head back and stared at the ceiling. Inhaling deeply, he contemplated his next step. *I was never good at this spy stuff, that was Angus's forte,* he told himself.

"Excuse us, sir," a voice from behind him came.

Turning, Taggert saw the woman and child from earlier standing behind him with a constable motioning for the security keypad on the door. "I'm so sorry," he replied, stepping aside for the threesome to walk past him and into the corridor.

Shoulders slumped, he strolled out into the midday sun just as a marked patrol car pulled to the front of the station. The glare reflecting off the vehicle's windows kept him from seeing any occupants inside as he turned up the boulevard towards his hotel three blocks away on Broad Street.

With his back turned, Taggert didn't see McDermott or Fletcher making their way into the building, just returning from their trip to question members of Callaghan and Higgins in Belfast. As the two Scotland Yard inspectors entered the building, Constable Ames greeted them with a message slip.

"Seems your suspect is back in town," she said, handing over the paper to McDermott.

Reading the contents, his eyes lit up at what he saw written. "Ames, go and change into some regular clothes, hen," he directed, nudging Andrew towards the administrative office. "Andrew, get with Sergeant Giles and have him prepare two officers as backup."

"What's going on?"

"Someone spotted our fella from the docks near the university," McDermott said. "We need to act quickly if we're to catch him in the act."

Chapter FOUR

Aberdeen, Scotland

The passing squall had weakened until the steady rain became just a drizzle. "Well, this'll be interesting," the constable said. Looking through raindrops dotting the windshield, he and his partner could see a gentleman walking towards their suspect. For the third week in a row, the two from Police Scotland's Drug Interdiction Unit (DIU) were tailing the associate professor from Saint Andrew's Medical School after receiving a tip he was dealing drugs on campus. The anonymous caller mentioned the scholar was a guest lecturer at Aberdeen University today.

Leaves rustled as the breeze freshened out of the west. The rain from earlier that morning cleansed the air, leaving a freshness for each breath taken. As he splashed through several puddles, CI McDermott was acting on his gut instinct regarding the suspect's involvement in supplying drugs to a student who killed his mate last week.

McDermott and his partner also wanted this professor, Calvin Benson, since he was also a suspect in the death of a dockworker. Just last month, he was seen talking with a man named Allen Doyle, who was later found murdered in the abandoned signal house. McDermott wanted to find out why they met and what they talked about.

As he entered the car park behind the university's Fraser Noble building, McDermott glanced around, noting the number of students walking in the vicinity. No one seemed to be heading in the same direction, so he continued tailing the suspect. Not far behind McDermott, Inspector Fletcher strolled in a parallel path with Constable Ames in a feigned act of conversation when they were actually providing back-up.

As McDermott drew closer, he spied two young men approaching Benson. The demeanor of the two made the inspector uneasy.

"Hey Prof, we need to talk," the pudgier fellow of the two men called out.

The sound of the man's voice caused Benson to turn as he recognized the two men to whom he'd dealt the last of his hashish three weeks earlier. "I'm not sure this is the best place to meet, do you?" Benson asked, looking about the car park.

"You promised us a score last Monday and you didn't deliver," the second, taller man declared as he produced a knife.

Benson's voice cracked as he answered, "I can't deliver what I don't have."

"Then when will you have it?"

"I'm not sure. My connection never showed up at our meet," Benson answered, unaware of Allen Doyle's murder at the signal house. "I'm hoping to get another order soon though."

As the three men gathered near Benson's car, McDermott had made his way behind the tall man armed with the knife. Fletcher and Ames noticed McDermott moving closer and made their way across the path towards the car park.

"What the hell's going on now?" the constable from the DIU asked his partner, watching their suspect being confronted by the two men, but now there were four converging near a red sedan. "Where did these two come from?"

"What about the other fella? He's getting rather chummy too," the second officer noticed as he got out of the car.

While creeping along behind a row of cars, McDermott drew his sidearm and checked to see he loaded it before coming up behind the three men. "Scotland Yard," he yelled while leveling the pistol at the knife-wielding man. "Hands where I can see them, gentlemen," he commanded. "You, drop the knife," glaring at the taller assailant. He could see Fletcher and Ames coming in from the side followed by two other men.

"Careful with the tall one; he had at least one knife on him," McDermott mentioned to Ames, who'd spun the man around to face him towards the car's boot. "Andrew, see to the pudgy fella, will you? Now Mister Benson, you and I will have a wee chat." He holstered his weapon while pulling their primary suspect aside. Before he could begin his questioning, the two constables from DIU were pushing past a

33

growing crowd of students lingering in the car park, observing the officers' actions.

"Hold on there. Identify yourself," the senior officer said, pointing to McDermott and placing his hand on his own weapon.

"McDermott, Scotland Yard," he answered, holding out his police identification. "Who the hell are you?"

The senior officer from DIU glanced at the billfold then looked at his partner. "Seems legitimate enough."

"My name's Inspector Cockburn," the officer with DIU responded. "Mind telling me what business you've got with this fella?" he asked with a point to the professor.

Fletcher and Ames stood off to the side, sensing the building tension between the two senior inspectors. As the men stood to face each other, Andrews' cell phone rang, breaking the silence. "Inspector Fletcher," he answered. "Yes, sergeant... I'll let the Chief Inspector know. And sergeant, have Mister St. James prepare two more sets. I'll have the names to you when we arrive. Goodbye."

"What was that all about?" McDermott asked.

"Sergeant Giles wanted you to know that Mister St. James delivered the paperwork on Mister Benson and that he's ready," Fletcher replied.

"And what might that be?" Cockburn asked.

"It would be a warrant for Mister Benson," McDermott said just as the police van was pulling up. Constable Howe and another junior officer got out and approached the group. "Howe, you and Ames see to these two. I'll see to the professor myself," he finished, escorting Benson towards the unmarked car across the street. As he walked away, he looked over his shoulder to the red Ford Focus and called out, "And make sure his motor is delivered for inspection too."

"I asked you a question. Where do you think you're taking them?" Cockburn demanded while grasping McDermott's field coat. His action was more reflex than confrontation, but the result was not what he expected.

McDermott looked down at the hand holding his coat then straight into the eyes of the inspector from Edinburgh. "If you want to use that hand for holding a pint, I suggest you let go," McDermott sneering back before turning to walk away. "You're more than welcome to discuss things with me back at the district office."

Inspector Cockburn stood watching McDermott lead Calvin Benson towards his unmarked police car. "I did nae think we'd cross paths with him this soon Sedgwick," he said to his partner.

"What are we going to do now?" Sergeant Sedgwick asked.

"First off, we'll introduce ourselves to the Superintendent, then find out what this fella knows about Benson," Cockburn said, turning away to walk towards their own unmarked sedan. "Come on, they'll be busy for a few minutes writing them up; we'll get to the office before them and get settled in."

McDermott opened the door, turning Benson's back to the rear seat to prepare to have his suspect sit in the backseat. "Mind your head when you sit down now."

Hesitating, Benson turned to the officer, asking a question for the first time. "What do you want with me?"

"You'll have a chance to answer questions once we're settled in at the station. Now come on... in you go." He maneuvered the man into the backseat just as Inspector Fletcher walked up. McDermott turned back to the crowd in the car park.

"Who are those two officers?"

McDermott glanced at his partner, giving his head a brief shake from side to side until he closed the back door. "I'm nae sure, Andrew. But I'm thinking they know who our friend is here. Let's get to the office and have a chat with Mister MacCallum, shall we?"

The ride from the university went by with little fanfare. Fletcher was learning the shortcuts through the city, with fewer admonishments made by McDermott, who had grown up in Old Aberdeen. Circling the offices for Police Scotland-Aberdeen, Andrew pulled into the parking garage.

After getting the door opened, McDermott reached in to help their suspect out of the backseat before passing him off to Fletcher. "See that Mister Benson is signed in, will you?" he asked walking towards the entrance and pushing the doors open for his partner. "I'm going to see Miss Sinclair about getting a few minutes with the superintendent."

McDermott soon passed the forensics lab as he made his way to the administrative office. "Conor, do you have a moment?" came the familiar voice of CI McIntyre as he stepped out of the lab.

"Can it wait for a few, Graham?"

"All right, but you need to see this report," McIntyre said, walking back into the lab.

CI McDermott strolled into the outer office of Chief Superintendent (CS) MacCallum. "Is the superintendent in, Miss Sinclair?" he asked before seeing Inspector Cockburn and Sergeant Sedgwick sitting beside her desk.

"Yes, he is, Inspector," the secretary replied. "You're more than welcome to see him after these gentlemen." Seeing the light on the phone bank go off, she rose from her seat and opened the door to announce Cockburn and Sedgwick.

Conor stood stone-faced, trying to grasp the reason for the two officers appearing ahead of him. As she closed the door, he stepped next to the secretary. "What did they say their business was?"

"They didn't," she replied. "They came in, presented their credentials, and asked for an audience with Mister MacCallum. Why?"

"Who are they working for?"

"They're with Police Scotland, Inspector," Miss Sinclair answered. "As a matter of fact, they're assigned to the Drug Interdiction Unit in Edinburgh if Inspector Cockburn's identification is correct."

Conor took a seat, pondering the reason for the sudden appearance by the two officers. Part of his briefing by his supervisor in London alluded to Police Scotland's lack of consistency with drug cases being presented to the Metropolitan Police force. *And now they've got a sudden interest in a suspect linked to my case*, he thought. The assignment of Fletcher and himself to Aberdeen began in pursuit of drug traffickers using the service boats out of the harbor. But now, they were being called upon to include their expertise with an investigation to include local dealers handling the hashish supplied by the French.

Voices grew louder as McDermott noticed shadows of feet gathering behind the closed door. Just as his partner Inspector Fletcher entered the superintendent's outer office, Cockburn and Sedgwick emerged ahead of CS MacCallum. "Fancy meeting you two again," Andrew blurted out.

Overhearing the comment, MacCallum replied. "Well, you've met these gentlemen have you, Inspector?"

McDermott got to his feet, speaking ahead of his partner. "Aye, they were at the university when we made our arrest of the suspect in Doyle's murder. Though we really didn't have a formal introduction now?" he answered, fixing his gaze on his counterpart.

Inspector Cockburn stared up at Conor, wanting to put the Scotland Yard officer in his place, but held fast to his original thought. "It was rather brief. The name's Cockburn, Hugh Cockburn," he greeted, holding his hand out. "And this is Sergeant Alan Sedgwick."

Acknowledging the greeting with a brief shake of his hand, the Scotland Yard inspector replied, "Chief Inspector McDermott," and, motioning to Andrew, "and this is Inspector Fletcher." He made an effort to keep the pleasantries to a minimum. "I'm sure you've given Mister MacCallum a full brief on why you were near our surveillance, haven't you?"

"Aye, I'm sure he'll be giving you your marching orders in due course," Cockburn said.

McDermott felt his face warm as the comment from Cockburn stoked his mistrust in the officer. Instead of lashing out, he stood firm, holding back his rebuke lest he embarrass himself in front of CS MacCallum. "Just so we're clear, Cockburn, if you want any information on my case, you'll come ask me," Conor said. "And that includes any suspects we've got in custody."

"Chief Inspector McDermott, I'm sure Inspector Cockburn knows all the standard protocols and will follow them," MacCallum said, the sternness in his delivery showing his disdain as the officers tried to establish their superiority. "Isn't that right, Inspector?"

"Aye sir," he replied without taking his eyes off McDermott. "If you'll excuse us, we've best get to submitting our reports. Come along, Sedgwick," Cockburn said, heading out the door.

With a wag of his finger, the senior officer directed his attention toward McDermott. "Chief Inspector, let's you and I have a chat," MacCallum said as he grabbed his cap and headed out the door towards the car park. "Miss Sinclair, please hold my calls for the next, oh, say… thirty minutes," he ordered, motioning McDermott ahead of him. As the men walked out of the building, they each were lost in their own thoughts.

MacCallum reached the furthest spot from the building before he stopped and looked at McDermott. "Foremost, Conor, those two men are part of Police Scotland, so they are obligated to serve in a capacity to protect the citizens as directed," he said. "And second, this is the first I've heard of their involvement into the drug dealing you've come across. Which begs the question I'm sure you wish to ask: why now?"

His arms folded across his chest, Conor accepted the rebuke from the superior officer. "Aye sir, it's crossed my mind," McDermott said. "And I know you're aware of what Mister Collingsworth briefed Andrew and me on before we arrived. To my knowledge, these two have nae been read in on my case."

"Yes, William mentioned your assignment. He mentioned you were to look at potential issues with inconsistencies in our handling of certain drug cases," the senior officer said, recalling the conversation with his friend and McDermott's supervisor. "But he didn't mention specifics. Is there something you can add that I don't know?"

The inspector shook his head. *He need not know about Edna*, he thought. "Nothing you don't already know sir," Conor replied. "So, what's the story with Cockburn? What his interest in this fella Benson?"

"Seems they have evidence tying him to drug dealing at Saint Andrew's in Edinburgh," MacCallum said. "Inspector Cockburn didn't go into details because they're trying to catch him with his supplier."

"Seems rather queer they show up now and not beforehand," McDermott said. "Did they have any paperwork to support their story?"

"No, they didn't. Now you mention it, they came in empty-handed," the superintendent replied. "Which means I'll be making a call or two back to Edinburgh for answers. Until then, I'd ask you be civil with them, but cautious."

"Aye sir, I'll do my best," Conor said. "I'd ask that you do the same when discussing things with Edinburgh," echoing the same concern. "If you'll excuse me now, CI McIntyre wanted to show me something in the Forensics lab." Making his way through the doors, he turned to his right and headed downstairs to the basement, meeting one technician at the counter. "Afternoon, Devin. Is the chief in still?"

"Aye, he's in his office, Inspector," the technician replied, motioning to the open door in the back.

Conor stuck his head in after rapping on the jamb. "Anybody home?"

"Come in Conor," CI McIntyre said while putting down the papers he was reading. "I thought you might want to see this." He pulled a folder from the desk drawer identified with the name *DUNBAR, A.*

"Will it give me the willies?" He was happy his field jacket hid the shiver caused by the mentioning of the assassin's name on the folder.

"Hardly. But it gives us a little insight into why he did what he did," the forensics chief said. "I had a friend at Gartcosh pass along samples of Dunbar's remains to the team at Saint Andrew's Medical School. They've been studying the brain of past killers looking for possible DNA links to their mannerisms."

Staring at the file, McDermott saw the words on the page, but did not comprehend the science behind it. "You mean the science-types think they can identify why a person goes on a killing spree?" he asked, flipping the page.

"To some extent, yes," McIntyre replied. "The more important part of that report is on page five though."

Conor flipped two more pages, coming to one labeled "DNA similarities." "I'm no a science-type Graham; what am I looking at?"

"Those are genetic markers," McIntyre said. "Based on information held in the national database, my friend was able to find a match. They show an individual out there who's a relative of Angus Dunbar. And based on those findings, there's better than a ninety-five percent chance it's his sibling, possibly even a twin."

"Did they have any further information? An address or phone number on the patient?"

"No, an anonymous individual provided the sample," McIntyre replied. "If I had to guess, it was from a home kit."

"You lied, Graham," Conor said as he handed the folder back. "Knowing Dunbar has a family member out there with the same tendencies does give me the willies now."

Chapter FIVE

Belfast, Northern Ireland

Michael Connelly sat in his private office, examining pages torn from an accounting book Blayne Taggert provided after the funeral for his twin brother, Angus Dunbar. Each line of the ledger had a date, location, and names recalling conversations he once had with the former hitman.

As he stared at the first page, Connelly noted the initial entry, the chance encounter with the former SAS sergeant. The cold night outside the pub in Haverfordwest near the college was busy with a mix of locals and college students. It was here where Connelly and several of his fellow Legionnaires had a drink with their British counterparts after finishing the training at the nearby airstrip.

Several SAS members kept close tabs on Dunbar, and Connelly found out the sergeant had trouble with drinking to the point they knew him to pull his weapon on innocent patrons. As the group was leaving, a few college students scuffled drawing the military members into the fray.

In a moment, Connelly saw the glint of light off the knife blade as Dunbar drew down on an unsuspecting student. Reverting to his training from his time in Corsica, Connelly subdued Dunbar, dragging him 30 meters out into the street. As the two men struggled for control of the knife, Connelly soon gained the upper hand and disarmed Dunbar.

"No one's ever done that alone," one of Dunbar's colleagues said, rushing up to Connelly.

"He's a drunk; it wasn't that difficult," Connelly replied as he tossed the knife towards the other SAS members. Standing over the fallen Dunbar, he looked down upon the soldier. "You best stay in the barracks the rest of the time or you'll be in the morgue," he half-joked, pushing through the spectators before the police arrived.

A gentle rap on his office door broke through Connelly's thoughts as his secretary Erin entered. "Mister Higgins, I took a call from Dublin;

they have canceled the nine o'clock conference call," the young woman said.

"Oh, thank you, Erin," He put the ledger pages on the desk. "Did Mister Callaghan offer a reason for canceling the call?"

"Actually, it was Roan who canceled it," she answered. Roan was the eldest son of the company's owner. Seeing the puzzled look on her employer's face, the secretary queried Michael. "Is there something bothering you?"

"I was just thinking. We've yet to hear from Mister Gilmore."

"All I know is his phone message says he's taken a sabbatical from the law firm," Erin said. "And that he'd be out of the country and have limited access to electronic mail service."

"Do you still have a copy of his office key?"

"Yes, it's amongst all the others for the floor," the secretary answered, walking towards her desk.

Michael Connelly stood up from his desk to join Erin in the outer office.

"Here you go, sir." Erin produced a ring with three keys strung together. "This one will open his office," she explained, holding the largest up. "And these two are for his desk and file cabinets."

"Thank you." Taking the ring and making his way to the opposite side of the building, Connelly came upon the office for his barrister and entered. He switched on the lights and made his way to the desk to unlock the drawers.

"So, Sean, what is it you have to hide?" he asked himself. Connelly rifled through the stack of papers and folders in each drawer, glancing at the contents within each of them. Pushed to the back, he found a daily planner from the previous year and thumbed through it. "Not very bright, were you?" he muttered, noticing an entry for the barrister's trip to Algiers to meet the drug trafficker, Louis Remesy.

Spinning around in the chair, Connelly unlocked the credenza. The top drawer had two spaces left vacant. *What did you have here?* he thought. Flipping past each tab, he soon came across one marked 'COLLEAGUES" and pulled the file out.

He came across a familiar name as he looked through the papers: Priscilla El-Sayed, Solicitor. Reading the document, he saw that the

41

young woman was a member of a public advocates firm in Edinburgh for the last three years. Before that, it listed her as an intern at a more prestigious law office in London.

Flipping the page over, Michael saw what he needed, a list of three phone numbers. He dialed the number listed for the private line to Priscilla's office in Edinburgh. A gentleman answered the call after four rings. "Continental Advocacies. Can I help you?"

"Yes, my name is Mister Higgins. I'm calling for Miss El-Sayed," Michael asked. "Is she available?"

"She's in consultations at the moment, but I can give her your message as soon as she's finished," the young man replied.

"Please have her return my call at the following number." Michael recited the number of the disposal cell phone he used with Sean Gilmore. "You can let her know I'll be available all day."

"I'll pass along your note, sir. Will there be anything else?"

"No, that was all. Thank you." Just as he was putting the folder back in the drawer, his driver entered the office. "Yes, Geoff, what is it?"

"Excuse me, Mister Higgins, but Erin was mentioning you being in Sean's office and I was just wondering if you needed any help?"

Michael looked at the young man for a moment. "What do you know about Mister Gilmore's filing habits? Seems he's got a few folders missing here," he noted, pointing to the open drawer. "You wouldn't know where the files are, would you?"

"Couple weeks ago, he asked that I forward two of them to his hotel in Aberdeen," Geoff said.

"Do you recall what they pertained to?"

"They were on two clients, I believe," the driver said. "One was labeled 'Dunbar' if I remember correctly, and the other had a French name written on the tab. But I honestly can't remember how to pronounce it or the spelling," his voice trailed off laced with a touch of disappointment.

"Was it Remesy?" Connelly asked.

Tilting his head to one side, the young man screwed his eyes shut to envision the spelling. "It started with R-I-C... but after that... I'm drawing a blank, Mister Higgins."

"Monsieur Adrian Richelieu," Connelly announced in a hushed and guarded tone.

Geoff snapped his fingers at the name. "Yes, that it," he replied.

Closing and locking the drawer, Connelly ushered his driver out of the office and handed him several bills. "I've got a few calls to make, Geoff. Why don't you get something to eat for all of us? Maybe a fish and chip supper," he suggested, patting the young man's shoulder. Reentering his office, he stepped up to his secretary. "Erin, please see I'm not disturbed until Geoff returns with our lunches," he mentioned as he walked into his office and closed the door.

Over the next thirty minutes, Connelly slowly read through the notes, digesting what the barrister's observations meant on each of the individuals. More importantly, the reason for keeping them. As he reread the information on the French shipping owner, he stood and paced, attempting to understand what he'd just seen.

Standing at the bank of windows, Michael Connelly watched as two tugboats were pulling a merchant freighter out to sea. "What more information did you have, Sean?" he muttered to his reflection. "And what do you have on Dunbar that I might not have known?" The windows vibrated briefly as a freighter's horn echoed across Belfast harbor as it headed out to sea. The shrill ringing of his cell phone from the desk drawer interrupted his thoughts. Pulling it open, he glanced at the number before answering the call. "Hello?"

The woman caller's body shivered hearing the Irishman's voice answer. "Mister Higgins? This is Miss El-Sayed returning your call from earlier. How can I help you?" she asked, though somewhat direct and forceful.

"I'll not waste your time Miss El-Sayed. I'm well aware you and my barrister, Sean Gilmore, were working together on a case in Aberdeen," the executive said turning his gaze back to the harbor. "I was wondering though… where is Mister Gilmore now?"

Priscilla appreciated having a private office. It kept her colleagues from seeing the color drain from her face at times like this. She had just spent an hour visiting her former classmate the day before yesterday at the visitor's section of Her Majesty's Prison (HMP)-Perth.

"Mister Gilmore excused himself from the Wallace trial after the sergeant attempted suicide," she said. "Since I was the lead counsel, he didn't see a need to remain on." The lie they'd agreed to after Sean's sentencing was well-rehearsed.

Connelly spun in his chair, staring out the window, his expression one of uncertainty. "And did he say what he would do after he left you there in Aberdeen?"

Priscilla sat down to pull out her chair and open her notebook. "Sean had mentioned taking a leave of absence," she said, glancing over the checklist of items her and Sean has decided to reveal for such an event like this. "He seemed rather spent from all the activity that was occurring in Aberdeen with Sergeant Wallace and the trial and such."

"I see. He didn't tell you where he was going though?"

"No, no... he didn't. I assumed it was back to Belfast to discuss the outcome with you," Priscilla recited, checking off another statement. Learning to lie to the Irishman was becoming easier though no less comfortable. "Are you telling me that Sean has gone missing?"

As he turned back to his desk, the Irishman returned his attention to the missing folders. "I'm not sure," Michael answered. "Are you aware of any documents he had dispatched from here?" alluding to the folders on Dunbar and Richelieu. "My secretary can't seem to account for several files Mister Gilmore was working on for me. And since he was in my employment when he began those inquiries, I consider them proprietary to my business."

Priscilla pulled open the drawer, glancing down at the files she swore to safeguard for her friend. Just looking at the one labeled "Dunbar" gave her chills, knowing of the man's behaviors outlined within. "I recall Sean receiving a package," she said. "But he said they weren't pertinent to the constable's trial, so he never made me privy to them." She felt her stomach churn as she listened to the questions. Glancing at the clock, she forced herself to lie once again. "I apologize, but I've got a counseling session in a few minutes; is there anything else?"

Michael contemplated his next step. "No, Miss El-Sayed. I've nothing else to ask for the moment. I'll have my secretary forward your retainer for the effort during the Wallace trial," he said. "If you get a chance to see Mister Gilmore again, I'd appreciate receiving a call. Have a pleasant day."

Priscilla felt her skin tingling at the thought of conversing with the Irishman. *How can he be so calm, and yet still dispatch a killer?* Pulling out the two folders, she opened the second one for the Frenchman Richelieu. Sean had said that if things got desperate, she could call in a favor from this man.

Back in his office overlooking the Belfast harbor, Michael Connelly looked over the handful of papers in the folder for Priscilla El-Sayed. The daughter of a Saudi Arabia Air Force pilot and an English mother assigned to the British consulate, she appeared to come from a privileged background. Educated at Oxford, first in her law class one spot ahead of Sean, who had been one spot below her.

"Well Mister Taggert, I believe I've got a task for you," Michael declared to the empty office. He was preparing to call the Scot when his intercom buzzed.

"Mister Higgins," the voice of Erin announced from the outer office. "Geoff has returned with our lunches, sir."

"Thank you, Erin. I'll be out in a moment," Michael replied. Dialing in the number for the Scot, he heard the chirp as it connected his call. After four rings, it forwarded the call so Michael could leave his message. "Good day, Mister Taggert. This is Mister Connelly. Please call back when it's convenient. I've got an undertaking for you," he said before ending the call.

Returning the phone to his drawer, Michael strolled out of his office to join his secretary and driver as they sat at the small table, dividing up the lunches. "What were the damages, Geoff?"

"It was four sixty-five today for yours," the driver announced. As he placed the change in front of Connelly, Geoff continued. "The cook was complaining the fishmongers are charging more per pound these days. He said the fisherman are demanding an extra five pounds per kilo of cod since the cost of petrol has gone up this year."

"What isn't costing us more?" the secretary asked. "Mister Sullivan asked us this past weekend to pay for our own drinks. He used to be quite generous but said the cost to have his deliveries has gone up. I mean, it's not like there are a thousand miles between here and the brewery at Saint James Gate."

"I recommend we enjoy what we have," Michael reminded them. "It wasn't long ago our families were having to go without, especially

45

during the wars. And let's not forget the suffering during the potato famine."

"Do you think Mister Gilmore's all right?" Erin asked, sensing her employer's concern for the barrister.

"I'm sure he's fine," Michael said. "I've got a friend who's going to look into things in the next day or two. I'd imagine we'll hear that Mister Gilmore is relaxing on the beach in Mallorca or the Bahamas."

Chapter SIX

Aberdeen, Scotland

Calvin Benson had gone from a university professor to suspect in a murder investigation in less than three hours. A constable led him into the interrogation room, and the stark coldness of the room took him by surprise. He noticed they had furnished it with a plain metal table and three chairs, each scarred from handcuffs and chains. The constable took the length of chain from his waist and ran it through metal on the chair as he sat him down. "The inspectors will be in soon," he said, closing the door behind him.

The control room's computers were manned by a constable prepared to record the interrogation of Benson, who sat in nervous silence waiting for McDermott and Fletcher to enter. As the technician adjusted the CCTV, the door for the interrogation room swung open and the Scotland Yard officers arrived.

Taking seats opposite the suspect, Fletcher set his notebook down and pulled a pen from his pocket while McDermott swung his chair to the side closest to Benson. As he placed a folder on the table in front of his chair, the chief inspector produced two photos from inside. He nodded towards the two-way glass and cleared his throat to let the technician know he was about to begin his questioning.

"I will be very direct with my questions," McDermott began. "You were seen with this fella several weeks ago..." He slid the first picture of Allen Doyle in front of the professor. Calvin Benson blinked hard as he saw the image. Before he could answer, there was a knock on the door. Fletcher rose to open the door to find a disheveled young man standing outside.

"Excuse me, sir," the barrister announced. "But they have assigned me as counsel for your suspect," He quickly showed the court document to the inspector, stealing a glance back at McDermott who just shrugged his shoulders and let the barrister in to the interrogation room. "If you'll excuse us, I'd like a few moments with... Mister Benson."

"You've got five minutes," McDermott announced as he grabbed the photo before exiting the room. Fletcher reached across the table for his notebook and pen and followed his partner outside. Stepping into the hallway, the inspectors noticed the two officers with DIU at the end of the hallway.

"What the hell do they want?" Fletcher asked.

"Aye, I'd say they're hoping for a wee peek at our guest," McDermott said. "Andrew, let the constables know not to allow them in the control room, will you?" He asked, nudging his partner down the hall. "I'm going to have a word with them."

With McDermott coming closer, Inspector Cockburn turned to his junior partner. "Mind yourself, I'll be doing all the talk," as he gave a stern look towards his partner, Sedgwick, before facing McDermott as the DIU officer greeted his arrival. "Finally come to invite us into your interrogation session, have you?"

McDermott stared back at the inspector. "You've not been read in to my case; so, the answer tae your question is no, you're nae invited," Conor said. "And for the record, unless I hear from my superintendent in London, you'll nae come near my case at all."

"That's not terribly courteous of you, McDermott," Cockburn replied. "We're trying to do the same, you and me. Don't forget that. It will always be about putting away the ones breaking the law and doing harm to others," he continued, folding his arms across his chest.

Before McDermott could reply, Inspector Fletcher walked up from behind. "They're ready Chief Inspector. And Sergeant Giles has been notified too." The constable outside the control room was standing fast in waiting.

"Cockburn, I suggest you and your partner go back to Edinburgh until you're needed," McDermott said. "No sense you wasting money sitting here in Aberdeen. I'm sure you'll read about our investigation in the dispatches."

Turning his back, McDermott walked away until he came to the door guarded by the constable. As he reentered the interrogation room, McDermott took a seat across from the suspect and his barrister while Fletcher drug another chair in from the hallway. "Before we begin again... please state your name for the record," McDermott said, facing the lawyer.

"My name is Erroll Turnbull, a barrister with the Public Defence Solicitor's office in Dundee," he replied. "And before we discuss dismissal of the charges against my client inspector, I'd like to see your summons," he requested, holding out his hand.

McDermott opened the folder on the table and handed over the summons. "I'm nae sure you'll find cause to request dismissal, Mister Turnbull," he said. "Your client Benson there is a suspect in a murder investigation."

"I'm sure upon my review of this, and seeing your evidence," he started, waving the summons, "I'll be able to substantiate my request," the lawyer said. Unfolding the document, Turnbull spent the next few moments reading the contents before glancing back to the two inspectors. "Don't let me stop you from asking your questions, Inspector," he said.

Fletcher glanced at McDermott, noticing the muscles in his neck twitching as the tension grew between the officer and the lawyer. The young inspector cleared his throat to break the silence. "Mister Benson, what studies are you involved in at the university?"

After stealing a glance at his lawyer, he looked back at the inspector. "I'm an associate in the Biomedical Sciences department," the professor replied. "With a specialty in Pharmacology."

McDermott peered at Fletcher, speculating what seized the young man to overstep his place in the room. Returning his attention back to the lawyer and his client, he purposely cleared his throat with a touch greater force than usual before asking his question. "You fancy yourself a chemist, Mister Benson?"

"Hardly, Inspector, there's no money in the mundane," he answered without realizing his lawyer was attempting to quiet him. "I mean, who wants to work a regular shift," he started, peering at the officers, "doling out pills all day to grey-haired grannies?"

McDermott pulled the first photo of Allen Doyle from the folder. "How do you know this fella?" he asked, pointing to the image taken by Fletcher three weeks beforehand. "And what business do you have at the docks anyway?"

Turnbull slid the photo across the table and stared at the group of men. "Who's who in this picture?"

"There's your man," McDermott with a stab of his finger at the figure dressed in the blue jeans and an Army field coat. "And this is the party in question." He tapped the image of the deceased dockworker he'd pulled from the folder.

"I'm sorry, Inspector, but this doesn't provide enough clarity to present to a panel of jurors," the lawyer declared. "Plus, look at Mister Benson; he's a proper lecturer for the university, not some slovenly attired derelict off a boat."

"Andrew, would you be kind enough to show Turnbull the evidence from his client's motor?"

Fletcher rose from the table and walked out the door, simply to return a few moments later with an evidence bag containing the weathered field coat from Benson's car. "Forensics got this from a search of your client's car just an hour ago," the young officer said. "Our forensics team couldn't find any soiled areas that would indicate your claim that the person from the picture worked the boats."

Before Turnbull could speak, Sergeant Giles followed a knock on the door, sticking his head inside. "Excuse me, Chief Inspector, this is for you," he muttered, handing over a folded piece of paper.

Accepting the note from the constable, Conor opened it and read. Inside, he saw the familiar handwriting of CI McIntyre, the forensic department head. Traces of drugs found in the suspect's vehicle matched the drugs seized on Standard-Apollo from June, with similar degradation noted by the forensics office in Gartcosh. This news brought a cruel smile to McDermott's face.

McDermott's back straightened as he folded the note. "Mister Turnbull, this session is over for the moment. Inspector Fletcher will be in touch with you when we will question your client again." He quickly pulled the picture away from the lawyer.

"I don't understand."

"There's an additional item which requires my attention. Until then, your client will remain in custody," he explained, closing the folder and standing. He peered out the open door at the constable standing by. "The suspect can be returned to the holding cells," he ordered as he walked away from interrogation.

Following close behind, Fletcher finally caught up with his senior partner at the elevator. "Why the sudden end? I thought we were pushing him to explain his relationship with Doyle?"

"Aye lad, we were going tae do just that," McDermott said, stepping in the lift and pushing the button for the second floor. "But Mister McIntyre found something out that's more important." He fanned the folder before the young inspector.

"More important than a possible murder suspect?"

"Aye. They scoured his motor and found traces of hashish," he explained as the doors opened and they made their way to the inspector's office. "And it's the same as what we got off the boat. Besides, Andrew, like the barrister mentioned in the room, Benson doesn't look the type, even for murder."

***

The debriefing room three floors above the interrogation area was quiet for the moment, allowing Inspector Cockburn and Sergeant Sedgwick to have a chance to converse without being disturbed. Keeping a watchful eye at the door, Cockburn settled into the chair before opening his folder.

"The way I see it, we've got two choices, Sedgwick," he started, sliding his report on Calvin Benson onto the table. "We can keep butting heads with the two from London or we let them do all the work."

"But what do you think they've got on the professor that we don't?"

"McDermott mentioned a murder," Cockburn said, scratching his chin as he leafed through his notes. "But we've no evidence he's the violent type, have we?"

"No, all we've managed was his arrest for possession when he was caught speeding along the A95," Sedgwick answered. "His defence on the charge was needing drugs for his studies on manipulating molecules or something like that," the sergeant added. "It was the endorsement by his department head at Saint Andrews to the chief superintendent that gave him his free pass."

Before the officers could continue, Constable Howe and another officer entered the room, wheeling in a cart with several file boxes labeled *L. WALLACE* across the sides. "Are you gentlemen lost?" Howe asked, surprised to see someone in the room.

51

"No, officer, we're just having a wee chat," Cockburn answered, a slight chill tingling his skin at the sight of the boxes. Ever since word about the former sergeant's treasonous activity filtered through Police Scotland, many of officers took extra care in the actions. Cockburn was no exception.

"They do not allow members of the public in this part of the building, so I'll need both of you to follow this constable to the lobby," he explained, nodding to his partner waiting by the door.

"That won't be necessary," the inspector said as he presented his credentials. "The name's Cockburn. Inspector Hugh Cockburn with DIU-Edinburgh. And this is Sergeant Sedgwick," he explained, nodding to his partner who was sitting opposite him.

"My apologies, Inspector," Howe answered. "Just so you know, we've a few cadets coming over to assist in reviewing these files," he explained, tapping his hand on the boxes. "You'll not have any privacy if that's what you're needing."

Before the inspector could answer, they heard keys jingling from a watchman's belt growing louder outside the room. Stomping of boots in the stairwell and the squeaking of rubber soles on polished tile announced the approach Sergeant McKee as she led six cadets into the room. "All right, keep the talking down," the woman demanded before she noticed the four men.

"Who are you?" she asked, seeing Inspector Cockburn standing next to Constable Howe. "Paul, who are these gentlemen?"

"I'm Inspector Cockburn with DIU in Edinburgh," the older officer replied as he stepped forward. "And this is Sergeant..."

"Sedgwick," the female officer said finishing the greeting. "Hello, Alan. Queer place to be running into you again," McKee answered before stepping alongside Constable Howe.

His cheeks became flush with embarrassment for being called out. "Hello, Annie," Sedgwick answered.

The inspector stood glancing back and forth between the two sergeants. "You two... you know each other?" Cockburn asked, wagging his finger between the two officers.

"Aye... we do," Sedgwick replied. "The sergeant and I went through academy training together."

Sergeant McKee noticed the half-dozen cadets just standing about as the officers were struggling to maintain a civil conversation. "Take a seat, two to a table," she ordered. "Constable Howe, find these two officers a space to work downstairs." She gestured towards Cockburn while averting her gaze from Sedgwick.

"Gentlemen," Howe quickly motioned towards the doorway.

Cockburn stepped towards the hall while Sedgwick skirted past the cart loaded with files the cadets would soon delve into for Sergeant McKee. "How closely did you know the sergeant?" Cockburn asked as Sedgwick joined him in the stairwell.

"Nae well enough to shag after a few pints, if that's what you're asking," the officer responded. His answer came in a hushed tone as the sergeant's colleague, Constable Howe, stepped through the first-floor doorway. "When you're grouped thirty to a squad, it's difficult to learn any intimate details, you know. But she held her own. Did nae take any guff from the fellas, you know? A real ball buster she was..."

The noise from both citizens and fellow constable crowding the first floor masked their conversation as they followed Constable Howe into the patrolman's space. "We've an empty cubicle here you can sit at until Mister MacCallum decides if you're staying," the young officer said, pointing to the space.

"Thank you, Constable," Cockburn replied sitting at the counter.

Watching Howe leave the area, the inspector turned to his partner. "Alan, I'm thinking you might need to renew your acquaintance with your fellow officer," he said.

"Why would I want to do that?"

"It might be our way of gaining an upper hand with the two from the Yard."

Chapter SEVEN

T he swish of pages being turned periodically along with echoes from
constables shuffling along the hallway were the only sounds heard
by the cadre of cadets. *Bloody numbers*, the lone female thought. Sitting
in the third-floor assembly hall, the young officer, along with five
others, were again tasked with searching stacks of computer printouts.
Three weeks ago, it was an office number in Glasgow of a criminal
syndicate member. And now, they were being asked to find a link in a
relationship between the former sergeant, Logan Wallace, and an
officer's number in Edinburgh.

Sliding a ruler along lines of numbers, she continued searching for
the corresponding match to what Sergeant McKee had written on the
whiteboard earlier. Each of the cadets had adopted their own technique
from a slip of paper with the target number written on it to noting each
number on the printout with a pencil mark.

"All right, it's time for supper," Constable Ames announced as she
entered the room.

"It's about time," one cadet sighed, rubbing his palms against his
eyes. "I was beginning to see spots, mind you."

Similar comments came from the others. "Look at it as a glimpse
into what police work is like," Ames said, waiting by the door. "Come
on, pack it all up. Don't forget to mark your place for when we come
back to it later."

As her colleagues gathered the loose piles of paper, the lone female
cadet lowered her face towards the sheet laid open before her.
"Constable Ames, I think I've got a match," the cadet decried, keeping
her finger on the line of the printout.

Ames looked down at the faint computer printing and then to the
board where the target number was written. "Well done, Mhairi. It's a
match," she said. Grabbing a pencil and a scrap of paper, she wrote the
date and time Sergeant Wallace made the call to the number CI
McDermott provided. "Leave a bit of scrap so we can come back to it
now," she suggested, sliding the paper to the cadet.

"We're all packed, Constable Ames," one cadet said, standing next to the cart now packed with the evidence boxes.

"All right then," Constable Ames replied. Walking to the phone hanging on the wall, she contacted the evidence room to ensure the custodian would be ready to receive the boxes. "Two of you wheel the evidence back; the rest of you meet in the briefing area," she directed.

Constable Ames left the cadets to return the boxes to evidence and hurried to the detective's office, hoping to catch McDermott and Fletcher before they left the building. "Come on, lads, move your arse," she ordered, pushing past several officers coming on duty.

Grasping the handle to the door, Ames yanked it open just as one inspector was reaching forward. The senior officer caught himself before hitting the wall as he stumbled past the constable. "Bloody hell, Ames. Why didn't you knock like the others?"

"Sorry, but I'm needing Chief Inspector McDermott," she replied, catching her breath as she strutted past him.

"He's in the back office with Fletcher," the officer answered as she walked away.

Ames skirted between chairs and desks crowding the room and stepped to the open door, glimpsing Inspector Fletcher flipping the pages of a folder. "Excuse me, Inspector?" she announced, sticking her head into the space.

"Yes?" Andrew replied without looking up.

Ames took a step into the office as she spoke. "I've got a bit of news for you and the Chief. One cadet found a match of the phone number to Sergeant Wallace's number."

"Just the one instance?" McDermott asked.

"Aye, but I've marked the spot," she answered. "Since it was the first instance, I figured if we had more, they'd come after this one."

"Well done, lass," McDermott said, holding out his hand for the note. "When do you expect the cadets to finish up the rest?"

"I've just sent them off to supper," Ames replied, brushing a strand of hair from her face.

"Andrew, let's gin up a wee note for the Mister MacCallum to read."

"And tell him what?"

55

Conor looked at the constable standing between him and his partner. Knowing the discovery that the former sergeant was communicating directly with someone inside the Drug Interdiction Unit would send ripples through the department, he paused.

"Constable Ames, do us a wee favor and have Sergeant Giles join us, will ya?" he asked, dismissing the young woman.

"Aye, I can dae that, if he's still about," the officer answered. "Anything else?" Her annoyance wasn't subtle, but McDermott didn't budge.

"No, but remind me to pay for your next lunch. It seems you've earned it," McDermott answered. Watching the young woman leave, he turned to Fletcher and waved the slip of paper. "If we can connect this Cockburn chap to calls that Wallace made 'bout the drugs, we've got our connection outside Aberdeen."

"You're assuming an awful lot, you know," Fletcher replied. "For all we know, Wallace was passing along legitimate information. Don't forget, he was the senior officer working with Mister MacCallum."

"I'm willing to wager he had others to contact when it came to the drugs," Conor said. "And when the time was right to move it from here to Glasgow, he made sure someone waiting on the other end," he continued as Sergeant Giles came to the door.

"You wanted to see me, Chief Inspector?"

"Aye... Marcus, have a seat," McDermott replied with a motion to the empty chair. Looking across his desk, he tried to read the constable's body language before asking his question. "Inspector Fletcher and I have a hunch we want to follow up on."

"But considering the sensitive nature, we're needing to be sure about whom we include," Fletcher added, peering over the computer screen.

Before he continued, McDermott raised his head, looking past the sergeant and out the door to make sure no one was eavesdropping on their discussion. "Who can you call upon in Edinburgh or Glasgow that's reliable?" McDermott asked in a hushed tone.

"Reliable in what way?"

"How do I put this? Let's say I want to know if you knew someone you can trust. Someone who's not the likes of Sergeant Wallace," the chief inspector said. "We might have more evidence on his misdeeds, and it might include others outside the force here in Aberdeen."

Sergeant Giles sat, his eyes darting between the two officers as he contemplated how involved he wanted to be in this case. "You know, Inspector, I might have a friend I could call on in Edinburgh. However," he paused to measure his response, "your little peek at the records didn't garner you any favors with the lads."

"Aye, I'm aware of that," McDermott stammered, embarrassed for violating the constables trust. "It's why I'm coming to you for help, as the senior officer, I'll have you. I'll be talking with the superintendent, but I'd like to get a wee head start so to speak," He wrung his hands nervously as he awaited an answer. "So, Marcus, do you know someone you can trust?"

While his partner was talking with Sergeant Giles, Inspector Fletcher toiled over the keyboard of his computer. Using the information provided by Constable Ames, he crafted a note they would pass to Chief Superintendent MacCallum regarding the cadet's discovery, and their sketchy hypothesis.

"What do you think, Andrew?" McDermott asked.

"I'm sorry, I wasn't listening," the young inspector replied before looking over the computer screen.

"It's possible Sergeant Giles knows a friend working in the home office we can trust," he said, "in the event Mister MacCallum does nae get a warm reception with our information."

"I've another tactic we can use," Andrew said. "But I'll need to gather a few bits of information first. Sergeant Giles, does this friend have any issues that could keep them from helping us? They're not in any trouble or anything of that sort?"

"Not likely, Mister Fletcher," the sergeant said. "Xander is a fair chap whose conscience will nae let him see anything bad go without punishment. He went so far as turning in his cousin for inciting a fight after a football match once."

"It's your call, Chief Inspector," Andrew was quick to pass the baton of responsibility to Conor. "If you're comfortable with the sergeant's colleague, I'll not argue the point." Hitting print on the computer, Fletcher turned and pulled the notice from the printer. "Here you go."

Conor read through the few lines before folding the note. "Seems rather sparse, but we've only got the one instance from the cadets. Marcus, give your mate a call and let him know we'll be in touch tomorrow or the next day."

Andrew pushed his chair in and grabbed his notebook. "I'll be back in a few." Strolling down the hall to the stairwell, the inspector made his way down to the forensics lab. As he pushed past several constables escorting their prisoners to the booking area, he turned the corner and entered the lab.

"Afternoon, Inspector," Constable Devin Eakins exclaimed, seeing Andrew enter.

"Hello, Devin," he answered. The overpowering stench of isopropyl alcohol was a vivid reminder of his time in the emergency room after his injury, enough for him to make an attempt to fan the odor from in front of his nose. "Is Inspector Gordon or Chief Inspector McIntyre in?"

"Aye, they're both in," he answered, nodding to the back office. "Still nae used to the smell of it?"

"No, I'm not." Skirting around the counter, Andrew walked past another technician, Kyle Patton, who had his head tilted over a microscope. Andrew gently knocked on the door frame of the office as he listened to the two officers conversing inside.

"Excuse me, Mister McIntyre, but can I have a word with you and Inspector Gordon?"

"Of course, Inspector Fletcher, please come in," McIntyre said, motioning to a seat next to Inspector Fletcher's companion, Sheila Gordon. "What can we do for you?"

As he entered the office, Andrew closed the door behind him before sitting. "As you know, CI McDermott and I are working to identify who's moving the hashish from the docks," he started and quickly flipped open his notebook. "And well, we believe Sergeant Wallace had possible accomplices in Edinburgh and Glasgow. I've a theory somehow other agencies are involved," the inspector said. "And I'd appreciate it if you could help me understand your procedures when passing information."

CI McIntyre leaned back in his chair. "You believe someone who sees reports submitted by us are using this information to mishandle the drugs seized by the police?"

"It's just a theory, but... yes. I'm wondering if Wallace was communicating with someone outside normal channels when it came to passing along his information. Or maybe there was someone else from another agency, like the Customs chap Baxter."

"Sir, we get calls from other agencies like Customs when they have evidence to transport," Inspector Gordon interjected. "We also have the university staff who do the blind testing on samples for us," she added. "I hate to admit it, but Inspector Fletcher is just pointing out what we already know."

"And what might that be?" McIntyre asked.

"Nothing is foolproof for passing information," Sheila replied. "Sergeant Wallace showed us that. Who's saying someone in Gartcosh isn't part of the drug smuggling ring?" Even Police Scotland's main forensic lab was subject to error.

"I understand your concerns, both of you," McIntyre said. "But since I've been in charge, we've never had samples mishandled coming or going to the lab." He leaned forward onto his desk. "And we've never had issues with the university, either."

"Our recent suspect is a professor at the university," Andrew said, flipping back a few pages. "He's an associate in Biomedical Sciences. He mentioned his specialty is in Pharmacology. And from what we know about the hashish seized earlier, he'd comprehend its makeup, don't you think?"

McIntyre ran his hand over his chin, the beginning stubble scratching his palm. "You've a good point, Inspector. But your suspect only had traces of the hashish in his clothing. The court could easily dismiss it as circumstantial since your investigation is on trafficking a greater quantity of the drug."

"But Graham," Sheila said, once again joining the discussion, "if this fella has the means of identifying the 'unknown' ingredient from the hashish, it seems likely he'd be on someone's payroll, don't you think?"

"I think your time with Andrew here is rubbing off," McIntyre said. "You're sounding more like a detective than a technician," he chuckled.

"But you make a good point, too. Inspector Fletcher, have you looked to see if this suspect Benson had a connection with Sergeant Wallace?"

"No, not yet. But it's also why I was looking into your procedures," Fletcher replied. "If Benson was part of the smuggling ring, he could have seen your earlier request at the university."

"You've given me a reason to look at our methods, Inspector Fletcher," CI McIntyre answered, getting up from his desk. "Inspector Gordon, let's pull our procedures folder and walk through each one, step-by-step. We'll start with the narcotics one first." He motioned the two officers from his office and the three approached the front counter.

"Thank you for your time, sir." Inspector Fletcher said, making his way around the counter. "If Chief Inspector McDermott and I learn anything from the suspect, I'll be sure to pass it to you as soon as possible."

"Excuse me, Inspector?" A constable walked into the lab holding a package. "You've a parcel from Gartcosh." The sensitive nature of the package was easily identifiable by its red and white striped exterior. "Sign at number 19 please," he instructed, holding out a clipboard.

Sheila took the clipboard and found the space for her signature. Signing the log sheet, she handed the clipboard back as the constable passed the parcel to her. "Thank you, ma'am," the constable replied as he left the lab.

"What could this be?" Sheila asked aloud to know one in particular while grabbing a pair of scissors from below the counter.

Andrew watched, getting a glimpse of how the officer handled what could only be some form of evidence being returned.

Sheila slit open the envelope, before setting the scissors down and reaching inside. She pulled out a weathered and dog-eared folder, its exterior stamped 'Confidential' and displaying the royal seal for the British Special Air Service. Several areas had been blackened out to avoid divulging personal information.

"I'll take the folder, Inspector Gordon," the senior officer said, holding out his hand.

"Is that the record for Angus Dunbar?" As a former Royal Marine, Andrew knew past military activities the former assassin could have been involved in would still be guarded, regardless of their time or place.

"Yes, Inspector Fletcher, it is," McIntyre said. "I'm hoping its contents will shed light on the notebook we found in his belongings. If the information is genuine, there are quite a few families who deserve to know why their loved one was killed." He slid the folder back inside the envelope and turned back to his office.

Chapter EIGHT

Edinburgh, Scotland

The couple stood nose-to-nose. The woman held her position firmly in front of her colleague from the courthouse. The gentleman raised his eyes to meet hers, his arms crossed in a feigned shield to the onslaught of verbal jabs he was taking from his adversary.

"Your client failed to submit the proper documents," he accused, waving his hand towards her.

Priscilla El-Sayed waited for the traffic to pass before replying. "My client had no obligation to submit immigration documents as the tenant," she countered. "And furthermore, your client already admitted he didn't care if he had refugee or immigrant tenants in the past. But he still made arrangements to make his flats available to them." Pedestrians looked on outside Edinburgh's Sheriff's Office on Chambers Street as the conversation went on.

Sitting across the street outside the café, Blayne Taggert took in the scene. The woman, regal in stature and standing firmly in place, appeared to be winning her argument. "What are you discussing?" he asked himself as he flipped the newspaper over.

Receiving the call from 'Mr. Higgins,' the alias Michael Connelly used, Taggert took to his assignment with delight. He'd taken a room in a hotel centrally-located to law firms and the Sheriff's Office in Edinburgh, confident he could track down his prey.

Connelly's instructions were straightforward: find out what the woman knows about Sean Gilmore, he recalled. Identifying Miss El-Sayed's office was easy given the name of the firm where she was employed. The difficulty for Taggert would lie in establishing her daily routine in the city.

In under an hour of beginning his surveillance, Taggert was able to identify the young Saudi woman. As he followed her from across the street, he could see her struggle between her upbringing and the trappings of her environment. Dressed in a conservative grey pantsuit,

Priscilla presented herself as any business woman would, battling for recognition in a man's world.

The suit was cut to hug her figure, yet also made to ensure her comfort while standing in the courtrooms of the Sherriff's Office. The contrast to that was her sole item linking her to her father's family: a scarlet-colored Hajib. The loose end of her Hajib fluttered easily as passing automobiles and trucks disturbed the surrounding air.

"Back to your office, are you?" Taggert muttered to himself as Priscilla turned into the parking structure entrance. He saw the woman hand over her ticket to the attendant who took off at a trot to fetch her vehicle.

As he watched, Taggert pulled out his tablet, selecting its camera function and beginning to discreetly saving images of the woman. Just as he snapped off the fourth image, an older model Volvo was pulled up next to her and the attendant stepped out to hold the door for the lawyer.

As Priscilla stepped to the door, she handed the young man a ten-euro bill. In a brief instance, she noticed Taggert across the street, a tablet pointed in her direction. She looked again as she got behind the steering wheel, but the man had disappeared as a bus passed the entrance.

Getting into the taxi, Blayne Taggert sat heavily into the seat.

"Where to, sir?" the driver asked.

Taggert recited the address for Continental Advocacies to the driver and opened the gallery of photos he'd just saved. He slid his fingers across the screen, the image of Priscilla El-Sayed's face filling the void. Can I keep track of you without the headscarf? he asked, knowing it was the only distinguishing item making her stand out from the crowd.

Just one street block behind the taxi, Priscilla maneuvered her car amongst the other drivers. *Who was that man?* she thought. In her mind she saw a man wearing khaki trousers and a dark-colored shirt under a tartan windcheater. His hair and beard were the same sandy brown color that could be said of most men in the city. Blinking, she refocused, trying to picture more detail. The blaring horn of a double-decker bus brought the lawyer out of her thoughts and provided her an instant's notice before she slammed on her brakes.

"That was bloody stupid of me," she exclaimed to the empty car interior. Glancing to the side, she caught sight as the bus driver exhibited his displeasure by flipping his middle finger at her.

"Piss off, old sod," she barked while waving her hand at him. She looked over her shoulder and spotted an opening and gunned the sedan around the red and white behemoth. After an uneventful ten minutes, Priscilla neared her office, but did not notice the gentleman standing at the corner as she pulled into the alley leading to the parking garage below the building.

Blayne had taken up next to the bus stop, leaning on the post with a newspaper in his hands., He glanced over the top of his newspaper to see the Volvo pulling into the lane between buildings and disappear. He noticed the lack of traffic and more important, police constables making rounds.

Noting which building housed the law office, he strolled to one side of the street and read off the names listed on the building. "So, when do you start your day and when does it end?" he asked himself as the municipal bus appeared. He looked at his watch, making a mental note to return later that evening.

Stepping onto the platform, Taggert paid his fare. "Do you happen to have a spare schedule?" he asked the driver.

The driver reached down below his desk and pulled out a multi-page pamphlet. "That'll be two schillings fifty," he said. Taggert took the pamphlet after paying the driver and sat down in the front seat behind the driver, looking over the route and times the bus made its stop.

***

"The superintendent will see you now, Inspector," the constable announced.

McDermott stood up and tapped on the door as he swung it open. As he stepped in, he noticed Chief Superintendent MacCallum reviewing yet another report filed by the constables. McDermott feigned a cough and stood at the front of the desk, waiting for MacCallum to acknowledge him.

Without looking up, the senior officer spoke. "What've you got now, McDermott?"

McDermott unfolded the note his partner Fletcher had typed up. "We've come across an instance of Wallace contacting DUI in Edinburgh," he answered.

MacCallum looked up from his paperwork, disdain edged on his face hearing the former sergeant's name associated with yet another questionable, and possibly a treasonous, act. "I'd expect you would, McDermott," he replied. "The sergeant had reason to make many calls while executing his duties."

"Aye sir, but nae from a private number," McDermott said. "This one came from his cell phone," he explained, sliding the notice on the desk.

This revelation brought a more serious look to Chief Superintendent MacCallum's demeanor. "Did you get the number as part of the listings associated with the case against Alistair Hunt?"

"Yes, one of the cadets came across it." McDermott shuffled slightly on his feet as he answered. "It's only the first, but Sergeant McKee is having them search for additional times Wallace might have called the DUI in Edinburgh."

"Is this another 'gut instinct' of yours that you're following?"

"I'm nae sure you'd call it instinct, sir," McDermott replied. "But it's awfully queer of Cockburn and his partner showing up now and not beforehand. Besides, we're still trying to establish how the drugs were handed off from the docks to Glasgow and Alistair Hunt." He wasn't afraid to admit that he and Fletcher were stumped. "There must be someone else, another link in the chain."

"You still have nothing from the suppliers?" MacCallum asked. "The tip we received was specific about the drugs in the gas bottles used on the service boat. With that information it should be simple enough to track, don't you think?"

McDermott dropped his head to his chest, his gaze fixed on the superintendent's nameplate perched on the desk's edge. Clearing his throat, he answered. "Aye, sir, but the bottle we seized did nae have any tag on it. It was like a plant or ruse to get us to look at ..." He slammed his hand on the desk at the realization. "How stupid of me," he stammered.

"What is it, Conor?"

"The bottle onboard the *Standard-Apollo* was a decoy," McDermott replied, running his hand through his hair. Circling the chairs fronting the desk, he came back to facing the superintendent. "The one item we've failed to look at after seizing the drugs were CCTV images from the weather office's cameras. Andrew caught a snippet of the Baxter murder on one of them."

"Are you saying we might have an image of drugs being handed off one of the other boats?"

"Not just any boat, sir, but the *Nordic Supplier*. The captain confessed to being the go between for the Irishman and the other captains."

Superintendent MacCallum sat back in his chair, hands together while his fingers propped up his chin. "You better move smartly if you expect to have any images," he noted. "I'll see that someone pulls the warrant from the files; this is still part of your initial investigation?" he asked, picking up his phone.

"I'm hoping you're wrong and they have nae recorded over that day," McDermott said as he turned away from the senior officer and headed out to grab his partner. Trotting down the hall, McDermott slowed just outside the inspector's room and waited for several officers to clear the door. He encountered several constable sergeants doing administration work as he entered the office, while hearing one trying to calm down a caller over the phone.

Before he could survey the room for his partner, Inspector Fletcher nudged his shoulder, causing McDermott to flinch noticeably in front of the other officers. "Damn you, Andrew," he exclaimed.

"It'll teach you not to stand in the middle of the doorway," the younger officer said, squeezing past the Scotsman and waving his ever-present notebook in the air. "I've got something that might help us with our questioning of Calvin Benson."

Pushing his way out of the office passed Andrew, McDermott said, "Tell me about it while you drive us to the docks."

The puzzled look on Fletcher's face was unmistakable. "What for?" he asked at the backside of his partner as they headed towards the car park. At nearly a slow trot, Fletcher caught up with McDermott just as he sat in the passenger side of the unmarked sedan.

"What's all the fuss about?" Fletcher asked, getting behind the wheel.

"The images from the CCTV cameras at the weather office," McDermott said. "How often are they recorded?".

"The clerk said they've got enough tapes for each day, why?"

"The drugs on the *Standard-Apollo* were a decoy," McDermott answered. "I'm thinking the captain on the *Nordic Supplier* was handling something bigger about the same time," he answered while watching the city pass by them.

"What gives you that idea?"

"Mister MacCallum was asking about the gas bottle on the *Standard-Apollo*," McDermott replied. "And how we haven't any luck of identifying who it belonged to," he added. "It dawned on me it didn't belong to any company. But someone meant us to seize it." He quickly grasped the door handle as Andrew turned the corner that led to the harbor. "Mind the speed limit while you're at it, too."

Fletcher smiled briefly, knowing his partner was regretting the choice having him drive through the city. "Do you think we'll find something being off-loaded that's suspicious, then?"

"Aye, I do, Andrew," he answered.

Parking in front of the building housing the harbor's weather service, the inspectors stepped out of the car and entered, with Fletcher leading the way. He caught the eye of a clerk in the middle of the office as he pushed the door open.

"Excuse me," Fletcher said, holding out his police identification. "I need to speak with Mister Argyle."

"One moment, sir," the clerk replied before picking up her phone. In less than a minute, an older gent with a slender build came through the side door. His greying hair was a wind-swept mess as he ran his hand through it in a vain attempt to look professional to the officer.

"Inspector..." The manager struggled to recall the officer's name.

"It's Fletcher," Andrew answered. "And this is Chief Inspector McDermott," He quickly motioned to Conor, who paced slowly behind him. "We'd like to look at your CCTV recordings for... the 3rd week of July," he explained as he glanced at his notebook to make sure his dates were correct.

"Certainly," the manager said. "If you'll come around the counter and follow me, I'll show you to our computer room." He held holding the swinging gate open for them an as they followed the manager, they saw staff members giving a brief to service boat captains, pointing out a weather system they could encounter while at sea.

"Here we are," Argyle said after unlocking the computer room. As they entered, Fletcher experienced the coldness of the room first, shivering under his sport coat. The manager stepped to a series of computer monitors and touched one screen. "You said the 3rd week, is that correct?" he confirmed, highlighting a file name.

"That's correct," Fletcher said, glancing at McDermott, who just shrugged his shoulders.

In moments, a series of images emerged. Each one had a date displayed, along with a compass direction. "You'll see that the day and camera location are noted on the screen," the manager said. "And while facing this wall, you are considered to be facing the harbor entrance, or due east as it were," he explained. "If you place the cursor on the image and hit the left button on the mouse, the image will enlarge."

"Thank you," Fletcher replied, sliding a chair over before taking control of the computer. He enlarged the image of the first day and then began the tedious work of scrolling through each one, looking for the *Nordic Supplier's* berth.

"There, that's her," McDermott nearly shouted in Fletcher's ear as he pulled up the image. "She's got a container lashed on the deck..." His voice trailed off as Fletcher selected the next picture, which showed a shadowy outline of a truck and trailer behind the crane on the dock. "And that's a lorry waiting for it. Can you make out the truck plates?" he asked.

"I've got them," Fletcher said, noting the identification of the truck and adding the description. "We shouldn't have any issues finding it." He tapped the figure's headpiece on the screen. "The chap standing next to the lorry appears to be Hindi or Sikh. That should narrow who we need to look into, don't you think?"

"Aye, it will," McDermott replied, studying the other images. Pointing to another image of the vehicle but from a different angle, he directed Fletcher to enlarge the picture. "Does this one look to have another fella in the cab?"

"The image is kind of grainy, but it looks to be someone," Fletcher replied. "Could it be the driver's helper?"

"Maybe, but what if it's the Irishman coming to collect his wares?"

Fletcher sat back, flexing his right hand over the keyboard. "He'd be taking quite a risk of getting caught, especially if he's the one behind the decoy delivery on the *Apollo*."

"Move on to the others," McDermott said, directing Fletcher to focus on the screen in hopes of finding another clue. "Look for the images with just the lorry."

Fletcher deftly selected a handful of images from the collection and displayed them on the screen for his partner to view. One by one, each image came into focus, the driver and his truck being the main object in each frame. "Who do we have here?" he muttered aloud.

"Seems like an official looking fella, doesn't he?" McDermott replied.

"Someone within Customs maybe..." Fletcher said before stopping himself. "Could it be Baxter? Damn it, how'd we miss that? It would make perfect sense. He signs off the documents for the drugs as a genuine transaction. Then he files fake ones away as proper inspections, making sure no one else handles it," he added. "Which puts Dunbar in the lorry's cab watching who is connected with the drugs," he announced, pleased with his deduction of the events.

"Wonderful synopsis, Andrew," McDermott declared. "But we're wagering that the person in the lorry is Dunbar and not the Irishman. Is there no way to clean up the images?' he asked, his eyes narrowing in his attempt to stare past the grainy picture.

"I'm sure Mister McIntyre could have Devin work on it. What are you thinking?"

McDermott paced behind his partner in the tiny room, his thoughts swirling at the possible accomplice or suspect sitting in the lorry. Looking down at the grainy image, he felt a nagging pain creeping across his forehead as he concentrated on determining who the mystery rider was.

"Make a copy; we'll let the folks in forensic do their magic," he said, leaving the air-conditioned room as beads of sweat trickled down his back. "And while you're at it, get a copy of the lorry numbers off to

Glasgow. Let them do some work for once. And see if London can help out with the container number, too," he added. "There's got to be a record of it being picked up or delivered somewhere" He strolled out of the building, hands stuffed in his pockets.

Chapter NINE

Belfast, Northern Ireland

As McDermott and Fletcher were viewing CCTV images at the meteorological office in Aberdeen, Michael Connelly was looking over production reports from the latest batch of drugs being manufactured. Circling a series of numbers in one column, he drew a line across the page to another set, noting the discrepancies between the two.

He took a gulp of his now cold coffee as he turned to his computer, which was preparing a draft notice to his senior manager at the Limerick facility, when his cellphone chirped. Picking up the phone, he saw the number and read the message display: *Have an answer, call when available, LF sends.*

"Well, Liam, what surprise do you have in store today?" Connelly asked as he selected a number on the call list. In moments, he could hear a chirp and a series of pulse tones as it dialed the number. After the third ring, an excited young voice answered.

"Mister Higgins, I didn't expect you to call back so soon," the Irishman replied.

"Well, Liam, I didn't want to wait any longer than necessary," Connelly replied. "What can you tell me about this discovery and the person who's collecting the thousand euros?"

"It was Liu Yang, the chemist from the University of Shanghai," Liam said. "She was able to break down the components and found the Algerians could add a PCP marker to the cannabis oil."

"Interesting," Connelly murmured. "Anything else?"

"Unfortunately, yes there is," Liam added. "It seems every time someone handles the drugs, the PCP begins to break down. Liu noticed the PCP became less potent after each instance of testing."

Connelly swiveled his chair and gazed out at the Belfast skyline. He hadn't considered the Algerian drug dealer, Nazim Aziz, would have someone with the skill to create the drug without some errors occurring.

Turning his attention back to his operations manager, Connelly considered how he could turn this misfortune to his advantage.

"Liam, I want you to move Miss Yang and her assistants to a separate area and advise her to prepare a sample of the hashish that won't breakdown. Let her know there's an added five-thousand-euro bonus to her and her associates if they can prepare the sample in thirty days."

Liam scrambled to write the message he would relate to the young woman as fast as his director spoke the words. "Will there be anything else?" he asked, holding the pen a fraction of an inch over the paper, ready to add to his task.

"The original plan is still in place," Connelly mentioned. "As they prepare the sample, they also need to consider preparing the anecdote to it," he added. "Remind them there's money to be made in curing the ailment, Liam. Don't let them forget that."

"Yes, Mister Higgins. I'll pass your wishes to them," he said.

"Oh… and Liam," Connelly said, recalling his promise, "let them know I'll see their bonuses are dispatched later today as well."

***

Across the Irish Sea in the fashion district of Edinburgh, a bustle of tourists and locals were making their way under cloudy skies. Nestled between a clothier shop and men's shoe store near Castle Street in downtown Edinburgh was a small jewelry retailer. Pulling her jacket tight around her shoulders, Priscilla El-Sayed made her way from her car to the shop, its miniature Spanish flag fluttering just over the entrance.

As she entered the small but organized shop, Priscilla was always pleasantly surprised at the sight. Long counters constructed out of gleaming glass displayed trays of engagement and wedding rings. Silver bracelets and earrings made with precious stones hung from clear plastic trees, showcasing their brilliance. In one corner were men's watches from various world-renown manufacturers and golden cuff links. She took in the jewels, always amazed.

As she closed the door behind her, she spied a woman with a monocle held firmly over one eye and a butane torch in her hand. "Buenos Dias, Priscilla, what a wonderful surprise," she exclaimed. Extinguishing the flame, the woman came out from behind the work bench to embrace her friend.

"Hello, Teresa," Priscilla replied, placing a kiss on each cheek of the woman from Cadiz. "I hope I didn't interrupt anything important."

"I'm preparing a new necklace," Teresa replied. "My supplier in Japan provided me with several beautiful pearls." She picked up the specimen tray that held the near translucent orbs on a bed of black felt.

"They're stunning," the lawyer exclaimed.

As she placed them back on the workbench, Teresa circled behind a display case with numerous pieces made of the finest Spanish silver. "Does something catch your eye?" she asked, sweeping her hand over the glass.

"Not today, Teresa," Priscilla said. "I need to ask a favor of you, though," she started, reaching into her jacket for an envelope. "I'd like you to pay a visit to our friend in Perth. It's rather important you see this passed to him."

This wasn't the first time she'd asked Teresa to act as a courier, passing along information to clients awaiting trial in one of Scotland's prisons. Teresa Munoz's debt to Priscilla El-Sayed was in the form of being the star witness in a corruption case against one of Edinburgh's more infamous slumlords. Priscilla also convinced her father to help Teresa establish her jewelry shop as an investment.

"When does your friend need to see this?"

"Sooner is always better," the statuesque lawyer replied, sliding the envelope across the display case.

Teresa took the envelope and placed it in her coat. "I've a few pieces to deliver to a client, so making a brief visit would not be out of the question," the young Spaniard said. "I'll see he gets this later this afternoon." She hadn't forgotten the visitor center hours at Her Majesty's Prison-Perth.

"Thank you, Teresa," Priscilla said. "Do let me know when you're done with the necklace. I might purchase it," she added, nodding towards the workbench.

"I'll see you get the first viewing when I'm finished," Teresa said while she brushed a few loose hairs back. As they exchanged their goodbyes, each woman contemplated what lay ahead of them for the day.

Teresa stepped to the door as the lawyer exited the shop. Flipping a small sign to show she was no longer open, Teresa locked the door and drew the security gate across the entrance. She picked up the precious metals and stones from her workbench and slid the trays into the safe before securing the door by spinning the antique dial several times.

As she looked about the shop, she grabbed her coat and checked for the envelope, certain it was still inside the pocket. Teresa collected her purse and made her way to the back of the shop where she set the security alarm before exiting the shop and locking the door behind her.

While her friend was closing up her shop, Priscilla strolled along the street toward the car park, unaware of the eyes following her from the bus stop. Blayne Taggert had taken notice of the jewelry shop the lawyer stopped at, but dismissed it since Miss El-Sayed had spent less than five minutes inside.

He glimpsed his target getting into her Volvo sedan, pulling on to the street, and heading uptown in the direction of the Sheriff's Office and the adjoining courthouse complex. "Another day defending the unjust," he muttered under his breath. Tossing the coffee into the trash bin, Taggert flagged down a passing taxi.

"Where to, sir?" the driver asked as Taggert settled into the seat.

"The courthouse on Chambers Street, if you please," the hitman replied, having lost sight of the lawyer's sedan.

With the taxi pulling away, Teresa Munoz maneuvered her BMW into the street behind the black livery vehicle to begin her hour-long drive to Perth. She pulled the envelope from her purse and slid her finger under the flap, exposing the contents. Underneath a single page letter, she found her compensation in the form of five crisp 100-pound bills. "Muchas gracias, Senorita Priscilla," she uttered. pulling them free.

With little fanfare or delay, she was soon on the motorway heading north. Pulling the letter out, she placed it on the steering wheel and read, memorizing the contents. *Sean, a former associate of yours, contacted me. He was keen to know your location, but I felt it best he not be told. He mentioned you had some documents he wished to have returned, but I didn't want to mention something out of turn. How do you think I should handle it?*

"What have you gotten into now, Priscilla?" Teresa asked aloud. Glancing back to the letter, she read the contents again, committing the dialogue to memory so she wouldn't arouse the suspicions of the constables working at the prison. After another thirty minutes of driving along the M90, the jeweler soon approached the outskirts of Perth.

With a deft touch of the clutch, she was soon negotiating the exit to Edinburgh Street where Teresa pulled into the car park designated for visitors to the prison. She set the brake and turned the engine off before she flipped down the visor to expose a small mirror. Rummaging through her purse, she found her lipstick and slid the glossy mauve color across her lower lip. She pulled back her raven-black hair, and grabbed the scarf tied to her purse strap, recalling her look from previous visits.

The dull grey walls of concrete surrounding the grounds again confronted her as she walked towards the entrance to the administration. Atop the walls were strands of gleaming razor wire, held in place by posts as rust stains streaking the walls told their age.

As she approached the storefront-like doors, they slid open as a mother exited, dabbing her eyes, her daughter in tow behind. Teresa presented her identification as she stepped to the front desk. "I'm here to see my companion, Sean Gilmore," she announced to the constable.

"Aye, sign the request log, please," the officer said while typing the prisoner's name in the computer. In moments, the information on the former lawyer for Michael Connelly appeared on the screen, which included the visitors who'd made previous visits. "And the nature of your visit, Miss Munoz?"

"I've some family news I need to pass along," the woman replied.

"Through the door to your left. A constable will announce when your party is available," the clerk said, directing Teresa to the waiting area. As she walked away from the counter, she approached the door which came to life, a loud buzz and the clank of the lock sliding open in greeting.

As she pushed the door forward, her senses were assaulted with the cold reality of confinement. A couple sat quietly on chairs bolted to the floor while a solitary television hung in the corner broadcasting a children's program. Across the room, another door would lead her to a room with the booths where she could pass along the information to Sean.

Moments after she sat, Teresa heard her name called as the entrance to the visitor's booths opened. She shuffled across the floor and passed the constable, who held open the door, waiting. "Number three, ma'am," he said as he pointed to the space.

Walking behind the various family members, she heard a myriad of conversations, snippets declaring innocence, and a few sobs from women looking at their sons through the plate-glass window.

As she stepped into the enclosure, she saw Sean, wearing an olive drab shirt, his hair looking flat and lifeless. Teresa could see the eyes of the former lawyer looking glazed over and sunken. Picking up the phone, Teresa sat on the metal stool and leaned in towards the window separating herself from the Irishman. "Good morning, Sean. How are you today?"

Sean smiled at the woman. For the last three months since they sentenced him, he'd kept to himself, avoiding the possibility of encountering someone who'd harm to him. "I'm no worse for wear," he replied into the phone. "What brings you to Perth?"

"It seems one of our schoolmates met an acquaintance of yours," she started. "He was a partner of a firm you both worked for and wanted to know how you're doing."

Sean leaned forward, resting his elbows on the ledge. "I'm afraid my former coworker and I had a falling out, so it's best he doesn't know about my current circumstances," he answered in a cryptic tone. "Unless he has my severance package," he laughed, a wry smile coming to his face. "That I'd be happy to take it off his hands."

"I don't know of any money deal you might have had," Teresa replied. "But he mentioned a series of files the firm considered proprietary and wants them returned. Also, our friend wanted me to pass along another message," she said. "Let your sailor friend know his vessel is captained by his former first mate." She hoped Sean understood Malcolm Spiers was now the captain of the Nordic Supplier.

A smile crossed Sean's face at the news that the ship of Clive Duncan was in good hands. The other news caused his chin to drop against his chest as he let out a heavy sigh. Looking up, his eyes narrowed, belaying a demeanor and appearance of serious resolve. "The notes in question are personal and need to be safeguarded," he said. "Tell our acquaintance under no circumstances are those files to be handed over... to anyone."

Even with the glass separating them, Teresa could sense the magnitude of Sean's statement. "I'll see the message is relayed correctly," she answered. "Is there anything I can do in your absence for your friend?"

Looking through the glass, Sean considered the offer from the young woman from Spain. He saw first-hand what evil Michael Connelly could unleash, whether provoked or on a whim. Using the former SAS sergeant Angus Dunbar to conduct the killings of at least three people who interfered in his drug empire gave Sean a moment of pause. "Yes, two things our friend needs to know," he replied.

"First off, remind our friend she can always call upon my cousin Adrian in France if she needs help," he said. It was his hope Priscilla would understand the message to contact the former Legionnaire who he'd dealt with in the past.

"And the second item?"

"I've two other former acquaintances, Erin and Geoff," Sean answered, spelling the names for Teresa. "They're not privy to my line of work. They deserve to be protected at all costs, if possible."

Looking at the Irishman and before she could respond, Teresa heard the constable's voice. "Time's up, booth number three," she said, the same time Sean heard the message on his side. "Take care of yourself, Sean," was the last thing she said before the handset went dead.

Sean acknowledged her with a nod of his head and a smile as a constable came up behind him. Getting him up from the chair, they led him from the call booth, leaving Teresa sitting alone for the moment.

As she replaced the handset back in the cradle, she slid the chair back and headed for the exit, passing the same constable who held the door open for her. She felt the sun warm her face as she left the building and searched for her car. Glancing over her shoulder, she noted the drab exterior. The thought of having to spend any time in prison gave her a chill.

Chapter TEN

Aberdeen, Scotland

With copies of the CCTV images in hand, Inspectors McDermott and Fletcher entered the forensics lab only to find the junior technician Kyle manning the counter. "Can I help you gentlemen?" he asked, looking up from the logbook he was preparing.

"Aye, you can," McDermott answered. "Where's Chief McIntyre?"

"The chief left early," Kyle replied. "Seems he had an errand to run."

"Then where's Inspector Gordon?" Fletcher asked, flustered at the young man's lack of urgency to provide information.

"She and Devin are on their way to the university," came the reply. "We've a call to assist in the school's security team in their investigation of a crime scene."

"Can you log these in as evidence, then?" Fletcher asked, placing the computer discs from the meteorological office on the counter. "They're part of the Wallace investigation."

As Fletcher waited for Kyle to log the evidence in, McDermott stepped out of the lab and into the hallway. Pacing across the tile floor, bits of the puzzle cluttered his mind from their case. Who was the mystery man in the lorry they saw in the video? If not the Irishman, was it the former SAS operative and assassin, Dunbar? And if it was Dunbar, was he there to protect the driver, or was he identifying his next target? In this case, the fella from customs, Calvin Baxter?

Running his hands through his hair and releasing a heavy sigh, McDermott felt a sense of loss at not having a chance to interrogate Dunbar before he was killed. And how does this professor fit in? Does he have a hand in the mix of the deadly drugs found on the *Apollo* from their earlier investigation? "Damn, too many questions and not enough answers," he muttered as Fletcher walked out of the lab.

"Did you say something?"

Before McDermott could answer, the public address system blared overhead. "Chief Inspector McDermott, contact Sergeant Giles, please," it announced, causing each man to glance at the other.

"What do you think it's about?"

"Maybe it's about his friend in Edinburgh," Fletcher replied, following his partner up the stairs. "Let's hope he's willing to help us learn what Cockburn and Sedgwick are so interested in."

Pushing through the crowd of constables, barristers, and a few civil servants making way to their respective posts within the building, the inspectors finally found Sergeant Giles. He was surrounded by four constables outside the senior constable's office, and they could hear him giving instructions on newly established patrols near the Council Headquarters of Aberdeenshire.

"Right now, listen up lads, we're expecting a civil showing at the protests," he said. "But keep your eyes open for some youngsters trying to make names for themselves, too." Turning, he saw the two Scotland Yard inspectors and finished his brief. "Go on now, and don't forget it's better to call for extra constables to help than for the medical folks to treat your wounds."

"Fine lecture, Sergeant," McDermott said, walking past the constables who were making their way out. McDermott couldn't help but notice a few directing distasteful looks at him. "You wanted to talk to us?" he asked, nodding towards Fletcher.

"Aye, Inspector. I got a call from a constable at the university," Giles said as he moved behind his modest desk in the office. Rifling through several dispatches, he grabbed several sheets in his hand. "Seems they've come across the same drug type from your Apollo case. Do you think your suspect Benson had a hand in selling it?"

McDermott dropped his head and sighed in resignation. His suspicions of the professor in custody leaned towards a buyer of the drugs, not a seller. "It appears he might be more involved than we thought," he said.

"The chief wanted you and Inspector Fletcher to meet with Inspector Gordon at the university to see if there's a connection," Giles mentioned. "Here some information." He handed over a transcript of the initial call from the school's security office. "The victims have been taken to the Royal Infirmary for treatment," he added.

McDermott grabbed the dispatch from the sergeant. "Andrew, you go and interview the victims," he directed, turning to his partner. "I'll go to the university to see if we've a connection between Benson and this latest event." Reaching over the sergeant's desk, McDermott grabbed the notepad and pencil from under a folder. "I'll be borrowing this for the time being."

"Fancy you wanting to have something to write with," Fletcher said, chiding his partner for taking the pad and pencil as opposed to his usual lack of note-taking skills. "Should I push the victims about their relationship with the professor?" he asked with a glance at McDermott.

"First, find out how they got the drugs," McDermott replied. "Afterwards, you can determine if they had any dealings with Benson. But remember, our first notion of the professor was about him being a buyer from Doyle, not a dealer at the school."

Approaching the police car assigned to them, Fletcher turned to McDermott. "How do you plan on getting to the university if I'm going to the infirmary?" he asked. The two locations were in opposite directions in the city.

"You'll be dropping me off first," the Scotsman answered, tugging on his field coat. "I suspect I can get a lift from the constables when I'm finished and join you at the infirmary before you're done."

"You don't think I can keep myself focused being around Sheila?" Fletcher asked, getting behind the wheel.

"It has nothing to do with you and Inspector Gordon seeing each other," McDermott replied. "I'm nae fond of hospitals, that's all. Besides, I'm an alumnus and I might be able to find out a wee bit more on Benson than you while on campus."

After twenty minutes of negotiating the city streets, Fletcher spotted the police van near the entrance to one of the buildings at Aberdeen University. "Here you go," he said, turning to his partner. "That'll be six-pence twenty," he teased, holding his hand out.

"Get on with yourself," the senior officer said as he climbed out of the car.

Pulling away from the university, Fletcher backtracked to Hutcheon Street where he turned right to join the rest of the traffic leading out of the city. Soon, he was pulling off the motorway, pleased with himself for not getting lost as he'd done in the past. Finding a spot to park, he locked the car and trotted towards the emergency entrance. The motorized whoosh of the sliding glass doors announced his entry as several members of the staff turned to address their next patient.

"Can we help you?" a nurse asked while the intercom screeched, requesting assistance in the radiology department.

"Yes. I'm Inspector Fletcher," Andrew replied as he held out his credentials. "I understand there were two individuals brought in from the university. They were being treated for possible drug-overdose," he explained with a glance at his notes.

"Aye, follow me, Inspector," the young woman said. Skirting passed one of the cleaning staff, his cart piled high with soiled linens, the nurse stopped at the central station to look at the large white screen behind her colleagues. Colored magnets, some with names and others with numbers, were skewered across the board. "Maggie, where the two from the university?"

"They'll be in rooms six and seven," the nurse replied, her voice trailing off from fatigue, the result of an extra eight-hour shift edged on her face.

Turning away, the nurse led Inspector Fletcher to the examination rooms. Standing outside was a constable from the station on Coningham Terrace. She tugged at the curtain, exposing a young man lying on the gurney. Over the bed, various medical devises chirped, beeped, or displayed the patient's vital signs. The young man appeared to be comatose to Fletcher. The only indication of life was the rhythmic beeping of the EKG machine, its lines cycling up and down on the screen to show a heartbeat.

"Has he said anything since he was brought in?" Fletcher queried the nurse.

"Nae much," the nurse replied. "The usual for a druggie. 'I'm dying... what I'd do this for...' that kind of talk." She shook her head. "The other one though, he was a bit more talkative," she explained, stepping out to the next room.

Glancing in at the patient, Fletcher noticed something familiar about the person lying in the bed. He glanced over at the bags of fluid hanging from the stand and the tubes running down to the needles, one stuck in each arm. The image of a tattoo gave the inspector a clue. "I know this chap," he muttered aloud.

"You do?" the nurse asked, surprised.

"I've seen him at a local pub near the university," Fletcher replied. Recalling the few times he and Sheila had visited the pub her friend Geoff worked, the young man was one of the crew who would come in and cleaned.

"Do you have his belongings?" Fletcher asked, returning his attention of investigating the possible connection to their drug case.

"Right here," the nurse said as she pulled a bag from beneath the gurney.

Before sliding the tray table in front of him, Fletcher grabbed a pair of gloves from the box hung on the wall. He then began to remove the articles from the bag: trousers, a shirt, and most importantly, the young man's wallet. Fletcher took out the university student ID card and held it up, making sure the photo matched the patient in front of him. *Niall Atchison.*

Movement from the bed caught Fletcher's eye as the patient turned his head towards the inspector. "Where the hell am I? And what are you doing rifling me trousers? Who the hell are you?" Niall asked, his speech slurred as he blinked in his eyes in an attempt to focus on the officer.

"You were brought in because you were overdosing on hashish," Fletcher answered. "By the way, my name is Inspector Fletcher," he added. "So, Mister Atchison, if this is correct, how about you tell me who sold you the drugs?"

Niall stared at the ceiling. Beeping from the EKG increased slightly, confirmed by the numbers displayed on the screen, showing the patient's heart rate was increasing. "A young lass gave me a wee bit to try," he said in a hushed tone. "Turns out it seems to be shit seeing how I'm here."

"And when did you make your deal for this wee bit of hashish?"

"About three months ago," he replied. "My friend and I, we made a trip to Southampton to do some research for our papers on a history piece regarding the Titanic... how's Quinn doing by the way?"

"I'm not sure," the inspector replied. "I'll leave it to the nurse to let you know. Now, what was the name of this young woman you met in Southampton?"

"Quinn and I just bumped into her at a pub," Niall answered, "over a few pints you know."

"So, in a single moment, you and your mate meet a local girl and decided to buy some drugs off her?" Fletcher asked, feeling the agitation build with every moment. "There was nothing special or unique about her?"

Niall let out a brief chuckle. "She was nae local, mind you," he replied. "She was studying at Portsmouth for the semester from St. Andrews. Turns out she was raised here in Aberdeen, too."

Fletcher stared at the young man, his mind working on the information from his statement. *Is it possible he's talking about one of the victims from the drugs off the French freighter?* he contemplated in silence. "Did she mention her name?"

"Aye, she called herself Pattie," Niall answered. "Said it was short for Patricia or something of that sort. She had no problem chatting about football or politics. It was almost like she was too friendly, now that you're asking about her."

The rustling of the curtain behind Fletcher caught him by surprise as his partner Chief Inspector McDermott stepped into the room. "Mind another visitor?" he asked, tapping the young Londoner on the shoulder.

"Not at all," Fletcher answered. "Mister Atchison and I were just discussing how he met his acquaintance in Southampton," he explained, waving his hand at the student.

"Oh? And what have we to say about him?" McDermott asked.

"Not him, but her. It was a young woman," Fletcher corrected.

"Really? Not what we consider normal in most drug dealing circles, heh?"

"It wasn't a drug deal, I'm telling you!" Niall declared. "She offered the sample to us like I said. Looking back, it seems she was trying to get rid of what she had." He closed his eyes for the moment.

"What makes you say that?" McDermott queried, pulling a chair in to sit on.

With his eyes closed, Niall continued. "She'd placed two small wads of hashish on the table while keeping a larger one in her hand. Said the two were for Quinn and I but the other was hers for the trip back to Edinburgh."

"Who's Quinn?" McDermott asked, looking at Fletcher.

"His running mate," Fletcher replied.

"And the lass was heading back to Edinburgh, you said?"

"Are you daft? It's what I said, isn't it?" Niall exclaimed, his patience thinning at being questioned about something that happened three months earlier.

McDermott leaned back in the seat, hands running through his hair. One of the deceased users of hashish identified in Southampton had been his niece, Edna. But was this young man telling him that she was actually one of the dealers instead of an innocent victim? "What did this lass look like? Her hair, eyes, anything you can remember?" his voice was sullen and low.

"She was nae a model-type, if you know what I'm getting at," Niall answered. "But she wasn't a matron for the elderly, either. She was just, you know, another lass in a pub."

As he picked his head up, McDermott clasped his hands in front of him, his fingers turning pale as they interlocked. *She was nae a plain Jane*, he thought. *She was a wonderful young lass with a bright future*, he told himself, restraining his anger at what he just heard. Closing his eyes, he could still see her waving at him from the dock with her floral dress swaying softly in the breeze as the warship he stood on pulled away from the pier.

Before the inspectors could ask another question, the nurse returned, this time with the doctor in tow who held the patient's medical file. "I'm sorry, gentlemen, but I'm going to ask that you withhold any more questions until after we treat the patient."

"Aye, we can do that," McDermott said, raising to his feet and tugging at the sleeve of his partner. "C'mon Andrew. We'll pass our findings to the sergeant."

The audible beep of the door sensor announced the departure of the inspectors as they strolled out of the hospital. "Where are you parked?" McDermott asked, scanning the car park.

"To the right, about three rows in," Fletcher answered as he led his partner towards the police car. "Are you alright?"

McDermott stopped, standing in the middle of the roadway. "No, I'm not," he replied. "The fella in there was describing my niece," he explained, rubbing his hand across his face as tears welled up.

"Your niece?"

"Aye, she was one of the victims Mister Collingsworth mentioned when we were given this case," McDermott added, pausing to sit on a concrete barrier separating the parking from the road. "I didn't want to tell you because I didn't want to believe she'd be using drugs." His chest heaved as he took in a deep breath. "I'm not sure why she'd call herself by another name though..."

"I'm sorry, Conor," the young Londoner said. "But we didn't have any evidence then that the female victim was peddling hashish," Fletcher said. "All we were told was she died and had signs of smoking the hashish, nothing more."

"Aye, I know. But you'll no convince me or make me believe she jumped off the roof of the flat, though either," McDermott said, recalling the manner of Edna Gallagher's death. "I'm still of the mind she was murdered, and I'm going to find out who's responsible one way or the other." He pushed himself off the barrier to rest his hand on Fletcher's shoulder. "Come on now, let's get back to the office."

Chapter ELEVEN

Edinburgh, Scotland

An old-fashioned brass lamp lit the surface of the desk and its contents. Its fluorescent bulbs gave off a cold harsh light across the papers scattered on the green marble inlay. With a large yellow highlighter reminiscent of Churchill's cigar, Priscilla placed a mark across the court transcript from her previous day's appearance at the Sheriff's Office.

As she picked up her tea, a series of chirps alerted her of a message arriving in her computer's mailbox. Sliding her chair to the opposite side of her desk, the lawyer entered a few keystrokes to allow a list of emails to appear on the screen. As she selected the latest one, she noticed it was from her friend at Jewelry Creations by Teresa. The file opened and she quickly scanned its contents.

"It appears I'll be buying a new necklace tomorrow." Pushing her chair back to the table, she looked over the pages to find the spot at which she'd stopped reading. She picked up her highlighter and found the last statement on the transcript needing her attention.

The sound of keys unlocking the outer door to the office caused Priscilla to hesitate, the pen hovering over the transcript. Getting up from her chair, she walked to the inner door and opened it just enough to see the outline of a man entering from the hallway. "Who are you and what do you want?" she stammered.

"Custodial services, miss," the man replied, pulling a cleaning cart through the doorway. As he turned around, Blayne Taggert, clad in fluorescent green coveralls, was now standing face-to-face with the lawyer holding information belonging to Michael Connelly.

"I thought cleaning was done on Wednesday?" Priscilla asked, now on the defensive. Already she'd felt something wasn't right just by the timing of the intrusive nature by the person. The strong scent of cleanser assaulted her eyes as Taggert pushed the cart further into the room.

"This isn't my usual building, so I'm not keen on the schedule," Taggert replied. "Besides, they called me in to work tonight, so someone decided I'm cleaning," he continued, pulling out an old-fashioned feather duster.

"Is it possible to come back later, say half-past nine?"

"I'm here now, so let's get this done, shall we?" Taggert pushed the outer door closed, locking it in the process. He quickly reached into the cleaning cart to grasp the polished mahogany handle of his weapon. "Seems you've information my employer wants," he added as the gleaming edge of a knife became visible. "Let's be civil and you won't get hurt."

"Who the hell are you talking about?" Priscilla asked, a nervous stutter to the question. She felt the muscles in her face tighten while she fought her desire to escape her intruder. "Did that Russian scum Tchaikovsky send you?" she asked, trying to gain the upper hand.

Taggert looked across the room at the women, a smug grin crossing his face as he twirled the blade slowly at his side. "You've no idea who sent me, do you? Most employers are rather fussy when their people keep things that don't belong to them," he said. "Seems you're keeping the whereabouts of a friend to yourself."

As the intruder spoke, Priscilla pieced together what was happening, recalling her earlier conversation with the Irishman, Mister Higgins, from the other day. Staring at the man before her, she met his gaze and wished she hadn't. His blue eyes sparkled in a mischievous manner, giving her a sense that Taggert considered the encounter festive in an odd sense.

Mustering up her courage, Priscilla stood steadfast while her mind screamed an impending assault to come before she heard the closing of the stairway door from outside the office. A flash of elation flowed across her face while Taggert turned towards the door just as the visitor tried the handle.

"Just a moment," Priscilla replied loud enough to be heard outside the office. Sidestepping the cleaning cart, she flipped the latch to unlock the door.

Sergeant Xander Holmes let go of the locked door upon hearing the woman's voice. Holding the packet containing additional court reporters notes, he took a step back and glanced down the hall in either direction. His radio squawked as other patrols called in situations they encountered while on the darkening city streets. This alerted Priscilla and her assailant of who stood outside waiting in the hallway.

As she unlocked the door, the barrister swung the door open against the stop, exposing the interior to the constable. "I didn't expect the royal treatment, Sergeant Holmes," she exclaimed. It was easy to recognize the officer from the courthouse, his slender build though obscured by police garb, showing through.

"Aye, it seems like it," Xander replied, taking notice of Taggert in the background and the cleaning cart between them. "Was I interrupting something?"

"It seems my supervisor gave me some poor directions," Taggert answered. "I was filling in for one bloke and not aware they care for this building on Wednesdays." He pushed the cart past Priscilla and into the hall and turned toward the elevator. "If you'll both excuse me."

"Hold on," the officer said, tapping Taggert on the shoulder. "Why was the door locked?"

As he turned back to glance at the officer, the former Royal Marine was quick to answer. "I must have bumped the latch when I was pushing in my cart before closing the door, nothing more. Why... is there a problem, Officer?" Taggert asked, his hand inches from the knife hidden beneath a cleaning cloth.

Sergeant Holmes glanced at Priscilla then back at Taggert. The custodian's response suggested nothing wrong, and neither did the neutral expression on the barrister's face. "No... no problem," he answered before entering the office and closing the door behind him.

As quickly as he could, Taggert wheeled the cleaning cart to the end of the hallway and the elevator. The doors slid open, and he pushed the cart in before selecting the lowest level. Taggert stripped off the coveralls as the elevator slowly descended and grabbed his sweater from the bottom shelf. Tossing the cleaning towel aside, he picked up his knife and slid it into its scabbard behind his back just as he reached the lower level.

Sergeant Holmes stood in the outer office, holding out the packet of court documents. "Judge Cavanaugh asked that I see you get these transcripts before Monday's convening," he said. He noticed her hesitation, as if she was elsewhere. "Is everything alright?"

Priscilla stood in the middle of the office, frozen in uncertainty. Her mind raced with numerous what if? questions, attempting to understand the repercussion of her dilemma if she let the officer know about the situation with Taggert. "Hmm...? Yes, I'm sorry, Sergeant," she mumbled. "The case has me going in several directions, I'm afraid." She grasped the packet from him.

Even though the woman was looking towards him, Holmes was getting the sense she was seeing someone else. "Are you sure things are all right?" he repeated just as the radio squawked too announce an incident nearby.

Having the dispatch summoning officers to respond gave Priscilla her chance to dismiss the constable. "You best answer the call; I'll be fine," she insisted, stepping to the door to let Holmes exit.

Sergeant Holmes grasped his microphone to answer the call while stepping out of the office. Striding slowly towards the elevator, he couldn't shake the sensation something was about to happen and he had stopped it from taking place.

Back in her office, Priscilla sat behind her desk, hands beginning to tremble as the realization of the encounter took hold. *It has to be the Irishman*, she told herself. She remembered the sudden call from the other day, his questioning about Sean's whereabouts. Sliding open her drawer, she pulled out a small ring of keys and turned, facing the hutch under the window. She unlocked the center drawer and pulled out two files. One showed the repeated use, its edges worn and feathered, while the other still showed signs of being newly purchased in color and the sparseness of papers it held.

Laying the files on her desk, she grasped the first feeling the knot in her stomach begin to form. Do I want to know what's inside? she asked herself. "Angus Dunbar is dead; he won't be coming back," she muttered while flipping open the folder. Her friend and colleague had compiled the information on the former SAS member as insurance against his employer, but to what end, she wondered. Scanning the contents, Priscilla took note of times and dates as she tried to comprehend the purpose behind them. Turning to the last page, she noticed the last entry. *M/V Joan of Arc*, Southampton, and it was dated this past April.

"What's the significance of your being here?" Flipping back several pages, she shoved her highlighter between pages keeping the contents visible. Selecting the 30th of April as a date, Priscilla searched her computer for any mention of peculiar activities.

In moments, the computer screen refreshed with the headlines of local officials investigating a third suspicious death, citing a dockworker killed on the job. "Sounds like an industrial accident if you asked me," Priscilla murmured. Reading further down, she noticed a familiar name associated with the investigation: *McDermott.*

"So... you started investigating a death in Southampton and it leads you to Aberdeen," Priscilla exclaimed, sounding once again like a lawyer and less of a potential victim. Reading the remainder of the article, she read of two other victims associated with the third, each of them identified as drug users. One, a sailor from the naval yard at Portsmouth was killed on his motorbike; the other, a female student, reported committing suicide by jumping from the roof of a four-story apartment complex.

Toying with her pencil, Priscilla struggled to connect the events in the last entry and what took place in Aberdeen. Did the Irishman dispatch Dunbar to kill those people? And if he did, what was his motive behind it? She turned the divider in the folder and came across a photo of the former SAS sergeant in his dress uniform, standing at attention. The appearance of the soldier didn't belie the fact he had become a cold, ruthless killer in the end.

As she looked at the picture staring back at her, she noticed a familiar feature, one she'd just seen an hour ago. The build and stature were somewhat similar, but it was the eyes. Yes, the eyes told the story, giving away what might go unnoticed by someone else in passing.

"Bloody hell," she gasped. Turning the last divide in the folder, she came across handwritten notes Sean had made. Priscilla read the entries, starting on the first page. Each one carried a date and location, along with the name Mr. Higgins. The descriptions that followed an entry began with a vague figure, until after the tenth, a clear picture had developed of the second party meeting with Higgins. "Sean was tracking Dunbar and Higgins each time they met," she stammered.

After reading two more pages, Priscilla found something causing her to freeze, her breath coming in a gasp. In October of last year, the note stated her friend Sean had observed Dunbar entering a bank in Cardiff. After he left, he met with another man in a local pub. "They embraced like family," she read aloud. The full realization of who entered her office finally came to light. "My God, a family member of Dunbar's is part of the conspiracy," she gasped.

Before reading any further, her thoughts were interrupted by the chiming of her cell phone. A reminder that read *21:30, begin yoga regime* greeted her as she picked it up. "Damn, where did the time go?" Closing the file on Angus Dunbar, she turned and slid into the hutch drawer, and glanced at the other. "I'll be looking you over tomorrow, monsieur," she promised, placing Adrian Richelieu's file on top of the other before sliding the drawer closed and locking it.

Chapter TWELVE

Aberdeen Scotland

Darkness shrouded the narrow streets of Aberdeen, with sporadic streetlights creating havens of safety in each circular glow. Conor McDermott strolled quietly along, lost in thought. The image of the shadowy figure in the lorry from earlier mocked his inability to close his case.

As he stood outside Ailene's rented flat, he cursed the emptiness waiting for him inside. For the third week, his lover was spending her time away after being called to the regional office for the Coast Guard and Maritime Agency in Liverpool. In hindsight, Conor knew it was best for both to have the break in their relationship. Since returning to Aberdeen in May, he saw the strain of his investigation affecting her in the number of increasing arguments.

After tossing his keys aside, Conor went straight to the hutch and poured himself a dram. He set the bottle down and shed his field coat before sitting. "I'm no closer to having anything on the drug shipments," he muttered. The warmth of the golden liquid cascaded down, but did little to help in solving the problem.

"If I don't have something to show William and the commander in London, they'll put someone else on the case," he muttered to the empty room. The whisky dulled his senses and he closed his eyes, but sleep was not an escape for McDermott. It wasn't long before his thoughts returned to a tumultuous period during his Royal Navy days.

Several young men, their summer uniforms a dazzling white contrasting against the ship's superstructure, bounded toward the waiting officer. "Permission to go ashore, left-tenant," one exclaimed. The three others crowded around, eager for a response.

The young officer manning the vessel's quarterdeck couldn't help smile at the crewmembers' enthusiastic nature. The *HMS Edinburgh* was finishing up several months of duty in the Eastern Mediterranean Sea. Now, after a week's sailing between Turkey and Greece, the ship was making its last stop before returning home to England.

"You all have your walking papers?" the young officer asked.

"Aye, we do," they answered in chorus, flashing their papers for him to see. The country of Malta required all foreign service members to carry a document at all times stating visitation requirements and rules of conduct with them while ashore.

"All right then, remember to sign the logbook," the officer directed. He tapped the notice affixed to the steel bulkhead near the gangway. "And don't forget when curfew takes place."

The first man finished signing the logbook and turned to the officer. "Permission to go ashore, Mister McDermott?" he asked while holding his salute.

"Permission granted," Conor replied, returning the salute. He repeated the exchange for each man, each who, after acknowledging the officer, spun around to toss a salute to the fantail, where the Union Jack hung in the afternoon sun.

"You'll not be telling Malcolm what I've been up to, sir?" Able/Seaman Smythe asked.

McDermott looked at the sailor, the young brother of his best friend. "As long as you behave, he'll not hear anything from me," the officer answered. "But... I can't promise keeping everything in after a few pints when we get back to Aberdeen," he chuckled as the young man scampered down to the dock and his waiting friends. Conor stood and shook his head, wondering what he and his friend Malcolm would talk about when it came to the young seaman.

Several hours later, Lieutenant McDermott stepped up to the ship's quarterdeck. "Heading out for a good time, I see?" the officer on duty asked.

"Hardly, Gilbert," Conor answered. "Just need a wee walk on some firm ground before we head home. Permission to go ashore?" he asked with a salute to his counterpart.

"Granted," the officer replied.

Returning to the ship after a few hours, McDermott made his way to the cabin he shared with three other officers, two of which were on duty. Conor stripped off his uniform and crawled into the coffin-like space and was soon fast asleep, knowing he would be back on duty himself come sunrise.

A fist pounded on the door, causing McDermott to jump out of his rack. "What the hell is it?" he shouted as he grabbed the door.

"Sir, you're wanted in the command center," the seaman stammered at the sight of catching the officer in just a pair of briefs. After quickly grabbing his shipboard clothes, McDermott dressed and made his way to the heart of the warship's operation space.

"Morn' to ya, McDermott," the officer in charge said.

"Morning? What time is it?"

"Half past two, I'm afraid," the officer answered as he sipped his coffee. "We've an incident needing a message to be transmitted. Seeing you're the only one who can access the secure tele-type to create the dispatch, we had to wake you."

McDermott shook his head slightly, clearing the cobwebs of sleep. Looking about the spaces, he noticed one of the enlisted men who was part of his communications department. "McPhee could have easily handled this," he noted, nodding to the young man.

"Normally I'd agree, but Commander Jones gave orders it had to be you," the officer as he handed McDermott a red folder.

McDermott knew whatever was inside needed to be treated with care. The color of the folder dictated the sensitive nature of its contents, and he was one of a few capable of handling it onboard. "Aye, I'll get on it right away," he said, relieving the officer of the information before stepping over to the small area where his communications equipment was located.

As he entered, McDermott pulled a curtain closed behind him, the only level of privacy as he prepared to transcribe the message. His heart sank immediately when he looked at the contents of the folder. The first page was a police report along with a notification from the local hospital regarding one of the crew. Written along the border was a name: *A/S Kyle Smythe.*

"Oh, hell laddie, what have you done?" McDermott whispered to himself. They had found Kyle unconscious near a local bar. While the police and medics tried to revive him, they had taken him to the nearest hospital, but it was too late. The police report noted they had found the seaman with several grams of hashish and a marijuana cigarette in his sock.

"That's nae like him," McDermott stammered as he wiped a tear from his eye. "What do I tell Malcolm?" He knew his best friend and the seaman's older sibling would ask about the circumstance the next time they met. Turning on the console, he typed in a few odd commands that allowed him access to the secret transmission mode for the radio. After nearly ten minutes, he'd finish composing the message, following the format dictated by the Admiralty for deaths of service members.

Before sending any message to Southampton, there was always the last act, the commanding officer's signature acknowledging the transmission. With the message finished, McDermott placed it in the folder before pulling the curtain aside. He stepped around a seaman and made his way to Commander Jones's cabin, just steps from the operations center.

McDermott hesitated, brushing his hand through his hair and clearing his throat before he knocked on the cabin door. The knocking seemed to grow louder in McDermott's mind and he wasn't sure why. The cabin door opened and yet he was surprised by the brightness of the light assaulting his vision.

"Conor. Conor, are you okay?" came the familiar voice of his partner Andrew as he felt the hand shaking his shoulder.

"What in God's name are you doing here?"

"It's nearly seven o'clock in the morning," Andrew replied. "Did you finish the bottle again?"

"What...? No, I did nae finish the bottle," Conor said. "It's just as full now as it was when I came home," he defended, pointing to the scotch on the cabinet shelf. "And how the hell did you get in?"

"The door wasn't locked," Andrew said. He could see the beginning signs of stress and fatigue setting in. He'd encountered the same while on a deployment in the Helmand province of Afghanistan, the men in his platoon having too many patrols and not enough rest.

As Andrew recalled the events of that deployment, he felt a growing slug of guilt occupy his stomach. Weeks before their tour was scheduled to end, he was leading a patrol into the foothills when they were ambushed. Fatigued from too many sorties and not enough rest, a simple leap turned into anything but. Andrew's left foot landed on a large stone as he jumped from his vehicle, causing his knee to twist in the opposite

95

direction. Amongst the hail of bullets and screams, he'd become a casualty, unable to lead the men.

"Fix me a cup of coffee, will you," McDermott said breaking through Andrews's thoughts of combat and self-inflicted failure.

"Are you going to wash up?"

"I'll do a wee splash of cologne; nae one'll tell the difference," McDermott replied as he headed towards the back of the flat and the bathroom.

Andrew stepped into the small kitchen, pouring yesterday's coffee into a mug before heating it in the microwave. Glancing at the counter, he could see Conor was becoming lazy in his housekeeping. Dishes were still piled in the sink, and the trash bin was full of takeout containers that smelled of fish and chips. "When do you expect Ailene back?" he asked, pushing aside a container in the small refrigerator to grasp the cream.

"I'm not sure," Conor replied as he entered the kitchen. "But I'll be needing to hire a cleaner soon." He took the cup of coffee with a quick, "Thanks. Let's get to work, shall we?"

"Shall I lock up then?"

"Aye, you can," McDermott said, tossing a set of keys at him.

When he was done, Andrew jogged up behind Conor. "You'll be happy to know there's a packet from Glasgow for you on the front seat."

"Aye? What's in it?"

"Don't know since it's sealed and addressed to you," Andrew replied while pulling the car away from the flat. "I'm sure it has something to do with the Gordon and Hunt case. They were looking into his calls and activities before we made our arrest, remember?"

"Don't let me forget to take this home. Let's have a wee look at what's inside, shall we?" he asked, setting his coffee mug on the dashboard so he'd remember it before running his finger under the flap to break the seal.

Inside were a series of papers showing business transactions and calls from Highland Stag Investments, the firm Alistair Hunt ran as part of his criminal empire greeted him. "I'm impressed," McDermott said. "They've not only listed calls, but found out who the receiver was." He turned the page toward Andrew to see for himself.

"Any names it should concern us about?"

"Well... let's see now," McDermott answered thumbing through the sheets. "We've several calls from Sean Gilmore, two from Cap'n Duncan," his voice trailed off. "And Hunt made two calls to Angus Dunbar himself."

"What about calls to Sergeant Wallace?"

McDermott thumbed through each page, reading the names. "Nothing."

"That's rather odd, don't you think?" Fletcher asked as he pulled into the station car park. "If the sergeant was passing info on drug shipments to Hunt, there must be calls, right?"

McDermott scratched his chin, realizing he'd have to explain his stubble to the superintendent if they met today. "But we know the cousin, Gordon, had something going on with Hunt. I'd wager he was the go-between." He looked over the last note as he opened the door to exit. "This is nae any good."

"What does it say?"

"Seems they found the lorry from our photo near a quarry outside Dumbarton," McDermott said. "The interior was gutted by fire, and the driver hasn't been found..."

"Dunbar?" Fletcher asked.

"Aye... tying off loose ends, I'd imagine," McDermott said.

As the inspectors made their way into the station, Sergeant Giles came forward to greet them. "Chief Inspector, I need a word with you," he said immediately, motioning towards the entrance to the constable's office.

"Am I included?" Fletcher asked.

"Aye, you'll both need to hear this," Giles added, following behind them into his office before closing the door.

"Is everything all right Marcus?" McDermott asked.

"Last night I took a call from Xander in Edinburgh. He mentioned having a run-in with a fella while delivering papers to the barrister on the Wallace case."

"But Gilmore is locked up in Perth, I thought?" Fletcher asked.

"It was the woman, Miss El-Sayed," Giles answered. "Xander mentioned she was a wee bit spooked at the encounter, but did nae mention anything."

"And why should this concern us?" McDermott asked, wanting to focus on the papers from Glasgow he held in his hands.

Over the next few minutes, Sergeant Giles explained what Xander Holmes had told him about the visitor to Priscilla El-Sayed. "And the way Xander described him, well... it reminded me of a fella who came looking for you the day you returned from Belfast."

"So, we had a news-type coming to ask a few questions," McDermott said. "It nae be the first time, you know, Marcus. What made this one fella stand out in particular from the rest?"

"There was something familiar about him I couldn't put a finger on, so I pulled the images from our cameras." He passed the photo of Blayne Taggert to McDermott. "I'd swear I was looking at the goon Dunbar, but I know he's dead and buried."

McDermott stared at the image. He recalled the information from Graham McIntyre, the forensics chief about a possible twin to the assassin being among the populace. "You're nae far from the truth, Marcus."

"What do you mean by that, Conor?" It was Fletcher asking now. "You know something about Dunbar? Does he have a brother we didn't know about?"

"Mister McIntyre had samples of Dunbar's DNA sent to Saint Andrews as part of a study," McDermott said. "They came across a possible match in the national donor database, but they listed it as 'anonymous,' mind you. He did nae know if it was man or woman, but this," he continued, waving the photo around, "confirms he had a cousin, or worse yet, a brother." Sitting back, he contemplated his next step. "Marcus, prepare a notice for distribution to the other stations, will you?"

He turned and looked at his partner, "Andrew, start on a communique for Mister Collingsworth. The people in London will need to know about this. Let's see if we can catch this bugger."

"Can I take a look?" Fletcher asked, reaching for the CCTV image.

"Here," McDermott replied as he handed over the sheet of paper.

Fletcher stared at the face looking into the camera. The hair is shaggier, he told himself. But the facial features and posture of the man spoke volumes. "I might... I mean, I think I know him," he muttered, handing the photo back to the sergeant.

"Really? Looking at just one photo...?" Giles asked. "And when and where did this take place, if you don't mind me asking Mister Fletcher?"

Fletcher shifted his gaze between the two officers. "If it's who I'm thinking of..., I was the officer of record at man's courts-martial," he replied matter-of-factly. "This fella, well.... the major had reason to see him drummed out of our unit. He was caught assaulting one of his own troops in the cargo hold of the *HMS Ocean*," Fletcher said. "It was while we made our way to the Persian Gulf."

Leaning back in the chair, Fletcher closed his eyes as he recalled the events onboard the ship. "I came across him using a blackjack on a private," the inspector said. "The young marine nearly lost his right eye because of the beating. They were both put ashore in Gibraltar, and that was the last I saw of either of them."

"How old was he then?" McDermott asked.

"Oh... he came out of the sergeant's school, which made him about 23 or 24, if I recall," Fletcher said. "He had the highest marks for any newly promoted sergeant coming to Four-Two in nearly ten years. He was put into the reconnaissance squad straight away and ultimately took over for the previous sergeant because of transfer."

"So, he'd be your age, then?" McDermott asked, having grabbed a pad and pencil from the sergeant's desk to jot down his notes.

"Yes, I'd suppose so," Fletcher answered with a shrug of his shoulders.

"Do you remember his name?"

"Yes. His name's Taggert. Sergeant Blayne Taggert."

Chapter THIRTEEN

Edinburgh Scotland

T he eye shadow was subdued but easily seen up close. "I look bloody awful," Priscilla El-Sayed muttered as she looked at her own reflection in the car mirror. Sleep last night came in fleeting moments, interrupted by bouts of restless anxiety and her appearance exhibited the aftermath. Each time she woke, the encounter in her office bombarded her thoughts with questions. Her intellect told her it was impossible for the former assassin Angus Dunbar to return from the grave. But yesterday's visitor had the same cold look in his eyes, and his posture and demeanor were nearly spot on to the killer from Aberdeen.

As she grabbed her purse and satchel, Priscilla sauntered into the office building. "Good morning, Billy," she greeted the freckle-faced member of the security crew.

"Good morning," he answered, blushing at the sight of the elegant woman from Saudi Arabia. "Here's your listing for today." Billy held up the names of clients scheduled for the meeting with her.

"Thank you," she answered as she stepped to the elevator. In moments, she entered the outer office meeting her assistant, Paul, staring at the computer screen. As he heard the door open, he picked his head up to see who'd interrupted his web surfing, greeting her with a wave of his hand. "Morning, Pri."

"And what are we watching this morning?" she asked as she glanced over his shoulder.

"It's the final test between Sri Lanka and England for placement in the Cricket World Cup," he answered, ducking his head back to the screen.

Shaking her head, Priscilla took out her office keys and slid one into the door lock leading to her office. As the key resisted against the tumblers, the door opened. "Paul, have you been in my office?"

"No... why?" he asked, not turning away from the match.

"I always lock my door, but it seems it wasn't shut," the counselor said. Peering through the gap between the door and the wall, Priscilla was cautious to see what lay before her. She pushed the door all the way open with her purse, casting a shaft of light across results of her late-night visitor.

Someone had pushed one of two chairs against the wall while a sheath of papers lay strewn across the floor. Flipping on the overhead light, she saw the office in complete disarray. Behind her desk, someone had forced each drawer of the credenza open.

"Oh, bloody hell," she exclaimed. "Paul call the police. Someone's been through my office."

"What...?" came the reply as he turned to peek passed her through the doorway. "Damn that's a fine mess," he muttered before grabbing the phone and dialing the local police station.

Pacing downstairs in the lobby for what seemed an hour, several constables soon joined Priscilla.

"Are you the caller?" the first constable asked.

"My assistant did," Priscilla replied. "My office... my office... I mean, someone got into... it appears to have been burglarized," she stammered as the realization of someone violating her personal space took hold.

"Let's go have a look shall we, miss?" the officer answered. After a brief time in the lift to the floor where her office was located, her assistant greeted them, sitting outside in the hall. "And this would be your assistant?" the constable nodded towards the young man.

"Yes, he is," Priscilla murmured under her breath.

As he glanced at the office title, he noted Priscilla was a law practitioner. "Have you had any skirmishes with your clients recently?" he asked with a tap of his pen on her nameplate.

"What...? Why... no, at least none I could discuss outside the court..." she stammered. "Oh, hell, Paul. I'm going to be late for my summons."

"I'm sure Her Lordship would understand your absence," he replied.

Before she could continue her protest, another constable interrupted Priscilla. His elfish-type stature was a contradiction to the muscles straining through his uniform. "Did you routinely keep important papers in your office? Maybe a summons or witness statements..." he asked, looking up at the statuesque barrister.

"Nothing more than the Sheriff's office allowed... why?"

"The credenza behind your desk took quite a beating, I'm afraid," the diminutive officer said. "It appeared obvious the party in question was after something you have."

"You're certain a past client didn't have a reason to return?" the senior officer asked again.

The entire time the event had unfolded, Priscilla had not put down her satchel. As she leaned against a small filing cabinet, she felt the shoulder bag, still holding the files she had taken home with her. "Oh God..." she said under her breath, yet still loud enough for the constables to hear. Sliding the bag in front of her, she peered in, confirming she still had the files entrusted to her from Sean Gilmore. She looked at the ceiling, her eyes shining as she looked at the two files for a second time, content in knowing this information was still safe.

"Is there something wrong?"

"No, not at all," she stammered.

Over the next hour a total of seven officers had poured over the office and asked questions of her and her assistant. Priscilla paced the outer hall, stopping only when asked. Leaning against the wall, she closed her eyes as a constable stood nearby.

Before she could answer another question, Sergeant Holmes walked out of the elevator, seeing the officer and her standing near the outer office doorway. "Miss El-Sayed, you've missed your appointment."

"I've had a run of bad luck it seems," Priscilla answered.

Holmes glanced past the forensic technician who was applying a dusting of powder to the door, highlighting a cluster of finger and hand prints. One thing he knew, the break-in was not random, having encountered the odd custodian last night. Pulling out his notepad, he flipped to the first blank page. "Can I have a word with you in private, ma'am?" he asked with a nodding down the hallway.

"Of course," she replied, stepping away from the office and further down the hall, which was now crowded with others trying to catch a glimpse of the activity. "Excuse me." She pushed past two secretaries gossiping as to what happened.

"Miss El-Sayed," Sergeant Holmes began, "this was nae a random act, was it? Your visitor from last night leads me to think you've gotten yourself into a spot of bother. Possibly with one of our least cordial citizens of Edinburgh," he continued, pointing out the barrister's list of former questionable clients. "The fella from last night might have been hired to make you drop one of your cases against the landlords, I reckon."

With each breath, Priscilla tried to calm herself. She'd learned from others of the officer's integrity and professionalism, and the questions were out of concern for her safety and well-being. What she didn't realize was the manner of holding her satchel in front of the sergeant. Since leaving the office, she'd clutched the straps so tight, her hands were now pale from lack of circulation.

"You've something important in there, don't you?" Holmes asked, nodding to her bag.

Embarrassed for portraying a woman easily scared, she looked down at the floor to hide the fact she was blushing. "I'm just caught up in all this, Sergeant," she replied with an attempt to loosen her grip slightly, but still keeping the bag close.

"Do you know of anyone outside the courts that might have a beef with you?"

Priscilla blinked at the question as a sudden image of Taggert's face flashed through her mind. "No... no one, Sergeant," she lied. *I've got to contact the Frenchman Sean mentioned.*

The diminutive constable appeared outside the office, looking at Sergeant Holmes. With a brief wave, he caught the officer's attention, causing him to turn from Priscilla for the moment. "What've you got, Thom?"

"We're needing a list of what was kept in the office, Sergeant," he said, his foot tapping in nervous anticipation.

"My assistant Paul can help you with that," Priscilla responded. As she turned attention back to the sergeant, Priscilla knew her next step wouldn't be easy. "Sergeant, considering the circumstances, I must ask for a continuance from Her Lordship Conway."

"Aye, she's already granted you until next Monday," the officer answered. "But mind you, you've only this one time or she'll call for a dismissal." They both knew the judge had no desire or temperament for delays.

"I'm well aware of the consequences."

The faint sound of pipes and drums could be heard as a local band practiced near a local car park. As the police continued with their investigation at Priscilla El-Sayed's office, a solitary figure sat on a park bench less than a kilometer away. The Prince's Street garden sat in the shadow of Edinburgh Castle which cast a wide swath across the space below it. Oblivious of the many tourists and locals making their way through along the gravel path, Blayne Taggert stared intently at his tablet.

"Not a damn thing," he muttered with a swipe of his finger across the screen to the next image. "Damn woman spent weeks with Connelly's barrister and she never kept a single note."

As the next image came into focus, Taggert's interest piqued. "What's so important that you need to write in Arabic? And who can I trust to decipher it for me?" As he sat contemplating his next step.

Two and a half hours to the northeast in Aberdeen, McDermott and Fletcher sat in the fish and chips shop owned by Malcolm Smythe, McDermott's childhood friend. Sipping at his coffee, McDermott struggled to piece together the sudden appearance of Dunbar's twin to his drug case. Each of them had their own ideas why, but Conor wasn't sold on any of them.

"It has to be revenge for his death," Fletcher said as he watched the cooks slicing the daily catch into filets for lunch. "I remember him having that demeanor and it's the logical choice."

"Aye, maybe you're right, Andrew," McDermott said. "But why now? Why come to the station when we were in Belfast the day before?"

Fletcher sat stoic, contemplating a theory to the former enlisted Marine's sudden appearance. He still considered revenge the motivating factor. Downing the rest of his tea, he wiped the back of his hand across his lips. "We're missing something... but I can't fathom what it might be." He sighed and sat back, dejected.

"I'm nae sure either," McDermott said, watching Sadie the young woman from Jamaica, setting up the register with cash. "But I'll not dismiss your idea of revenge though. You could be right, but it's the who or what in this situation I feel we're not getting a grasp on."

Just then, a uniformed officer appeared at the front of the shop, tapping the back of her hand against the glass.

"We're not open until ten-thirty," Sadie shouted over the cook's music.

"I'm here for them," Inspector Gordon mouthed while pointing at Fletcher and McDermott.

"Let her in, Sadie; she's here for us," McDermott said, motioning to the hostess.

"Thank you," Sheila replied as Sadie undid the latch to allow the constable to enter.

"Nae worries, hen," Sadie replied.

Fletcher stood up, pulling an empty chair to the table for his companion and fellow inspector to sit on. As she shed her cap and coat, she leaned in and gave Andrew a peck on the cheek before sitting.

"Aye, there'll be none of that here," McDermott chided the young woman.

"Sadie, do you mind fixing another tea, please?" Andrew asked before sitting back down.

"You've kept Andrew so busy we've nae had ten minutes to ourselves," Sheila replied with a smirk. "Anyway, Marcus said you came down here. I thought you'd both like to see these as soon as possible." She handed over a folded piece of paper to McDermott.

"What is it?" Andrew asked.

"The cadet's finished scouring the phone listing last night and came across several numbers associated with Alistair Hunt."

McDermott listen to the two inspectors while he reviewed the list of names and their corresponding telephone numbers. Some of them are cell phones, he told himself. And a few seem to be landlines. "You've one here for London?"

"Aye there is…" Sheila answered as she took the tea from the waitress and started to stir it as she placed it in front of her. "And someone called it to and from on five separate occasions," she recalled. "Hunt called it on two separate instances, and the other caller made contact three times. Two were text message transmissions, and the other a call."

105

"Mister McIntyre's right; you're becoming more adept as an investigator than forensics technician," Andrew said.

"But it is still forensics, mind you," she replied. "The queer bit is who made the calls. We've identified Hunt with what Glasgow provided, and we linked the other two calls made by the Irishman."

"If that is the case, it seems like Connelly has someone in London he can turn to," McDermott muttered.

"Who's Connelly?" Sheila asked, shifting her focus back and forth between Andrew and McDermott.

"Conor has a feeling that our 'Mister Higgins' from the drug trafficking is actually a gentleman named Michael Connelly in Belfast," Andrew explained to her. "Seems the surname Higgins was his grandfather's, who started the company Callaghan and Higgins back in the early '30s."

"But we've nae proof of that," McDermott replied, scratching at the growing stubble on his cheeks. "The only connection is the single call from Cap'n Duncan to the office in Belfast. But I'd wager he's up to his arse in something illegal just by his smug attitude." As he glanced back to the list of numbers, one set caught his eye, causing him to flip the paper over then back again.

"Did you not realize, hen, you had the mystery caller's number listed twice?" McDermott asked, staring at Sheila.

"No, I didn't," she replied, taking the paper from him. "Where did you see it...?"

"Look for the cell number for Gilmore, the barrister," McDermott replied while sliding his empty mug across the counter towards Sadie. "Give me another if you will hen..." he winked.

Sheila passed the paper to Andrew so he could see what McDermott was trying to point out. "And so, we've the barrister and the crime boss contacting the same person in the greater metropolis of London," he pointed out. "What do we do with the information... call the number?"

McDermott perked up just as Sadie came to him with a fresh cup of coffee. "It's nae a bad idea," he said. "You can go about like you're one of those solicitors from the telly." He drummed his fingers against the cup in thought. "Once we get the name of the person answering, you apologize and hang up."

"What if the number leads to a cell phone?" Andrew asked, playing the part of devil's advocate. "Who's saying they'll answer if the number registers from a desk at Police Scotland, then what?"

A grin he couldn't contain emerged through his five-o'clock shadow. McDermott's eyes grew wider at the realization they still had a means of making the call without identifying themselves as police.

"You've got an idea you want to share?" Fletcher finally asked.

"We've the barrister's cell phone in evidence," McDermott blurted out, unable to contain himself any longer.

"Aye, and that's where it'll be staying, too." This announcement came from Sheila once again making her case as the forensics technician for Police Scotland. "You'll nae tamper with evidence by making additional calls on it."

"Aye, we can and we will," McDermott stated. "And I've precedence on my side since we're still in the middle of the case." Getting up from the table, he looked at the other two inspectors. "Come on," he insisted, pulling Fletcher's elbow. "I've been itching for a break," he declared. "And I don't want to let this one going by the wayside now."

Chapter FOURTEEN

Chief Inspector McDermott strolled towards the superintendent's office to discuss his desire to use seized evidence to contact the unidentified callers or recipients from Inspector Gordon's earlier list. As he did this, Inspector Fletcher retired to their shared office, pushing past several desks occupied by constables working on their reports, while others were taking calls from harried citizens filing complaints.

As he sat at his desk, Fletcher unfolded a second copy of the phone listings Inspector Gordon had given him. Wonderful girl, thinking of me like that, he smirked while grabbing a pencil and notepad. Reviewing the names, he soon jotted them down from most important to least. At the top he placed Sean Gilmore, barrister for the Irishman. Below was the crime boss Alistair Hunt, then Gordon Wallace, the still missing syndicate member. Then came Robert Burns, Hunt's barrister who was still missing.

"I'd wager a quid or two Burns and Wallace are stewing away together," he muttered while making a note to the side. The next listing, he wrote was associated with the same number someone called the most, identifying it as Unknown #1 on the pad. Before he could jot down the next number, the familiar buzz of a text on his cell phone stopped him. Pulling it from his jacket pocket, he read the text: Don't forget about our dinner, Sheila.

Andrew sent back a quick "okay," and just as he was setting down the phone, an idea came to mind. "It's bloody brilliant," he stuttered as McDermott came through the door, a dour look to his face.

"I take it Mister MacCallum wasn't keen on your idea?" Fletcher asked.

"Well... he did nae say yes, but he also did nae say no either," McDermott replied. "But instead he mentioned the need to discuss it with George Hamilton at the Sheriff's office. He's a wee bit worried we'd be exceeding our ethical jurisdiction, even mentioning entrapment he did." He let out a sigh as he sunk into his chair. McDermott glanced at his partner, who was sporting a Cheshire cat-like grin. "Why the silly grin?"

Fletcher leaned forward. "I've got a solution," he answered, picking up his cell phone. "It still lists my number for London," Andrew said. "Which means we can still use your ploy as a solicitor after a fashion. Like you said, if we can just get a name, we can gather a summons for a proper search."

McDermott looked over the desk at his young partner. It was over eight months ago when he was first assigned, and Conor had his doubts about whether he would finish the first week. But now, Andrew was showing true signs as an investigator, thinking for himself and conjuring up possible alternatives to explore. "When do you make the call?"

Andrew blinked, not because it caught him unaware, but for not being prepared with the next step. "I'll need a few minutes to figure out some questions." He rolled over the top page of his notepad to expose a fresh sheet. "Now, let's see... there's a greeting," he muttered under his breath, the pencil dancing across the empty lines under cursive musings crediting his education.

"I'll be back," McDermott said as he left the office. Pushing through the stairway door, he headed to the basement and the forensics lab. He nearly fell on his wallet as he turned the corner and encountered the remains of a drunkard's evening meal on the floor. "Who the hell left this mess...?" he muttered, shaking his foot and sending the sour remains against the wall.

"Sorry, Inspector," came a voice from around the corner. "I was needing a clean bucket for this one," the janitor exclaimed as he placed the 'wet floor' placards around the mess. Tossing a rag for the inspector's shoe, he added, "Don't worry, it's clean."

McDermott gave his Chukka boot a quick wipe before tossing the rag onto the cleaning cart. "Nae worries," he said as he continued to the lab. Pulling open the door, he entered the secure environment where boxes of evidence sat next to a cart, the clear baggies filled with an article or piece of evidence. "Morning, Gavin," he greeted the senior constable at the table filled with numbered boxes of evidence bags for each case file laid neatly in a row. In the back room, McDermott saw crowded metal shelving, evidence lockers, and the computer station for cataloging everything being held.

"Aye, it still is," came the weary reply.

"Still filling in on the evening shift?"

109

The technician turned to face McDermott. "Aye, it's my last night," Gavin answered with a yawn. "The chief is giving me an extra day off to get myself ready for days again. Thus, I'll be off till Tuesday next week," he replied as he finished up his notes. His demeanor becoming more cheerful at the prospect of extra days off work. "Is there something you need?"

"Aye, I was wondering if they have sorted the videos from the weather office," McDermott said.

Gavin turned to his counterpart who was still logging down the evidence. "Alfie, did Kyle ever finish with the CCTV files?" he asked, pulling the hard-bound evidence log from under the counter.

"I believe so," the technician replied without looking up, "since he complained about how bored the job was looking at nothing."

Thumbing through several pages, Gavin found the entry for the CCTV images brought in by Inspector Fletcher. "Give me a minute..." he muttered as he turned away from McDermott and entered the evidence room. Going to a keypad, he entered the code to unlock the drawers, where he soon found a folder nearly an inch thick. After pulling it out, he slammed the drawer shut and swiped several keys to reengage the locks.

With a resounding thud, he dropped the folder on the counter in front of McDermott. "Each image properly printed for your viewing pleasure," he joked. "You'll find we bunched them by day and time, just like the computer file," he explained. "Hope you enjoy the show, Inspector," Gavin added with a touch of sarcasm.

Opening the folder, McDermott flipped each of the pages, the captured images a grainy display of the Aberdeen harbor. After a dozen, he stopped flipping. "Why do these first nine pictures seem different?"

Gavin came over from the table and spun the folder towards him. As he kept his finger in the place where McDermott stopped, the technician flipped the first few pages. "They took these first ten on the 13th of July," he explained, pointing to the time stamp, "and these are from 2nd of August."

McDermott stood, struggling to recall why the first date sounded so familiar. As he continued to wrestle with his thoughts, each puzzle piece fighting to find its proper place, the chief of forensics, Graham McIntyre, walked through the doors behind him. "Fancy seeing you here, Conor," he greeted, placing his hand on McDermott's shoulder causing the inspector to spin around, fists at the ready to assault the interruption. "Mind yourself, Inspector," he laughed, grasping McDermott's outstretched hand, his grip holding the punch at bay.

McDermott quickly straightened his coat. "Sorry Graham, you caught me thinking."

"What has you so worked up?"

"I can nae remember why the 13th of July sticks in my mind," he answered with a point to the time stamp on the image in front of him. "I know it's important, just did nae know why," he sighed.

"Wasn't that the day at the docks?" the forensics chief said on the way to his office.

McDermott's eye lit up hearing the forensics chief mention the event at the harbor that culminated in Angus Dunbar's death. "I can nae believe I'd forget that, Graham, but you're right," he said. Starting with the first image, McDermott studied it, looking for any telltale sign he and Andrew might have missed.

After scrutinizing the first four images, McDermott noticed something odd on the fifth. "Graham, I need a magnifying glass or something," he shouted. Putting his finger down on the image to keep track, he looked towards the back room.

"Here you go, Inspector," one of the young technicians replied, handing over the glass loupe.

He took the handle and placed it in front of his face. As he drifted across the image, he stopped, blinking quickly. "Gimme a pencil, will ya?" he asked, holding out his empty hand.

McDermott glanced at the pencil to distinguish where the point was. Once oriented, he drew the tip closer to the grainy portion of the image he fixated on and drew a crude circle. "What do you see there?" he asked, handing the loupe to the technician.

The young man hesitated for a moment. Taking the magnifying glass, he bent over and examined the spot McDermott circled. "I'd say it looks like a foot," he answered. "But it's hard to tell for sure being near the shadow of the roof edge."

"Go and get Mister McIntyre for me," McDermott said, dismissing the technician. Putting the loop back in front of his eyes, he spent a minute concentrating on the image again. Just as Chief McIntyre stepped to the counter, McDermott turned the page to a new image.

"Have you found something?"

"Aye, a wee sliver of a boot," McDermott explained, flipping back a page. "Right on the edge of the shadow. It's nae very clean, but I'll buy the first pint if I'm wrong."

Taking the magnifier from McDermott, the forensics chief looked over the image, then turned to the next page, then the next before stopping. "Kyle, reprint this image, but turn down the contrast and boost the sharpness on the settings."

"What is it, Graham?"

"I'm not sure at the moment," McIntyre said, glancing at McDermott. "They capture the images every 60 seconds, and looking where you circled, the image changed on the third capture."

"Here you are, sir," the technician said handing over the corrected image.

With the adjustment to the image, a shadowy figure was now visible. The figure, now facing the camera, was in the act of disassembling a weapon. The remarkable piece of the image was the fact he was doing so while looking up and not at the rifle.

"This is your shooter," McIntyre pointed out. "And he appears to be well versed in his weapon," he added.

"Is the image good enough to send to Gartcosh?" McDermott asked.

"It's certainly worth a try," McIntyre replied. "I'll give their chief a call and let him know the image will be sent soon..." his voice trailed off.

"Something wrong Graham?"

"Well... it's just a feeling, mind you," he started. "But during my time with the Black Watch, the gunners would bet on stripping and assembling their weapons during their downtime. They'd blindfold each other to make it fair, but I'll have to admit, a few of the fellas were scary good at it."

"You saying this fella on the roof was a para-type?" McDermott asked. "Possibly an SAS-type like Dunbar too?"

"Quite possibly," McIntyre said. "The best way to hunt your prey is to think like them... to be one of them really," he added. "And who better than a member of your old unit, or someone close to it to be the one hunting you down?"

"I'm nae liking the thought we've another loon out there, gunning people down Graham."

"But we haven't in the last four weeks now, have we?" McIntyre asked.

McDermott straightened up from the counter. "Since you've gone and mention it, we've nae had any serious incidents," he said. "At least not the types who are familiar with using firearms." He paced the room, lost in thought. Just as he turned his back to the door, his partner Andrew Fletcher came through, wheezing from lack of breath.

"I've got a name," he gasped, waving his notepad in the air.

Chapter FIFTEEN

Dublin, Ireland

S itting in the backseat of his Jaguar, Michael Connelly watched the rolling hills and various farms of the Irish countryside pass by. "Mind your speed, Geoff. No sense getting cited in a foreign country, is there?" he warned his chauffeur and bodyguard.

"I'll be careful, sir," the Ulsterman answered as he maneuvered the luxury car around slower traffic. "We should be in Dublin by supper time if traffic stays the same," he said. "Where are you supposed to meet your manager again?"

"At the Wynn's hotel, near the harbor," Connelly replied.

Soon after the Scotland Yard inspectors left, Michael Connelly made a call to Liam Finnegan, his production manager, expressing his desire to meet him later that day. As he was talking with Liam, Connelly had his secretary make the arrangements for the overnight stay where they could meet.

The closer they came to Ireland's capital, the more congested the traffic became. Scores of buses and lorries made maneuvering the sedan a test of patience and skill for Geoff. The car was a family heirloom, passed from Michael's father to him when he returned from his service with the French Foreign Legion. Connelly loved basking in its luxury when he could, so it became his personal mode of transportation whenever he traveled by car.

After passing the airport, traffic thinned out, allowing them to make their destination at the scheduled time. As Geoff watched the valet pull their bags from the boot, Connelly entered the hotel to register. He strolled to the front desk, where a wiry young man with ginger hair stepped forward.

"Glad to see you arrived safely, sir," Liam said, holding out his hand.

Connelly shook hands with his plant manager from Limerick. "Thank you, Liam. It's rather therapeutic to see the countryside from time to time." He turned to see Geoff enter with their bags. "You two have met before, haven't you?" he asked, motioning to his driver.

"Just the one time if I recall," Liam said, extending his hand.

"Pleasure to see you again," Geoff answered as he shook hands.

"I've seen to both of you being registered; here are your key cards." Liam held out two small envelopes. "You're on the third floor as requested, sir. I'll give you a hand with this," he insisted, grabbing Connelly's bag as he showed them to the elevator. The need to be on the 3rd floor was borne more out of his foolish superstition that the power of the triad or three would somehow protect him.

As they stepped out onto the third floor, Connelly turned to his driver. "Geoff, if you don't mind," Connelly said, "Liam and I have business to discuss this evening, so you're free to entertain yourself tonight. But don't forget I've a nine o'clock reservation tomorrow morning with my mother I mustn't miss."

"I'll see you're on time, sir," Geoff said, grateful for some free time. Looking down, he noticed his room was down the opposite hallway from Connelly's, which suited him fine.

Connelly made his way to the hotel lounge soon after getting settled into his room, where Liam had already secured a secluded corner table. "Thank you for making the arrangements, Liam," the executive said. "Am I early?" he asked, glancing at his watch.

"No, sir," Liam replied.

"Then they're late I presume," Connelly said of the guests they were expecting.

"They're on time," Liam said, motioning at the two Asian women towards them.

Dr. Liu Yang and her assistant Xi Feng made their way to the back booth. Each of the women were a stark contrast in appearance to most Chinese. While Liu exhibited a slim, yet taller than average image then a typical Asian woman seen on television, Xi was just the opposite, her full and muscular build akin to a gymnast's physique.

"Ladies, a pleasure to see you again," Liam said. "May I introduce Dr. Liu Yang and her assistant Xi Feng," He motioned to each woman individually as Michael rose to his feet. "This is Mister Higgins."

115

"A pleasure to meet you both," Connelly said while gently shaking hands with each of them. "I'm looking forward to hearing of your progress tonight."

"I'm looking forward to eating," Xi exclaimed with a chuckle.

A sudden barrage of Mandarin, a language foreign to each man, from Dr. Yang berated her assistant for being so rude to their guests. The rebuke was sufficiently stern as was evident by Xi's submissive posture as the lecture ended. "I apologize for Xi's rude behavior," Yang said. "But she's picked up some poor habits while working here in Ireland." Her steely eyed glare reminded the assistant of her position.

"It's quite alright," Connelly said, embarrassed to have witnessed the exchange.

"On a more pleasant note, I'd like to thank you for your generous gift, Mister Higgins," Dr. Yang said, bowing slightly toward the Irishman. *The additional money will go far to help with my defection from Peking's eyes*, she thought.

"I believe in rewarding productive employees," Connelly replied. "Of course, I see your achievement as just the first step. I can promise your stipends will be made tenfold for you and your assistant when the final product is available."

Xi Feng's eyes grew wide, imagining the sum of money someone could give them for their work. But knowing of Yang's concern about the results caused her gaze to dart between the Irishman and her superior while she fought hard to remain silent. He doesn't know, she told herself.

Liu Yang sat quietly across from the two men. Identifying the mystery component within the sample of hashish was easy. So much so, it was actually Xi who'd come across the marker identifying the phencyclidine hydrochloride, or PCP. "I'm grateful for your trust in our abilities," she said just as the waitress brought their appetizers to the table.

Connelly waited for the waitress to finish serving before he continued with the discussion. "I am interested in the effort to maintain the agreed upon timetable though," he said. As he stabbed one of the grilled scallops from the porcelain tray, he resumed his questioning. "You see, I've another transaction that is aligned with your development of the drug and anecdote, doctor." You can sense my concern, can't you?"

Dr. Yang was torn between reaping the financial reward that would come working with the Irishman or admitting her failure. Either way, she knew her time working outside of Communist China would end soon. As she sipped her wine, Dr. Yang concocted a half truth, attempting to gain the upper hand. "Mr. Higgins," she began with a forced smile, "the completion of our initial work will certainly meet your timeframe. However, you understand producing the quantities you require will require having satisfactorily tested both the drug and its counter-drug."

"I'm not sure I understand," Connelly said. Looking over to Liam, the young man from Dublin just shook his head. "Is there a problem re-creating the mixture... or is it the anecdote?"

Dr. Yang finished her wine before answering Connelly's query. "As we develop each sample to the potency you asked for, the outcome is consistent. But when we take the sample and divide it to create additional portions, the PCP loses its potency."

Connelly sat back in his chair, struggling to comprehend what the micro-biologist was trying to explain to him. "You're saying each time you handle the host sample," he said, leaning forward, "the next portion is not as strong?"

"I haven't been able to determine if it's the PCP or the hashish causing the deterioration," Dr. Yang replied. "Each instance differs slightly from the previous one. Because we can't produce the drug in consistent quantities over ten grams, we're at an impasse to create its anecdote." Her voice was clearer in expressing disappointment more than her expression.

Connelly drained the remaining gin and tonic in one gulp. Sitting across from the chemist from Shanghai, he saw his dream of a correcting his family history when it came to a united Ireland slip from his grasp. "Liam, why don't you and Miss Feng get a wee breath of fresh air. The good doctor and I need a moment alone."

"Of course," Liam replied as he ushered the Asian woman from the table.

Several awkward moments passed which allowed Michael Connelly to consider how to phrase his ultimatum to the chemist. "Dr. Yang," he began, "I'm sure you can comprehend the importance of your work I've asked you to undertake, can't you?"

Dr. Yang felt the same sense of dread she'd encountered working in the state-run facility outside Shanghai two years ago. Produce your quota or else, she recalled. Looking back at the Irishman, she saw the same intimidating look the managers had in China, but Connelly didn't have a pistol in his hand, just a fork.

"Even with my skills, I can't bend the laws of science, Mister Higgins," she answered. "Until I can determine the reason for the molecules releasing and produce a suitable binding agent," the chemist said, "I'll only be creating an inferior product. And I'm well aware, it is not the outcome you prefer." She picked up the water glass, a slight tremor to her hand.

Connelly could see the fear not only in the woman's actions but also in her eyes as they flittered about the room. "I can promise, no harm will come about because of your difficulties in the lab, Dr. Yang," he said. "But I've made another transaction based on your discovery, and I'm not about to see it fall through because of this setback. To that end, I need you and your assistant to return to the laboratory and find an answer."

"Did we lose two patrons?" the waitress asked, approaching with their orders.

"They needed some fresh air," Connelly answered. "They'll be in a few minutes from now." As the waitress delivered the food, the Irishman contemplated where he could concentrate his effort to insure the chemist wouldn't fail him.

"Earlier you mentioned having a stable source at... ten grams, wasn't it?" Connelly asked while cutting his lamb shank. "Could you reproduce the drug efficiently in those quantities without losing its potency?"

"Yes. To this point we've done just that," Yang answered. "Anything greater and it begins to break down," noticing Liam and Xi returning to the table.

"So... you're saying you could develop the anecdote based on those quantities, correct?"

"If I did that, you'd be hard pressed to find a buyer," the woman replied. "Unless you intend to sell the drug at that particular quantity,"

Yang said, nodding at Xi. "And by doing that, the anecdote itself would need to be twice the size to be effective."

"What have I missed?" Xi asked, the speed of her Mandarin surprising the two gentlemen.

"We're going to be busy, just like we were in Shanghai," Yang delivered in a more educated form of Chinese.

"I'd ask you to converse in French to make it easier for me," Connelly said with a forced chuckle, put off by their sudden change in languages. "I'm not as skilled in linguistics as I'd like to be." What did they just say to each other? he asked himself, still smiling politely.

"I'm sorry," Yang replied with a slight bow to her guest. "Xi was just mentioning the food looked delicious. I recommend we eat before it grows too cold."

"I'll second that," Liam replied, sliding his salad aside.

"Here's to a productive period to come," Connelly said raising his glass. Staring at Liu, he considered what else was spoken between the two women. The chilled water did little to quench his apprehension about introducing the PCP-laced hashish amongst attendees to several music festivals throughout Ireland this fall.

As the evening progressed, Connelly did his best to be cordial and refrained from discussing the chemist's work. Instead, he focused on learning more of the two Asian women, with an imperceptible questioning of their backgrounds that Liam might have omitted from their dossiers.

"If you'll excuse me," Liu said, raising from the table, "I need a moment to freshen up." She grabbed her clutch and, without looking at her assistant, stepped off towards the women's room across the dining room.

"Certainly," Connelly replied, coming to his feet, as did Liam.

With her companion absent for a moment, the men sat back down and Connelly turned to Xi. "So, what is it like working for Dr. Yang?"

Xi finished the mouthful of cod she'd just consumed before answering. With a wipe of the napkin across her lips, she chose her words with care. "She's an exceptional technician," she began. "To watch her work... her skill and patience are truly remarkable. I can only hope to be as accomplished as she is in the laboratory when we return to Shanghai."

While Xi was answering the questions posed by Connelly, Dr. Yang sat quietly in the last stall, doing her best to ignore the gossip between two others. With her notebook balanced on her lap, she wrote down what she'd suspected from the earlier discussion. *It will please the chairman to know what I've discovered*, she considered. Tearing the page out, she folded the paper until it fit into the aluminum cylinder.

As she left the bathroom, a robust and muscular man sporting Maori tattoos nudged Dr. Yang along one arm. "I'm so sorry," the man replied, steading the doctor before she fell. Unless one was skilled in dead-drops, the passing of the cylinder went unnoticed.

"That's quite alright," she replied. "I should be more mindful, but thank you," she said, brushing past the courier. As she pulled her chair from the table, she wrinkled her nose slightly. "Will anyone be having dessert?"

Xi noticed the facial expression, the signal Dr. Yang had passed along something to the courier who'd been assigned to accompany them when they left Shanghai.

"I'm stuffed," Liam answered, pushing his plate away.

"Unless you ladies wish to have something, I'll have to pass as well," Connelly said.

"If that's the consensus of the gentlemen, I recommend we pass as well," Dr. Yang said with a bow toward Xi, who openly showed displeasure of their meal finishing prematurely.

Connelly waved the server to the table, advising her they would be passing on dessert, and requested the bill.

With their meal complete, Dr. Yang took the opportunity for her and Xi to depart. "Thank you for this evening, Mister Higgins," she said with a slight bow to the host. "I'll keep Liam informed as to our progress."

"I look forward to hearing from you soon," Connelly replied. As the women faded from sight lost in a throng of pensioners entering the hotel, he turned to Liam. "I want you to contact your friend at Phoenix Park and find out any additional items about Xi Feng. Something tells me she's more than a lab technician."

Sitting in a pub three blocks away, Geoff Brennan took a sip of his stout, savoring its frothy and creamy head spilling over the rim. His dismissal by his boss was a much-needed break after the three-hour drive from Belfast. Now, watching a trio of young ladies across the bar, he could relax.

At the same time Geoff was admiring the young ladies, two patrons step over to where he was sitting, their looks one less of acceptance and more of disdain. Each of them was sporting the same rugby jersey, denoting a local club from Dublin. Sensing the closeness of the taller gent, Geoff spun on his stool to face the Dubliner. "You've a question you want to ask me?"

"Yeah, I do for that matter," the footballer replied, setting down his pint. "We're not keen on tourists coming to town just for a fling with our ladies," he explained, nodding to the table of women Geoff was admiring earlier.

Geoff was no stranger to fending off the occasional drunkard, but he was wary of the second man catching him off guard. Lifting his pint, he took another sip.

"I've always enjoyed conversing with locals in their own pub," he replied as he set the glass down. "But you..." the drunk slurred, "you don't strike me as a patron of that fine gentleman's hospitality," he said with a nod to the bartender, who was making his way over.

Colin Munster worked hard for fifteen years making his dream of owning a pub a reality. And over time, he'd learned a few hard lessons when it came to ruffians trying to make a name for themselves at the expense of the pub's décor. "You're not thinking of lashing out at this fella, are you?" the barkeep asked, tapping the rugby player on the shoulder.

"Mind your own self," the footballer replied as he pushed the hand off him.

Geoff saw the expressions of the patrons behind the rugby player change from amusement to shock, warning him of the other player's action before it happened. Ducking to his right, Geoff avoided the full force of his punch, which landed against his shoulder.

The reaction by Geoff caused the bartender to lunge for the player before he could engage Geoff. But his move was a split-second slower as he missed grabbing the man's arm. The first man swung at Geoff, catching the Ulsterman's arm, which he raised in defence.

Soon, the pub was a melee of screams and broken glass. Chairs and tables were pushed aside as the patrons scrambled to avoid the fighters, which now numbered four. The bartender subdued the second player to the floor as Geoff warded off a slew of punches before landing his own on the first man, knocking him to the floor.

Regaining his feet, the first man prepared to lunge at Geoff. Before he could take a second step however, an arm reached around his neck and dragged him downward to the floor in quick fashion. "You've had enough?" Connelly shouted while squeezing the man's airway closed.

With a brief nod and a few shorts gasps, the man relented, his crimson complexion growing paler.

"Where'd you come from?" Geoff asked his employer.

"The clerk at the hotel mentioned you asking about a quiet place for a stout," Connelly replied. "Seems you had found one." He pushed the footballer away before handing over a half dozen fifty-euro bills to the barkeeper. "This should handle the damages."

The barkeeper shook his head. "Your man didn't start it though," he replied, in an attempt to refuse the cash.

"Still... he did spill his Guinness," Connelly said looking over the pub's interior. "Payment for cleaning up the mess." He pushed the money into the barkeeper's open palm. "Have a pleasant evening." With a few swipes, Connelly brushed off his slacks before tugging on Geoff's arm.

As Geoff glanced about, he was soon in step with his employer and heading back to the hotel. "I'm glad you showed up, but I wasn't in any trouble, mind you," he said. "I mean... I could have handled them by myself, you know..."

"Of course, you could've, Geoff," Connelly replied, slapping the Ulsterman's back.

Chapter SIXTEEN

Aberdeen, Scotland

The woman glanced at her companion. "I'm no sure 'bout this," Sheila said fiddling with the note. "We should wait to hear from Mister MacCallum, don't you think?" Tugging her sweater over her knees, she curled up in the easy chair, watching Andrew pouring the wine.

"Any other time I'd agree," Andrew replied as he set the glass in front his companion. "But Conor and I think this might give us the break we need on the case."

"Well, I'm nae sure I trust your partner after he stole a look into my file," she said. Several weeks earlier, Chief Inspector McDermott had entered the personnel office and obtained information on Sheila's mother. This led them to call on her and question the relationship she'd had with her employer, Alistair Hunt, and his crime syndicate in Glasgow.

"I wasn't happy to hear he did that, either," Andrew replied, sitting across from Sheila. "But in the end, it helped in getting Hunt arrested."

"And my mum's never felt worse because of all that," she exclaimed. "For better or worse, Alistair Hunt gave my mother a chance after dad died, she appreciated that fact. If it wasn't for the job and her friend Alfie, she'd be lost, you know."

"This is just one of four numbers from the telecoms which they can link between our suspects," Andrew said. "If it leads us to the buyer... then we can close the case."

"Then what? You pack up and go back to London," Sheila said. "I'll end up paying the rent for this flat myself, then wouldn't I?" she asked, her lips curled in a childish pout.

Andrew looked at this wine. He knew at some point he'd have to decide regarding their relationship. He wasn't ready to let Sheila know he'd plan on discussing a possible transfer to Police Scotland with Chief Superintendent MacCallum. "The way we're going on this case, I'll be here well into next summer," he laughed.

"I'm nae sure of that," Sheila said. "I overheard Miss Sinclair making a call to London last week, and she asked for your supervisor, I'll have you know. I'm thinking Conor overstepped his grounds again and Mister MacCallum wants him gone."

"Let's worry about that when the time comes," Andrew said. "Now... how about you make the call and scratch one item off our list before turning in? I've even jotted down a few questions in case the person who answers is the chatty type."

Sheila took the questions and looked them over. Chuckling at the last one, she tossed the paper on the table. "You think I can pass as a punter, do you? What if the person wants to place a wager... then what?" she snickered. Taking Andrew's phone, she took in a deep breath and dialed.

With her fingers, she gave her companion a sign of how many times the phone had rung on the other end. On the fifth one, a man answered, his breathing slightly labored. "Hello... this is Ethan."

"Yes. Hello, sir," Sheila began. "I'm assisting Metro Police with their public out-reach endeavors; I was hoping you'd be willing to support the local emergency personnel fund raiser," she read off an item Andrew wrote.

"I've seen the flyers around the barracks and already gave my pledge to the sergeant last week," Ethan Taylor replied. "I've ten minutes to get to muster so if you'll excuse me, I'll be going."

Her eyes widened while her mouth fell open in shock hearing the man openly discuss his occupation. Gathering herself, Sheila replied. "Thank you, sir. Can I get your name for the records so we don't call again?" she asked, grabbing a pencil from the table.

Ethan heard the woman's question just before he disconnected. "It's Constable Taylor, from the Heathrow detail," he said. "Can I go now?"

"Yes, once again, thank you, sir," she replied, staring at Andrew, who was like a statue on the sofa. Ending the call, Sheila replaced the cell phone in her hand with the wine, which she emptied in one gulp. "Andrew, this man said he's a constable," she explained, learning of their mystery caller with Hunt and Gilmore now. Getting up, she made her way into the kitchen.

"He said that? You're certain he mentioned constable?" Andrew asked, not wanting to believe there was another officer on the crime syndicate payroll. "Did he say where he was assigned? Or what his rank was?"

Sheila took the bottle from the kitchen counter and poured more wine. "He replied as a constable," she said, placing the near empty bottle down, "and said he had ten minutes to make muster at Heathrow."

Andrew ran his hands through his hair, pulling his head back while closing his eyes. "It makes little sense..." he uttered aloud. "How can constable in London be of use to Hunt? And what information can he pass along to a barrister?"

"What if it's just a temporary posting?" Sheila asked.

Andrew looked at the woman, trying to comprehend the situation, and like his partner McDermott, put the puzzle pieces in their proper position. "If that's the case, he's fresh from his training, or he's there because of something else."

"So how do we find out about his standing?"

Andrew glanced at the clock. "It's too late for the normal admin staff to be working in London, and this is too sensitive to discuss with just anyone," Andrew surmised. "We'll get with Conor in the morning. It might be we'll have to talk with Mister MacCallum and Mister Collingsworth directly about what we know." He was quick to empty his own glass. "Did you leave me any or should I open another?"

***

McDermott stared at the screen, the words filling the document putting the chief inspector into an apparent coma. It was the tenth witness statement he'd read regarding the suicide of the university student near the docks of Southampton.

Using the mouse, he selected several files and placed them side-by-side across the screen, making his task easier, though the print was smaller. "There's something here I'm missing," he muttered. With a slow sweep of a pen on the glass, McDermott read each statement word for word, looking for the golden ticket.

"Came out the door...noticed a dark-haired gent running from the flat," was part of the first account from one male student. "A fella jogging down the path by the flat nearly struck me down," was another. McDermott grabbed a pad from his partner's desk and jotted down, scribbled really, the description. Selecting three more files, he was now looking for the dark-haired man.

"Scouring the archives, Chief Inspector?"

McDermott picked his head up. Glancing at the doorway, he saw Constable Drusilla Ames leaning against the wall, her arms crossed like a secondary school administrator. "Aye, you might say that," he answered. "Are you needing something from me, hen?"

"No..." she said. "I've just never seen you stay in without Mister Fletcher nearby. At least not since you coaxed me to open the records room." Stepping into the office, the young woman pulled out a chair, sitting across from the Scotsman.

"You're still fuming about that, are you?"

"No, I'm well over it now, Inspector," Drusilla said. "Sergeant Giles took his pound of flesh to make Mister MacCallum happy. He said it was more on you for telling me to bend the rules, though."

McDermott winced at the reminder for having the young constable allow him into the restricted space without permission. "Aye, the good sergeant reminds me about it every day now." The chief inspector felt his actions were justified if it brought them closer to arresting their suspect. In this case, it allowed him to direct his partner to question Inspector Gordon's mother, Janice. This gave them information on their suspects, Alistair Hunt and his hired gunman, Angus Dunbar.

Still, McDermott knew his actions had consequences, and he once again stood at the bottom of a hill looking to others for help in regaining the top. This time it was Sergeant Giles's fellow officer in Edinburgh who he hoped could provide a clue on the Inspector Cockburn's sudden appearance and interest in his case.

"Can you tell me what is it you're trying to find?" the constable asked, invading his thoughts.

"Oh... just making sure there was nae something Inspector Fletcher and I might have missed," he said. "Do you mind seeing if the kettles on the boil? I could use another cup," he asked, raising his tea cup above the desk.

"Aye, I'm sure the lounge is still open," she replied with a spin away from McDermott.

Looking back at the computer, McDermott returned to his task. Selecting the last three interviews, he scanned through each statement. His perseverance paid off on the last one. This witness recalled getting shoved aside in the building's stairwell. Once again, the description was a dark-haired gentleman. However, the constable's interview notes included the review of CCTV images from the flat.

Deep in thought again, it caught McDermott off guard by the appearance of Constable Ames. "Here you go," Drusilla said before placing the tea near him. "I did nae know what you took in it, so I brought a wee bit of everything." She dropped packets of sugar, creamer, and honey on his desk.

"You're a saint, hen. Do you mind helping out just once more? I'm trying to locate a file for this interview, but I'm nae seeing where it would be."

"Let me see," Ames replied, pulling a chair next to McDermott.

McDermott slid his chair to the side, watching the officer's hand maneuver the cursor across the screen as she selected one icon or tab after another. In moments, she leaned back in the chair, a wave of her hand to the computer showing she'd finished. "There you are, Inspector McDermott, all the images associated with the case number," she beamed.

"I owe you more than a lunch, hen," he answered leaning in past her. Scanning the listing of images, McDermott counted nearly eighty or more being held in the folder. Almost half lined up with the constable's report identifier. The others had just a time stamp in the corner. Selecting the first, the two officers were greeted with an exterior view of the flat, and in the corner, a yellow drape laying over the deceased.

"You're looking into a death investigation?" the woman asked.

"Aye... murder it was," McDermott spoke in a matter-of-fact manner, the tightness in his eyes as he stared at the image never wavering from the cloth. Taking the mouse, he closed the image and selected another further down the list. This one showed the interior of the flat entrance, the image capturing damage to the wall, a slight blood stain evident against the paint.

"I'd say it was quite the ruckus," Ames said.

McDermott didn't hear her. Selecting another image, he saw a grainy image of party-goers, pints in hand, the odd cigarette dangling from a mouth or fingers. Though not clear, he could make out the faces. With the next image, he found what appeared to be the person he was searching for. The picture showed one man pushing back another as if they were scuffling. The first one had his head up enough McDermott could recognize the face.

"Ames, I need you to open this case file in admin," he said, handing her a slip of paper.

"You're getting me in hot water again, aren't you?"

"Don't be so daft; it's my investigation file," he said. "Go and print out the last three pictures and bring them back, will you?" Staring back at the computer, McDermott swore the man was same he'd seen before from his drug trafficking case.

While Constable Ames retrieved the photos from Admin, McDermott looked over the other images. Two others captured the same man, allowing the inspector to note his appearance and clothing with better detail. Ten minutes later, Ames returned handing him the printed images.

"They're a wee bit off," she said, handing over the photos taken at the Southampton docks.

"Thanks, hen," he replied while holding the first one up to the screen. "Do you see the same person?" Before the constable could answer, he put the second one next to the screen. "How 'bout this one?"

"Aye, I'd say you've a fifty-fifty chance of making them out tae be the same fella," Ames agreed. "For sure the hair style looks the same, and they might be the same height and build. But for a court to rule they're the same, you'd be hard pressed to win the argument if you asked me."

The third image gave McDermott a clue as to whom he needed to contact next. In the print-out, the man was standing along the rail of the freighter being used for drug trafficking, and the French police would have the information he needed. *For Edna's sake, I need to find this fella*, he told himself.

Chapter SEVENTEEN

Gartcosh, Edinburgh, Scotland

The computer's hum could be felt more than heard as technicians slid chairs and stools across the linoleum floor, scraping slivers free as their wheels caught seams. Along one wall, several carts were lined up, each holding labeled totes. The plastic bins all held small bags of evidence waiting to be examined.

In one corner, a technician peered at a computer screen, selecting images of men from the system to compare to their sample. Every five seconds, a new face appeared and in moments, a series of dots emerged before it connected together them with digital lines mapping the contours. If the face didn't meet certain criteria, they labeled it as a non-match and discarded. But if the face matched the minimum, they saved it for further examination by another technician.

This routine had gone on for over seven hours as the computer, linked to the European Union database in Brussels, scanned the nearly ten million entries within its database. Leaning back in her chair, the woman yawned, stretching her arms overhead.

"Haven't found a date yet?" her co-worker asked, mentioning the running joke they had when searching for a male suspect.

"A couple of possibilities are out there," the first one answered. "But I've nae found any Ewan McGregor-types yet." A brief flash of red caught her eye as she turned back to the computer. "Seems I've got an 85er," she said, indicating the percentage the image matched the sample.

The second technician wheeled her stool over to the screen to take a look. "The butch cut does nae help. Pull it off and dress it up a wee bit and see if it helps."

The first technician saved the image before selecting the enhancement program. Like a Hollywood makeup artist, she had a range of colors, styles and accessories to choose from. Opening several tabs, she soon was selecting a hairstyle to add to the photo over the nearly clean-shaven scalp of the man. Next, she used her stylus to tag the skin-tone tab, and 'painted' the face with a slightly darker complexion. "What dae you think, Helen?"

"Aye, that's your man," the second technician pointed out. "Go ahead and wrap it up."

The first technician selected the updated image and saved it to their system along with the original sample provided by Chief Inspector McIntyre of Police-Scotland Aberdeen. Marking off the steps she used, the technician's final act was to label the image Pasqual Sequin.

While the lab technicians in Gartcosh were putting the finishing touches to their work in Aberdeen, Constable Kyle Patton was suppressing a yawn. As they compiled the information at the main forensic lab outside of Edinburgh, an automated response was sent to the requestor noting the work had been completed. This alert flashed on the screen as Kyle was cataloging evidence.

"Another damn notice," he exclaimed while he forced hands and arms into action, adding the notice to the department's list of queries being answered. Noting the time-stamp the department submitted and when it was returned, Kyle perked up. "Mighty nice of them to act so swiftly," he chided, typing in the information. Distracted by both the notification and his fatigue, Kyle didn't hear the door when his supervisor entered.

"Who's being so nice now?" Chief McIntyre asked, surprising the young man.

"Sorry, sir, I didn't hear you come in," Kyle replied, his attention renewed in the presence of the department chief. "We got back a query from Gartcosh."

"Anything significant?" McIntyre asked as he unlocked his office.

"They're results of a facial scan Chief Inspector McDermott requested from the other day," the technician answered. "I finished logging in the notice when you came through the door."

McIntyre came out of his office pulling on his starched lab coat. It was the first of several acts he undertook every day before beginning his work. Looking over Kyle's shoulder, he caught a glimpse of the file. "I'll look it over in a moment. Is the coffee made?"

"I didn't have any last night," Kyle replied. Instead, he held up an empty can of a popular energy drink, nodding towards the bin where three other empties were visible inside. "But I can fix a pot if you'd like."

"Please do," McIntyre answered, turning on his computer to review the information they'd just received. With a deft touch, he'd inputted his security code to access the system and soon had the file open. The first image was the one from the rooftop he'd submitted, while the second and the third came from the lab in Gartcosh. *Interesting*, he thought, studying the first image.

Kyle entered with a cup of coffee for his chief. "Kyle, what do you make of this picture?" he asked, tapping his knuckle on the computer screen.

Stepping around the desk, the young technician rubbed his eyes for a moment before looking. "Seems like one of our booking photos if you're asking me," Kyle said, nodding at the picture of Pasqual Sequin. The CCTV image showed the Frenchman, a member of Papillion Transport and former Legionnaire. In it, he sported a closely cropped haircut and blank expression similar to one of many hooligans from a football match.

McIntyre listened closely to the young man's description. "There something else about it though? But I'm not quite sure..." he began, strumming his fingers on the desk. With his eyes closed, McIntyre did his best to conjure up similar images in his mind. Then it hit him. Pulling open his desk drawer, he pulled the file for Angus Dunbar and flipped open the pages to his service photo. There, staring back at him was a familiar sight: a young man scared and alone, suddenly immersed into military life. "This man was in the armed forces," McIntyre exclaimed, stabbing the image in front of his young technician.

"Are you sure?"

"I'd bet an extra day on your next holiday," McIntyre said. "The only problem is whose army he served in... When is Devin due to report?"

"He'll be in by half-past seven today." Kyle replied, glancing at the wall clock. An hour and a half left before I can leave, he told himself.

As the two men in the laboratory discussed their colleague's arrival, Inspector Gordon made her way into the room. "Morning, gentlemen," she exclaimed. "Fancy seeing you so early, Mister McIntyre. Kyle, don't forget to pick up before you sign out," she warned, pointing to the empty can on the counter.

"I'll see to it right away," he said, shuffling over to it and grabbing the waste bin.

"Speaking of early, you're in ahead of your normal time aren't you, Sheila?" McIntyre asked.

Surprised, the young woman hesitated before answering. "I've had a wee idea bugging me about the Hunt case, so... I thought I'd look into it before we got too busy," Sheila replied. "Andrew... I mean Inspector Fletcher, gave me an idea on one suspect I need to follow up on."

"Don't spend too much time on it. I've an idea some things will pick up later," McIntyre assured her, slurping at his coffee from earlier.

As she took a seat at one of the computers, Sheila quickly logged on, selecting the Metropolitan Police link to the officer's contact page. She selected the locator tab and put in the recipient's name from last night, Ethan Taylor. In seconds, a profile page emerged on the screen showing his current assignment and previous position to include personal information such as address, birthdate, and hometown.

Andrew needs to know this, she told herself while grabbing the phone. Dialing his office extension, her companion soon greeted her. "Andrew, I've got something you need to see right away," she stammered.

"All right, give me a few minutes," he said before hanging up.

Five minutes passed by before Inspector Fletcher entered the lab. While strolling up to Sheila, he coughed as the acrid chemicals and vapor from Kyle's cleaning assaulted his airway.

"Are you ok, Mister Fletcher?"

"Yes, I'll be fine," he replied, suppressing another cough. "I recommend you get another fan going to blow the stench outside."

"You sure you're ok?"

"I'll be fine," Andrew repeated. "What's so important?"

"This is," Sheila explained, pointing to the computer. "Your mystery number is this constable, Ethan Taylor," she said. "He worked in your office."

"Bloody hell," he said. "If he did, then it explains how Sergeant Wallace knew about Conor and I before anyone else." A call from Metro to here wouldn't be amiss."

"What's next then?"

"See if you can find any more information on Constable Taylor: birthplace, next of kin, current address..." Andrew said. "I've got to let Conor know." He gave Sheila a quick peck before rushing out. Bounding up the stairs, he nearly bowled McDermott over coming out of the stairwell.

"What's all the fuss?" McDermott asked, halting the door just inches from his face.

"The number between Hunt and Gilmore..." Fletcher stammered, catching his breath. As he made sure no one else could hear, he continued. "It belongs to Constable Taylor, the one from our office in London."

McDermott was at a loss for words at this news. Scratching his brow, he struggled for the moment on the impact of having a corrupt officer identified again, this time one close to his case. "Are you sure about this, Andrew?" he asked, turning away to sit down outside the community service office.

"Sheila made the call last night, and she feigned being a solicitor," Fletcher said, gazing at McDermott, who'd leaned over, head in hands in disbelief. "She said he couldn't talk because he was heading to muster at Heathrow."

McDermott got to his feet, brushing back his hair. "Come on then, we'll give Mister Collingsworth a call and pass along what we know."

Before they could reach their office, which they shared with other senior constables, Sergeant McKee walked up, waving a single sheet of paper. "I've some info to give you, Inspector," she said, her voice bubbly and higher pitched than usual. "Seems someone called your mystery number four other times in the last six months," she explained as she pointed out the highlighted text.

McDermott took the paper from the sergeant. He noticed the times and dates associated with each call. "Thanks, Annie," he said. "And make sure you let the cadets know I appreciate their effort, too." His smile was the most genuine she'd seen in weeks. Passing the paper to his partner, McDermott made a quick decision on their next move.

"Andrew, look into the dates; see if you can link them to any drugs being moved in our case," he said. "And get with Mister McIntyre, too; see if he's had anything transferred along these dates."

"And what about calling Mister Collingsworth?"

"I'll handle that right after I see Miss Sinclair about getting time with MacCallum." With the decision made, he strolled away towards the superintendent's office, his pace quickened with a purpose.

"I've never seen him light up like that before, have you?" the sergeant asked Fletcher.

"Not in recent memory," the inspector answered, worried the flood of new information might once again cloud his judgment like it did in South London nine months ago.

Sitting at his desk, Fletcher pulled their case file and reviewed the dates they'd compiled of the drug trafficking. He saw two of the six dates aligned with the case from when calls were made by Sergeant Wallace. The other four instances occurred before their arrival in Aberdeen. Returning the case file to his drawer, Fletcher made his way back to the lab.

While his partner tracked down the communication links on the drug trafficking, McDermott sat across from Superintendent MacCallum. "While we're waiting on Mister Collingsworth, I was wondering if you'd heard from the Sheriff's office on the summons? Or maybe from Mister Hamilton?" he asked while pulling his field coat taunt across his shoulders.

"Um... yes I have," MacCallum replied. "Seems you're in the clear to contact those 'mystery' numbers. But only under the premise of identifying the number to a caller in the case," he explained, tapping his finger on the desk. "And nothing more until someone delivers a proper summons," he added just as Miss Sinclair announced the call was ready.

"Good morning, Bruce," Superintendent Collingsworth answered. "I was surprised to get a request for a secure call this morning; is everything all right? McDermott's not causing too much of a fuss... or is he?"

McDermott's head straightened up hearing his supervisor in London make the inquiry. Before he could open his mouth, MacCallum held up his hand, signaling to hold his thoughts for the moment.

"He's being rather civil for the moment, William," MacCallum answered. "I wanted to have him on this call. Provided you don't have any reservations that is."

"I take it both of you have something to tell me," Collingsworth said, looking out at Churchill Gardens below his office. "I've no worries," he added.

McDermott paused for a moment before he cleared his throat. "Morning, Will," he said. "How's the garden coming along?"

"Not as well as my rose bushes," Collingsworth replied. "You and Bruce have information needing passed, do you?"

"Aye, sir," McDermott said. "I've done some back checking on our investigation, and I'm of the mind to have the death of Edna Gallagher corrected to murder based on my findings."

"And how have things changed?" Collingsworth asked, knowing the case involved McDermott's niece. "The coroner's inquiry was rather thorough in this matter. Anything you have better be concrete to gain a correction from them."

"Aye… I know," McDermott said. "But the investigators might have missed a fella who was present when the death occurred." McDermott spent the next few minutes explaining his hypothesis into the French sailor off the Joan of Arc being at the party, and drugs being linked to the ship.

"What do you say, Bruce?" Collingsworth asked his friend and fellow superintendent.

MacCallum glanced at McDermott before answering. "I've seen what your man has put together, Will, and it might deserve a second round. The biggest problem would be getting information on this sailor."

"I'll see what I can do from this end," Collingsworth said. "Conor, have a courier hand the information you have directly to me. Now, you mentioned a second issue, didn't you?"

"Our investigation into this drug trafficking is turning into a rotten onion, I'm afraid, Will," MacCallum started. "Seems we've uncovered another series of questionable communications from here in Aberdeen."

135

"Something linked to your sergeant, I suppose?"

"Aye, sir, but it goes beyond a local angle," McDermott answered ahead of the senior officer. "We've a problem at the home office in London. Fletcher has learned several calls from our suspect in Glasgow were made to a constable there in our building."

"What are you saying? We've a snitch amongst us, McDermott? Here in London?" Collingsworth asked, his tone and question challenging the evidence his senior inspector and partner had gathered.

"It appears so, Will."

"Who is it?"

"We've identified him as Constable Ethan Taylor," McDermott read from his note from Andrew. "He's assigned to Heathrow's security detail, which makes him a perfect conduit to push drugs through the checkpoints."

Collingsworth sat back in his chair, his expression blanching, growing paler by the moment. He knew the young officer's posting at England's busiest airport was only temporary and he'd return to his department soon. "Wrap up all your information on him, I'll take care of him on my end," he directed McDermott. "Bruce, I'll keep you informed. Are we done?"

"Aye, Will, for the time being," MacCallum said "I'll be in touch if McDermott and Fletcher have anything else. Cheerio." He disconnected the call before turning to McDermott. "Will's going to have his hands full for a few days. You best get the files together so we can add it to the courier's pouch for the afternoon."

While McDermott and MacCallum discussed their findings with London, Inspector Fletcher once again fought the noxious smells of the forensics lab. He was there to review four other instances where drugs being moved might have been compromised with Chief Inspector McIntyre. "This goes back to my suspicions from last week on how your samples are being handled," he pointed out to the forensics chief. "Sergeant McKee and another constable came across these."

"I've had Inspector Gordon go over those and they all check out," McIntyre said.

"But what department, though?" Fletcher asked. "You've got what, three or four separate locations handling evidence. Who's saying they've got everyone under constant supervision?"

"Before we send everyone into a panic, let's look at your information against our records, shall we?"

Fletcher handed over the list, which McIntyre took and walked over to the counter displaying the department's log books. He reached under and grabbed the one labeled "Drugs" and flipped it open to the last page. "No dates since your arrest of Sergeant Wallace," he said. With a flip of the page, he placed his finger on the last entry. Sliding his finger upward, he read off the dates and locations, stopping at one matching Fletcher's.

"We've a match?"

"A lorry driver was stopped at the MOT station on the A95 with a marginal amount of cocaine," McIntyre read. "We sent this off to Gartcosh since our machine was down." While reading upward, he came across another instance. The chief closed his eyes, recalling the circumstances on the case involving Sergeant Wallace supplying parties unknown with sensitive information on drugs being moved. The last two entries were the same.

"And what is the constant between them?" Fletcher asked.

McIntyre leaned on the counter, eyes closed as he contemplated what Fletcher asked. "Each occurrence was accounted," he began. "Our records show the evidence being signed for, log sheets endorsed at each point they're handled."

"And who else knew of these processes?" Fletcher asked, his thoughts drifting back to his time as a Royal Marine. *Higher ups knew your process for any patrol action you took*, he told himself.

"These are standard steps for every station," McIntyre replied.

"And those include advising the higher ups as well?"

"Well, of course we'd... of course," McIntyre muttered, slapping his hand down. "We'd advise Edinburgh for everything. You're thinking they advised someone like Cockburn, aren't you?"

"Conor has his concerns on him being around now that we've started to close the loop on the key players," Fletcher said. "It's a matter of identifying the 'what' and the 'whom' and right now he's becoming a prime candidate."

"I'll need to make a call," McIntyre said. "I don't want my colleague at Gartcosh caught off guard if Edinburgh sends the commission around asking a bevy of questions."

Chapter EIGHTEEN

Belfast, Northern Ireland

Rain spattered across the window, tap dancing its way along the glass as it was pushed by the wind. The gloominess of the morning matched Michael Connelly's demeanor. Spending time in Dublin with the chemist was supposed to bring better results. Instead, all he heard was reasons behind the delay in producing his own version of the PCP-laced hashish he stole from the Algerian Nazim Aziz who went by the alias of Louis Remesy.

Strolling to the end of his office, Connelly poured himself another cup of coffee. Looking up at his grandfather's picture, he contemplated what he would say of the young man's actions. "It's all for the best," he muttered, lifting his cup in salute. "But would you do the same if you could?"

The chirp of the intercom interrupted his period of reminiscence. "Sir, there's a Mister Taggert here to see you," Erin mentioned.

"Send him in please," Connelly answered as he took his place behind the desk.

In a moment's time, Erin was escorting the Scotsman through the door.

"Thank you, Miss Malone," Taggert said with a slight bow of his head. He tossed his damp peacoat across the wing-back chair, much to the disdain of Connelly seeing the fine leather abused.

"You wouldn't have something a wee bit stronger than coffee?" Taggert asked, nodding towards the cup in the Irishman's hand.

Spinning his chair, Connelly reached in the credenza behind him and drew out the crystal decanter and two glasses. "I'd mention the time of day, but then I wouldn't be a kind host, would I?" he teased, pouring each of them a drink.

"Good health to you."

"Slainte'," replied Connelly in Gaelic.

"I've looked into the affairs of the Saudi woman," Taggert said. "It seems she had a few notes written in Arabic from the trial, but nothing else. All her files related to cases in Edinburgh, but none for Aberdeen. Are you sure she'd have information on your barrister?"

Connelly sipped at his whisky before answering. "I'm not sure of anything," he said. "It's why I wanted you to look into her activities. She and my former barrister had to exchange information at some point."

"I've the impression she'd nae give up anything without a fight," he figured, draining the rest of his whisky in a single swallow. "Now mind you, I only went through her office, not her flat. If you're asking me to do something along those lines, you'll need to pay me up front."

Connelly glanced at the Scotsman, contemplating what he wished to have him undertake next with finding information on Sean Gilmore. As each day passed, the opportunity of locating his barrister grew more remote. "And what of you finding your brother's killer?" he asked, changing the subject.

"It was nae a shooter with Police-Scotland," Taggert admitted. "Talking with the lass from the boat, she mentioned the kill shot coming from a rooftop. The police reported the weapons team taking Angus out. So, it begs the question... who else had the means of killing my brother?"

Connelly reclined his chair, his hands brought together as though in prayer. "Most people would say the best manner to subdue a killer is to think like one," he said aloud. "Wouldn't you agree?"

"You saying another SAS-type did the job?"

Connelly hadn't considered another par-military member would have a grudge against the former sergeant, but the possibility existed. Certainly, one of the men from the Legionnaire camp in Corsica would be more than capable, recalling his former time in the elite unit. "Your brother and I didn't converse enough to discuss past acquaintances," Connelly answered. "Still, I'm not sure who would've known Angus would be in Aberdeen...."

"You something else to add?" Taggert asked, noticing the Irishman's expression.

Connelly finally realized why Sean Gilmore might have had a file on the French shipping owner. He had connections with one or more Legionnaires, he concluded. "It seems my barrister had a secret I wasn't

140

aware of..." the Irishman admitted. "Do you have any contacts outside the UK?"

"No, why are you asking?" Taggert replied, becoming defensive.

"My barrister had the means of contacting someone in France," Connelly said. "It's possible this person would have the means to dispatch mercenaries to quell your brother."

"If that's true, it could be one of any group out there," Taggert said, rubbing the back of his neck. "You know Angus trained with almost every service in NATO, right? And we can't dismiss someone here on the home-front either."

The office fell silent as each man exchanged glances, neither man dismissing the other's statement but also not offering support for them. "So where does that leave us?" Connelly asked.

Sitting outside the building, two officers of the PSNI sat in the unmarked van waiting for their suspect to emerge. "Is this the first time you've helped Metro, Sergeant?" the young constable asked.

"No, it's not," Sergeant Kennedy answered. "They assigned me to guard several delegates during the Good Friday talks. They didn't all come across as stuffed shirts, you know."

"What about this time, though?"

"Well, this time is different," the sergeant said. "This chief inspector, he's on edge. Something is driving him and I think it goes beyond the case he's investigating." The glint of sunlight flashed across the windshield as the sliding doors parted. "Here we go," he started, nodding to the top step of the office structure.

Taggert looked back. The meeting with the Irishman wasn't what he expected. He's keeping me in the dark on something, he told himself. Pulling the collar of his coat up, he stepped through the glass doors while glancing up and down the street for the ride he called.

"That's our man," the constable said, looking at the image supplied by the supervisor.

"Yes, it is now, isn't he?" Sergeant Kennedy said as a red minivan pulled close to the curb. "His host called a taxi for him. Let's keep a close eye on him, but not enough to be noticed now."

Ten minutes passed as the constables followed their suspect. "He's not heading to the train station," the constable said, nodding to the road sign when they passed it. "Catching a flight maybe?"

"Seems like it," Kennedy said, picking up the radio microphone. As the taxi continued on the A2 expressway, the destination for Blayne Taggert became obvious. Without proper summons, the constables for PSNI could only watch as a key suspect in Scotland Yard's investigation proceeded to leave the country. Following the taxi, they pulled past while it dropped the fare off at the airport terminal.

"We'll make a full report when we get back to the station," Kennedy said with a glance at his partner. "But first, let's get a quick bite. I'll buy the first round," he suggested as his partner maneuvered the van away from the airport.

Word from Chief Constable Darcy in Belfast about their suspect came as a sudden jolt to the Scotland Yard inspectors in Aberdeen. The bright spot in the communique was confirmation that Taggert's picture from the CCTV cameras provided enough clarity for an identification. Everything else the PSNI officers passed was mundane and nearly useless to them.

"It looks like Darcy's constables didn't care to find out what flight he was on," McDermott sighed, his head dropping against his chest. "And they wonder why we go in with a chip on our shoulder. He could be on any flight heading anywhere." He picked his head up, to look at Superintendent MacCallum.

"It appears they were rather lax in their observation," MacCallum said. "But mind you, there could have been a reason they didn't follow him into the terminal."

McDermott's frown did little to hide his true feelings for what happened in Belfast. "We don't even know if he met with Connelly, do we? All we've got is he went into the same building, and that's it, isn't it?" His face reddened as his frustration grew.

MacCallum could see the case taking its toll on the inspector. The more time passed between when clues were found and acted upon, the colder the case became. And in the long run, the harder to justify the effort in solving it. He'd seen good constables succumb to the pressure, several taking their own lives like Wallace did. Conor was too good a man for this, he told himself. "Go and have a few hours to yourself," MacCallum said. "That's an order."

"I've got too much going on," McDermott said, rising to his feet.

"And I'm telling you to go have a pint and forget today," the superintendent replied. "No officer is as more important than the next one. You're pushing too hard, Conor; you're not seeing things clearly and you need a break."

A knock on the door interrupted their discussion as Miss Sinclair peered inside. "Excuse me, sir, Inspector Fletcher needs a word with both of you." He swung the door to let them see McDermott's partner standing behind her.

"Come in, Fletcher," MacCallum said. "Have a seat." Nodding to his secretary, she closed the door behind the officer. "What's so important?"

Struggling to find the right words, it conflicted the young inspector on how to broach the subject he wanted to pass along. "Seems we've identified who Sergeant Wallace might have been contacting in Edinburgh," he started.

Once again, MacCallum faced dealing with the corrupt constable's actions. "Go on then, tell us... who's the culprit this time?"

"Well, sir... as you know..." Fletcher hesitated with his delivery. "We've identified numerous calls from Wallace's phone, and well, sir..." he stammered.

"Damn it, Fletcher, just tell me," MacCallum exclaimed, his patience expired.

"It's Sergeant Sedgwick, sir," he admitted, dropping is gaze to the floor.

MacCallum exhaled. "Now... wasn't that much easier, Inspector?" the senior officer asked. "So, what else is there besides the number at Sedgwick's desk tying the two of them together? There needs to be more than just a call if we're to rid Police-Scotland of all these scum officers."

For the next twenty minutes, Fletcher explained how drugs being sent from Aberdeen were tracked, which included communicating the movement to Edinburgh. As someone did this, they routed the paperwork through DUI where Sergeant Sedgwick would note the type and quantity of drugs. Records showed he would contact Sergeant Wallace, who in turn relayed the departures back to him.

"You see, sir," Fletcher continued, "the key was finding Sedgwick's number associated with Alistair Hunt's office. Inspector Gordon came up with the idea to cross-reference numbers after we identified Constable Taylor's on Sergeant Wallace's phone. We've now established how the drugs moved from here to Glasgow."

"I think we all need a pint," MacCallum said, grabbing his hat. "Come on, I'll buy the first one," he declared, leading the two inspectors out of the office. "Hold my calls, Miss Sinclair. We'll be back in an hour or two." He strode past his secretary's desk, the look on her face one of sheer surprise.

"Yes... of course, sir," the woman replied.

As the three officers strolled through the door of The Archibald House, the hostess showed them to a corner table. Their presence didn't go unnoticed as several constables were finishing up their ploughman's lunch. "We'll have three lagers and a large order of chips," MacCallum said to the hostess, placing his cover on the wall hook.

"Right away, sir," the young lass answered.

"You think this is a good idea, do you?" McDermott asked.

"I'm fed up dealing with pariah the likes of Wallace," MacCallum said, shedding his uniform coat and placing it next to his cap.

"I didn't mean..." Fletcher said before the superintendent cut him off.

"It has nothing to do with you, Fletcher," MacCallum answered just as the drinks appeared. "It has everything to do with individuals like Wallace who become constables. After they're settled, then they turn around, betraying the populace's trust in taking advantage of their status in the community. That's what irritates me." Grabbing his pint, he saluted the two inspectors before gulping down the ale.

"And you see it as a reflection on yourself," McDermott said. "But you know as well as anyone, it's nothing on you or your position." The waiter was quick to bring plates and the basket of steaming chips to the table. "It's greed, pure and simple." Taking a fork, Conor stabbed at the chips, placing them on the plate before dousing them with malt vinegar.

Andrew took a sip from his pint. "But how do you make it better?" It was Fletcher asking now, wanting to learn from the senior officer.

MacCallum looked at the young man from London and saw the raw form of a fine inspector standing at the split in the roadway. "You make sure the one's following you know you've their interests at heart," he answered. "Then you squash those who betrayed you... and you do so as hard as possible." He grabbed several chips to munch on, a shrewd smile lingering on his face.

"If that's the case... how would you deal with Sedgwick?" McDermott asked sprinkling more of the vinegar and salt on the chips he piled on his plate.

The senior officer peered over his glass at Conor, choosing his words carefully as he felt the effects of the lager clouding his thoughts. "He probably considers his actions as minuscule in the grand scheme. I'd say catching him in the act is always satisfactory in my books," he continued. "In the earlier days, I'm sure kicking the shit out of him would be acceptable, too."

Fletcher nearly choked on his lager hearing the superintendent converse so bluntly. But he was beginning to understand everyone needed a release from the pressures or it would consume them. "So, we develop a ruse to catch him would be your recommendation?" he asked.

"Aye, and the more the merrier will make it easier," MacCallum said while the waiter brought the second round of pints to the table. "You've Benson... where is he in all this? He's your bait." Sliding chips onto his plate, he stabbed a few with a fork and fed the alcohol in his stomach.

"But do we let the likes of Cockburn in on our plan?" McDermott asked. "If something goes wrong, we'd be making an enemy instead of an ally, you know."

"I've talked to his chief; he's reassured me Cockburn and Sedgwick have... been following up on a legitimate investigation on Benson. They believe he's getting the drugs here during his monthly lecture and selling them in Edinburgh."

"Well then, Cockburn was telling the truth," McDermott sighed. "I'm nae keen on setting the professor off without asking about what he and Doyle were meeting about last month. If he confesses to making a buy, then I'd consider asking for reducing his time at Grampian. But he

145

also has to give us the next fella passing the drugs through Hunt's network."

As the three officers continued their discussion, Sergeant Giles walked through the door. Searching the room to catch McDermott waving him towards their table. Sauntering up to the officers, he noticed the empty pint glasses. Everyone deserves a wee break I guess, he told himself. "Excuse me sir," addressing MacCallum, who just finished his second lager. "We've just gotten notice Chief Inspector McDermott's suspect passed through the entry point at Edinburgh's airport."

"Taggert?"

"Aye, the constables followed him to the Garden Inn," Giles read from his notepad. "They saw him registering. When they questioned the clerk, she told them he was there for at least 4 days."

"Why were constables in Edinburgh directed to conduct a tail on this suspect?" MacCallum asked, now drinking water instead of another lager.

"Well... the Chief..." Giles began.

"I had him establish a bulletin to all stations," McDermott said. "I had the sergeant identify Taggert as a suspect in a crime against one of Her Majesty's Judicial officers. I made Giles aware Taggert paid a visit to Sergeant Wallace's barrister several nights ago."

"The Saudi woman?" MacCallum asked while waving the server to the table. "The tab if you please," he asked before turning back to the men. "Are we sure about this?"

"Sergeant Holmes confirmed..." Giles began, but McDermott cut him off.

"Aye, it's the same one."

"We believe Taggert was contacted by this Irishman, Connelly, somehow and persuaded him to shadow the woman," Fletcher said, jumping into the discussion. "It's possible..." His voice trailed off as he contemplated the theory why Taggert was tailing Miss El-Sayed.

"What's possible, Andrew?" McDermott asked, holding out his hand for the bill the server was bringing to the table. "I'll handle this."

"Well, we know Gilmore had discussions with Connelly, but he's been locked up now. It goes without question the Irishman doesn't know about his barrister," Fletcher said. "Which leaves Miss El-Sayed as the only contact who knows of his whereabouts in his mind."

"I'm wondering if this Gilmore chap has something on Connelly?" McDermott wondered, handing over the bill which included a healthy stipend for the server. "If I were the barrister keeping separate records, I'd want to make sure they were in hands I could trust."

"The best place to put the pieces together is the station, gentlemen," MacCallum said, rising from the table. Sliding his jacket back on, he grabbed his cover before heading to the door. "Sergeant, have Miss Sinclair set a kettle on. We'll be needing it. What's your plan for the next step, Conor?"

"With what we know about his brother, my first instinct is to nab Taggert before he can dae any harm to the woman," McDermott answered. "Then we'll make a plan for Sedgwick."

"What about Connelly?" Fletcher asked.

"We'll hunt him down last when we see what his barrister is hiding," McDermott replied, leading the others back to the police station.

Chapter NINETEEN

Several cars passed the police vehicle as if they didn't care of the possible consequences for breaking the speed limit. "When we've finished this case, where do you think Mister Collingsworth will assign us to next?" Andrew asked following a string of lorries on the A90 towards Edinburgh. Glancing over, he could tell McDermott was listening, but unsure if he cared. "This is the first time I've been on a case outside London, you know."

"Worried about you and Sheila, are you?"

Andrew glanced at his partner as he maneuvered the police car around a tour bus. "Aren't you concerned about yourself and Ailene?" he asked. "Sheila and I've found a comfortable niche being together, I'm not sure I want to see it ruined by being reassigned."

"We've a few more months before William has to decide," Conor said. "Besides, you need to concentrate on getting us to Perth in one piece. And mind you, after we see Gilmore, we'll have the evening to meet Giles's friend about Miss El-Sayed," he continued, closing his eyes and resting his head against the window.

With the two-hour ride behind them, McDermott and Fletcher found themselves outside HMP-Perth, where the former barrister for Connelly was incarcerated on a four-year sentence for conspiracy against the crown.

Strolling up the path, someone logged the inspectors in and escorted to the Governor's office by a civil constable. "Here you are, gentlemen," the officer said, motioning to the outer office for the prison's senior official.

"Good morning," a stocky, compact woman greeted her visitors. Miss Colleen Monroe was kindhearted, soft-spoken but managed the facility with a firm grasp when needed. Fletcher and McDermott would soon experience this firsthand as they took their seats after returning her greeting.

Closing the door behind them, Miss Monroe took her place behind her desk. "It's my understanding you wish to have a private consultation with one of our residents," she said, cutting to the heart of their visit.

"Yes ma'am," McDermott answered. "Our investigation points to your resident as you call them having additional information on a suspect in a capital crime. We'd like to have a more relaxed environment to have our discussion in the hopes he'll assist us."

"And what do you have to say?" the woman asked, glancing at Andrew, who was sitting next to his partner, notepad and pen ready to make a note of anything significant.

"Chief Inspector McDermott is the senior officer. I do what I'm required..." he answered, the growing redness on his cheeks as a sign of embarrassment.

"It's Inspector Fletcher's theory that your resident has additional information, ma'am," Conor said, fending off the insult. "He and our forensic team have pieced together various points of evidence leading us here."

A brief ring announced the governor's assistant was entering the room. "Excuse me, Colleen. The resident is waiting."

"Thank you, Jeffery," she replied. "Inspectors, if you'll follow my assistant, he'll escort you to the interview area." She shook each of their hands as she dismissed them.

Andrew leaned in and whispered to Conor, "She didn't seem too happy with us, did she?"

"She's in a difficult job," Jeffery replied, sensing what Andrew was telling his partner. "What with budget cuts, lack of support from the higher ups, and the liberals... oh God, they're a fine lot to complain. Here we are, gentlemen," They stopped outside the security checkpoint. "You must surrender your sidearms."

Each inspector placed their weapon and spare rounds in the locker, signing the logbook before the constable would allow them to enter. "You'll find your man in room number three," the constable announced, releasing the lock to the entryway to let McDermott and Fletcher proceed.

Sean Gilmore sat, his handcuffs removed but the waist chai secured to the ring of the metal chair, reminding him he wouldn't be leaving after this visit. An audible clang announced the lock disengaging on the door. Turning to meet the visitor, he shifted his weight on the cold slab of stainless steel, unable to get comfortable. His anxiety quickly faded, replaced by disbelief upon seeing the Scotland Yard inspectors entering.

"I wouldn't have expected seeing you two so soon," the Irishman said, shaking his head. "You've come to let me know they commuted my sentence, have you?" His mind raced to comprehend the sudden appearance.

"If you cooperate, it may come to that now," McDermott said, sitting across from the felon. "We've something more serious to discuss, so let's nae start with the funnies, shall we?" he chided as he pulled a single sheet from his field coat. "Seems your former employer has a new friend." He slid the image of Blayne Taggert in front of Gilmore. "Look familiar?"

The eyes of Angus Dunbar's twin brother stared back at the barrister, giving a sinister yet mischievous look to the man. "I've not met this person before... who is he?" he asked, even though he already knew the answer.

McDermott took a breath knowing he had to reveal something to the barrister. "His name is Taggert, Blayne Taggert," the officer replied. "He's been in contact with your employer, Michael Connelly."

Tilting his head to the side and pursing his lips, Sean was just a little more than confused about the image and the inspector's idea he knew the man. "I'm sorry, but I've no idea who he is," he answered, sliding the image across the table.

"Andrew, if you did nae mind..." McDermott said, nodding to his partner.

"Blayne Taggert was born in Dundee, and was the twin brother of Angus Dunbar," the inspector said. "He served in the Royal Marines before being discharged after a court-martial for assaulting a fellow Marine," Fletcher recounted without looking at his notes.

With one hand, Gilmore slid his chair closer to the table allowing him to lean on it. His curiosity piquing his interest, he queried the inspectors for more information. "Why the different surname?"

"Family members recall the mother having difficulties raising the two boys and sent one to a cousin in Kilmarnock to be reared," McDermott said. "Now, the reason for us being here is simple: your man Connelly sent Taggert after Miss El-Sayed, and I want to know why."

He stabbed a finger on the image, the tone of his speech low and directed towards Gilmore.

"I'll tell you what I know," Sean replied. "But... I want your personal assurance Priscilla is afforded police protection until this is all over."

McDermott looked at the Irishman, knowing he had limited means of protecting the Saudi woman. "I'll do my best to see she's looked after until we get our hands on Taggert," he answered. "It's all I can do for now."

"All right," Sean said. "The other day, Priscilla sent her friend to see me so she could pass along some information regarding a call from Connelly," he started, choosing his words carefully. "You see, I've had concerns about Michael's intentions for some time, and well... I made myself an insurance policy."

"You've something on Connelly?"

"He's looking for two files I had Priscilla take possession of while we were in Aberdeen," Sean continued. "One is a dossier I compiled on Angus Dunbar, and the other is on a French citizen." Pausing, he took a deep breath before continuing. "As it turns out, when Michael began running the distribution operation, Callaghan's older son Roan noticed shipments missed labeled for type and quantity. He contacted me to look, discreetly mind you, into Michael's daily business transactions. It's what led me to act in the capacity I did as his barrister."

"So, they asked you to spy on Connelly on behalf of the family?" Andrew asked, a smirk of amusement edged on his face. "Why didn't they just call the police? It wouldn't be the first time one family member had another jailed."

"Roan did after he suspected that someone leaked their experimental cancer drug to a competitor," Sean replied. "I had two meetings in Dublin with a Sergeant Fahy regarding a meeting Michael had with his factory manager."

"This is all well and good, but what can you tell us to help put Connelly away?" McDermott asked, his patience wearing thin at the lack of anything of substance.

Sean dipped his head in resignation, knowing if the information he spoke of made its way to the wrong people, he would be killed, prison cell or not. "You've got me in a predicament, Inspector McDermott," he said. "Damned if I do and all...." He leaned back in the chair inhaling deeply.

Dictating for nearly thirty minutes, Sean Gilmore gave the two Scotland Yard inspectors the information they would need to have Michael Connelly arrested and put away for a long time. The one bit of information he refused to relinquish though was his French contact in Marseille; keeping this from being divulged would ensure his safety once released from prison.

"I'll do my best to keep my end up," McDermott said, hearing what he wanted. Getting up, he pushed the call button by the door. "Come on, Andrew, we've got another stop before calling it a night."

"Give Priscilla my best, will you?" Sean said as McDermott and Fletcher left.

The inspector's next stop was an hour south in Edinburgh. Fletcher drove towards the capital while McDermott scribbled on a notepad, placing names in a line. "The only thing Gilmore did nae provide was how Connelly contacted Hunt and his cronies in Glasgow," he muttered, placing several dashes under the syndicate's name.

"You think Sedgwick will give us someone?"

"Aye... maybe... only if he's keen on saving some of his skin," McDermott sighed, brushing his hair aside. "We might want to have Mister MacCallum contact the superintendent in Glasgow... what's her name?"

"You mean Chief Superintendent Cameron?" Fletcher replied. "I think she goes by Grace if I remember what Sheila mentioned when they first met."

"Aye, that be the one," McDermott said. "We'll need her help in having someone looking into the next fella." Glancing up, McDermott noticed the road signs for entering the Scotland's capital. "Mind you'll want to take the A90 to Queensferry Road; it'll be quicker," he explained, directing his partner off the expressway toward the main police station.

The last fifteen minutes went by with little talk. Pulling into the car park, Andrew found a space and shut the sedan off. "Quite a change to what we have in Aberdeen," he noticed, looking up at the multi-storied structure. "But it certainly beats the granite and wrought-iron look."

"Come on, let's not waste any time," McDermott said, climbing out and heading to the entrance.

Before the two inspectors had gotten to the door, Sergeant Giles's friend, Xander Holmes, met them. "Welcome, gentlemen," he greeted, holding out his hand. "I'm Sergeant Holmes with the Sheriff's office."

"Chief Inspector McDermott," Conor replied, accepting the officer's hand. "This is my partner, Inspector Fletcher."

"A pleasure, Sergeant," Andrew said as they shook hands.

"If you'll follow me, we can get tonight's activity over with and get you settled in," Holding the entrance open for them to pass through, he continued, pointing to the constable's station just past the entry point. "If you'll just sign the log. Oh, and you can keep your sidearms while in this facility too," he mentioned as he noticed the inspectors unholster their weapons.

After a few minutes, Sergeant Holmes led McDermott and Fletcher through a labyrinth of hallways until they came to an office with another constable sitting at his desk. "Gents, this is Sergeant Myles Cavendish."

"Evening," Cavendish answered before returning to his computer.

Taking a seat, McDermott cleared his throat before beginning. "Sergeant Giles has informed you about what information we need and who we need to meet with?" he asked, looking at Holmes before glancing at Cavendish. "Has someone advised him to our visit?"

"Aye, Myles and I share our responsibility with the same zealous attitude," Holmes replied. "And Marcus let me in on your tendency to take actions before asking too, Inspector," he continued, teasing McDermott with knowledge of the inspector's review of personnel records in Aberdeen. His smug attitude had the intended reaction of putting McDermott in his place.

"So... Marcus told you, did he?"

"Aye, he did, but it's nae important for the moment," Holmes said. "Now, what else can you tell me about this character stalking my barrister? Marcus said he did nae have anything on him."

"Go ahead, Andrew," McDermott started, nudging his partner with his elbow.

"Very well..." Andrew said. "The person of interest is Blayne Taggert, a former Marine and the twin brother of Angus Dunbar." Over

153

the next ten minutes, Fletcher laid out what they knew about each man, and the importance of seeing Priscilla El-Sayed safeguarded.

"You're saying another gunman offed a former SAS-type?" Holmes asked, his surprised expression almost comical. "And now his twin is working for the same employer? And where does Miss El-Sayed become involved in all this?"

"Her companion in a trial had information on the former assassin's employer," McDermott added, jumping into the discussion. "He passed it to the woman; now Taggert is trying to figure the best way to get it back." Pinching the bridge of his nose, his eyes squeezed shut as his frustration returned. "We've an agreement with the barrister to see that Miss El-Sayed is safeguarded until all this has blown past."

Just then, the phone on Holmes's desk buzzed. "Sergeant Holmes," he answered, stabbing the speaker button.

"Your client is in the conference room, Sergeant," the constable on the other end said.

"Thank you," Holmes replied. "Gentlemen, if you'll be so kind," he started, waving towards the door, "we mustn't keep a lady waiting now, should we?"

McDermott and Fletcher exchanged glances at the sergeant's declaration as they followed the officer down the hallway. "You had her brought in?" McDermott asked.

"You wanted to see her... didn't you?"

"Aye, but I did nae want her to being defensive when we talked either," the chief inspector replied. "I don't see her being too happy sitting across from me now."

After a constable escorted her into the meeting room, Priscilla took a moment to check her make-up, subtle as it was, though it didn't need fixing. The sound of the doorknob turning brought her attention to the entrance.

Opening the door, Sergeant Holmes stepped into the conference room, holding it for the Scotland Yard inspectors as they strolled past him.

"Sergeant, what's the..." Priscilla began, but never finished her statement. The sudden appearance of the man in the faded field coat followed by the more dapper-dressed gentleman was enough for her to surmise what was taking place. "What the hell do you want?" Her eyes appeared cold and lifeless, staring back at McDermott.

"Aye... good evening to you too," McDermott answered, pulling a chair out at the opposite end of the table. "I did nae expect the sergeant to have you brought here. But it's better than in the tombs, isn't it?"

"I'll ask just once more... what do you want?" Priscilla demanded, picking at invisible lint from her blouse. Her smile was polite, but lacked the genuine concern for what the inspector had to say, or so she thought.

Andrew and Sergeant Holmes sat watching the two thrust and parry with their verbal assault, the distrust each had for the other clear by their body language and manners.

"You've had a visitor lately, haven't you?" McDermott said, a strange calmness in his delivery. "He's nae one to take lightly, hen, and I'm here to see you're not put in any harm," his gentle and soothing tone attempting to lessen the hostility between them.

"How do you know who's come to see me?" Priscilla asked, stealing a glance at Holmes, who'd lowered his gaze to avoid hers. "Sergeant Holmes, did you call these gentlemen here today?"

Shaking his head, Holmes replied. "No, they contacted me, God's truth," he promised, raising his right hand up.

"Miss El-Sayed... Priscilla..." McDermott set his shoulders back, sitting more upright. "In Aberdeen, you were made privy to your fellow barrister's employer, and an associate of his too, weren't you?" he asked, letting the question linger. "This associate had a twin, and I'm of the mind he was the one paying you a visit."

Priscilla listened, the shock of hearing the inspector describe what had just happen causing her to blink in rapid succession as she tried to process what was just said. "A twin? Are you certain...? I mean... how?" she stuttered, knowing they confirmed what Sean Gilmore had observed in his notes.

"Priscilla, we know Sean Gilmore asked you to hold several files for him," McDermott continued. "We chatted with him in Perth just an hour ago; he told us one is on Dunbar, the other on a French citizen. All we're asking for is the file on Dunbar," McDermott said, the plea for her help coming easily. "Gilmore agreed to let us have the file, just until we catch this fella..."

"I gave Sean my word though..." the woman replied, eyes moistening with tears, overcome with regret for betraying her colleague. "He said the information wasn't to see the light of day," She used a delicate linen neckerchief to dab away the tears before squaring her shoulders in a brief act of defiance. "Who's saying I haven't disposed of them?"

"You're nae the type," McDermott said softly. "You've faith that you'd see Mister Gilmore again and be able to pass them back, don't you, hen?"

"You've still got the files, Priscilla." It was Sergeant Holmes adding his voice to the discussion now. "They're in your satchel, aren't they?" he asked, pointing to the bag wedged between her leg and the arm of the chair.

Priscilla stole a glance to her side. *Damn constables and their keen sense of observation*, she reflected. Looking at Sergeant Holmes, a child-like smirk grew from her lips. "You were always keen on seeing things weren't you, Xander?" Taking a deep, pained breath and closing her eyes, she undid the buckles and laid the flap over. "I've your word inspector, you'll see they're kept safe?" she confirmed as she pulled out Dunbar's dossier first.

"Aye, hen, but we'll just be needing Dunbar's. You can keep the other," McDermott answered.

"I'll see the other is kept safe if you want?" Holmes offered.

Priscilla hesitated, her hand on the file. "I'm not sure..." she replied. How can I assure Sean's trust? she asked herself. "Give me an evidence bag, then," she finished, conjuring a solution to her dilemma.

As Sergeant Holmes went to retrieve the envelope for Priscilla, she turned her attention back to McDermott. "Well, Inspector, how do you intend to see I'm protected from this Taggert fellow? Round the clock escorts to and from my flat, maybe?"

The thought of escorting the barrister brought a smile to McDermott's face he couldn't hide. "I was going to leave that up tae the good sergeant," he declared just as Holmes returned with the large evidence bag.

"Thank you," she said, taking the bag from the officer. Pulling the file from her satchel, she deftly slid it under the flap before anyone could read the exterior of the folder. With a flourish, she pulled the seal from the security tape off and pushed the flap closed, fastening the envelope closed. "There you are," Priscilla announced as she slid the folder to McDermott. "I trust it will be returned in the same condition when this is all said and done?"

Pushing the envelope in front of his partner, McDermott replied. "If you'll do the honors, Andrew."

Taking his pen out, the junior inspector annotated the date and time on the outside of the evidence before holding his pen up toward the sergeant. "If you don't mind seconding the custody of the parcel sergeant," he asked with a glance at Xander.

As Fletcher and Holmes handled the evidence which Priscilla watched over, McDermott drummed his fingers on the file of Angus Dunbar, anxious to read what was kept inside. Watching his partner finish taking possession of the file, he shifted in his seat. "Xander... do you know a good fish and chip shop?"

Chapter TWENTY

Edinburgh, Scotland

The low reverberation of discussions between constables was constant inside the Drug Intervention Unit offices each day. But this morning, they were eerily subdued as word spread about a Russian heroin dealer being apprehended the night before. Sergeant Sedgwick sat at his desk, reading the dispatch with a cruel smile etched on his face.

"Hope the Kremlin is happy now," he chuckled as his partner rounded the partition.

"What's that you're saying, Alan?" Inspector Cockburn asked.

"The lads finally caught up with Chekov dealing with the Turks near a nightclub in Portobello," Sedgwick replied, reciting the dispatch. "Seems once he finished getting a haircut, he stepped into a handful of disgruntled users. The doorman to the club had to call in the local patrol."

Cockburn slumped into his seat; his first act was fumbling through a drawer for the bottle of aspirin he kept. He could sense a trickle of sweat form near his right eye, the lingering effects of watching the rugby with his mates still present.

"You didn't get much sleep, did you?" Sedgwick asked.

"Billy over at the Rose 'n Crown had a wee party for the fellas watching the test from Sydney last night," Cockburn answered, working his mouth to combat the pasty remnants of drinking too much. "Can you fetch me some water?" he added in a low groan to his partner.

Sedgwick strolled out to the nearest vending machine and returned with a liter of water for his partner. "I've been looking into this case in Aberdeen," he explained, handing over the bottle. "I found out it did nae start there with McDermott, you know."

After he opened the bottle, Cockburn dropped four tablets into his mouth before chugging the half the water out of the bottle. "God, I hope that helps," he muttered. "You were saying the case in Aberdeen didn't start there. So where did it begin?"

Sedgwick pulled a folder from his desk, flipping the cover over. "Seems after McDermott botched a case in south London, they assigned him one in Southampton. Metro was handed a drug trafficking case linked to three deaths. But they had no suspect, though they found one victim with a note leading them to Aberdeen," he finished, slapping the folder closed.

Cockburn's headache kept him from focusing on what his partner was saying. Since their return from Aberdeen without the suspect Benson, the inspector had his partner dig into the case being handled by McDermott. With another long pull on the water bottle, Cockburn drained the remains, a slight dribble making its way down his chin. "He mentioned they were holding Benson as a murder suspect, didn't he?"

"Aye, but it couldn't be one from Southampton," Sedgwick replied. "We had him being tailed a week before then. Besides, he's never acted out or been involved in any fights we know."

As the aspirin worked on his hangover, Cockburn ran his hand across his forehead, wiping away the ever-present sheen of sweat. He tried to will the dull ache away by pressing his fingertips against his temples. "Well then, we know Benson's not the suspect for those killings... who's murder would it be, then?" he asked, squinting towards the constable.

"According to the dispatches I've seen, they've had a half dozen violent deaths in the last three months," Sedgwick said. "All the murders had drugs associated with them except for two of them."

"And what made those two so special?" the senior officer groaned.

"One was at the hands of some deranged veteran who was offed by a Special Weapons constable onboard a boat," Sedgwick answered. "The other was a Borders agent who was robbed on the docks. Seems someone knifed him during the robbery."

"Really now, they identified the one killed by the constable as a veteran?"

"Aye, some former SAS-type suffering from PTSD went on a rampage according to a constable with the weapons team here in Edinburgh," the sergeant said with a smile. "They said it was quite a shot, through the window and all."

159

The enthusiasm in the sergeant's voice as he described the killing did little to soothe the inspector's hangover. Cockburn pushed himself away from the desk. "I'll be back in a few, just need some fresh air," he started, strolling towards the door. In a few minutes, he was outside, sidestepping a group of smokers polluting their lungs with nicotine.

Each step in the fresh air helped Cockburn clear the fog of last night's drinking. *I've got to be more careful, I'm nae a youngster these days,* he scolded himself for overindulging. So, the last three months have been busy for Aberdeen? I remember one dispatch mentioning the Border agent, but not this veteran. I need to read up on McDermott's case too, just to confirm what Sedgwick is saying.

Turning the corner, the inspector approached the rear entrance to the station when he saw a member of the weapons squad unloading his kit. "Morning to you, Willie," he greeted, waving at the constable.

"Same to you, Inspector," the officer replied. As Cockburn grew closer, the constable got a better look at the inspector's appearance, which was less than his usual dapper self. "You look rather knackered, Hugh; what gives?"

"Had a wee bender last night watching the rugby from Sydney," Cockburn answered, his cheeks growing rosy. "Willie, do you remember reading the dispatch on the vet in Aberdeen?"

"When was that? All we've heard from those fellas was the senior sergeant offing himself in the cells waiting trial," the officer said. "Oh... and they had one of those rave parties near the university where a fella was stuck by his mate. Why, is there something I should know?"

Cockburn shook his head. "No, probably just a pub story getting out of hand by one of the lads," he replied. "I'd not worry about it until you see it in the papers," he finished, patting the constable on the shoulder as he trudged down the sidewalk.

Glancing back, Cockburn watched the constable carry his bag and weapons case into the building. "Well, Sedgwick, you've either taken to spreading tales, or you're seeing things before the rest of us," he muttered. Slowing his steps, he contemplated how the sergeant knew of the dealings in Aberdeen. As he completed his lap around the building, the inspector decided to check on the events his partner had related to him.

"Feeling better?" Sedgwick asked as he watched Inspector Cockburn take a seat at his desk.

"Aye, for the moment," Cockburn said. Tapping on his keyboard, the inspector began the task of reviewing the case file on the drug trafficking in Aberdeen. "What did you do with the Benson file?"

"It's on the computer," Sedgwick replied. "Look under the active files on the Z drive. I was just looking through them last night, so it should still be there."

Cockburn squinted at the screen, searching for the drive. In a moment, he'd found it, which led him to the file on the university professor. Pulling out his folder from the drawer, Cockburn selected the notes he took after their brief encounter with Benson and McDermott. As he glanced between what he'd written and then typed the previous day, he saw several corrections.

"Did you correct this file?" he asked, looking at his partner.

"What?"

"I asked if you did something to my file while you were looking it over," Cockburn snapped at Sedgwick for the second time. "Seems a few statements aren't what I put in the other day."

Sedgwick edged back in his seat. "I did nae touch your file," he replied. "You sure you recall what you typed in there? I mean... I've me own record to submit, too," he answered in an attempt to rationalize.

Cockburn held his head in his hands, then looked back at his partner, his lips pressed together to create a thin line. "When you're done with your report, I'll want to see it," he said. "And I'll be expecting it by the end of your shift today." Closing out his report on Calvin Benson, he began searching the larger file labeled "Aberdeen" for McDermott's case.

With the file located, Cockburn got up from his chair as the information was streamed to his computer. Strolling out to the vending machine, he grabbed a cup of coffee before returning to his desk. The screen lit up with the first page as he moved his mouse around.

The first page was the typical police administration jargon: name, rank, assignment, etcetera. Selecting the second page, Cockburn began to see information on the chief inspector's notices on the current case. *All this began in April for you*, he read. McDermott and his partner were following up on the event from Southampton. *Made an arrest of a ship crew for trafficking hashish*, he noticed. *Why didn't you stop with that score, McDermott?* Cockburn asked himself.

A tap on his shoulder from a constable caused him to jump. "Inspector Cockburn, you've a visitor."

Looking up, he noticed Sedgwick was not at his desk. "Who is it?" he asked, peering up at the officer.

"The fella claims to be a chief inspector."

Cockburn closed the files before pushing away from his desk. Walking past the door, he tossed the coffee cup in the trash bin, its remains adding to a collection of stains on the wall. He glanced toward the stairwell and noticed the disheveled and harried look of Conor McDermott. Dodging a few constables, he soon found himself coming face-to-face with the officer from Scotland Yard. "I did nae expect a visit from you."

McDermott shuffled his scuffed-up Chukka boot at the stain before looking up to answer his counterpart. "I'm nae the type to create a fuss," he began, "but there's something you need to know." As he leaned against the wall, he scanned the hallway. "Can we have a bit of privacy?"

Cockburn nodded down one end of the hall. "Aye, there's a meeting room this way," strolling to his left. "You on your own today?" he asked, noting the absence of McDermott's partner.

"Andrew's minding the car," McDermott replied.

Cockburn hit the light switch, turning the darkened room aglow under the fluorescent lighting. Pulling a chair out, he offered it to McDermott before sliding one out for himself. "So, you've some news you'd like to share about Benson?" the DIU officer asked.

McDermott sighed. "I wish it was that easy," he said. With his hands placed on the conference room table, he looked over at the inspector. "Cockburn, we've had... the Aberdeen staff have had a rough go of it recently," he began. "You've seen the dispatch on their senior constable, haven't you?"

"You mean the one committing suicide? Aye... I heard 'bout it," Cockburn said.

For the next ten minutes or so, McDermott read Inspector Cockburn into his case of the drug trafficking that began in Southampton and eventually led them to Aberdeen. He also provided details on the university professor's meeting with the murdered dockworker. "Seems the sergeant knew of our assignment before we were being dispatched," McDermott said.

Cockburn leaned back in the chair, hands resting on the growing paunch his desk job was contributing to over the last few months. "You telling me this Wallace fella had something on you from London?"

"Aye, and we've found out he's been in contact with other officers," McDermott started, trying to ease the blow about to be delivered. "Turns out Wallace also was linked to a dead Customs agent..." he began to explain before Cockburn cut him off.

"And what does all his actions have to do with DIU?"

McDermott knew he needed to inform Cockburn of his partner's involvement. He also wanted to rid himself of the burden of knowing Sedgwick's chance of manipulating reports on the drug trafficking through Edinburgh. "We believe one of the other officers is your partner," he said. With that single statement, McDermott felt relieved to the point he actually sat up in his chair.

"You've no right accusing my sergeant of being dirty," Cockburn replied emphatically, his finger pointing at McDermott. "You want to blame someone, you better have solid proof," he added. "I've read part of your file, McDermott. You're trending towards a dismissal if you screw this one, aren't you?"

The Scotland Yard inspector sat back, accepting the verbal onslaught and allegations. He knew Cockburn was right; he was given one more chance by London to prove his worth to the Metropolitan Police. If he didn't come through, there was a very good chance he'd be dismissed. "I'm aware I've had a few muck-ups of investigations in the past, but London's seen fit to give me another go on this case," he said. "Plus, Fletcher and I've proof on Sedgwick."

"You'd be hard pressed to convince me of that," the inspector muttered under his breath. Now on the defensive, Cockburn sat across from McDermott, his gazed set square on the Scotland Yard officer. "And since you've nae paper in your hands, I'd say you're full of it."

McDermott reached into his field coat and produced several sheets of paper. "We tracked the cell number Wallace used when calling a syndicate boss in Glasgow," he pointed out. "It's the same number he called here in the building. Do you think it'll be one of the numbers in your office?"

The dull ache of the hangover caused his head to throb. It also made accepting the news harder. "Let's say for your argument, you're right. What do you want me to do about it?" he asked, his hands open in mock defeat.

"Nothing for the time being," McDermott replied. "He's just one of several fellas we need to connect to the trafficking between Aberdeen and Glasgow. But you could start a wee set of notes on his behavior."

"Snitch on my own partner," Cockburn said, grimacing at the suggestion. "And what is it I'm keeping an eye on, heh?"

"Anything you think is beyond what he should know about or should be doing," McDermott said, sliding the sleeve up on his coat to look at the time. "I've a 1300 meeting with the Chief Superintendent in Glasgow." Looking down at the inspector, he continued. "I know it's nae easy to hear the truth, but I wanted to make sure you heard it from me now before it was done at trial," he finished, offering his hand in goodwill.

"And when does my super get the courtesy of a call?" Cockburn asked. "He'll no like being blind-sighted by all this, you know."

"Mister MacCallum was scheduled to make his call later today," McDermott said, walking out of the room and towards the exit.

The DIU officer sat in quiet, considering what he'd just been told by the Scotland Yard inspector. *Earlier this morning, Sedgwick mentioned things even I had little to no knowledge of,* he thought to himself. *But why would the sergeant become involved in something like this?* Every thought he had playing the devil's advocate only led to more questions. As he trudged through the door, he flipped the switch to plunge the room into darkness.

"Well, how'd Cockburn accept the news?" Fletcher asked as his partner slid into the sedan's passenger seat.

"Like I thought he would, denying it at first," McDermott answered. "But I've an idea he knows something might be amiss with the sergeant already. Let's go, we've another meeting before supper," he reminded his partner as they settled in for the hour-long drive to Glasgow.

As Andrew hummed to himself, McDermott watched the fields pass by. With the information passed to Cockburn, he was left to determine the best manner to snare the sergeant as part of the growing corruption case within Police Scotland constable ranks. The gentle rocking of the car soon lulled him to sleep.

The blaring horn of a passing lorry woke McDermott, the suddenness resulted in hitting his head against the window. "What the hell?" he muttered, rubbing his eyes as he watched the truck speed past the police car.

"Don't look at me; I didn't make him do it," Fletcher said, noticing the scowl on his partner's face. "Besides, we're almost there." He nodded to the exit off the M8 expressway and in less than five minutes, Andrew was pulling into a spot outside Glasgow's Police Scotland headquarters building on Stewart Street.

McDermott got out, tugging at his trousers before setting his field coat squarely on his shoulders. "Come on. With any luck, we can get in a few pints before supper," he suggested, waving the young inspector towards the entrance.

Chapter TWENTY-ONE

Limerick, Ireland

The squealing brakes of the Prevost tour bus announced another party of tourists' arrival. In minutes, couples, both young and old, were soon disembarking as the driver and hotel valet pulled bags from storage bins. Amongst the group, Safia Amine stood off to one side while her escort, Ismail Ghazi, tended to their luggage.

After checking in, the couple met in the hotel's café where they ordered a light meal. "How long do we have to find this young Irishman?" Ismail asked, sipping the water brought by the server.

"Your master wishes to have us return by the end of the week if possible," Safia replied. "Whether or not we have the information, but obviously with evidence is better for both our futures. My contact said we should have no problem locating our target."

"And how confident are you in this information?"

The woman paused, her anger coming forth at Khalid's servant soliciting information. "My informant has never wavered or placed me in difficult situations," she replied. "And our target has a schedule which hasn't unchanged over the last six months. So... I'm very confident."

Ismail was not used to having a woman placed in charge, but for this excursion, his master's direction was to follow Safia's direction and protect her at all costs. "Are we to begin this evening? We don't even know if the target is here in the city yet."

"Will you be like this the entire time?" Safia asked, the directness of her question failing to hide her displeasure. "I've faith in my contact, and if you continue, I'll have him detain you while I return."

The rebuke had the desired effect as the young man sat back, his face holding a sullen and neutral expression. *I've never had to deal with a woman like this*, he thought to himself. The next twenty minutes passed quietly as they ate. Reaching out, he took his water and finished. "I'm ready," he said, ready to complete the task and return home.

"Here, this should cover the expense," Safia said, dropping several 10-euro notes on the table. "I'll be outside waiting."

Meanwhile, across the River Shannon, several young Irishmen sat around a table in a small pub, sharing a laugh. It was early, so their banter wasn't disturbing anyone except a few tourists who'd stopped in to soak up the local ambiance.

Liam Finnegan tilted his pint back, finishing his stout. "Here you go. I'll cover the next round," he offered as he tossed some money onto the table. The last few months were taking their toll while he played escort to the Chinese chemists working for his employer. He was grateful for the added money, but felt his experiences were being wasted.

"So, Liam, when's your next trip to Dublin?" one friend asked.

"It's up to my employer," Liam replied. "If he needs me, I'll be happy to go. Staying in a posh hotel, meals paid for," he bragged, grabbing the fresh drinks being delivered and lifting his in salute. "You'd think I was someone's band mate."

"But you've no mot on your arm this time, do you?" The young ginger-haired man was never shy around women, and rarely without a date.

"I'm 'fraid my work would scare one off," Liam joked, but knew his occasional time with Dr. Yang would give off the wrong impression to the others. Taking a long pull from the glass, he wiped the back of hand across his face. "Besides, they'd only be after my money." Looking at the reflection in the mirror situated behind the barkeep, he noticed it was near time for him to pick up his elderly mother from the shops. With one last guzzle, he polished off his drink. "That's enough fellas; I'm off," he announced, sliding on to his feet from the stool.

"We'll be seeing you on Thursday then...?" one friend chimed in.

"I'll be here, and you can buy the first," Liam replied slapping his fellow patron on the back. With a wave of his hand at the barkeep, he was soon skipping down the steps onto the street. He ambled along the sidewalk, dancing around a family outside the McDonald's, the mother and father bribing good behavior from their children.

The late summer day had brought plenty of sunlight, but also some wind as it blew between the buildings. As he neared the bookstore his mother worked at, Liam was treated with a glimpse under a young woman's skirt as a gust of wind from a passing bus lifted her fabric.

Shaking his head at her frantic effort to retain some modesty, Liam pulled the door open.

Across the street, Safia noticed her target enter the store. "Right on time," she muttered. She saw Ismail standing near the entrance to a local department store, trying his best to remain in the shade, and motioned for him to join her.

"When will we begin?" Ismail asked, his patience for watching the pedestrians waning.

"He's in the bookshop," Safia nodded across the street. "He'll be out in a few minutes with his mother, according to my source," she informed him, glancing down at the city map she took from the hotel. "They'll take a bus to her apartment, and then we'll see where he goes from there." She made quick work of folding the paper back to its original size.

"Your informant seems very competent," Ismail said. "So much so, I'm wondering why I'm here.".

Will the insolence never stop? Safia pondered. "You're here to ensure the information we learn is passed to your master," she said. "I don't expect trouble, but I would rather be ready in any event."

Half a block away, Garda Sergeant Seamus Fahy and his partner munched on their food, watching their suspect enter the bookstore. The plant manager for the pharmaceutical company Callaghan and Higgins was their main "person of interest" in a human trafficking case. The past twelve months had seen a marked increase in the international workforce for the company, but several of the new employees had also triggered immigration flags.

"You think he's getting a kickback for bringing in prostitutes?" the young constable asked Fahy.

Slurping the last of his cola, the sergeant paused before answering. "You've cracked the case have you, Murphy?" Fahy replied. "Our man has shown no sign he's pimping any of the workers. And if you read the briefs, you'd see that most if not all are chemists or technicians."

Duly admonished for his speculation, the young officer hung his head. "I'm just considering the number of women they have seen him with during our surveillance," he replied. "And who's saying his visit to Dublin with the two Asian's wasn't to have them meet up with a client."

Sergeant Fahy chuckled. "We already know who he met with," he said. "The dossier on the gentleman has him as the company operating officer. And they weren't anywhere in the city we didn't have someone watching them either." He wadded up his sandwich wrapper and cup. "Be a good fella and toss this in the bin, will you?" he asked, handing the trash to the young officer.

As the constable took care of their trash, Fahy noticed Liam Finnegan and his mother leaving the bookstore. "Come on, it's time for a bus ride," he muttered with a tug on Murphy's sleeve. As the officer headed to the kiosk, he did not notice the Middle Eastern couple making their way to the stop.

After a brief twenty-minute bus ride, Liam helped his mother from the bus and walked the last thousand meters to her flat. The two officers with Garda Síochána (Irish National Police) watched as they stepped off, noting the location and stop. Safia and Ismail did the same, but hesitated to follow them.

"I'd say we're about ten minutes from Roxboro Station," Fahy muttered to his partner. "We'll get off in two stops and hoof it. Someone there can get us back to the car."

"What about our gentleman friend?" the constable asked.

"He's off the bus, so we'll have to catch him again later," Fahy responded under his breath while shuffling to the exit.

Chapter TWENTY-TWO

Glasgow, Scotland

Trudging out along Campbell Street, McDermott and Fletcher made their way to the local eatery recommended by Superintendent Cameron earlier in the day. Ascending the stone steps, they opened the door to the eclectic shop. "The name suits it," Fletcher said, pointing to the neon display of a potbelly pig and peacock butterfly in the windows.

"I'm more interested in their food," McDermott answered as he followed his partner.

After someone seated them and they placed their drink orders, McDermott glanced about before speaking. "Is it possible a full class of cadets could be in on our smuggling? Like... make a pact to control it, be their own syndicate?"

"I'm not sure a full cadre of thirty would all go along with it," Fletcher replied as the waiter served them their drinks. "But if you consider we've hit on individuals of the same rank, it could be feasible." He picked up his gin and tonic, nodding to his partner with a silent "cheer" before taking a sip.

"Aye, good health to you," McDermott replied, taking up his pint. "Who's the senior man out of the lot so far?"

Fletcher took a moment to reflect on the question. "So far we've only come across the two sergeants, and Wallace was the senior man," he said. "And Chief Superintendent Cameron didn't have any indications of a sour lot here when we briefed her."

"It does nae mean she'd know right off," McDermott said. "I'd bet a new pair of Chukkas she has something in the works by now. Besides, we know London sent out a notice to the commissioner about the corruption, who was to brief each district superintendent, right?"

The increase in police corruption within the force being managed by Edinburgh had not gone unnoticed by Independent Office for Police Conduct's office in London. Most of the evidence was leading to extortion of witnesses and claims of excessive police brutality with suspects in custody. The mis-handling of drug evidence in a case in

Portsmouth is where McDermott and Fletcher had been brought in to the mix.

"You think Cameron only briefed certain members?" Fletcher asked as their server brought out a small plate of marinated olives and a sliced baguette and pesto sauce. "She doesn't seem the type... She seems as tight-fisted as MacCallum. You saw how she was when we pinched Hunt."

McDermott took a slice of bread and placed a touch of pesto in the middle. "Aye, I remember," he replied before taking a bite. "I also recall her being keen to hear him out like she wanted to know if she'd have any issues with what he knew."

Fletcher sat back, his mind racing to piece together possibilities. Finishing his drink, he caught the attention of their server to bring a second drink to the table. "If we consider your theory, we'll need to see if the sergeants even went through training together. Who takes the lead on that effort?"

"I'll give London a call in the morning. They can do it for us," McDermott replied as his platter of fish and chips were set before him. His eyes grew big seeing the portion of cod hanging over the plate, the batter a golden brown. "I need to ask who their fish monger is here and tell Malcolm he's losing money."

"Back to our dilemma with this Connelly fella..." Fletcher said as the server brought his meal to the table. "Do you think we'll get something on him from Hunt's testimonies?"

"We've already got what the barrister told us," McDermott said, dousing his filet with some malt vinegar. "All we need is Hunt to admit meeting Connelly and we'll have cause to draw a summons. As long as Connelly stay's in Belfast, he'll be ours for the taking."

"And if he doesn't stay... then what?"

"We'll leave it to William and the pundits in London to fight with Dublin if he heads south to the plant. And if he skips to the continent, I'm sure London will see fit to notify INTERPOL."

As McDermott finished his answer, Fletcher contemplated where this case was leading them. It started with drug smuggling in Southampton, three deaths, and then the encounter in Aberdeen with the former SAS sergeant Dunbar being killed. Now, they were hunting down a group of corrupt constables instead, apprehending their suspect in the drug smuggling. Some investigations are never routine, I guess.

***

The morning hustle of constables changing shifts was never easy for a meeting, and now Fletcher and McDermott were caught in the middle with Sergeant Trotter at the Stewart Street station. Most of the officers wore hi-vis coats under their bullet-resistant vests, while others had their kits slung over the odd shoulder. "Miss Cameron had these picked up last night," the sergeant said, handing McDermott a folder.

"Are those the transcripts?" Fletcher asked as he squeezed past several officers that were headed to their patrol cars.

Flipping the folder open, McDermott glanced at the contents. "Aye...mostly procedural," he noticed as he pulled the first page out. "Sergeant, you've a room we can sit in for a wee bit?"

Trotter showed the inspectors to the office he shared with two other sergeants, Trotter waved them to an empty set of chairs. "The lads are both on the evening shift, so you'll have quiet for 'bout an hour," he assured them, looking at his watch before heading out of the room.

Each of the inspectors took turns reading the court recorders script of Alistair Hunt's testimony. It was Fletcher who came across the first nugget of dialogue. "They asked Hunt about his dealings with a suspect named 'Higgins,'" Fletcher read. "And his answer corroborates what Sean Gilmore told us in Perth," he continued. "Hunt described knowing of an arranged meeting between Higgins and a vessel captain at the Edinburgh Zoo."

"Clive Duncan of the *Nordic Supplier* I presume?" McDermott asked.

"There's no direct mention of names," Fletcher answered, flipping through the manuscript.

McDermott closed his eyes before rubbing his hand across his face, a heavy sigh coming forth. "We've got the Captain already admitting to the arranged shipment, right? And we've evidence Hunt has talked with Connelly who was addressing himself as 'Higgins' in all this... So... all we need tae do is tie the meeting between Connelly and Duncan and the calls with Hunt."

"And how can we make the connection between them?" Fletcher asked as Sergeant Trotter returned.

"Am I interrupting something?" the sergeant asked.

"No... but you've perfect timing," McDermott said. "We need to have the prosecution in the Hunt case request to prepare a summons for a search of the Edinburgh Zoo," he added. "It needs to include all CCTV security feeds of the grounds."

"You're daft," Sergeant Trotter replied.

"You're thinking about the CCTV images from the harbor, aren't you?" Fletcher asked, the realization of his partner's plan suddenly hitting him.

"Aye... we link Connelly to meeting Duncan at the zoo and make our case he's the intended buyer behind the hashish," McDermott said, his cocky smile appearing. He sat back, his chest expanding with pride as he successfully put together another series of puzzle pieces.

Sergeant Trotter picked up the phone and put the wheels in motion to see if the inspector's theory could be played out. As he spoke to his counterpart at the Sheriff's office off Saltmarket Street, Inspector Fletcher's cell phone rang.

Looking at the number, he answered. "Hello?"

On the other end, Sergeant Xander Holmes in Edinburgh was holding a dispatch notice from the evening watch. "Inspector Fletcher, Holmes here in Edinburgh," he began. "We've a sighting of your suspect."

Fletcher's mind flooded with a thousand questions he wanted to ask the sergeant. "Do you have a constable keeping an eye on him?" he asked, waving a hand at McDermott to be quiet. McDermott nodded several times as he heard what steps the Edinburgh sergeant was taking. Looking at his watch, Fletcher replied, "We'll be there in two hours. Good work, Sergeant."

"What's that all 'bout?" McDermott finally asked.

"Sergeant Holmes said the evening watch found Taggert, and he's still in Edinburgh," Fletcher said. "We've got to go right now. Sergeant Trotter, a pleasure meeting you." He shook the officer's hand and pushed past him.

"What about your summons for the CCTV feed?"

"Keep after it, we'll be back," McDermott shouted over his shoulder as he rushed after his partner. "I'll give the superintendent a call!". As he exited the building, he found Fletcher already had the car turned around, its strobe light affixed to the roof.

"You know we've no need for the lights, right?" McDermott said, sliding into the passenger seat.

"It'll get us through traffic," Fletcher replied while beginning to maneuver toward the entry point for the M8. As the inspector joined the flow of traffic, the blue strobe did its job. It gave the unmarked car passage as motorists parted allowing the inspectors to make their destination in just over an hour's time. Fletcher pulled off the motorway, and he was soon parking in front of the District Headquarters on Saint Leonard's Street where they noticed Sergeant Holmes waiting outside.

"You made excellent time, Inspector," the sergeant greeted Fletcher.

"He had a good navigator," McDermott chimed in. "Where's our suspect?"

"They saw him near the shopping district downtown," Holmes replied. "One patrol noted he was sitting outside a local coffee stand making notes or something."

"That's not enough to bring him in," Fletcher said. "He's suspected of impersonating a custodian for the moment, hardly a capital offense."

"Sergeant, can you take us to the shop?" McDermott asked.

"Aye, give me a minute to fetch a car," Holmes replied before heading up the steps of the office building.

"What are you thinking, Conor?"

"I want to keep this fella from doing the same thing his brother did," McDermott answered, the intensity of his stare denoting his feelings against the deceased brother. "If they're cut from the same cloth, there's no telling how he'll react."

The awkward silence between the partners was soon broken as Sergeant Holmes emerged, pointing to the row of marked vehicles behind the inspectors. "We've number 22. I had dispatch send a message out to the patrols. We'll be meeting one near the shops." He slid behind the wheel while the other two took their respective seats, McDermott in the front and Fletcher behind him.

After negotiating the downtown traffic of taxis and buses, Sergeant Holmes soon neared the location where Blayne Taggert had last been seen. As the sergeant pulled the car into a vacant spot at the curb, two other officers emerged from the corner coffee shop.

"Sergeant Holmes," Constable Baird greeted, tipping his cap to the driver. His partner tilted her head to the side to glimpse the other occupants.

"Moonlighting as a taxi now, Sergeant?" Constable Kerr teased.

"There'll be none of that or I'll see you walking the Tower grounds," Holmes growled back as McDermott and Fletcher exited the car. "Chief Inspector McDermott and Inspector Fletcher, Constables Baird and Kerr."

"Our man was sitting by the coffee shop there?" McDermott asked, pointing to the corner.

"Aye... and facing so he could look down Rose and Castle," Kerr answered, pulling out her notebook from her vest. "An earlier patrol noticed he was writing on a tablet every so often," she added.

McDermott dodged a passing bus loaded with tourists as he strolled towards the corner. Stopping near the entrance, he glanced up the street to his left, then slowly surveyed the shops to the right until he had scanned the scene in front of him.

"Fancy telling me what you're thinking?" Fletcher asked.

McDermott stole a glance at his partner before waving Sergeant Holmes over. "How far is it from your courthouses? Could someone make it to one of the shops for lunch?"

"Nae likely; you've got the mall to negotiate plus the park," Holmes replied.

McDermott walked across the street once again. Looking around, he took in the shop locations, trying to piece together a reason behind Taggert's need to be in this specific area. He also was trying to fathom if Priscilla El-Sayed would have reason to be there.

"Do you think Taggert followed the barrister to this area before?" Fletcher asked.

"Aye, but why... why here and what was she doing here," McDermott replied.

175

"There are a few wee shops that might have caught her fancy," Constable Kerr offered.

"Sergeant, is Miss El-Sayed in any sessions this morning?" McDermott asked.

Holmes pulled out his notebook where he slid out a schedule. "Aye, she's a summary hearing," he read off the slip before glancing at his watch, "in twenty minutes with Lord Calvert. We could catch her right after she's done."

"Andrew, you stay with the constables," McDermott said. "The sergeant and I will go see Miss El-Sayed and find out what might be so interesting to her along this street."

"And I'm doing what...?" Fletcher asked.

McDermott got into his partner's face. "You've seen Taggert up close," he said. "Put yourself in his boots... think about him doing a reconnoiter along the street. What would he be looking for? Go back to being a Royal Marine on the ground."

"All right then," Fletcher responded. Turning to the constables, he presented them with his plan as McDermott and Holmes returned to the patrol car. "Constables Baird and Kerr, is it? I'm going to need you about 50 meters behind me while I play scout," he explained, outlining his plan. "I want you to consider where our suspect could hide or stash a motor, a weapon, or has a companion he could call upon."

"And what is it you're going to do?" Baird asked.

"I'm going to think through why he's here and what he's seeing," Fletcher responded. "We'll begin here and head east to the end of Rose Street, is it? Cross over and return heading west. Questions?" Each of the constables returned his question with a brief nod of acknowledgment. "Talley-ho then," he exclaimed before heading away from the coffee shop.

As Fletcher strolled along Rose Street with constables in tow, McDermott and Sergeant Holmes had made their way to the Sheriff's office. Exiting the lift, they found Priscilla El-Sayed waiting to enter Lord Calvert's courtroom.

"Miss El-Sayed... a moment please," Sergeant Holmes said loud enough to garner a few heads in the hallway to turn in his direction.

Priscilla turned at the officer's hail and blinked hard at the gentleman behind him. "Come to turn yourself in, Inspector McDermott?" she asked, ribbing the inspector.

"I'd be better off at Saint Giles's receiving absolution from the priests," McDermott replied. "I've a question you need to answer." He glanced at the constable ushering patrons into the courtroom. "I need to know what you're doing on Castle or Rose Street."

The question caught Priscilla off guard. "I've an acquaintance who has a shop nearby," she replied. "Is there something I need to know?"

"We'll fill you in after your session," McDermott said, nodding in the constable's direction coming to escort her. "You're no in trouble, so did nae worry about that," he assured her as he watched her disappear inside the room.

They left the two men standing in the hall. It was Sergeant Holmes who spoke first.

"She might not be in trouble, but what about this shop-keeper?" he asked.

"We need to find out who this person is," McDermott explained. "And make sure nothing happens to them or to Miss El-Sayed."

Chapter TWENTY-THREE

Teresa Munoz didn't take much notice of people who made their way between the shops during the day. She did, however, focus on the customers who came in and browsed her display cases. This morning it was a husband and wife from America looking for something "uniquely Scottish," as the wife said.

"Don't you think these are so cute?" the woman asked, holding up a pair of silver earrings adorned with amethyst-shaped stones representing a thistle.

"You actually like those thorny bushes?" the husband replied.

"The Scots consider the thistle flower their national symbol," Teresa said, mediating the couple's discussion. "The richness and depth of the amethyst contrasts well against the silver stem and leaves," she continued, using her best negotiating skills to persuade the woman.

As the couple discussed the impending purchase, Blayne Taggert entered the shop. "Good morning," he said, greeting the patrons and Teresa.

"Is there something I can help you find?" Teresa asked.

"Not at the moment," Taggert said. "If I have any questions, I'm sure you'll be able to answer them," he added, twitching his nose as he smiled at the woman from Cadiz.

Turning her attention to the couple, Teresa saw they were ready to make their purchase of the earrings and a matching necklace. "A wonderful choice; these sell for £235.00 pounds," she said as she wrapped the pieces in a silk-covered box.

The gentleman from Colorado stood embarrassed for the moment. "You'll have to excuse me; I'm still not sure on your money," he expressed, his wallet open to expose a myriad of dollars, pounds, and euros.

Spying his credit cards, Teresa playfully snickered to herself. "My apologies for looking, but your green card there will work for this occasion."

"Now there's a smart businesswoman," the husband replied, handing over the card.

In a few minutes, the couple was exiting the shop with their purchase in hand. This left Teresa and Blayne Taggert alone. What Teresa failed to notice was Taggert had circled the shop until he stood next to the entrance.

As she slid the tray of precious stones into the display case, she glanced up to her customer. "Well sir, what is it I can help you with today?" she asked.

Reaching for the door, Taggert flipped the closed sign and twisted the lock.

"What do you think you're doing?" Teresa demanded, stepping back against a display case while panic quickly replaced her business demeanor.

"You and I need to have an uninterrupted chat," Taggert said. "Shall we adjourn to the rear of your shop?" he suggested, pulling the trench knife from under his coat for her to see.

The woman, her eyes now wide and fleeting trying to determine a plausible means of escape, edged around the counter. Keeping her tormentor occupied would be the greatest ally she knew. Someone will come, I'm sure of it, she told herself. While stepping back, Teresa's hip rubbed across a switch, sending her polishing wheel into motion. The sudden whir of the motor caused her to jump aside, but in doing so, allowed her to activate a silent alarm.

Taggert froze the moment he heard the motor spin up to speed, the sudden noise nearly causing him to drop his knife. He chuckled as the woman panicked while she attempted to shut the device off. "I'd hate to think you did that as a distraction," he mused as he stepped next to the last display case.

"What is it you want?" Teresa stammered as her breathing quickened.

A horn from a delivery van pierced the back of the shop. Taggert stopped his approach for the moment, expecting the bell to ring at the rear exit. When nothing happened, he glanced over his shoulder towards the front before speaking again. "How well do you know Miss Priscilla El-Sayed?"

Teresa's mouth parted as she lifted her eyes to the ceiling offering a brief prayer of thanks that she wasn't the target. "She's a customer who

179

appreciates custom pieces," she said. "She's come in on several occasions to discuss having items fabricated, nothing more."

Just a block away on his return leg of his surveillance, Inspector Fletcher was slowly walking along, contemplating his adversary's potential target when Constable Baird approached him from behind.

"Excuse me, Inspector," the officer said, "but we've been alerted to an alarm in the vicinity," securing the radio onto his jacket.

Fletcher saw in the young man's eyes he and his partner was preparing to respond, with or without him. "All right, you lead the way," Fletcher replied, instinctively placing his hand over his sidearm as they trotted off in the direction the alarm originated.

Nearing the corner opposite of the coffee shop, Baird stopped and turned to his partner. "Kerr, you stay with the Inspector, I'll go around the back," he delegated as he pulled out his baton, which he snapped to its full length.

"All right, Ivor, but you be careful," Kerr replied. Pulling out her own baton, she also grabbed her microphone to inform dispatch they were investigating the alarm.

Fletcher approached the jewelry shop window, hugging the wall of the adjoining shop. Peering in past the security grates and display items, he saw the back of a man and a woman who stood in an open doorway. "You knock... I'll cover you," he nodded to Constable Kerr, his weapon held low in front of him.

Stepping to the door, Constable Kerr grabbed the handle to find it locked. Glancing back at She used her baton to rap on the glass after a quick glance back at Fletcher. "Hello, Police-Scotland doing a security check," she declared.

The sound of metal on glass caused Taggert and Teresa to both look toward the storefront. "Just a moment," the woman replied as Taggert slid the knife under the front of his coat.

Fletcher glimpsed movement in the man's right arm. "He's got something in his hand," he muttered to the constable just as Teresa was unbolting the entrance.

"Can I help you?"

"We've been alerted something activated your alarm," Kerr answered. "If it's all right with you, we're here to conduct a safety inspection to make sure everything is fine. Sir, I must ask you to make your way forward," she directed at Taggert. As Kerr was giving her commands, her partner came over the radio.

Taggert did his best to keep the officer from getting a good look at his face, but Inspector Fletcher noticed similarities from an individual in his past. The stance, the hair, and profile reminded the inspector of the former sergeant in the Royal Marines. "Taggert?" he asked.

The natural act of responding to one's own name was Blayne Taggert's undoing as he spun around to face the voice. The features were the same minus the close-cut scalp of a service member. Facing the former lieutenant, Taggert noticed the second officer appear in the doorway, giving him the needed edge to escape the police.

In a calculated risk, Taggert bolted towards the rear of the shop just as Constable Baird entered the front. He burst through the rear door with every ounce of his weight, stumbling head-long into the alley. Sprawling against the delivery van still parked behind the business, he soon was sprinting towards the opposite end of the promenade that made up the shopping district.

The sudden burst of action caused Constable Kerr to grab Teresa Munoz and pull her from the shop, passing her to her partner and safety. Inspector Fletcher pulled his weapon and moved in the opposite direction, chasing after the suspect.

Fletcher was able to glimpse Taggert as he exited the shop, nearly twenty meters separating them now, running away before he turned out of sight. As he took off in pursuit, Fletcher dodged several shop owners who were exiting their businesses to find out what the commotion was about.

As Fletcher made his way to the corner where he last saw Taggert, he slowed before making the turn. The distance between the two was the same as he noticed several pedestrians helping an elderly man to his feet.

Pushing past the scene of onlookers, Fletcher turned into another alley. This time it was crowded with garbage bins, pallets and near the end, a cordoned off area where construction workers set barricades around the building to facilitate repairs. But now, there was no sign of Taggert.

His passage had been blocked by the construction, and Taggert leaned heavily against a garbage bin catching his breath. Glancing to his left, he noticed a shop door open slightly, offering him an escape.

As Taggert slipped into the shop, Inspector Fletcher had reached the edge of the first bin. He slowly began his advance with his weapon drawn, each step calculated and with a purpose. His repetitive training in the Marines took hold as he swiveled his head from one spot to another. Looking back slightly, he noticed the same door as Taggert. The wail of sirens warned other constables would arrive soon, but he wasn't prepared to wait and see if the suspect would still be there.

As he held his gun in one hand, Fletcher pulled the door aside and peered into the darkened shop. A flash of blue reflected off the windows. "No time like the present," he muttered before stepping into the shadows.

The metal hinge squealed in protest, which alerted Taggert to someone entering behind him. In his haste to escape, he did not consider that a shop being renovated would have the front entry barred and locked. Cursing under his breath, he knew he needed to defend himself.

Fletcher, aware of Taggert being armed in some fashion, proceeded with due caution. As he slipped past one door leading to the front, he braced himself against the other, waiting for the assault.

The crunch of footsteps on crumbled mortar alerted Taggert. From his position crouched behind a tarp-covered ladder, he sensed where the inspector and former Royal Marine would approach from. As he peered into the shadows, he saw a glint of light reflect off the officer's pistol. In a calculated move, Taggert lunged out from hiding while he swung his double-edged knife towards its intended target. At any other instant, the blade would have slit through the flesh till it struck bone. But Taggert's attempt was partially successful due to a tangle of electrical cords laying on the ground.

Fletcher caught enough movement to raise his arm in defense, but did not see Taggert's weapon until it was too late. The beveled and sharpened edge of the knife, ground down to a mirror finish, sliced both fabric and flesh without protest. The wound to Fletcher's arm appeared quickly as blood oozed freely from the knife's entry. "Damn it!" Andrew screamed, looking at his arm.

As he tumbled backwards onto the floor, Fletcher brought his pistol up and fired three successive rounds at his attacker. The gunfire sounded like cannons in the enclosed space as it echoed off the walls. The first and third bullets missed their intended target, but the second found its mark. The 40mm projectile tore through flesh and tendon of Taggert's shoulder with enough force to shatter his humerus. Grimacing in pain, he dropped the knife as he staggered back from the impact.

Fletcher fought to regain his footing while Taggert reached down to grab his fallen knife with his good arm. Bringing his pistol up, Fletcher took aim. "You know I've gotten good with both hands since leaving Lympstone," he said, leveling the gun in his left hand.

As he got to his feet, Taggert glanced at the wound as the blood oozed freely down his arm. "You ruined me... you whimpering snob," the former sergeant spat as he grimaced under the pain.

As the two men stood apart, members of the Specialist Firearms Unit entered the back accompanied by Constable Baird. Shouting commands to both to drop their weapons, one officer drew his Taser while the other held up his machine-pistol.

As Taggert turned toward the officers, the first one noticed the movement of the knife and discharged his Taser at the Scotsman. The sudden release of nearly 1,500 volts caused his muscles to spasm and convulse as he fell to the ground. As the charge was released, Constable Baird and the SFU officer subdued Taggert, restraining him with their handcuffs.

Baird took his radio and alerted the officers standing by outside that medical crews could enter. As this was all going on, Fletcher had found a box to sit on as he grew light-headed from the blood loss.

While two paramedics tended to Taggert's wound, the Scotsman stared at Fletcher. "This isn't over Left-tenant," he said. "I'll get another chance, you'll see... you won't deny me of my redemption... I'll get my rightful status put back," he continued.

"You'll need to go to the hospital," the medic said, looking at Fletcher as she tended to his arm. "I'm thinking a few stitches are in order," she suggested as she wrapped the gauze over the wound.

"It's only a flesh wound," he teased, the forced smile his attempt to put on a brave face for her.

His partner McDermott, along with Sergeant Holmes, had heard the altercation and made their way to the scene. "Excuse me," McDermott said, pushing past the constables outside the shop. Walking in, he saw the chaos of too many officers milling about. To one side he saw the SFU members discussing the events, on the other, medics tending to Taggert and Fletcher, with just a single constable overseeing the treatment.

"Sergeant Holmes, make sure you've two people escorting the suspect," McDermott directed just as a medic wheeled a gurney next to Taggert. Getting the suspect settled, the medics strapped him down as constables placed his good arm against the rail where he was again handcuffed. "And let's get the spectators moved out so a proper investigation can take place," he continued as he stepped alongside his partner.

Crouching down to examine the weapon, McDermott shook his head before addressing his partner. "Fancy a former soldier who brought a knife to a gun fight?" he joked, nodding towards the Fairbairn–Sykes styled fighting knife on the ground.

"Seems so," Fletcher said, his voice weak. "Pretty foolish of me rushing in, right?"

McDermott stood silent, knowing this wasn't the time or place to begin dissecting his partner's action in the melee. "We'll chat about it over a pint later," he said. He stepped aside as the medics helped Fletcher onto a gurney and wheeled him out.

Chapter TWENTY-FOUR

Dublin, Ireland

BBC and SKY News, along with other television stations, were busy broadcasting the events in Edinburgh from yesterday. Each station used different cell phone images obtained from local citizens and tourists alike showing both Taggert and Inspector Fletcher being wheeled into separate ambulances from the crime scene.

Michael Connelly sat in the hotel café, sipping his coffee while he watched. *Damn it*, he thought as he saw Taggert. The image burned itself into his mind, the realization another individual with knowledge of him and his dealings was apprehended.

"Is it 'must see' telly?" his driver asked munching on his toast.

"What...? No, it's just not a common occurrence here in the Isles, that's all," Connelly said. "If you watch broadcasts in America, police shootings seem to happen once or twice a week. Though. I thought the constables in Scotland were more civil over here, that's all."

"I'd swear the other fella there is the one who came visiting with the PSNI from last week," Geoff said, sipping his tea. "Difficult to see with him being covered up, but the other fella following behind him looks familiar, too."

Connelly didn't need to stare at the image; he knew it was the same man, which confirmed his suspicions about one of the wounded men on the stretchers being Blayne Taggert. *What did you get yourself into?* he wondered. "So, Geoff, what's on our agenda today?"

Reaching into his coat pocket, the driver pulled out a neatly typed note card. "You've a nine o'clock meeting with Mister Callaghan and the board of trustees," he replied. "They planned the meeting for two hours according to Erin. After that, you've an early dinner with Mister Finnegan at the distribution center in Limerick," Geoff added. "Barring any traffic, that is."

With a glance back at the television, now broadcasting rugby scores, Connelly finished his coffee before answering his driver's monologue regarding the day's activities.

"Well, then... no time like the present," Connelly announced as he pulled out money for the bill. Handing the cash and the bill to a passing server, the two men left the café. In moments, they stood at the valet station where a runner brought forth the vintage Jaguar, its coat a lustrous British racing green. Sliding into the back seat, Connelly soaked up the scent and feel of fine leather as his driver pulled out into the morning traffic.

Meanwhile, in Police-Scotland District Headquarters (Aberdeen), Inspector Sheila Gordon paced the floor of the forensics lab. She'd taken a call from CI McDermott last night, where he mentioned he and Andrew would return in the morning. The call was brief with no explanation why they needed the extra night in Edinburgh.

"Can you no sit still?" Devin asked, watching the woman stride about like a caged animal.

Her piercing gaze told the young technician everything he needed to know.

"She's concerned about the Inspector," CI McIntyre said as he entered the lab from his office. "If you could spare me a moment, Inspector."

"Aye, just a moment though," Sheila said, heading to the back room. As she entered, she sat across from her supervisor, her nervous anticipation evident in her fidgeting as if movement would make Andrew appear in the lab faster.

"Mister MacCallum spoke with me earlier this morning," CI McIntyre said. "Seems McDermott and Fletcher were involved in an altercation," he continued, avoiding her gaze. "Inspector Fletcher was... how do I put this...?" he started, stumbling over his own words.

"Oh, for God's sake, Graham, just tell me," Sheila demanded. "I'm no wee lassie."

McIntyre cleared his throat before continuing. "A suspect wounded Inspector Fletcher during an altercation," he said. "The suspect had a knife and gave him quite the cut across his forearm from what we're being told."

Sheila fought to restrain her emotions but to no avail. She gasped and leaned forward, resting her arms on the desk. "How bad is it?" she asked.

"I'm not..." McIntyre began, but stopped when he saw Inspector Fletcher enter the lab. "You can ask him yourself," he added with a nod behind the woman.

Spinning in the chair, Sheila saw Andrew, his right arm in a sling over the top of an aqua-colored surgical scrub. "Andrew," she cried, rushing to his side. Throwing her arms around him, she placed a kiss to his cheek. "What happened?"

"Easy now, it's still a bit tender," Andrew said, returning her kiss. Over the next twenty minutes, the inspector related how he ended up wounded from hearing about Taggert's presences in Edinburgh, the alarm at the jeweler's shop to the confrontation in the empty shop. "The surgeon said there's no permanent damage, no tendons severed or blood vessels needing fixed," he said.

"Well, now you can add this scar," Sheila said, tugging gently on his sling, "to the one on your knee."

As Inspector Fletcher described the events, McDermott was upstairs, sitting in MacCallum's office relating the same story, but with details of his conversation with Inspector Cockburn of DIU.

"I had the feeling I was nae telling him anything he didn't already suspect," McDermott said of Cockburn's reaction to his partner's possible involvement in drug smuggling. "He had the look in his eye he was just given a free pass."

"His superior was none too pleased to hear about it," MacCallum said. "But he also said he wasn't surprised since his chief constable has put them on notice after the IOPC report in February identified instances of poor policing." Picking up his tea, he took a sip before continuing. "How's Inspector Fletcher?"

"I think he learned a valuable lesson yesterday," McDermott said. "He's lucky this Taggert fella stumbled on some debris or the outcome could have been worse. The surgeon at Royal Edinburgh said he'd have no issues with his recovery, just keep his arm immobile for a fortnight so the stitches don't tear."

"That leaves you without a partner," MacCallum said.

"What? I'd nae thought about being alone on the case from here on out," McDermott snickered. "None of the other lads want to take a spell with me?"

"You've the balls for asking that question, you know?"

McDermott knew looking at Inspector Gordon's record tarnished what little reputation he had with the officers in Aberdeen, but it provided a clue leading to Alistair Hunt's arrest. "If he's no worried, I'd like to have Sergeant Giles help," McDermott replied, making his case for the constable.

The chief superintendent glanced over his cup. "I'd normally say no to any specific request, McDermott. But you're in luck since Giles has been studying for the Inspector's exam, so it be good for him to have the added exposure." Setting the cup down, MacCallum continued. "But if he starts to pick up your bad habits, I'll see you're put behind a desk."

McDermott grinned. "Thank you, sir. But it will put you a man down, won't it?"

"Ordinarily, yes," MacCallum said. "But with Fletcher confined to a desk, the office won't be left empty. And you recall Sergeant McCord, don't you? Well he's being transferred in from Victoria Station, so the force will still have a senior constable present."

"I better be letting Andrew know he'll be regulated to the desk," McDermott said, getting to his feet. "Will you be letting Giles know of his reassignment?"

"I'll have Miss Sinclair prepare the memorandum," MacCallum replied. "Until then, it'll remain between the two of us, understood, Inspector?"

"Aye, mum's the word."

Traipsing down the stairs, McDermott hummed a tune as he made his way to forensics. He pushed through the door and saw Andrew sitting with his companion Sheila while the technicians Devin and Kyle were busy cataloging evidence.

Seeing McDermott enter, Inspector Gordon began her tirade on being left guessing at Andrew's condition. "I've a good mind to scalp your arse," she exclaimed waving a finger while finishing the lecture, which brought forth a few muffled laughs from Devin and Kyle.

"It'll cost you a few night's supper if you want to get back in her good graces," Andrew added with a smirk.

"I'll start a tab then," McDermott said. "Now, you've got something from Edinburgh Zoo, didn't you?"

"Aye, we did," Inspector Gordon answered, swiveling in her chair. "Devin, what have we got from the images captured at the zoo?"

The young man grabbed a folder and strolled over to the other officers before answering. "We've determined these images here are of the vessel captain," Devin said, sliding three photos across the desk before adding another one. "And this picture here is the best one showing the suspect with his barrister."

McDermott picked up the one with Sean Gilmore and Michael Connelly. The time stamp was the key. It would prove the period between the call from Clive Duncan on the Nordic Supplier, the meeting, and then the delivery of the container in Aberdeen.

"But without the driver, we've no idea where the container was delivered," Fletcher said, shifting his wounded arm into a more comfortable position in the sling. "And the constables in Glasgow have yet to find Gordon Wallace or Robert Burns," he added. "And your assumption of Dunbar being in the lorry's cab isn't any good now with him being dead."

McDermott paced the room. *It's Connelly*, he thought. *He's the key to the drugs. He'll know where they are*, his decision on the matter is now final. "Andrew, you'll need to contact London, have them secure a summons we can have issued by the folks in Dublin," he said. "Make sure it covers all of Callaghan and Higgins properties. Get a separate one for the office in Belfast if need be."

"There's one piece missing I can add to," Inspector Gordon said. As she took a folder from her desk, she handed a paper to McDermott. "I've found our connection to the constable in London," she said proudly.

"I almost forgot about him," Fletcher answered.

McDermott said nothing; he was too busy reading the printout: Ethan Taylor, born in Paisley Scotland to Moira Hunt and Benjamin Taylor. It listed Moira's older brother as next of kin, Alistair Hunt of Glasgow. Reading further, McDermott paused momentarily, the ramifications he saw being more serious. "Says the constable was accepted to Metropolitan Police in 2005, assigned to the communications office of the Drug Enforcement Task Force."

"That's how Sergeant Wallace knew about us so quickly," Fletcher exclaimed. "What other information do you think this fella might have passed along?"

189

"I'm nae sure..." McDermott replied, scratching the back of his neck, frustrated he didn't see the signs earlier. "I'll wager there's a few other instances we'll tie back to him, though," waving the sheet in the air.

McDermott handed the sheet back to Inspector Gordon. "Add this information to our packet going to London, will you, Andrew?" he said, motioning to his partner. "Let Mister Collingsworth know I'd like to be present when he detains this constable."

As the officers took in what they had just heard, Sergeant Giles entered the lab. "Am I interrupting something...?" he asked, noticing everyone turn to look at him.

"Nothing you shouldn't be hearing. Come in," McDermott replied.

"Mister MacCallum mentioned you'd need a hand with Inspector Fletcher on the mend," Giles said, nodding toward Andrew fidgeting with his sling.

"Did he now?" McDermott asked, feigning surprise at the comment.

"And what am I supposed to do?" Fletcher asked, just as shocked.

"You'll be busy putting the paper trail together," McDermott said. "We've got all the pieces in front of us now; they have to be sorted out and connected. And I'll need your keen sense of protocol for discussing things with Chief Constable Darcy."

Before Fletcher could protest, Constable Howe came into the lab. "Chief Inspector, I've a printout for you from your office in London." He handed over the sheet of paper and turned to the Sergeant, who was no longer in his uniform. "You off watch now?"

"Special posting," Giles said. "Sergeant McCord will man my desk for a few days. Don't get on his bad side," he warned.

"Gerry is filling in here?" Inspector Gordon asked, not hiding her surprise hearing her former sergeant was being reassigned.

"Aye, for a wee bit," the sergeant replied before moving closer to CI McDermott to read the printout. "Anything I need to know about?"

"Your first assignment, Giles," McDermott started, handing the paper to him. "Find the common thread between these groups as they apply to our case." He then turned to Andrew. "See he gets a brief on where we are with things. I'll be up in the office," he said before heading out of the lab.

As McDermott and the others in Aberdeen were discussing the latest evidence against Michael Connelly, the Chief Operations Officer sat with other board members of Callaghan and Higgins in downtown Dublin.

As the stately clock chimed nine o'clock, Rubert Callaghan was wheeled to the head of the table in the expansive boardroom. The assembled members all rose out of respect as someone brought their meeting to order. The elder executive took a sip of his tea, a noticeable tremor to the cup. As he set the cup down, he spoke. "You may begin," he started, looking towards his senior assistant and eldest son Roan.

For the next sixty minutes, several of the lead chemists provided updates to the company's latest efforts. From their work on a cancer detection drug to one that would ease those suffering from psoriasis and the need to scratch, each one painted a rosy picture of success.

Connelly sat near the end of the table, listening to the discussion but not hearing the words. His mind was awash with various scenarios facing him with Blayne Taggert's arrest for assaulting a constable. Having been given records of his meetings with Angus Dunbar by Taggert, he now worried the twin had done something similar.

"Michael, how goes our expansion onto the continent?" was the question that broke Connelly from his thoughts. Looking up, he saw fourteen pairs of eyes staring back at him, as Roan Callaghan placed him center stage for the board members to judge.

Surprised, Connelly quickly offered a feigned apology while he went into his speech regarding efforts to place the companies approved drugs into the European markets. "We've negotiated with several distributors in the south of France, and will move towards Spain later in the year," he read from his notes. The elder executive shook his head in approval while others jotted down notes on the pads they had on the table before them.

"After we've adjourned, I'd like a word in private, Michael," Roan said, ending the COO portion of the meeting. After adding a few comments and soliciting the members for theirs, he called the meeting to an end. As he rose to his feet, he saw to his father's exit as the others left the room.

Connelly sat, waiting for the doors to close before saying anything to the owner's eldest son. "Something on your mind, Roan?"

Roan walked to Connelly's side of the conference room table, sitting on the edge before he spoke. "Someone has made me aware the Garda are looking into the activities of your manager in Limerick," he said.

"And what might those activities be?"

"The police are preparing to open an investigation into trafficking of civilians," Roan said. "Seems you've requested quite a number of chemists from offshore. And the Garda are of the mind it could be for something... illegal."

Connelly listened to the accusation with a keen ear. Why would the Garda consider something amiss, and how is Liam involved? he asked himself. "I can assure you Roan, I have sent all the proper documents through the necessary channels to see these people allowed in to the country legally," he said. "I'd be happy to discuss it with your source if need be."

The facial expression didn't change, but Connelly noted Roan's cheeks twitch at the last part of his statement. "When the time comes, you be ready to answer the questions. And don't expect your mother, God bless her, to be of any help in protecting you either." Her absence from the board meeting today was due to her failing health at a local care facility.

Connelly took in a deep breath, calming himself before answering. "Rest assured, Roan, I'll be ready," he started as he got to his feet. "If there's nothing else, I've an appointment to make."

Chapter TWENTY-FIVE

Sergeant Giles looked over the list of cadets McDermott handed to him earlier. Several of the names on the list he knew firsthand. Logan Wallace, the deceased sergeant from Aberdeen, and Trotter from Glasgow were in one class. And then there was his class, with the names of his coworkers in Aberdeen: McCord and McKee. Last was his friend in Edinburgh, Xander Holmes, along with Sergeant Sedgwick from the Drug Interdiction Unit in Edinburgh.

"Besides being constables, what is our common link?" he muttered to himself, flipping the page. Here he saw the last group, with the name of Ethan Taylor circled. "You're not part of Police Scotland, are you?"

Sliding out the next page, Giles saw the name of each District Headquarter and two telephone numbers. He noted one number as Logan Wallace's, the other of Sean Gilmore, the barrister who defended him. He searched through the list until he found one inconsistent entry. It was a call from Logan Wallace to a number in the Glasgow station on Baird Street. He turned to the desk computer and searched the roster of constables assigned to the post.

McDermott stood in the doorway, observing the sergeant's method of tracing the numbers across the pages. "Any luck, Marcus?" he asked, breaking the sergeant's concentration.

"Nothing you and Mister Fletcher didn't already put together," he said. "But it seems the cadets missed a number when they were searching earlier," the sergeant added. "It's for one listed in Glasgow; and it's nae the district office, mind you."

As Giles glanced back at the computer screen, he noticed a list of officers for Glasgow's Baird Street station appear. Taking the paper with Wallace and Trotter's name on it, he held it up. "We've a match," he exclaimed.

"Who is it?"

"A fella by the name of Ross," Giles explained. "But he's listed at the station as a special constable."

"Why would Wallace have reason to contact him?" McDermott asked. He tapped Giles on the shoulder. "See if there's any record of investigations between the constables and officers at DIU. And see if you can get a full bio on this Ross fella while you're online, too."

"Where are you going?" Giles asked.

"The chief superintendent needs to know this so he can make a call," McDermott said over his shoulder. Why the hell does Ross sound so familiar? he asked himself. As he descended the stairs, he slowed his pace until he stopped at the bottom step.

McDermott pulled the door open and strolled into the lobby just as Sergeant McCord from Victoria Station was meeting with his counterpart, Sergeant McKee. The two made quite a sight to the other constables. McCord, his sturdy and thick physique reminding many of his time on the police rugby squad, just the opposite of the female officer. McKee, though a half-meter shorter, she would never be mistaken for a gymnast, but police work suited her saucy, spitfire demeanor with a temperament twice her physical size.

"Morning, Sergeant McCord," McDermott said, reaching the two constables.

"Chief Inspector," the officer replied, shaking hands with Conor. "Malcolm sends his best. Says you're still welcome when you've got time."

"Aye, it's been a while, hasn't it?"

The sergeant turned to his fellow officer. "So, Annie, what's the pace like?"

As he left the two officers, McDermott walked straight to the Chief Superintendent's office. Here, Miss Sinclair set him aside as she escorted several members of the city council out after meeting with MacCallum. Their discussion centered on how the police handled a minor protest near the council building from last week. McDermott stood to one side, smiling politely as each member passed. As the last one left, he stepped forward. "Miss Sinclair, can the chief spare a moment?"

"Just a moment," the woman replied, knocking on the inner door. "Sir, it's CI McDermott. He needs a moment."

"All right, but you've my permission to drag him out when the next appointment comes in," MacCallum said loud enough for McDermott to hear.

Sliding by the woman, McDermott smiled. "Thanks, hen."

MacCallum sat, twirling his pen in one hand while he waited for McDermott to say his piece.

"We've found the possible link in Glasgow," the inspector started. "Sergeant Giles noticed we missed a number our former Sergeant Wallace had called. It leads to the Baird Street Station and associates the number with a special constable's desk there."

"So that's it then, you've got your trail to follow?"

McDermott shook his head. "It's not just that. We've also linked a meeting in Edinburgh with Captain Duncan and the Irishman from last month. The CCTV stamp shows it happening a week before we raided the *Standard-Apollo*, which we believe was a ruse for a larger delivery."

"But you've no physical proof yet of another delivery, do you?"

"Not yet, but we've CCTV images of this Connelly fella meeting the captain," McDermott replied. McDermott explained what they learned about the images of a lorry being on the quay when the Nordic Supplier was docked. He also added that the driver was missing, and someone found the lorry torched in a quarry near Dumbarton.

"Is the district headquarters staff in Glasgow aware of this?"

"Aye, we briefed CS Cameron when we saw her the other day. She's got her inspectors checking on things with the constables in Dumbarton."

"I recommend you gather all the evidence together and create your report," MacCallum said. "Make sure you keep it in sequence; it'll make the prosecutions effort easier."

As MacCallum directed McDermott on his next steps in Aberdeen, Priscilla El-Sayed was sitting at a spare desk in her Edinburgh office. Pulling out her cell phone, she glanced at the face to make sure she had service before dialing the number in her hand. Someone answered after several moments passed by.

"Bonjour, Papillion Transport," the woman on the other end said. "How may I direct your call?"

"I'd like to speak with Monsieur Richelieu," Priscilla replied. "Inform him it is an associate of Monsieur Gilmore."

"One moment, please."

Priscilla could hear a series of clicks over the phone as she was put on hold by the receptionist. After nearly a minute, a man's voice came on the line.

"This is Monsieur Richelieu; how may I be of help, Mademoiselle El-Sayed?" Gregory Arsenault greeted the caller using his alias.

Priscilla looked down at the folder she'd opened while waiting for the call to connect. Inside, she read Sean's note regarding how to address the Frenchman. "Monsieur, I was given your information from my friend in the event I needed your assistance," she began. Over the next ten minutes, she explained the circumstances of Sean Gilmore and her call from the Irishman, Michael Connelly. "It seems my associate is concerned Mister Connelly will begin something leading back to your business if he's allowed to continue."

Gregory Arsenault sat in his chair listening with great interest. The last several weeks, he and his associates had done well to minimize their exposure to the authorities, but this new development could place all that in jeopardy.

"You say his name is Connelly?"

"Yes... it seems he was using Higgins as an alias," Priscilla mentioned. "Does this help you any?"

"Possibly. And you wish for me to confront this man and stop him?" he asked. "I've a shipping firm to manage, not an army to command Mademoiselle El-Sayed. Plus, it would not be something easily accomplished within the borders of another country."

Priscilla sat chewing on the end of a pen as she listened to the Frenchman. "I understand. It appears someone misled my associate when he directed me to you regarding your abilities, it seems," she said. "I apologize for the intrusion then, Monsieur Richelieu."

"Please mademoiselle, I didn't mean to give you the wrong impression. Allow me to make a few calls," Gregory said. "I may have an acquaintance who could be persuaded to have a conversation with your Monsieur Connelly." He glanced over at his business partner, Louis, who'd just entered the room. "I'll call back in... let's say thirty minutes."

"I'll expect your call, then," Priscilla said. "Au revoir monsieur."

Gregory looked at the handset as it buzzed. Setting it on the receiver, he looked at his associate Louis with a puzzled look on his face. "Seems the lawyer for the Irishman needs our help."

"What type of help?" Louis asked. "Are we to testify on his behalf at trial?" he chuckled.

Gregory picked up the notepad and tossed it at his friend. "His employer's name, does it ring a bell to you?"

The Frenchman turned the pad over to see the name Connelly then Higgins printed next to it across the top. Louis Clement picked up the pad and stared at the name. "I don't recall anyone by that name," he said, stroking his well-trimmed beard. "And we both know the reliability of an alias."

"Still, if this woman is pointing us to the person responsible for the British Navy hunting down one of our ships, it might be worth paying him a visit," Gregory said. "He might have the means to cover the costs of maintaining the Joan of Arc." The oldest ship sailing for Papillion had suffered a minor breakdown on its last voyage and the repair costs would severely impact the company's bottom line.

"Extortion? But if he has information on Papillion, it could backfire on you," Louis said as their associate Hector Pichon entered the office.

"Am I interrupting something important?" Pichon asked.

"Seems someone has given us an opportunity to meet the person responsible for stealing the last delivery to the Scots," Gregory explained, handing Pichon the pad.

"Is the first name correct?" Pichon asked, his incredulous stare back at Gregory a surprise.

"You know someone by that name?"

"We had two Irishman on Corsa. If it's the same one I remember," Pichon said, "he was cunning and smart, but his ego was also out of this world too." Pichon paced back and forth before speaking. "But, if it is him, it would explain how he could contact the Scotsman, Dunbar."

"You said 'was;' is he dead?" Louis asked.

Hector Pichon related to his associates about an operation he and his Legionnaire team were involved with while deployed to the Ivory Coast in 2004. "We were assisting the 3rd Engineers during their project in the bush and he went missing," he said. "I recall he was with three others and they were patrolling the brush, safeguarding the equipment from vandals. The corporal mentioned there was shouting, a handful of shots, and then he was missing."

"And the team did a sweep of the area?" Gregory asked already aware of the answer.

"At daylight, we found his weapon. It took two more days and nights of searching until we found parts of his bloody and torn uniform hanging from a tree," Pichon said. "The captain called everything off afterwards, reporting him as a casualty of the terrain and the animals."

"But no sign of a body," Gregory whispered to himself. The three Frenchman sat in silence, each wondering if the effort would be worth the reward.

"If this man is the one from your unit, would you want to see him returned to Corsa and placed on trial for desertion?" Gregory asked.

"It would be fitting if it was him," Louis said. "But we didn't exactly leave on the best of terms either." Smoothing out his moustache, Louis considered his next question to his colleagues. "It would be poetic justice to see him pay for setting the SAS sniper after the vessel captain though."

"Then it's settled," Gregory said. "You two will go pay this man, this Higgins... or Connelly if the woman is correct, a visit and see what information he has on us. And while you have his attention, persuade him to forget about the two lawyers."

"That's it?" Louis asked. "You don't think we'd be risking exposure by leaving the country again?"

"If we have a chance to silence a threat, I consider it a risk worth taking, wouldn't you?"

Louis threw his hands up in mock surrender. "We're assuming quite a lot based on this woman's call, you realize?" he said, questioning the reason behind his associate's decision. "And if it turns out to be nothing, then what?"

"Bring me back some Waterford crystal then," Gregory said, picking up the phone to contact Priscilla El-Sayed.

Chapter TWENTY-SIX

Glasgow, Scotland

Sergeant Giles wasn't used to being out of uniform in the performance of his duties, but he was getting accustomed to it working with CI McDermott. However, this was the first time since he left the police academy that he'd been in Glasgow's District Headquarters where they were to meet with Chief Superintendent Cameron.

"Do you think our man's on call today?" Giles asked.

"It's best he's not, then we can have him brought here instead of Baird Street," McDermott replied. As the two officers entered, they logged themselves in before heading to CS Cameron's office.

As the lift stopped and the doors opened, McDermott nearly bowled over Constable Weir as she turned to step inside. "Mind where you're going, hen," McDermott said, grasping her as she stumbled back.

"Mind yourself," the officer replied, slapping McDermott's hand from her arm before noticing the credentials hanging from his neck.

"Anything wrong, Barbara?" Sergeant Trotter asked as he walked up on the three officers. "Oh... hello, Marcus. What's the occasion?"

"Morning to you, Kevin," Giles replied.

"You know these two gents, Sergeant?" Weir asked, straightening her coat.

"Morning..., Chief Inspector McDermott..., isn't it?" Trotter queried.

McDermott gave the sergeants a moment before answering. "Right on point; is CS Cameron in? She's expecting us," he said, stepping aside for other constables walking the halls.

"Aye she is; this way," Trotter replied with a motion to the office.

A few moments later, McDermott and Giles were sitting in Chief Superintendent Cameron's office as she read over their report regarding the drug trafficking and the possible police corruption. "You've quite a lot going on here, McDermott," the woman spoke, flipping through the sheets. "All the players, but none of them holding any drugs."

"Inspector Fletcher and I are having a summons prepared for a search regarding that," McDermott said. "We've identified members of the syndicate involved with the trafficking to this point; the arrest of the drug buyer is the last in our investigation."

"Here in Glasgow?"

"Ah, no ma'am. We've narrowed our findings to a firm in Ireland."

"And the arrest we made last month is only the beginning, I supposed?" Cameron said. "Wasn't this person the one responsible for soliciting for the drugs you seized in the first place?"

McDermott was growing impatient with the banter from the chief superintendent as she pointed out the holes in his investigation. "I don't mean to be disrespectful, but my plan is to catch the bastard who started it in the first place."

CS Cameron slowly closed the folder in her hands, setting it back on the desk. Tapping a finger, neatly manicured and polished, against the folder, she fixed her gaze on the senior inspector. "I can empathize with you, McDermott, but you of all officers understand the need for procedures and protocol."

McDermott felt the jab hit home as she delivered the rebuke. "Yes ma'am, I'm quite sensitive to that," he replied, his shoulders slumping dejectedly. "But you're aware I've other reasons to see this end, too."

"Mister Collingsworth has made me aware of your circumstances," she replied. Before she could continue, Sergeant Trotter stuck his head into the office. "We're ready when you give the word, ma'am."

"Make the call," she said, rising to her feet to lead them to the conference office. "Shall we get this done gentlemen. We've prepared a pseudo ceremony to bring this Ross character into the office."

The three officers were marched to the front of the conference room where the chief superintendent stood behind a podium. With their backs turned, McDermott and Giles walked up from behind until they were just a few paces away.

"I apologize for pulling you from your duties, gentlemen," Cameron said reading her notes. "But we've an occasion that required your attendance. Special Constable Ross, front and center please," she commanded. As the officer stepped forward, the other two constables took several steps backward, leaving him alone before the senior official.

"Ma'am, Officer Ross standing by," he said with a salute.

Before CS Cameron could say anything else, McDermott stepped forward and grabbed the officer's shoulder, spinning him around. "You..." he exclaimed. "This is nae the first time I've seen you, is it?"

Ross stepped back, his eyes widening in fear and disbelief from the confrontation. "I'm not sure," he stammered. "Maybe at a football match..."

"Gentlemen, we've a proper place for asking questions," Cameron said through their encounter. "Sergeant Trotter, escort Constable Ross to interrogations. Chief Inspector McDermott, we'll need a minute to prepare things," The audio and visual recording of the meeting needed to be set up.

"Chief Cameron," Giles said as she stepped toward the stage. "Can one of your officers provide an up-to-date bio on the constable?"

"Constable Weir, see to the sergeant's request if you will. And then meet us downstairs." As Cameron stepped away from the dais, she approached McDermott's side. "Who is he to you, McDermott?"

"I've the mind to link him to Hunt's syndicate," the chief inspector said. "He paid a visit to the cells after we liftit two of his cohorts in Aberdeen."

"Let's see what he has to say for himself before passing judgement, shall we?" CS Cameron said, nudging McDermott towards the hallway. Walking to the lift, they made their way to interrogation where Sergeant Trotter stood by outside along with Sergeant Giles.

"Here's his bio," Giles said, handing McDermott a sheet of paper.

"Sergeant Trotter, did he have anything on him?" McDermott asked.

"Let's see....," Giles started, glancing at the booking sheet, "wallet, keys, a ticket from a punter's booth at Celtic Stadium..." the officer replied. "Usual stuff, really. Why?"

"No cell phone, though?" McDermott asked.

"Oh yeah, he was relieved of that too," Trotter answered.

McDermott turned to Giles. "Get the number off the phone and pass it to Inspector Gordon in Aberdeen. Have her check it against calls made by Wallace and the others," he directed the officer. "And don't waste time on it either."

"Constable Weir," CS Cameron said, "make sure the sergeant gets the information without any fuss. If Mister Dobbins has an issue, have him call me."

"Yes ma'am," Weir said, trotting after the sergeant.

As he sat in the interrogation room, Jimmy Ross squirmed on the metal chair as he stared at the mirrored glass facing him. The faded blue walls of concrete did little to calm him as he anticipated what was to come next. A key turning the lock caused him to turn around.

"Sorry for keeping you waiting," Chief Superintendent Cameron announced as she waited for the inspector to close the door.

McDermott slid a chair out for her before taking his own seat. Glancing over the bio sheet Giles gave him, he saw the details: place of residence, date of birth, next of kin, physical features. "Mister Ross, what is your position with Police Scotland?" McDermott asked.

"Before I answer questions, I've a right to know what am I charged with?" Ross asked defiantly.

"To the best of my knowledge, you haven't been charged with anything," Cameron said, her voice smooth, soft in tone, and very much in control.

"Then what's this all about?"

"The Chief Inspector has asked a simple question. Can you provide him a simple answer?"

Ross took a deep breath and leaned his elbows on the cold steel table. "I assist in coordinating the civil constables at all sporting events in the city proper," he replied. "And now I'd like to know why I'm being questioned."

"Fair enough," McDermott said. "There's an ongoing investigation which began in Aberdeen. Several calls were made to your desk at Blair Station from the District Headquarters there and I want to know why." He paused for the moment to catch his breath. "So, I'm asking, who do you know in Aberdeen?"

Ross blinked. "You're serious, right?" He snickered as he sat back in the chair and let loose a chuckle before resuming his gaze at the two senior officers. "I'm a Special Constable working in a station. Don't you think I'd be answering calls from another district?" he asked, carefully controlling his voice and tone addressing the senior officers.

Cameron's eyebrows lifted as the constable stated the obvious while McDermott sat stoic.

"I've never been east of Edinburgh in me life, and I can nae recall anyone I know living in Aberdeen."

"You expect us to believe you've lived your entire life in Glasgow? How dull," the woman uttered.

"Aye," Ross replied. "My father worked at the railroad yard, and mum took care of us three kids," he continued. "That is until me older brother joined the Army and left for a spell before coming home, oh, 'bout five years ago."

"And your other sibling?" Cameron asked.

"My sister Gladys," Ross answered, "left after meeting a mechanic working for a transport firm in Dumfries. Gave mum and dad a wee grandson last year."

McDermott's posture stiffened hearing about the officer's brother. Much like the similarities between Blayne Taggert and Angus Dunbar, McDermott was realizing his next suspect might not be this officer, but his older brother.

"Chief, can I have a word in private?" McDermott asked, getting to his feet.

As he closed the door behind him, McDermott led CS Cameron to the side.

"What is it?" she asked.

"I'm thinking the fella I saw was this older brother Ross just mentioned," he said. "If they are family, then they'd look the same."

"But what about your phone calls from Sergeant Wallace to this constable's desk? Don't you think something like that holds credence?" Cameron asked.

"Let's just say your constable gets a call from Wallace," McDermott began, "and he passes the information to his brother?" Placing his head against the wall, McDermott gently bounced his forehead off the surface. "But why do that? Why didn't Wallace call the older brother directly?"

"If you have your reservations inspector, we've got to let him go," Cameron said, knowing there was no case to keep Ross. "I'll let him know it was a case of mistaking him for someone else."

"We've proof of the calls though," McDermott said with a glance at the senior superintendent. "I can nae dismiss what I know. And this fella is either a fantastic liar or a poor sap in the wrong chair."

As the officers discussed the dilemma facing them, Sergeant Giles rounded the corner and approached them. "You'll not believe this, Inspector, but we've a hit on the numbers for Alistair Hunt, but it's not what you think."

"I'm nae a mind reader Marcus; what are you saying in King's English?" McDermott asked.

"Inspector Gordon looked over the calls associated with Hunt, and the phone number at Blair Street would have been a match," the sergeant began. "But she found the number for the constable's desk is off by one number."

McDermott, confused by the statement, repeated what he'd heard. "It's the wrong number by one? Wallace mistakenly calls another police station because of a single digit?"

"That gives us nine possible others he could have called," CS Cameron chimed in ahead of the two men.

"Aye, but Inspector Gordon called a technician with Sprint-Europe and confirmed the number's correct owner," Giles said. "And she found out it list the number having called Alistair Hunt a half-dozen times in the last year alone."

"So, it seems this fella Ross is off the hook then," McDermott said, letting out a brief sigh as he rubbed his palms across his eyes. "But if they meant the call for his brother, then he'd be liable to mention our questioning and ruin everything...."

"I'll take care of that," CS Cameron said.

McDermott had the look of a man defeated. "I'm going to need a few minutes," he said, heading for the stairwell. "Go on, I'll see you at the car in a wee bit, Marcus."

Giles walked behind him, but was pulled aside by CS Cameron. "Let him go; he needs some time to sort things out Sergeant," the woman said. "I'll have Sergeant Trotter escort you back to the lobby."

McDermott made his way to the car park at the back of the building. Walking out of the gate, he leaned against the brick wall. I'm so close to getting this bastard, he told himself. As he closed his eyes, he considered what he had accomplished and what he and Fletcher had missed so far in their investigation.

Minutes passed until he sensed someone standing nearby. Picking his head up, he saw Grace Cameron a few meters away, her arms crossed in front of her. "You've something to say?" he asked the woman as she stepped closer.

"I've had Ross sign an affidavit to the effect that what we discussed is confidential," she said. "He agreed to keep things quiet until you tell him otherwise." As she leaned against the wall next to McDermott, she continued. "You're smart enough to know you can't catch all the criminals in this world. Sometimes we miss and that's why we get ourselves smarter for the next go 'round."

"Aye, I know, but I've lost someone I was meant tae protect," he said as a few tears rolled down his cheek. "I'm nae sure I'll have my family's trust if I don't at least try to redeem myself to them."

CS Cameron knew McDermott had made the investigation personal by his statement. "You're not alone in the effort," she reminded him. "You're a step closer today than yesterday. And tomorrow, you'll be another one to solving the case," the senior officer added just as Sergeant Giles pulled up in their patrol car.

McDermott ran the back of his coat sleeve across his face. "I see my driver is getting antsy." As he stared off at nothing in particular, he exhaled long and slow before straightening himself up from the wall.

As Giles pulled forward, he rolled down the window. "Inspector Fletcher called," the sergeant said. "Seems we're to get home and pack our bags for a wee trip to Dublin. He mentioned getting a call from London an hour ago."

"No rest for the wicked," McDermott said to Chief Superintendent Cameron as he slid into the passenger seat. "We'll be sure tae give you a brief when we get back."

Chapter TWENTY-SEVEN

Aberdeen, Scotland

The police car pulled to the curb in front of a row of tenement flats, their weathered granite facade showing streaks of rust from window sills. In keeping with the city's unofficial status of having the most colorful doorways, each of the entries displayed separate hues of the rainbow, the prominent ones being red.

"Give me an hour and then come back," McDermott said, sliding out of the car. "Don't forget we still need to meet with Mister MacCallum before we leave."

"Aye, I'll be ready, Inspector," Giles said as he pulled away.

McDermott took the key from his pocket and grabbed the door handle. He hesitated, feeling the knob turn in his hands. As he opened the door, he was greeted by the sound of the kitchen drawer slamming shut.

"Ailene, is that you?" he asked, sliding his hand over his pistol.

"Who else would it be?" came the agitated voice of a woman.

Conor shed his field coat in the front room as he made his way towards the kitchen. Turning the corner, he saw her. A sheen of sweat on her cheeks, chin, and forehead magnified the effort she was expending to clean up his mess. As did the tone in her voice directed towards him. Clean dishes lay dripping in the rack on one side of the sink while the remaining dirty dishes sat piled in the sink under spent bubbles.

"I'm gone just a fortnight and when I come home, it's to this mess," she exclaimed, her voice cracking. "Did you not think to pick after yourself from time to time?"

"I've no excuse," Conor said, hanging his head in shame. "This case has me running ragged," taking a step closer to his companion. "And it's nae getting any easier. I need to grab a few things..."

Ailene stopped cleaning and looked at Conor. "We need to talk about this," she started, her underlying tone meaning something else. "You know, it excited me when you called about your posting," she uttered. "And I was hoping with time... well, I'd hoped you would have matured some from our last go 'round."

Conor's chest heaved as he took in a deep breath, the weight of guilt weighing on him for treating his lover like this. "I'd say it'll get better, hen, but I've no control over work..., and you know that," he said. Stepping to her side, he pulled her close, wrapping his arms around her. "I'll let Mister Collingsworth know I need some time when this is all done," he whispered, leaning against her.

Ailene pulled away from him and leaned against the counter. "They've asked me to take the manager's post in Liverpool," she said, a sense of pride to her statement. "Someone told me they've a need to straighten things up and my name keeps getting mentioned."

"When?"

"After the first of the year," Ailene replied. "It'll give you time to find a flat of your own if you're staying past Christmas. And I'll have time to get my things collected and ready for the mover's too," she finished, exchanging glances between Conor and the floor.

The sudden news of Ailene's departure was sinking in. Conor felt his chest tighten as he felt sad and alone, the same sensation he felt when his mother had passed away. His shoulders drooped in resignation as he tried to accept the news.

"If you've a minute, can you toss these in the trash bin?" Ailene asked, kicking two full plastic bags next to the kitchen table.

"Aye... I can," Conor said with a wry chuckle.

After he dragged the trash outside, the remaining time between them was spent in a somber silence. As Ailene continued to clean, Conor went to the bedroom to pack what few clothes he had. The clock ticked down as they both withdrew from the other, the sadness of their plight growing with each sweep of the second hand.

"Will you be long on your trip?" Ailene asked.

"Long enough to serve a summons and question the suspects," Conor answered, entering the front room of the flat with his bag in hand. He set the overnighter on the floor before grabbing his field coat from the sofa and putting it on.

"You and that damn coat," Ailene said, looking at him from the kitchen. "Have you ever thought to wash it?"

"What...? And lose its character?" Conor said. Looking at his companion, he took a step closer, preparing to say something when there came a knock on the door. "That'll be Sergeant Giles." Opening the front door, McDermott saw the constable with a smile on his face.

"Ready when you are, Inspector," Giles greeted.

Conor turned back to Ailene, wanting to say something to ease the pain of leaving, but was lost for words. Ailene came to him and placed a brief kiss on his lips.

"I'll be here when you're done," she whispered, tears forming in the corner of her eyes.

"Aye... and I'll be back too," Conor replied, kissing her in return. Glancing at the sergeant, he nodded towards the car. "C'mon Marcus, time to catch our flight." He paused a moment before grabbing the overnight bag and walking out the door, shutting it behind him gently.

While McDermott and Giles briefed Chief Superintendent MacCallum on what they learned in Glasgow early that day, Michael Connelly was being whisked along the highway between Dublin and Limerick. The Irishman was deep in thought having been chastised by Roan Callaghan about hiring workers for the company.

The stark white appearance of the concrete structure where Callaghan and Higgins Limited prepared their products was just like many others in the industrial area in western Ireland. On one side, delivery trucks parked in one of four bays waiting to be loaded with finished product for transporting to market. Michael Connelly had seen it before, but for his driver Geoff, it was his first time as he pulled the vintage Jaguar into the parking lot's VIP spot.

Inside the manufacturing center, technicians clad in clean-suits scurried from one station to another, while specialists operating tools and machinery producing thousands of tablets and pills did their jobs in robotic unison. Connelly walked through the reception area and headed for the secured inspection station, which required a temperature-controlled environment.

An electric cart appeared out of nowhere carrying Liam Finnegan up to the executive where he greeted Connelly as he donned his own clean suit. "Good afternoon, Mister Connelly," the young man said, jumping off the vehicle.

"Yes, it is afternoon, but I'm not sure if I'd consider it a good one," Connelly said, a sour tone to his voice. He was still reeling from Roan's lecture earlier after the board meeting. Turning to the young man as he slipped cloth booties over his shoes, Connelly weighed asking Liam about any police activity at the facility. "Liam, have any of the technicians or chemists asked about their work here?"

The young man shook his head. "They've not made any demands to my knowledge, sir," he replied. "Only thing I've overheard from time to time was the lack of eateries near the facility. With our mix of ethnic workers, it's hard to please everyone."

"After I'm done having my discussion with Dr. Liu, I'll need to have a private word with you," Connelly said. Pulling the entrance door open, he was greeted with a rush of air. As the two entered and closed the outer door, they felt the pressure change and their ears pop as the air exchanger kept the environment pristine.

Dr. Liu sat at the station, peering through her microscope, hands sweating under the rubber gloves. Bits of blackish-brown microbes of hashish floated in the saline solution as she catalogued the reaction to the drug's reaction to the chemical. The shadow of a figure stepping next to her brought her head away from the instrument.

"Mister Higgins, I didn't expect a visit from you," the Chinese scientist greeted the executive. "Liam, you should have told me he was coming for a visit."

"I was in Dublin for a meeting and wanted to see how you were progressing," Connelly replied. Glancing at the other technicians about the room, he could see their effort was present, but it still lacked a useable product he could market.

"We will be ready to produce product by your requested date," she said bringing a smile to Connelly's face as she explained what they'd accomplished.

"I'm glad to hear that. I'll let you return to your work," Connelly said. With Liam in tow, he exited the secure laboratory, stripping off the Tyvex suit and tossing it in the bin labeled "Burn" across the top. "Now Liam, let's you and I have a talk, shall we?"

Using the service cart, Liam drove to his office near the shipping bays. They climbed up some stairs and Liam held the door open as Connelly entered the small room overlooking the distribution spaces. "Is

209

there something wrong?" he asked, taking a seat across from the executive.

"I will be frank with you, Liam," he started. "I need to know if you've gotten into any trouble. Anything having to do with the Garda recently? Something here at the plant with any of the workers?"

The young man sat quietly for a moment, his eyes not moving off from his superior. "I've not had as much as a citation for drunk in public," Liam stammered. "I've never even been cited while on the motorway, either," he added.

Connelly heard Liam, but was thinking of what caused Roan to make the accusation earlier in the day. He mentioned irregularities with documents for the workers, he reminded himself. "Liam, who handles the workers documentation when they arrive?" he asked.

Liam blinked. "I've no clue, Mister Connelly," he replied. "I come to the factory and I make sure we ship our product out. And I've been keeping an eye on the handful of workers you identified for your project. I've never been involved in the recruitment or settling of the chemists or technicians."

"You're right," Connelly said with a glance toward the ceiling. Dropping his head in his hands, his frustration grew. "I should have known, shouldn't I?" he muttered to himself and rising to his feet. "Seems someone misled me, Liam. I'm sorry for getting you worked up."

"Is there something going on I need to know about?"

Connelly put his hand on the young man's shoulder in a fatherly gesture. "No, Liam, there's nothing at the moment. Just my foolish paranoia I'm afraid," he chuckled. "Keep an eye on the doctor, though," he said as he made his way towards the exit.

As he walked out of the building, a grey and angry sky greeted Connelly. His driver noticed him step out of the facility and had the back door open for him. Settling onto the supple leather seat, Connelly closed his eyes and took stock of his situation. "Geoff, I think it's time to call it an evening, what do you say?"

"I'm fine with that," the driver agreed, pulling the Jaguar out of the parking lot and northeast toward the center of town. "Do you fancy anything special for supper? I can call ahead to The Savoy and see if we can get a table reserved next door."

Michael Connelly didn't hear Geoff's question as he continued to reflect on what it brought to his attention by Roan Callaghan. Questionable entry into the country? Why does he think I've anything to do with bringing illegal workers into Ireland?

Exiting the motorway, Connelly's driver negotiated the evening traffic through town as they made their way to the luxury hotel in the city center. Before Geoff could stop the Jaguar at the set down area of the hotel, a concierge member had already opened the passenger door to let Mister Connelly exit.

"Fine motorcar you've got, sir," the attendant greeted the executive.

Connelly gave it a loving glance before answering. "Yes, she is, isn't she?"

"See it's handled with care," Geoff added as he held out the key and a 20-euro banknote.

"We always do, sir," the pimple-faced young man replied, accepting the keys while Geoff handed the bags off to another attendant.

Michael Connelly laugh inwardly at the exchange, knowing Geoff was just as possessive about the vintage car as he was. "I'm sure the property insurer will see it's looked after properly, Geoff," he said as he stepped toward the entrance.

A uniformed doorman assisted in pulling the glass and chrome door open for Connelly. The hotel's name hung over the receptionist's counter, its gold lettering shimmering in the lights hanging in the lobby. As he walked up to the long front desk, situated to his left, several uniformed employees stood, waiting to check Connelly and his driver into their rooms.

As Geoff followed his employer, one steward stepped forward to collect the luggage on a trolley for room delivery. "Thanks," Geoff said to the young man, slipping him a five-euro bill.

"How my we assist you?" the young woman asked Connelly as he stepped to the counter.

"I've a reservation. The name is Connelly," he replied.

"Just a moment," the woman replied as she tapped her fingers across the keyboard. "Yes. We have two rooms, Mister Connelly: an executive suite and a standard. Is this correct?"

"Yes, it is," Connelly smiled.

"I also see we've reserved a table next door for you; dinner for two at 8 pm, correct?"

"That's right."

In moments, the young woman had completed the registration process and they could hear the whir of a printer spitting out the form behind her. "Please initial here, here, and here; then sign at the bottom," she said, highlighting the areas for Connelly to sign.

As he gripped the pen, Connelly scribbled his initials and signature onto the powdery softness of the invoice, its high-quality paper soaking up the ink like a sponge.

Chapter TWENTY-EIGHT

Belfast, Northern Ireland

They could hear the crackle of the security officer's radio over the low murmur of passengers standing in line. McDermott and Giles stood behind the kiosk, waiting for the supervisor to confirm their credentials.

"Is it always this bad?" Giles asked.

"No, no it's not this bad when we're conducting official business," McDermott said, his reply loud enough for the officer behind the counter to hear. An older couple stood in the line next to them, the woman's discounted perfume wafting over them and causing Giles to sneeze.

A second indiscernible crackling over the security officer's radio announced someone had cleared them to enter. "Welcome to Belfast, gentlemen," the harried clerk said, handing over their police credentials.

McDermott just nodded while accepting his paperwork. Shouldering his overnight bag, he pushed through the crowd gathering around the baggage conveyors. Giles followed, keeping his bag in front of him as a buffer against the unsuspecting travelers.

As he neared the exit, McDermott saw the constable, his bottle-green uniform a sign of his service with the PSNI, holding a sign with his name above the crowd. "Giles, to your right," he said over his shoulder, motioning toward the officer. Approaching the constable, McDermott stood aside while a family of seven made their way towards the exit, with three of the five children pulling on a piece of luggage.

"I'm McDermott, Officer...," he said taking the last few strides toward the constable.

"Special Constable Meyers, at your disposal for the evening," the young man said. "I've a car waiting to see you both to the hotel," he explained, nodding toward the street. "And tomorrow Sergeant Kennedy will pick you up."

"Let's get on with it, then," McDermott said.

SC Meyers noticed Sergeant Giles following them. "Is he with us?"

"Oh, aye, he is," McDermott replied. "This is Sergeant Giles of Police-Scotland," he said, pulling him forward. As the three men made their way to the car, the roar of an outbound flight filled the arrival area of the airport.

"Mister Darby has you set up near downtown," Meyers said while maneuvering into traffic and heading away from the airport. "He made sure you'd have a chance to grab supper, so there're places nearby," he started, mentioning a few eateries near their hotel. Half an hour later, SC Meyers pulled up to the stately old hotel on Victoria Street where McDermott and Giles would stay, at least for the night.

While SC Meyers settled the registration, McDermott and Giles asked one of the concierge staff for a recommendation regarding the local pubs. With their rooms secured, the two men from Aberdeen soon found themselves poised on the edges of their stools, working on a hot meal and cold beers.

"Inspector, if you arrested this fella in Glasgow for his involvement in the drug trafficking, what are we doing in Belfast?" Giles asked. "Seems we're off our pitch on this one."

"You're not wrong in thinking that, Marcus," McDermott said, finishing his second pint and grabbing a few chips from his plate. "The authority in conducting this investigation still rests with Metro in London. Since Andrew and I started this case, we've got the means to investigate within the kingdom."

"And if the fella you're looking for crosses over the border, then what?"

"You can read about it in the papers," McDermott replied. "This fella's no getting away with what he's planned. Besides, Andrew and I have London working on smoothing out the feathers in Dublin if need be."

Giles finished his ale. "Seems like a lot of fuss for something that's not going away."

McDermott glanced at the constable, considering his next choice of words carefully. "Marcus, why did you become a constable, heh? Sense of duty, steady pay, something else maybe?"

"It's just something I've always thought of," the constable replied. "I was always keen on the American movies about the G-men, you know, Eliot Ness types."

A broad smile crossed Conor's face hearing the honesty behind the young man's answer. "And behind your reason for being a constable is the answer to why I'm the Chief Inspector I am today," McDermott said.

"And what's that?"

"Simply put, it's perseverance," McDermott stated, leaning back for the server to take his plate. "In our case, drugs will always be the obstacle in the path of a decent society which must be overcome. And the deadlier the drug, the more dogged our attempts need to be."

"But what about the people clamoring to legalize marijuana? Surely we need tae heed their wishes at some point?" Giles asked in protest.

"Be careful, Marcus," McDermott replied. "Once you let the political pundits and citizens sway your decision making, that'll be the chink in your armor. As long as we've laws telling us it's wrong, we'll never be questioned for our actions for doing the right thing."

The constable shook his head. "You sound like the lecturers at university," he chuckled.

McDermott grinned at the compliment. Finishing his beer, he slid off the stool and put his hand on the constable's shoulder. "Best we call it an early evening, Marcus. Who's tae say what tomorrow will bring." He quickly glanced at the bill before placing money on the counter.

The clamoring of trash bins being emptied woke McDermott. With a toss of his arm, he slid out of bed, stepping to the window to see the offending party. Below in the street, the lone vehicle pulled forward as two men hoisted barrels heaped with garbage to the lift which slung them skyward. "It's no like the old days," he muttered in the dark.

As he sat back on the bed, he looked at his watch. 4:30 in the morning. McDermott dressed and headed downstairs. As he stepped off the lift, one of the evening staff bumped into him.

"My apologies, sir," the young man said. "Is everything all right?"

"Aye, just need a bit of fresh air," McDermott replied as he continued towards the front entrance. Stepping outside, Conor strolled across the street where he took a seat on a stone bench outside the front garden area of St. George's Church.

"It's nae like St. Mary's chapel," he muttered, examining the stone building with its carved crests above the entrance. A single lamp hung suspended over the doors leading into the Anglicans' place of worship.

Under the muted glow from the streetlight, Conor pulled out the photo of his niece. The face of a cherub stared back at him. Soft curls of hair hung over her shoulders.

"You went and grew up tae fast, didn't you? And with a mind of your own, you might have done something foolish," the Scotsman whispered as several tears crept down his face. The young girl in the summer dress, holding the hand of the naval officer, just stared back at him.

The commotion of a delivery truck caused Conor to turn as he watched the vehicle turn past the Albert Memorial clock and head towards the riverfront. As he noticed the time, he felt the growing pangs of hunger. With one last look at the photo, he folded and slipped it back into his pocket. Sweeping his thumb across his cheek, he flecked the few tears from his face before heading back to the hotel.

While McDermott sat outside St. George's Church in Belfast, a vintage Jaguar maneuvered through the city of Limerick, its occupants making their return drive to the Northern Irish capital. "Sorry to have you up so early, Geoff, but I need to finish a few things from the board meeting," Connelly said, reading a document under the overhead light.

Suppressing a yawn, Geoff spoke. "I'm ok with it. Makes getting through Dublin a little easier. With any luck, we'll be at the office before ten o'clock. Unless you want me to stop at the residence first."

"No, to the office first will be fine," Connelly said, not noticing the passing countryside this trip. As he undid the buckles from his briefcase, he slid out his notepad and grabbed a pen. For the next few hours, Connelly planned his activities for the next several weeks.

***

The hotel's restaurant became busier the closer it came to the eight o'clock hour. McDermott had already finished two cups of coffee and was working on his third when Sergeant Giles joined him.

"Am I late?"

McDermott glanced up. "No, no you're not, Marcus. I just had a few things come to mind that woke me, so I decided to have a cup early that's all."

"No sight of our escort?" Giles asked as he poured himself some coffee from the carafe.

"Aye, no yet, I'm afraid," the senior officer replied. "I don't think anyone will be waiting for us when we serve our summons at this time anyway." Before they could continue, the server brought McDermott's breakfast and laid the plates down.

"Yours is coming up," she said, nodding toward the sergeant. "More coffee?"

"Aye, and a few more of the wee creamers too please," Giles said as he doctored his cup with several. He looked back to McDermott. "What are you hoping to find with our summons?"

McDermott finished buttering his toast before answering. He noticed a hostess greeting a family of four with menus and crayons and coloring paper for the kids, which brought a brief smile to his face.

"Inspector?"

"Sorry Giles, just a wee thought had me amused," McDermott said. "Our goal is tae find something tangible to link the Irishman to Alistair Hunt and the drug trafficking. Notes on a ledger, a calendar entry, some written ideas..."

"Sorry for the wait," the server said as she returned with the coffee and her companion placed Giles's food on the table. "Do let us know if you need anything else."

"Quite the feast," Giles remarked, looking at the plate, his sausage still sizzling in its own drippings. "Will the PSNI types be helping with the summons?" he asked as he sprinkled a dash of salt to his eggs.

McDermott wiped his mouth before answering. "They'll be holding the door while we do the work," he said. "They've not been fully read in on the case. Besides, I'm nae sure which side of the fence the sergeant sits on."

"I've not been read in fully," Giles exclaimed.

"True, but I've a sense you'll nae compromise things like the PSNI could. Besides, I'm thinking you'll be working with Andrew and I for a few more months," he said, finishing his coffee.

"As long as it means a few pounds more in my pay," Giles quipped as he swirled a bit of sausage amongst the yolk from his egg. "I'll need that just to pay for a new suit," he added. "I'd hate to think the extra money would only allow buying something like yours." He jokingly waved his fork at McDermott's faded field coat, its sleeves showing bits of fraying fabric.

McDermott was beginning to like having Sergeant Giles around. He'll make a good inspector given time, he told himself, slicing off a piece of blood pudding. "You need to balance the costs of your kit and keeping it clean," McDermott said. "I can go a few weeks and nae worry about this. Andrew has two or three sport coats to himself."

Just past the hostess, Sergeant Kennedy was trying to look beyond a group of businessmen into the café. Stepping around two executives discussing their bottom line, he spotted CI McDermott sitting with another gentleman. He avoided colliding with a server whose arms were full of plates from one table.

"Morning, Inspector McDermott," Kennedy said. "And who's your new associate this trip?"

"Giles, Sergeant Marcus Giles," McDermott's companion said. "Police Scotland-Aberdeen," he greeted shaking the Irish officer's hand.

"Fair enough," Kennedy asked, pulling a chair over to the table and picking up the carafe. "Do you mind...?"

"No, not at all. Seeing how your department is paying for it anyway," McDermott said, handing the sergeant the bill.

Kennedy's eyes widened as he was taken by surprise by McDermott's gesture. Giles sat staring ahead, fighting back his urge to laugh at the Irishman's reaction. "Seems only fair being your host," Kennedy answered as he grasped the slip and looked over the amount.

The chiming of a cell phone interrupted their discussion. "Sorry, it's mine," Giles announced before reaching into his coat pocket and looking at the number. "Seems the office is calling," Giles explained as he answered. "Hello?"

In Aberdeen, Inspector Fletcher heard the sergeant answering. "Good morning, Sergeant. Is Chief Inspector McDermott with you?" He glanced at the wall clock in hopes it wasn't too early to call. "And can you put him on the phone?"

Giles handed the devise to McDermott. "It's Inspector Fletcher for you."

"Aye Andrew, what is it?"

"I had a call from PS Glasgow and Miss Cameron," Fletcher began. "She ran down more information on this Ross fella you questioned the other day. Seems he was straight up with his duties at the sporting venues. On a hunch, she had the security footage at Celtic Stadium reviewed and it showed the constable working the VIP boxes."

"And that means what to us, Andrew?"

"She said there's several frames of Constable Ross with Alistair Hunt," he answered. "And there's one more thing. Hunt was with another man. Seems the constable and the other fellow knew each other quite well since they exchanged more than a handshake. Turns out Hunt was a major supporter of the football club."

McDermott considered how to best use this new information to his advantage. "Andrew, have CS Cameron monitor this fella until I return. Don't let her detain the constable until then, you understand?"

"I'm not sure she'll accept my authority, Conor," Fletcher stammered.

"Then have Mister MacCallum make the call, but you make sure you're in the room when he does," McDermott directed his partner. "You make sure he understands we need to keep the constable in check."

"I'll do my best," Fletcher replied. "That's all I've got for the moment. I'll call after meeting with the chief superintendent and my visit to the infirmary. Cheerio."

"Good news?" Sergeant Kennedy asked after the call had ended.

"Aye, a wee bonus from an interrogation session the other day," McDermott replied as he failed to hide a smirk. "Marcus, get your kit together and we'll meet you outside. Sergeant," getting to his feet, "time to go."

Chapter TWENTY-NINE

Unlike most receptionists' desktops that are cluttered with everything from files, memos, and papers, Erin Malone prided herself on being neat and orderly. Her desk held just the basics: a computer screen and phone console while the computer tower sat underneath. As she hung her sweater, she leaned over the file cabinet and turned on the stereo, filling the office with pleasant sounds from an instrumental group.

With her superior, Michael Connelly, still in Dublin, she had the whole floor to herself. She made herself a cup of tea and sat in front of her computer, checking on solicitations, emails, and scheduled calendar events. Humming to the music, she was caught by surprise when Chief Inspector McDermott and the two sergeants entered.

"Good morning," McDermott said.

The sudden appearance of the police had Erin's heart racing from the surprise. "Can I help you?" she stuttered. The absence of her employer made this encounter even more frightful to the young woman, clear by the tingling sensation of hairs rising on her neck.

McDermott pulled out the summons for the young woman. "We're here to conduct a search of the spaces," he explained, placing the paper on the desk. "You're welcome to stay seated here under Sergeant Kennedy's supervision or you can accompany me as I look over everything."

"What are you looking for, though?"

"It nae be fun if I told you," McDermott said with a gruel smile. "Is your superior..., his name's Connelly, isn't it? Is he in yet?" he asked, pulling on a pair of gloves Giles handed to him.

"No, he and Geoff are in Dublin for a board meeting," Erin replied, a noticeable tremor in her voice. "You're welcome to wait till he returns."

"The summons is for the offices of Callaghan and Higgins," McDermott said, looking for a starting point. "And since you're an employee who's present, we can begin while someone of authority can be summoned."

McDermott's statement spurred the young woman into action. Picking up the phone, she selected the speed dial option for her employer. After the second ring, Michael Connelly answered the call. "Good morning, Erin," he said. "I didn't expect to hear from you. Is everything all right?"

Placing one hand against her forehead for support she answered, her voice cracking. "I'm afraid not, sir. Seems the police are here with a summons." She felt powerless under the circumstances.

"It's all right, Erin," Connelly said, trying to calm the young woman. "Geoff and I are on our way. I'll be in the office soon."

"Where are you?" she asked, causing McDermott to turn towards her from the files he was scanning.

"Geoff, how soon to the office?" Connelly asked his driver.

"Should be about thirty minutes if the traffic is sparse," the young man replied.

"Erin, I'll be there in about a half-hour according to Geoff," he answered, feeling the vintage auto pick up speed. "Do your best to be polite and keep the officers in your sight if possible. I'll contact Mister McGrew to come by as quick as he can."

As she hung up the phone, Erin swiveled her chair until she faced CI McDermott. "Mister Connelly will be here shortly." She forced a smile though the stress continued to mount.

"Aye, that'll be helpful," McDermott replied. Sliding one folder back in the cabinet drawer, he drew out another. Bloody ledgers and invoices, he told himself. "You mind handing me a slip of paper, hen?" he asked, holding out his hand.

Erin obliged the inspector and tore a sheet from her notepad.

With his pencil, McDermott scribbled out some dates on the paper and handed to Sergeant Giles. "Here's your cue to what we need to find."

As each officer reviewed his individual files, the minutes passed, and the opening of the office door brought a halt to their search. "That'll do for the moment, sir," the booming voice of Connelly's colleague announced.

"Who are you?" McDermott asked as the heavy-set gentleman closed the door.

"I'm counsel for Mister Connelly," the man replied. "And until I review your summons, I'd ask you to refrain from conducting any further search." He settled into the chair opposite Erin. The weight of the man caused the chair to creak, but held up under his sizeable girth.

"I'll ask again. Who are you?" McDermott demanded, his tone more forceful and direct as he stood over the lawyer.

"It's Desmond McGrew, esquire. Now, can I please see the summons?" he asked, holding out his hand.

McDermott withdrew the document from inside his field coat.

As he unfolded the paper, the lawyer drew out a pair of spectacles reminiscent of Ben Franklin. Settling the spindly frame to the bridge of his nose, McGrew and turned to the first page of the document and read. Sporadic nods of his head were the only signs of life from the lawyer.

Downstairs, the green Jaguar belonging to Michael Connelly pulled up to the entrance behind the PSNI patrol car. Constable Flynn noticed the vehicle and walked towards the driver's window.

"Geoff, go and get the car cleaned up," Connelly said, sliding out the back as the officer made it to the car. Sticking his head back inside, he added. "And see it's filled with petrol, too." He closed the door before trotting up the stairs. "Morning, Constable," he said with a wave trotting up the stairs.

In moments, Connelly stood outside his office. Gathering himself, he closed his eyes in an attempt to slow his heart rate. After feeling his pulse subside, he grasped the handle and entered the outer room to see four familiar faces and one stranger.

In unison, Erin, Mister McGrew, and the three officers turned to face Connelly, who was greeted in various tones and voices. "Morning, sir," Erin said as calmly as possible. Getting to her feet, she took a small pile of messages off her desk.

"Thank you, Erin," he replied, taking the notes. "Seems we've a need for some coffee," he added. "Please prepare a pot and bring it inside when it's ready." He pushed past McDermott to enter his office. Connelly looked back as he held the door open. "Mister McGrew, a word in private, if I may?"

McDermott followed behind the lawyer into the executive's office.

"This is a private consultation," Connelly announced, raising his eyebrows, to stress his smug attitude toward the inspector. Waiting for the Scotsman to back away from the door, he glared back with a smirk.

McDermott knew this was not the place to create a scene, but he was becoming more agitated with the Irishman acting as if rules didn't apply to him. Stepping aside for the lawyer to waddle past, he turned to Sergeant Giles. "Marcus, stay here and be cordial with the lass. Sergeant Kennedy, let's have a wee talk," he started, heading into the outer corridor.

As the officers stepped out of the office, Connelly addressed the barrister holding the Crown's summons. "What does Scotland Yard want with me, Desmond?" he asked as he stared out the window towards the harbor.

"I'm surprised you called me in the first place, Michael," McGrew replied. "Where's that young man we seconded to you? Gifford was his name, wasn't it?"

"You mean Gilmore," Connelly said. "He's taken a sabbatical until Christmas," he lied. "Now, what can you tell me about the summons?"

"The summon addresses the need to search the company records and all associated documents within the property," McGrew said. "Which includes all electronic devices on the premises." He folded the document up before continuing. "Michael..., is your grandfather's company in some sort of trouble?"

Connelly was pleased to have his back to the lawyer. It made lying to him much easier than seeing his face. "I can assure you, Des, the company's fine," he chuckled. "Unless the health firms on the Continent turn down our cancer treatment drugs, that is."

"Then why is this ruffian from Scotland Yard here?" the older man asked.

Connelly hesitated for the moment. Turning to face the barrister, he provided an answer he hoped would carry credence with the gentleman. "I've no criminal past, so I'm not sure what their motives are," he half-shrugged, confident he wasn't portraying the secret behind the raid.

In the corridor outside the office, McDermott and Kennedy stood alone for the moment. "Sergeant, can you see if Mister Darcy can spare an unmarked motor?"

"Why?"

"I need to see where this fella Connelly goes from here, you know have him followed discreetly," McDermott answered, glancing about the hallway. "I need to know where he lives so I can have another summons prepared to see his place searched."

"Your summons doesn't cover his private home?"

"No, just the offices associated with his company at the moment," McDermott admitted.

Before he and Kennedy could discuss anything further, Sergeant Giles stuck his head out the doorway. "Chief Inspector, I've something to show you," he said, nodding towards the office. As the men returned, Giles flipped open a folder exposing a call ledger. "I noticed this," he mentioned with a point to the bottom right corner of the page. Contact C. Duncan-Nordic Supplier at the following number.

Someone had written the message in pencil, using very neat handwriting. McDermott noticed the date and time of the entry, glancing at the young woman who nervously twirled a mechanical pencil amongst her fingers. With a slight lean, he whispered to Sergeant Kennedy. "Can we get a female constable dispatched?" he muttered, nodding towards Erin.

"I'll see to it straight away," the sergeant replied before stepping out of the office.

Connelly and McGrew came out of the executive's office. "Thank you for being so understanding," Connelly said. "According to my counsel, you've a requirement to search the offices. I'll not keep you for your task, Inspector." The lawyer walked past, as he returned to his office three floors below where he stood.

"Marcus, you can keep checking the files," McDermott said as he closed the folder in his hands and moved to step past the two Irishmen. "I'll check on Mister Connelly's office. Oh..., and I'll have a cup of the coffee when it's ready hen."

As McDermott entered the executive's office, he turned to his left and searched through a set of filing cabinets. Drawer by drawer, the inspector pulled out folders, finding much of the same records. Invoices, Bill of Lading accounts, and notices of payment were being kept. "You and your secretary keep the same files?" he asked the Irishman as he closed the last drawer.

"No. Erin keeps certain accounts at her disposal while I keep older ones in these," Connelly replied, pointing to the cabinets. You won't find what you're looking for here, he told himself with an inward smile.

McDermott stepped across the room and ran his hand across the leather wing-back chair until he stood before the founders of Callaghan and Higgins Limited. "What secrets are you two keeping from me," he whispered to the image, sliding a hand behind the picture frame.

"I can attest there's no wall safe behind the picture," Connelly announced as Erin came into the office with the coffee service. He sensed her nervousness and reached for her hand. "It's going to be all right," he reassured her.

McDermott walked behind Connelly's desk and knelt before the credenza. Sliding back one door, he saw several types of liquor. "I see you fancy yourself a whisky drinker," he noted, holding up a bottle. "Tae bad it's a blended version." feigning to read the label even though he already knew how the drink was produced.

"I take it you prefer an unblended whisky?"

"Aye. There's nothing finer than the smoothness of a single malt from the River Spey," McDermott replied. "Or a dram steeped with smoky peat from an offering off the Isle of Islay."

The Irishman demonstrated a sense of comfort in close proximity of the Scotland Yard inspector. "If we'd met under different circumstances, I'd offer you a drink inspector," Connelly said, sipping his coffee.

As McDermott stood, he turned to the last space needing to be searched: Connelly's desk. As he pulled the chair away and sat, he pulled the center drawer open out of habit. "You've nae breath mints?" he asked, rummaging through the contents. One by one, he selected a drawer and opened it until he came across the last. Locked. "Something in here worth protecting?"

Connelly stood and walked behind his desk, pulling the center drawer to get the key. Dangling it from his fingers, he stared down at McDermott. "If you must look."

McDermott accepted the key and slid it into the lock. With a turn, he accessed the contents, once again finding folders with corporate information and nothing of substance. That is until his fingers grazed a thicker bound folder. Sliding the drawer against the stop, he pulled the old-fashioned check book into the light of day. "Fancy signing one of these over?" McDermott asked.

"You willing to accept a bribe inspector?"

"No, I'm a better man than that," the chief inspector answered, sliding the book back and closing the drawer.

A ruckus outside the office caused both men to turn their attention towards the entry as Geoff Brennan came through the door. "Hey Erin, what's going on?"

While the receptionist answered Connelly's driver, McDermott got to his feet. "I'll be returning shortly," he started, walking into the outer office. "Sergeant Giles, see if Sergeant Kennedy's returned if you will."

Before Giles could push the button to the lift, the doors parted, letting Kennedy and a female constable out. "Chief Inspector was wondering if you'd be back. Marcus Giles," he added, extending his hand to the woman officer. The sergeants and the constable made their way back into the office to find McDermott leaning against the file cabinets.

"I'll be taking my leave now," he said. "Miss Malone, is it? If you'll do me the pleasure of accompanying this officer, we'll be on our way?"

Erin's confused look spoke volumes. "What did you just say? Why do I need to leave? Mister Connelly, I've done nothing wrong," she replied, glancing around as if looking for an answer.

"What's the meaning of this, McDermott?" Connelly demanded.

"I've a few things I'd like to ask the young lass," he said. "You're welcome to send your barrister to the... which station are we going to, Sergeant?"

"Musgrave Station on Victoria," Kennedy answered.

"There you have it Connelly," McDermott declared. "But I'd send him soon; I won't be waiting for counsel to ask my questions. Rest easy now." He noticed Connelly's face muscles tighten. "I'll get me answers one way or the other."

Connelly grabbed the phone from Erin's desk, contacting Desmond McGrew and explaining the situation. Hanging up, he looked at Geoff. "I'm going to need the car; can you meet Mister McGrew at the police station?"

"I've my car across the way," the young Ulsterman replied.

"Good, go see to Erin and make sure she's cared for when the police are done," Connelly said, feeling the stress of the unknown bearing down on him. "You got the rest of the day off unless I call for you," he sighed, heading into his office before closing the door.

Hearing his driver leave, Connelly walked over to the credenza and slid the door open. With the Waterford decanter dangling from one hooked finger, he stood at the window. He wondered if he'd just dodged another IRA-type bombing today, in hopes it was enough. What does Scotland Yard know about me? What did they find that involves Erin?

The questions the police were asking caused him to doubt his efforts. Clouds, black and turbulent, gathered to match his mood. Soon, a sheet of rain pinged against the glass, like it was trying to get in at him. He took a swig of whisky and watched his plan for clearing his great-grandfathers name during a time when he fought uniting Ireland appear to dissolve around him.

Chapter THIRTY

Erin Malone provided little resistance as the officer steered her holding her arm as they entered the police station. They could hear muted voices over the intercom system as they passed through the secure doors that lead to an interview room.

CI McDermott pulled Sergeant Kennedy aside before entering. "Do you have a technician that can record our interview?"

"We're well staffed, Inspector," Kennedy replied. "Mister Darcy said you'd be given every courtesy, and it includes getting a copy of your questioning session of the young woman. Are you going to give him any time with the woman?" she asked, nodding towards the portly figure of Desmond McGrew.

McDermott entered the room ahead of the sergeant and the barrister. "He'll have a few minutes after I'm done." Like most interrogation rooms, someone furnished this one in typical fashion with a plain metal table and several chairs, one of them equipped with handcuff rings. In the center of one wall was the ever-present mirrored window, and in each corner a small CCTV camera, each with a single red light on.

"Before you begin, I'd like a few moments with Miss Malone," McGrew said as he squeezed himself onto the chair, the metal frame groaning in protest. "I want to know why you've singled her out for questioning."

Sergeant Giles stood in the corner, watching and listening to the barrister, but it was his assistant who was garnering most of his glances. The young woman's willowy figure reminded him of a Highland dancer. Except most wouldn't be seen in a mix of plaids and stripes, he told himself as her blouse and skirt appeared to be from a second-hand bin.

"Mister McGrew," McDermott began, "you'll have plenty of time to counsel Miss Malone in a few moments." Turning his attention to the secretary, he leaned onto the table, bringing his hands together as if in prayer. "Now then, hen," he began. "In your capacity as Mister Connelly's secretary, you've occasion to answer all his calls, don't you?"

The claustrophobic sensation of being in a locked facility would give most people a temporary case of laryngitis. But for Erin, it did not differ from being in a new pub, singing with her friends in front of strangers. She felt the hand of McGrew as he tried to control what she said, but she pulled away from him and stared into McDermott's eyes.

"Seems silly to ask a question you've already got an answer for," she replied in typical proud Irish fashion.

"It would seem so," McDermott said. "But can you tell me, do you remember answering a call from a fella by the name Duncan? It would have been...," he looked at Sergeant Giles, "what was the date, Marcus?"

The constable shook his head, recalling how Inspector Fletcher warned him about McDermott's habit of not writing things down, especially important information. Now he was living it first-hand. He flipped open his notebook and read, "Second week of July, between the 11th and the 14th."

"Miss Malone?"

Erin screwed her eyes shut. Assuming the worst-case scenario, she felt trapped. If she acknowledged taking the call, then it was sure to lead to the police arresting Mister Connelly. Picking her head up, she looked at the barrister McGrew before answering. "As I said, Inspector, I answer a lot of Mister Connelly's calls."

"Miss Malone, for the record, you've done nothing wrong," McDermott said, struggling to keep his tone civil. "I've evidence calls were made from Aberdeen to Callaghan and Higgins office in Belfast. More directly they were to your desk, I'm just needing you to confirm answering, that's all."

"This is nonsense, McDermott," McGrew bellowed, his pudgy mid-section quivering. "She just confirmed receiving calls, isn't that enough for you?" His hand slapped the table with a resounding thud, scattering several pencils to the floor.

The sudden outburst caused Sergeant Giles to edge closer to the table while Kennedy leapt to his feet, his chair clanging onto the floor as it toppled over. McDermott, however, sat still, keeping his gaze on Erin Malone.

"Miss Malone, after you took the call, do you know if Mister Connelly returned it right away?" he asked. "Or did he wait a few minutes, maybe an hour...?" He was struggling to keep his voice level and his tone neutral.

With a huff, the Irishwoman answered. "Mister Connelly was on another call, so I slipped him a note," Erin replied. "I assume he called after he was done," she shrugged.

McDermott took the lone pencil from the table and used to tap out a tune. "Do you remember taking any calls from a gentleman who addressed himself as Alistair Hunt?" he asked, moving on to the crime syndicate head in Glasgow.

"I've already said I answer the phone; you can't expect me to recall all the names, do you?" Erin replied, protesting the inspector's question as the pressure of being in the police station grew. "If I did, I'm sure something related it to some business arrangement," she added as her face reddened, tiny bits of sweat forming on her brow.

McDermott let out a sigh. He knew he didn't have any evidence against the young woman, especially for just doing her job. And it was becoming clear she'd never been privy to conversations that Connelly had with others being investigated.

"One last question before I finish," McDermott said as he feigned a cough. "Do you know the number of your employer's cell phone, Miss Malone?"

The young Irishwoman chuckled. "He's no got a cell phone," Erin replied. "He's rather old-fashioned like that. If he can't sit at a desk and pick up the phone and call you or better yet, speak face to face, he'll say it's not important."

It wasn't the answer McDermott expected, but it confirmed the woman didn't know everything that occurred behind closed doors. Getting to his feet, he gestured to the door. "You're free to leave. And thank you for your cooperation."

Erin was the first to get up as Desmond, McGrew's assistant, helped him to his feet. Kennedy held the door open and instructed the constable outside to escort the trio past the secure areas to the front lobby.

Watching the group leave, Kennedy turned to the Scotland Yard inspector. "Was that it? A few questions regarding phone calls. I thought you were getting something of substance, Inspector."

"I confirmed she took the call from one of my suspects," McDermott said. "And I also learned she's no in the room when Connelly has his conversations, either." He ran his hand through his hair, his own frustration growing.

"Why ask about the cell phone, though?" This time, Sergeant Giles asked the question.

"Almost all the communications have been by cell phone," McDermott said, glancing towards the constable. "Andrew and I lucked out finding the communique between a ship captain and the office. The biggest problem we have is the regular phone records will show calls across Britain, Ireland, and the Continent. It'll be like trying to find a wee wildcat in the forest to catch Connelly saying something incriminating."

As the three officers debated the success of the interrogation, Geoff Brennan paced the sidewalk outside the station. He caught sight of his friend Erin Malone and the two barristers walking through the doors. "Are you all right?" he asked, trotting up the steps to her.

"I'm fine. What are you doing here?"

"Mister Higgins told me to make sure you were ok." The use of their employer's alias was out of habit. "What did they want with you, anyway?"

Erin spend the next few minutes going over what happened in the police station. "Seems odd they only wanted to know about me answering the phones," she said, following Geoff towards the car park. "And it was only 'bout two gents Mister Higgins had business dealings with."

"Nothing illegal doing your job," Geoff said as he opened the door for Erin.

"Why are you driving your car?"

"Mister Higgins told me to leave his at the office," the Ulsterman replied, starting the engine. As he pulled the car from the lot, he slid neatly between two buses as they headed back to the office.

"Oh, and the last question was odd," she explained. "The inspector asked me if I knew Mister Higgins's cell phone number. I don't recall him even having one."

"But he does. I've seen him take calls while we're out and about. You don't remember when he wigged out thinking he lost it after golfing several weeks ago?"

Erin shook her head as she slid out of the car.

"It dropped out of his golf bag into the boot of the car," Geoff answered. Strolling up to the entrance from the parking garage, the two made their way to the lift and their employer's office on the twenty-first floor, only to find the door locked.

"You've keys?" Geoff asked.

"Yes, but shouldn't Mister Higgins still be here?" Erin answered as she began digging into her purse.

When the door opened, Erin and Geoff found the things as they had left them, with the notable exception of the inner office door being left open. "He's never left his door open before, has he?" Geoff asked, creeping towards the open door.

"He's very protective of his privacy, you know that," Erin replied, thankful for having her companion in the room with her. "It's out of character for him to leave and not close it."

Geoff pushed open the door and peered inside the executive's space. Standing in the room's center, he spun around, looking for anything that could be considered out of place. The only item he'd never seen left in view was the crystal decanter sitting on the credenza behind the desk.

Something's not right. Returning to where Erin sat, Geoff just shook his head. "He's not here now," he confirmed, settling in the easy chair near the doorway. "You know, I've never had Mister Higgins ask to leave the motor car before."

While his two employees attempted to piece together why he left, the Irishman was making his way south towards Dublin. Filled with a sense of dread not knowing what evidence Scotland Yard had against him, he fled. In the process of leaving, he now enjoyed the exhilaration of handling the vintage British car on the open road. Its twelve-cylinder engine purred like a contented cat, and Connelly was comforted by the tuned suspension absorbing the road's irregularities with ease.

As he neared the border, the chirping of his cell phone drew his attention to the satchel on the passenger seat. Connelly slowed, pulling the Jaguar off to the side. The number was from the corporate office in

Dublin. Under it, he noticed the symbol showing the caller had left a message.

Thumbing through the digits, Connelly activated the recording.

Michael, this is Roan. When you get a moment, please contact me at the office. It seems your manager in Limerick has got into a spot of trouble with the Garda, and your assistant called voicing her concern. That's all for now.

Connelly laid his head against the polished steering wheel. "What have you done now, Liam?" he muttered. Not only am I being confronted with issues by Scotland Yard, now the Garda are snooping around.

Focused on the growing list of dilemmas, Connelly did not hear a patrolman's BMW motorbike pull behind him. The uniformed officer stepped off the bike and approached the driver's window. Tapping a gloved hand on the glass startled the driver enough he bolted upright from his position.

"Is everything all right, sir?"

Connelly heard the constable speak, but didn't understand his question. As he reached along the door for the lever, he rolled the window down a few inches to address the officer. "I'm sorry, did you say something, constable?"

"Is everything all right? Do you need a lift?" he asked, looking over the vintage vehicle.

"I'm fine," Connelly said. "I pulled to the side to answer a call," he explained with a wave of his cell phone to the officer. "I'm not the type to try to drive and concentrate on the other parties talking."

The patrolman nodded, still mesmerized by the condition of the Jaguar. "You've done a good job keeping this motor looking so clean. You've kept it in the garage, haven't you?"

Nodding politely at the comment, Connelly kept a smile on his face while trying to think of a way to leave. "I'm not one to be rude, but I've a business counseling to broker in Dublin..."

"My apologies," the patrolman said. "Just want to keep the motorway safe and all. You have a pleasant day." He waved to Connelly on his way to his destination.

With a twist of the key, Connelly brought the twelve-cylinder to life, and with a cautious glance, maneuvered the car back into traffic. Looking in the rearview mirror, he saw the patrolman still staring, his admiration for the car on full display. "Now, to see what Liam's gotten into," he said before continuing his trek towards Dublin.

Chapter THIRTY-ONE

Dublin, Ireland

The Garda's immigration bureau was unusually busy for this time of day. Liam Finnegan stood in line against a wall with a group from Senegal, waiting to have his fingerprints recorded before the officer took his physical measurements and photograph.

"Well, well... you're a regular, aren't you?" the Garda officer said, viewing the computer screen of Liam's past transgressions.

"It's been a few years," Liam replied. He was careful to keep his distance from the counter as denoted by the faded footprints painted on the floor. "I'm a much cleaner version of my former self."

The officer scoffed at the declaration, handing over the booking sheet, still warm from the printer. "He's all yours, Sergeant Fahy."

"Let's go." Fahy tugged on Liam's elbow to lead him away from the remaining suspects. As each man passed the threshold, they soon left behind the noise and activity of the processing space.

"This is rather pleasant," Liam said, noting the subdued conversations that filtered out of the various offices they strolled past. He couldn't help but sneak peeks in the rooms with open doors. "I've never been here you know."

"That's refreshing to hear," Fahy said, guiding him around the corner. At the end of the hallway, Sergeant Fahy's inspector stood waiting near an open doorway. "Now, mind your manners and all will go well for you." Fahy led Liam into the room and settled him on a chair. As Fahy strolled past, he gave the booking sheet to the senior officer.

"Now, Mister Finnegan, I'm all for fair play," the Garda inspector began. He pulled a photo from a folder and slid it in front of Liam. Someone had taken it outside the factory in Limerick and showed him with Dr. Liu Yang and her assistant Xi Feng. "How about you tell us what your role is in the obtaining workers for Callaghan and Higgins."

Liam exchanged glances with each of the officers as if they would provide him with an answer to their own question. "Let me get this right," he said. "You think I'm responsible for hiring the chemists and technicians. And how do I accomplish this? I've never left the country!"

"But you're the manager of the facility, aren't you?"

"More like a custodian," Liam said, searching for a reason he was being questioned. "I make sure the staff has the means of getting in the building and what they produce gets forwarded to the packaging building."

While his plant manager was being questioned by the Garda, Michael Connelly was pulling into a parking garage in Dublin. As soon as he found an empty space, he parked his Jaguar and trotted over to the elevators. Once in the lift, Connelly selected the correct floor and caught his breath, rushing to Roan Callaghan's office once it stopped.

Though unannounced, Connelly bounded into the executive's office. Behind the big, expensive-looking desk, Roan spun his chair about, making it creak from his size. "It seems you got my message."

"You sounded concerned," Connelly replied, taking a seat opposite of Roan. "So, what has your informant with the Garda conjured up about Mister Finnegan?"

"You've a brass set accusing me of having an informant with Garda." Roan leaned onto the desk, bringing his fingertips together to form a steeple. "Seems young Finnegan has been cooking the documents for some workers. Garda Immigration noted there are more members coming from off-shore to work for us than normal. And the last three weeks, Finnegan has been escorting several Asians around town," Roan continued while getting up from his seat.

"And what's wrong with him giving someone a lift?"

Roan stepped to the small beverage cart and poured himself a glass of water. "According to the Garda, after being seen with the certain Asian woman, an individual the police know approached her. Turns out, he's a handler for the Chinese consulate."

"And you want to blame Liam for your mistake?" Connelly asked with the jab of a finger toward Roan's face. Connelly's rage upon hearing the reason for Liam's arrest caused the anger to spill over. "You're the one who manages the staffing. You're the one who does all the negotiations with these government officials..."

The executive stood quiet, gazing out the window. "There are two ways we can address this," Roan said.

"I'm listening."

Connelly let Roan Callaghan speak his mind. The executive didn't admit he was responsible for hiring chemists and technicians, but he agreed checks into their past weren't as thorough as they should have been. The last part of his discourse caught Connelly by surprise.

"The board has given me a vote of 'no confidence' and I need to find a way to redeem myself to my father," Roan said. "They've seen the transactions I've negotiated and feel the company should have benefitted more"

"And you felt sacrificing Liam would save your arse?" Connelly exclaimed. "And what of him? He's been loyal to both me and the company for nearly five years."

"It was too easy," Roan said. "He's a former drug user for God's sake, Michael. I insinuated to the Garda it possibly involved him garnering extra money to supply his habit," he explained, sinking into his chair. "What's one less burden on the system, anyway?"

Connelly felt powerless for the moment as the vacant look on his face showed. "I'll not see you defile this young man's name," he said. "If you're in need of redemption, go see the vicar. And another thing; you need to call your friend at the Garda and have Liam released." He stood from his chair and moved to the door. "You do that, or I'll go to your father with what you're trying to do," Connelly threatened before walking out of the office.

Back in Aberdeen, Inspector Fletcher returned from his physio appointment free of the sling. The knife wound he suffered from Blayne Taggert had healed enough, allowing the doctors to permit him to return to full duty.

As he sat at his desk, Andrew returned to scrutinizing phone records of Callaghan and Higgins in Belfast. Like most of the calls, they centered on locations in the United Kingdom, with a few coming from different countries on the continent. As he flipped the page, one set of numbers caught his eye for the second time.

"Where are you calling from?" he asked the empty office. As he highlighted the number, he spun his chair to face the computer and typed the digits in the field to conduct a search. The computer signaled the end of the search with an audible beep as the screen flashed. His search had found the call originated in Durbin, South Africa. "Who are you doing business with here?" he murmured as Sergeant McKee entered.

"Since you asked, it be you, Inspector Fletcher," the constable joked.

Andrew looked up. "Sorry about that; I've a bad habit of talking to myself since I began working with the chief inspector," he chuckled, sliding the chair away from his desk "What can I do for you Sergeant McKee?"

"The university staff provided a set of images from that rave party last week," McKee said as she handed over a folder to Fletcher. "They came across a few crude pictures of a motor leaving the car park in the vicinity where we found the lad who was stabbed by his mate."

Andrew shook his head. "I'm not part of the investigation; why are you bringing them to me?" Nonetheless, he opened the folder and pulled out the first image. "Looks to be a Ford Cosworth... with a single occupant, probably a man..." Andrew scratched the side of his head. "I've seen this motor before; I think..." Looking at the second image, Andrew leaned closer to it, his eyes narrowing as he concentrated. "Is that...?"

"Your professor? Aye, it's Calvin Benson," McKee replied.

"Is this the cleanest image?"

"Inspector Gordon sent copies to the lab at Gartcosh to see if they could enhance them a wee bit," the sergeant explained. "But the time stamp and date places him in the incident's vicinity. With the crime's severity, I'm thinking it'll be worth accessory to the fact if he sold the lads hashish," McKee added with a smug look to her face.

"You seem rather pleased with yourself, Sergeant," Andrew noted, handing the folder back.

"Just glad to get another drug peddler off the streets."

"Do we know who was filing the initial report?"

"I am once the super signs off on it," the sergeant answered.

Andrew leaned back in his chair. He knew his partner had discussed their theory of several sergeants passing info regarding the drug trafficking and someone assigned one to DIU with Inspector Cockburn.

"All right, Sergeant, just make sure we have copies added to the Wallace files, too," he reminded her, picking up the phone.

Before the constable left, Inspector Fletcher dialed the number for Cockburn's desk in Edinburgh. On the fourth ring, he got someone to answer. "DUI, Sergeant Sedgwick; how can I assist you?"

"Yes, Sergeant, this is Inspector Fletcher in Aberdeen," Andrew answered, "is Inspector Cockburn available?"

"Sorry, sir. He's out for the moment. Can I help you with something?"

Fletcher was leery about sharing the information about Calvin Benson with the sergeant since they considered him to be part of the trafficking group. "Just let him know to call me before five o'clock," he said with a glance at his watch. "I'll be in my office all day."

"Of course, Inspector," Sedgwick said, looking at the phone before setting it on the receiver. Glancing around the office, the sergeant made sure he was alone before pulling out a small notebook from his shirt pocket. As he flipped it open, he jotted down the date and time as a reminder to look for information coming from the district office in Aberdeen.

Meanwhile, Inspector Fletcher nodded to Sergeant McKee. "Make sure you note having our conversation on your report," he said. "But keep Benson's name off it as our suspect for the moment." The Scotland Yard inspector spent the next few minutes briefing the sergeant on his and McDermott's theory that Sergeant Sedgwick was part of a larger conspiracy.

"You'll let me handle cuffing him?" the sergeant asked, her eyebrows raised in anticipation.

"I'll see that CI McDermott knows of your request," Andrew replied. "Any special reason?"

"Let's say it's a wee payback for something from our training days," McKee replied, her smirk having a devious undertone. "You see, Alan had a notion of being a lady's man and made it known a little too often with me and the girls. He went too far during our field training on apprehending and subduing suspects."

"I take it he was too hands on?" the inspector queried.

The sergeant's lip curled upward as recalled the incident. "Aye, and then some," Ames replied. "Cost him a day in the infirmary when he groped me on the last day," the officer said. "But he also cost two girls their posting 'cause they caved in before they could finish their training."

As Fletcher heard the story, he knew it would help the woman settle a score. "I'll make sure you're the lead when the time comes," he said. "And I'll make sure the chief inspector doesn't step in as well."

"Sheila said you'd understand. If you have nothing else, I've got to finish putting the packet together." She grabbed the folder off Andrew's desk before leaving the office.

Fletcher watched the sergeant leave as he turned his attention back to the phone listing for the business in Belfast. "Now, where was I," he muttered, thumbing through the papers. He found the mark for the number in South Africa and then another, this one identified as incoming. As he slid his finger along the paper, he noticed the date. "That was just a week ago." The date coincided with the initial visit he and McDermott had made to Callaghan and Higgins.

Grabbing the phone, Fletcher contacted the communications center located two floors above him. "This is Inspector Fletcher. I need you to record the following outbound call from my number. I also need you to connect me with the international operator. I'll wait."

A moment later, Fletcher had the constable from communications join him. "We're all set inspector, just dial your party's number," came the direction.

Andrew wasted no time in punching in the phone number from the listing. His mind raced to his next step, unsure what was to come from his actions. After several excruciating seconds, he heard a chirp and click as it made connections.

"Gazelle Transport; how can I direct your call?" the woman answered in Afrikaans.

The Scotland Yard inspector hesitated in his response when he heard the call being answered.

"Hello, can I help you?" the woman asked again, this time in clipped English.

Fletcher heard the voice again. "I'm sorry, my Afrikaans is rather rusty," he replied. "Is your supervisor there? This is Mister Higgins calling for him..." He used the Irishman's alias, unsure how the woman would respond.

Chapter THIRTY-TWO

Belfast, Northern Ireland

Conor McDermott, along with Sergeant Giles, followed Sergeant Kennedy through the hallway of PSNI headquarters in Belfast, heading to the administrative space and Chief Constable Darcy. As they approached the lobby near the senior constable's office, the sergeant slowed as they came upon a group gathered near the memorial wall.

"In closing," the senior officer continued, "I'm reminded of the struggle former members of our provisional police force overcame. And PC O'Brien was one many who exemplified strength in faith and country," Chief Darcy declared to the family and friends of the former officer. "We'll always see him as a stalwart member of the community to which he served."

The station chaplain stepped forward and offered the benediction to the ceremony, bringing an end to the memorial service. After acknowledging several members of the family, the senior officer made his way to McDermott and the two sergeants.

Chief Darcy stepped away from the ceremony to greet the three officers who stood aside from the gathering.

"I take it the officer was no a recent victim of some secular turmoil," McDermott said, noting the ages of the family members.

"He was the last survivor of a bombing near Drumcree," Darcy said. "Have you finished your business with Callaghan yet?" he asked as they headed to his office.

"Aye, but just for the moment, mind you," McDermott replied, following behind. "But I've still got a few items being looked at in Aberdeen before I can place Mister Connelly under arrest. Until then, I'd appreciate it if you kept an eye on this fella for us."

Chief Darcy scoffed at the request. "Scotland Yard doesn't have the manpower to do a proper surveillance, does it?"

McDermott bristled at the rebuke. "Didn't you mention just the other day someone could see it as historic? Metro and the PSNI working together?" he asked. "Now's your chance to show London what you've got."

It was Darcy's turn to hesitate as he thought through McDermott's comment. "Sergeant, contact the watch supervisor at Musgrave and get his schedule. We'll see what we can muster for a surveillance team."

"Mister Darcy, I don't want to push, but I'm keen to find where this Connelly fella's home might be," McDermott said. "I'll be asking for a summons to search his residence once I've finished going through his office."

"Sir, you've a packet from London on your desk," the secretary said.

"Thank you, Noreen," Darcy said as he strolled into his office. Grabbing the envelope, he sat behind his desk where he pulled out a flick knife from his drawer, and slit it open.

"Odd to see a police chief blatantly courting a felony for an illegal weapon," McDermott noted, seeing the switchblade in Darcy's possession. "A souvenir from your youth, I take it?"

"It was my father's, just so you know," Darcy replied. "He brought it back from Germany after the war." He turned the knife to show the inspector the Schutzstaffel symbol for the German military unit. "He was part of the 7th Dragoons who fought at Armen."

"Then he certainly earned it after those campaigns," McDermott said. "Now, back to this Connelly fella. His secretary confirmed taking a call from one of our suspects. Our problem is Connelly's calls with the others was most likely done by mobile phone, and I've no had a chance to look it over."

"And getting your hands on the phone would let you look at the call log," Darcy said as he slid out a folder from the overnight envelope. Glancing at the cover page, he held it out for McDermott. "This is for you."

With a puzzled look, McDermott took the folder from the Irishman. He flipped it open and saw the letter from Chief Superintendent Collingsworth. "Seems I've got my summons for the remaining assets for Callaghan and Higgins Ltd. Hold on to these will you, Giles?" he asked, handing the folder to the sergeant.

"So, you're off to Dublin now?"

"We've no motor for the trip," McDermott replied, embarrassed for not planning past his time in Belfast. Feigning a cough, he glanced at the senior official. "Eh... you wouldn't happen to have a spare we could borrow for a day or two, would you?"

Darcy chuckled at the request. "I'll see Sergeant Kennedy gets you to the airport. You can rent one from one of the outfits," he said. "I'm sure the Yard can pay you back on your expense account."

Embarrassed, McDermott bid the senior officer good day and walked out of the office where Sergeant Kennedy was waiting for the two Scotsman. "Seems you're to drop us off at the airport, Sergeant," McDermott said, strolling past him.

While McDermott was securing a rental at the airport, Michael Connelly sat alone in a spare office of Callaghan and Higgins' office in Dublin. Pulling out his cell phone, he scrolled through the numbers until he found the transport firm in Limerick to negotiate the movement of a container from the processing center to a warehouse outside of Donegal.

Connelly's next call was to his associate Kurt VanHoorst to delay the shipment from South Africa. Once again, he scrolled to the number and selected it. As he waited for it to make the connection, he went to the door and locked it to insure this call wouldn't be interrupted. After five rings, someone finally answered his call.

"Gazelle Transport; how can I direct your call?" the woman answered in Afrikaans.

"This is Mister Higgins. I'd like to speak with Mister VanHoorst," Michael answered in clipped Afrikaans.

There was a brief pause on the other end as the woman hesitated. "Excuse me, sir, but did you say your name was Monsieur Higgins?"

"Yes, Mister Higgins from Belfast."

"One moment, sir," the woman replied as she stared at the two blinking lights on her phone.

Just then, the arms dealer VanHoorst entered the office, shaking the rain from his hat. "What's line is Mister Higgins on, Hannah?"

"Both," she answered pointing to the flashing lights. "But I believe the man on line three is your colleague," she added, "only because his accent sounds more genuine."

Confused, VanHoorst hovered his hand over the phone. "Are you sure?"

"I'm not entirely positive," Hannah replied with a shake of her head. "But the first caller sounded... how can I put it... He was more articulate when I answered. And he sounded surprised, too," she added. "Oh, and this other man asked to speak with my supervisor, not you by name as usual."

The arms dealer picked up the phone and selected the line.

"This is Kurt, how can I help you?"

The tone of the South African caught Michael Connelly off-guard as he listened to his associate answer. "Kurt, it's Michael Connelly. Did I catch you at a bad time?" he asked in Afrikaans.

Hearing the Irishman address him in his native language eased VanHoorst fears for the moment. "Michael, does anyone else have this number?" When questioned, he briefly explained what his secretary had relayed to him.

"Of course not," Connelly said. Then the realization struck him as his face turned ashen with the memory of Scotland Yard's visit to his office. Getting to his feet, he paced the office staring out the window but not seeing the city below. Connelly's mind raced. "Wait... it might be someone has the number besides myself. Kurt... it's possible the authorities have it."

The Afrikaner's face reddened with anger. "How, Michael?"

Over the next few minutes, Connelly told his associate what he surmised had happened, from the trial of the police sergeant in Aberdeen and the disappearance of his lawyer through the recent visit by Scotland Yard inspectors. "It's possible the police have gotten your number as part of their investigation."

"So, this other Higgins who called, he could be with the police?" VanHoorst asked. "And by calling, they now have the alias for the company fronting my operations." His voice rose in anger. "You're a good man, Michael, but you're not my only customer you know," he reminded him, getting the discussion back to business. "If I'm forced to choose, I'll protect myself by any means."

"I understand, Kurt," Connelly said, leaning his head against the cool surface of glass.

"I'll handle this," the arms dealer said. "And when I'm done, I'll contact you when I'm ready to continue our discussion on our current transaction," as Kurt ended the call.

Connelly stood silent in the Dublin office, staring at his cell phone after the call disconnected. He could understand the South African and his desire to maintain his anonymity since he'd done the same operating his criminal activities. The sound of someone grasping the door handle brought his attention back to his current issues. Stepping to the door, he flipped the latch and pulled it open.

"I'm sorry, Mister Connelly," a young man said. "Ah... Mister Callaghan would like to see you in his office when you're free."

"Would that be Roan Callaghan?"

"Yes, it would be. I'm sorry for not clarifying."

While Michael Connelly returned to meet with Roan, in his South African warehouse, Kurt VanHoorst turned his attention to the blinking light on his secretary's phone. "I'll take this call in my office, Hannah," he told her before walking into the back room.

As he swung his chair around, VanHoorst settled into it, easing his brawny frame against the back. Groaning in protest, the chair came to rest as he leaned towards the phone. Punching the button, he began the conversation. "Hello?"

In Aberdeen, Inspector Fletcher was surprised at the respondent being male after a woman initially answered his call. "Whom do I have the pleasure of speaking with?" he asked, twirling his pencil.

VanHoorst grinned. *Time for a little cat and mouse*, he sensed. "This is the foreman for Gazelle Transport," he said. "Who am I speaking with, if you don't mind answering," he added.

Fletcher hesitated for a brief second before answering. "My name is Mister Higgins."

"Mister Higgins is it?" VanHoorst said. "What is it you want, sir? You have a product needing moved? Maybe some furniture or office equipment?"

"I've products needing transported from Marseille, France to Dublin, Ireland," Fletcher replied, going along with the information from their investigation.

VanHoorst sat up in his chair. He knew his associate had dealt with the French in the past, so hearing of the location only heightened his suspicions of the caller's intent. "My trucks don't travel that far. I recommend you contact another provider," he said, ending the call before it really began.

Fletcher slammed the phone down in disgust. "I knew I pushed it too hard," he stammered as the constable from communications walked in. "Was I on long enough to establish a trace?"

"We lost the signal just after they passed it from Lagos, Nigeria, sir," the officer said.

"Africa?"

"Yes, sir, it went through an exchange there before it pinged in Nairobi and then went dead."

"All right," Fletcher said, hanging his head in defeat. "Give everyone my thanks for making the attempt. Make sure when you're done cataloguing it, there's an extra copy for my report," he added, sweeping his hand over his face.

Fletcher closed his eyes, trying to envision what type of scheme the Irishman would have with a firm somewhere in Africa. With a kick of his foot, he spun his chair around, eyes still closed in thought.

"You'll make yourself sick doing that," a familiar voice exclaimed.

"You can always hop on and join me," Fletcher answered as he stopped spinning and looked up at his companion Sheila Gordon. "Or better yet, we'll buy one for the apartment," he added with a smirk.

"Aye, we could. Are you ready for lunch?"

"In a minute," the inspector said. Taking the folder with his notes on the call he'd just made, he slid the lot into his desk drawer and locked it for safekeeping. Before he could grab his jacket, the phone rang.

"PS Aberdeen, Inspector Gordon," Sheila said, grabbing the call.

Sitting in the rental car heading to Dublin, Fletcher's partner McDermott was surprised to hear the woman's voice answer. "Aye you can, hen," he said. "Put your better half on if he's decent."

"You're awfully cheeky this morning," she said, handing the phone to Fletcher. "It's Conor."

Fletcher took the phone. "Morning, Conor. Did you manage to get the packet from Mister Collingsworth?"

247

"Aye, we've got it," McDermott said before filling him in on their current effort with Michael Connelly. "Once I get Chief Darcy's information on Connelly's home, I'll need you to have another summons prepared to have it searched."

"Anything else?"

"Aye, you're a better driver than Sergeant Giles by a hair," he chided the constable as he maneuvered them closer to Dublin. "But not by much mind you."

"He's in fine tune," Fletcher said after hanging up the phone. Looking at his companion, he picked up his sport coat and motioned towards the doorway. "Now, what's for lunch?"

Chapter THIRTY-THREE

Dublin, Ireland

Michael Connelly sat across from Roan Callaghan as the CEO spoke on the phone. He hated hearing half the conversation, but was happy to know the executive was talking with his Garda informant.

"Yes, I'm sure we submitted the information in error," Callaghan said apologetically. "Yes, and I'm well aware your assets are being used based on a false report, but I'm certain it's not the first time it occurred."

Connelly listened as the conversation drug on. The more Roan talked to the officer, the more it sounded like he was also covering for previous transactions. Or more important, a future one. *He's apologizing to this officer like he's insuring him he'll still get paid*, he reasoned. If he was using Liam as the scapegoat, I'd say he's the one being sought after.

"Thank you, officer, I'll be in touch," the CEO said before ending the call. Turning to face Connelly, he noticed a smile which made him uncomfortable as the younger man settled back in his chair with exaggerated casualness. "Your man will be released within the hour."

"How much will this cost you?" Connelly asked. With Roan, it was always money being the symbol of his place in society. Losing it was more painful than a kick in the balls, and Connelly knew it.

"For the sake of conversation, a month's pay for one of your technicians," Callaghan said, picking up his coffee mug but noticing it was empty. He knew the cost was twice what he mentioned to Connelly because the Garda official in immigrations wanted an extra 5,000 euros. A "penalty fee." he called it.

"Well then, it seems one of your contacts is getting greedy and you offered up my manager," Connelly replied. "Just how many of these 'technicians' have you brought in illegally just to increase the company's bottom line?"

"It's not the number mind you. It's who was brought in," Callaghan said. "One of the technicians recruited in Hong Kong turns out to be an agent for the Chinese government," he admitted, explaining how the Garda constable approached him.

Connelly sipped at a glass of water, collecting his thoughts. There were nearly a dozen chemists and technicians who worked at the facility fitting that description. Of the Asians working, more specifically those of Chinese descent, it involved two in developing his hashish cocktail. "It appears you've just offered me a seat on the board," he said with a smug look on his face. "That is... if you want me to keep quiet about our discussion."

Callaghan felt his body become tense at the statement. As his blood pressure rose, the heat flushed through his body, pushing droplets of sweat to his brow. "You'll want to leave and meet your man at immigration," he said, standing behind his desk. "And don't forget, I'm the one with a friend in Garda... not you."

While Michael Connelly was in discussions with Roan Callaghan about the immigration issues, two men stepped out of their rental car outside the office building. As one man grabbed a knapsack from the backseat, the other unfolded a tourist's map to identify landmarks to their location.

"Do you think Gregory trusts the woman too much?" Hector Pichon asked his partner.

Louis Clement looked up from the map. "Gregory does nothing without careful thought," he said. "And he made a good argument for tracking this man down if he's responsible for nearly losing the *Bonaparte* to the Royal Navy."

"I'm more interested in seeing if this was the coward who broke from our code," Pichon said as he hefted the knapsack onto his shoulder. "Besides, we can't hand this Irishman over to just anyone, you know. Do you think Gregory can contact someone in Castelnaudary?" That was the French Foreign Legion training site southeast of Toulouse.

"Let's find the man before we worry ourselves about getting him to 'The Farm,'" Clement replied, glancing at the high-rise buildings that dotted the landscape of downtown Dublin. "According to the woman's information, the office is this way," he explained, pointing west along the River Liffey.

As the two Frenchmen approached the building where Michael Connelly was located, the Irishman was just leaving the office of Roan Callaghan. He returned to the spare office, knowing he'd have a short drive to the immigration center where Liam was being held. His concern wasn't just Liam though; it was also on which of the Chinese was the agent for their country.

As Connelly closed the door behind him, he marched to the stairwell, looking up and down the hallway to ensure no one saw him leaving. he quickly trotted down the four flights of stairs and stopped short of the exit to catch his breath. Glancing outside, his only concern was two women smoking in the designated spot for employees near a park bench.

With a tug on his jacket and a sweep of his hand through his hair, Michael Connelly stepped out of the building and strolled towards his car. He pulled the keys to his Jaguar out to unlock the driver's door just as he noticed another car pull into a spot in the adjoining aisle across from him.

"Damn it... if that's not Connelly," Conor McDermott exclaimed as Sergeant Giles pulled their rental into the parking space. "What the hell is he doing here ahead of us? Marcus, get on your phone and give the Garda a call; I'm thinking we'll need them," addressing the sergeant. He got out of the car and waved. "Mister Connelly... so happy to see you again."

Connelly froze. He contemplated fleeing the scene, but knew it would only complicate matters. "I work for the company," he said, "so why wouldn't I be here. Aren't you outside your jurisdiction anyway, Inspector?"

McDermott walked up to the Irishman while Sergeant Giles stood to the side. "London's been busy," he said, holding out the summons. "And besides, I've only had the pleasure of seeing your private office in Belfast, not the proper company spaces." While the inspector and the executive faced off in the car park, two spectators took in the scene from nearby.

"You think one of them is the police?" Hector Pichon asked.

Louis Clement studied the three men closely before he answered. "Two of them might be. One of the men facing the other is the senior man and the other standing to the side is his partner," he guessed, pointing out McDermott and Giles. "But the other man... I'm not sure of."

Pichon studied the Scotsman from his vantage point. The disheveled appearance of the Scotland Yard inspector tugged at his memory, but the appearance of Sergeant Giles was a mystery. "If I didn't know better..." he muttered under his breath.

"What is it?" his companion asked.

"The one in the potato-skin looking coat, I think he's the one we saw in Aberdeen," Pichon said, recalling the events when he and his partner Pasqual Sequin eliminated Angus Dunbar. "He was on the dock directing the other officers."

"And the other one, was he there too?"

Pichon shook his head. "No, this officer's partner was well-dressed. Almost like a bank executive, not a policeman. All the others were in uniform, some with weapons, but most didn't carry one."

As the Frenchmen exchanged views on the officers, Connelly stepped closer to this car. "You must excuse me, Inspector, I've an appointment to keep," he started, pulling the driver's door open and stepping behind the wheel. "And besides, I'm sure you'll find someone inside willing to give you a grand tour."

McDermott grabbed the door, keeping it open. "Aye, I'm sure some poor fella or lass could show me about, but you're the executive here. You don't want to be rude twice in one day now, do you?" He pulled the door against the stop, waiting for Connelly to exit.

The Frenchmen kept their distance while watching the exchange before Clement spoke. "The one in the field coat is someone of authority, if you're right, Hector. But what does that make the other man?"

"It's too bad we didn't get a picture from the woman," Pichon said, shifting the pack onto his other shoulder. "So, now what? If those two are police, we'll be lucky to have any time to ask about this character Connelly we're looking for."

Just then, two police cars pulled into the car park. The three men turned when they noticed the Battenburg-marked vehicles, their markings reminiscent of Curacao liquor and Meyer lemons, entering the car park. With a wave, Giles motioned them towards where he stood while McDermott and Michael Connelly remained next to the Irishman's car.

One officer slipped out of the lead vehicle and approached Sergeant Giles. "I'm Garda Inspector Quinn. Did you make the call?"

"Aye," Giles replied. "Sergeant Marcus Giles of Police Scotland," he answered, showing his identification to the Irish officer. "The chief inspector there," he started, pointing to McDermott, "and I are serving a summons on this business. And that gent is a possible suspect." He pointed to Michael Connelly.

Quinn strolled over to the Jaguar sedan where McDermott and Connelly had been talking. The inspector let out a low whistle as he admired the vintage car. "She's a beauty," he said, extending his hand over the rear fender, hesitant to touch the metal. While two officers held their position near Sergeant Giles, the officer who drove with Quinn approached the trio.

"You've identification, gentlemen?" the Garda officer asked as he pulled his notepad out.

McDermott stepped aside from the car before flipping his field coat open, not wanting to nick the paint job. In a brief second, he displayed his holstered sidearm to the Irish officer while extracting his identification.

Before he could yell an alarm to his fellow officers, Quinn saw the crested stamp on McDermott's identification papers of the Metropolitan Police in London. "You're a fair bit off your grounds, aren't you..." he asked, examining the Scotsman's information, "McDermott."

"And you are...?" McDermott asked, pulling back his papers.

"Garda Inspector Patrick Quinn," the Irishman replied, producing his own identification for McDermott. "And I suppose you've proof you're here on official means."

"Aye..." McDermott said with a wave towards his partner. "Marcus, give us the summons will you. You see, Inspector, I'm in the middle of an investigation and this good fellow," he pointed to Connelly, "was just preparing to show us about his office."

Connelly stood opposite of McDermott. Opening his wallet, he pulled his license out for Quinn to examine. As the Garda inspector glanced between the photo and the man before him, he appeared to be satisfied.

"You've done a bit of travelling to be here, Mister Connelly. Whiteabbey? Isn't that just north of Belfast?" he asked as he noticed the location of his residence.

"Just a bit, Inspector," Connelly replied, shoving his license back into his wallet.

Giles handed the folder to McDermott, who gave it to Quinn. The Garda officer scanned the document, glancing up at Connelly every few seconds. "Says here your part of Callaghan and Higgins Limited; is this true?" he asked, nodding towards the Irishman from Belfast.

As Connelly was preparing to discuss his role with the company, Roan Callaghan appeared through the side door and approached the trio next to the Jaguar. Connelly stopped his explanation as Callaghan drew closer.

"Seems they have delayed you, Michael," he said.

"And you are...?" McDermott asked ahead of the Garda inspector.

The Irishman tilted his head slightly hearing the highland accent come from the inspector. "Roan Callaghan," he started, offering his hand. "I'm the Chief Executive Officer for Callaghan and Higgins Limited. And you are not from around here, are you?"

As he pulled his identification out for the second time, McDermott introduced himself. "I'm Chief Inspector Conor McDermott of Scotland Yard. And I'm here to serve this summons as part of an investigation," he explained, holding up the folder.

Callaghan turned to the Garda inspector. "And you?"

"Garda Inspector Patrick Quinn, sir."

The growing group of men in the car park had caught the attention of the company staff, and quite a few had come outside to see what was happening. The chirping of a cell phone caught everyone by surprise. Embarrassed, Sergeant Giles turned away as he answered the call.

"If you'll indulge me for a few moments, I must have my solicitor present to review your summons," Callaghan said, looking at McDermott. "And while we're waiting, Michael and I can discuss the protocol for your search."

"Excuse me, Chief Inspector," Giles said, approaching the men still conversing around the Jaguar. "I've a message from Aberdeen for you... in private," he explained, holding up his cell phone.

"Excuse me for a moment. Oh..., Mister Callaghan is it? It's best you call on your barrister; you and your staff might need representation." He strolled over to the sergeant and turned his back to the others. "What is it, Marcus?"

"Inspector Fletcher received information on the container," Giles said. "The numbers were genuine enough, and they came up on a manifest here in Dublin. And this was the registered destination point when leaving the docks." He pointed to the address for the Callaghan and Higgins lab facility in Limerick.

"Keep it to yourself for the time being, lad," McDermott said. "I want to see what we're told by this Callaghan fella before we arrest Connelly. But..." he tapped on the sergeant's notepad, "be ready to pass this to Inspector Quinn so we can have the Garda's help."

Chapter THIRTY-FOUR

The jet touched down at Ireland's Shannon Airport just after two o'clock. The pair of officers from Aberdeen stood quickly as the plane parked at the terminal, wanting to avoid the rush of passengers during the exit. Striding up the jetway, Inspector Fletcher protected his arm from the harried business-types pushing past him.

"I'm surprised Mister MacCallum agreed to let me join you," Inspector Gordon said, following her companion towards the rental car kiosks.

"I requested you come along because if we find this container, you'll need to get samples for the investigation," Fletcher replied. "And I will not wait for someone to process things through normal channels."

"So, Inspector Fletcher, what's our first step going to be, sir?" she giggled, her demeanor mocking his senior officer status.

Andrew stopped in front of the men's room near baggage claim. "I need to pee," he exclaimed, handing her his satchel. After a few minutes, he returned grabbing the bag from her shoulder. "Do you need a minute to yourself?"

"Best I do it now is that what you're saying?" she teased, handing over her bag and purse for Andrew to hold. After what seemed like ten long minutes, Sheila returned.

"You get lost?"

"I can't stand next to some bloke at the trough like you," Sheila replied. "And there are only so many stalls. Not to mention the mothers and their wee bairns in a trolley."

After standing in line for nearly thirty minutes, the two inspectors secured a rental car and were soon making their way towards their hotel in Limerick. The countryside passing by was postcard perfect with a hodge-podge of stone walls separating the farmland. In the distant hills, they could see herds of sheep and cattle grazing.

"This place looks beautiful, but it's got nothing on the Highlands," Sheila said, taking in the scenery. "I mean its nae flat mind you, it's just that, well... it's all rolling hills and turf."

"Enjoy it while you can; we'll be busy shortly," Andrew replied, watching the GPS unit on the dashboard lead them to the hotel. "As soon as we check in, we'll need to get to the facility and start looking for the shipping container."

"And what if the box is nae there, then what?" Sheila asked.

Andrew had considered this on the flight, but didn't want to dwell on the possibility. "If that is the case, then we'll search their records to find out where it went to next," he said. "According to the records on file, this is the only lab in operation Connelly would have access to."

"And what about getting help from the local officers?"

He glanced between the road and his companion. "I guess we'll stop there beforehand to let them know we're here and what we're doing." Conor would have considered it, he told himself.

Sheila pulled her cell phone out to search for their hotel and the closest station. "There's a Garda post just around the corner from the inn," she said, turning the screen so Andrew could see it.

At the same time as Inspectors Fletcher and Gordon were making their way to Limerick, Chief Inspector McDermott and Sergeant Giles were searching the office of Michael Connelly. They did this under the watchful eyes of Callaghan's lawyer, who was still confused as to the reason for the summons.

"Nothing, Inspector," Giles said, slamming closed another file cabinet drawer.

McDermott shut the last of the desk drawers he had searched. "Aye, it's rather mundane, he replied. "Almost as if he knew we'd come looking," he muttered under his breath. "I'd like a word with Mister Callaghan and Connelly, if you please." He gestured to the young secretary made available to oversee the search with the lawyer.

"It might help if you'd let me know what you're after," Inspector Quinn said from the corner as he watched. "Some of these folks will go home soon, and you won't be able to question them if the need arises, you know."

McDermott thrust his hands firmly on his hips as he surveyed the room. *Connelly doesn't come here often*, he thought.

"Mister Callaghan is waiting in the boardroom inspector," the young woman said, hanging up the phone. "If you'll just follow me."

In moments, someone showed the three police officers and lawyer into the expansive room. It was situated with comfortable chairs around an oblong table while glasses and pitchers of ice water sat on a teak tray in the center. Sitting at the head was Roan Callaghan, his fingers fluttering nimbly as if he was playing a sonnet. "Did you find what you were looking for, Inspector?"

McDermott strolled to the head of the table. "No... no I didn't," he said as his eyes scanned the room. "Where's Connelly? I asked him to be present."

"He went to the men's room," Callaghan said. "He'll be back in a minute."

"He's nae privileged to use yours?" he asked, pointing to the door behind the executive.

"Even executives like to mingle with the workers," Callaghan replied nonchalantly.

McDermott looked at the Garda inspector. "Quinn, have two of your men search the building and look for Mister Connelly," he directed. "Make sure they look in every room, too." Gesturing to his partner, he added, "Marcus, you go with them. Find out where he's at and bring him here, to me."

Once the Scotland Yard inspector requested his presence in the boardroom, Michael Connelly knew he needed to avoid being questioned in front of Roan. Feigning the need to use the men's room, he was soon stepping outside the building. Glancing around, he noticed the Garda officers sitting in their car, but facing in the opposite direction of his Jaguar.

In a slow trot, Connelly got to his car and was soon sliding behind the wheel and heading onto the roadway. His departure went unnoticed by the Irish police, but not by the two former Legionnaires who'd been waiting outside.

"Where do you think he's going?" Louis Clement asked his friend.

"I'm not sure, but he's in a hurry," Hector Pichon replied as he pulled their rental car into traffic to follow the Irishman. Keeping their eyes on the vintage sedan wouldn't be a problem as most of the vehicles on the road lacked the style of a Jaguar. As he entered the M7 expressway, Hector noticed they were heading west. "If he keeps heading away, we'll miss our rendezvous," he muttered.

"I'm still waiting for Gregory's call," Louis replied. He knew they only way to see their target returned to France was by avoiding the use of commercial airlines. Their partner Gregory Arsenault was calling in a favor to make things easier for Louis and Hector.

With Connelly and the two Frenchman on their way to Limerick, Sergeant Giles and the Garda officers returned to the boardroom. Here they found Inspectors McDermott and Quinn waiting with Roan Callaghan. "Chief Inspector," Giles announced entering the room, "Connelly's not on the premises."

McDermott turned to Callaghan, who sat without emotion or reaction to the statement. "Your man is a suspect in my investigation, and in his absence, I'm going to consider you an accessory to his actions. Inspector Quinn, we need to locate Mister Connelly. Can you have the stations put out an announcement to the Roads Policing units for the Jaguar?"

"I can have it done straight away," Quinn replied. "What's the charge he's violating, though?"

"He's wanted for drug trafficking and accessory to at least one, if not two murders in Aberdeen," the chief inspector announced. This caused Callaghan and his lawyer to approach the Scotland Yard inspector.

"You've proof to those accusations?" Callaghan asked. In the back of his mind, Roan was struggling to determine how he could use this information to his advantage. *If Michael is the target, then I can sway the Garda's investigation away from me,* he told himself.

"It's part of the summons," the corporations lawyer said. "But why hasn't Mister Connelly been apprehended before now, Inspector? If he's your prime suspect, and you haven't seen fit to detain him, I could argue in sessions your tactics were entrapment."

"You'll both receive a full explanation when Connelly is found and detained," McDermott said, walking out of the boardroom. "Sergeant Giles, get the car ready."

With knowledge Connelly fled the building, McDermott considered what the Irishman's next step might be. As he caught up with Garda Inspector Quinn, he pulled the officer aside. "Quinn, how far is it from here to Limerick?"

"Oh, about two, maybe a two-and-a-half-hour drive depending on the amount of traffic leaving Dublin, why?"

McDermott explained the theory he and Inspector Fletcher had pieced together regarding Connelly's involvement in the drug trafficking case. "If I had to wager a few quid, it's possible he's headed there," McDermott finished.

Quinn looked at his watch. "He's had a thirty-minute head start. I'll see if the Traffic units have anything on him. And I'll see if they can scan the CCTV along the way too."

McDermott marched up to the rental where Sergeant Giles sat waiting for him. "Marcus, you've got the address to the lab site, don't you?" he asked after opening the door.

"Aye, they listed it on the summons," he replied, opening the folder.

Quinn trotted up to the rental car where McDermott and Giles were. "Central just identified a late-model Jaguar heading west on the M7," he said. "They saw it on CCTV passing a turnoff for entering Johnstown."

"How far ahead is he?"

"Oh, nearly 35 kilometers at best," Quinn replied. "My superintendent said I'm to assist as needed. It'd be best if you want, I'll lead and you can follow behind."

"Aye, let's go before its tae dark to see," McDermott answered, closing the door.

With Garda Inspector Quinn leading, McDermott and Giles followed as they entered the motorway and headed out of Dublin. With blue and yellow markings, it was easy to track the Garda sedan, its flashing lights allowing them to proceed through the traffic with little fanfare as drivers yielded to them.

Sergeant Giles kept his attention on the Garda vehicle as he glanced at CI McDermott sitting across from him. "What do you think he's going for, this fella Connelly?" he asked, breaking the silence.

McDermott turned slightly in his seat before answering. "I'm nae sure, Marcus," he said. "I've been trying to piece this together to see his motivation, but nothing fits."

"According to Captain Duncan, the container was loaded with at least fifteen to twenty-thousand kilos," he explained, recalling his arrest of the seaman from the Nordic Supplier. "That's a lot of dope to be sitting around."

"What if this Connelly fella is using the company to make his own? And this is just a wee starter for him until he's got his brew ready?"

Before McDermott could answer, Giles's cell phone chirped with an incoming message. Digging it out of his pocket, he handed it to McDermott. "See who it's from if you do nae mind," as he kept his focus on the road ahead.

Conor slid the device open and was greeted with three blanks fields. "What's your access code?"

"Oh, sorry. It's zero-zero-seven," the sergeant replied.

McDermott chuckled at the officer's use of the movie icon's signature moniker for his security code. "Fancy yourself a spy-type, do you, Marcus?" The screen changed, and it revealed the message.

"It had more to do with a young lass telling me I resembled Sir Sean Connery a few years back," Giles replied. "I even had the movie score as a ringtone when she called," he chuckled.

"Well, for the moment, we'll just have you act like Constable Sergeant Giles of Police Scotland and not some agent for the Crown," McDermott said with a grin. "Concentrate on the motorway and don't mind the snoring," He leaned against the window as they continued following the Garda towards Limerick.

Chapter THIRTY-FIVE

Limerick, Ireland

The production facility was a stark contrast against the rolling emerald hills, the buildings for Callaghan and Higgins Ltd. spanned three football pitches in width. Clouds obscured the sunshine or the white-painted concrete would have blinded the four officers as they exited their cars near the shipping entrance.

"Inspector Fletcher, exactly what are we looking for again?" Garda officer Burke asked.

"We're searching for a 12-meter container," Fletcher replied.

"Amongst all these?" the officer exclaimed, waving his hand across the lot dotted with over thirty containers of various size and color.

"It won't take long if we split up." Inspector Gordon tore a slip of paper from her notepad. "Here's the number of the container we're looking for," she explained, handing a slip to the two Garda officers.

"And what are we doing when we find it?" the second Garda officer asked.

Fletcher hadn't considered how they would keep the container secured once if they found it. His first concern was hoping to find it with the drugs still inside. "I'll look for your superintendent to help us when that time comes," he said. "Until then... let's find it first, shall we."

"We better move on it; one of those might be here to transport the box," Burke pointed out. "Sean, get someone from the office to hold those fellas from taking their loads," he directed.

While the Garda officer went into the facility, the other three spread out and searched through the trailers with the shipping containers loaded on them. As each of them approached a trailer, they quickly read off the numbers stenciled on the side.

As Inspector Fletcher stepped around one trailer, he saw one lorry backing up against an empty trailer. Soon, he noticed an industrial lift truck, its orange safety strobe flashing in the fading light, make its way towards the end of the facility. Looking off to his left against the building, he saw a container resting on the pavement.

The roar of the lorry echoed off the building as the driver backed against the trailer, a loud crash-like sound announcing the hitch and fifth-wheel making contact. The lift truck was now positioned along the side of the container, its driver seen talking on his radio.

Inspector Fletcher abandoned his search and trotted towards the lone shipping container and the lift truck. A squeal of metal against metal pierced the surrounding area as long forks of the lift truck slid into pockets of the container. With a rumble from its engine and smoke bellowing from beneath, the lift truck strained as it picked up the box.

"Hey, hold off there," Fletcher screamed above the din while quickening his pace. Approaching the vehicle, he waved his arms, attracting the operator's attention for the moment. He waved his hand to motion for the box to be lowered.

"What the hell's going on?" came a voice from behind the inspector.

Fletcher turned and came face to face with a member of the facilities shipping department, escorted by the Garda officer. "Who are you?"

"John Casey; I'm the evening supervisor," he said.

Pulling his ID from his coat, Fletcher introduced himself. "I've a summons to search these facilities," he explained, holding up the court papers. Looking at the shipping box, he held up his slip with the written number from their CCTV image. It matched. "And I'm going to begin with this box."

Inspector Gordon and the other Garda officer heard Fletcher and made their way to where he now stood. "What's wrong, Andrew?" she asked, stepping next to her companion. "We heard you shouting from across the yard."

"This is it," he said with a point to the container.

"Officer Burke, this is now a crime scene," Inspector Gordon explained, pulling a pair of gloves from her pocket. "See we have space cordoned off for at least thirty meters," she directed. Walking around to the end, she noticed the door held a lock and security seal. "Andrew, these numbers don't match the manifest."

"Do you have the key?" Fletcher asked looking at Casey.

"There in the office," he replied.

"Officer Burke, if you'll be so kind as to escort Mister Casey to his office and retrieve the keys," Fletcher said. "Inspector Gordon and I will prepare the area." He pulled a mobile phone from Sheila's purse.

"Calling Conor?"

"No, Sergeant Giles. You know Conor doesn't carry a mobile with him," Fletcher replied searching for the constable's number. Looking up at the lift operator, he added, "You can go get a cup of tea; this won't be getting loaded anytime soon."

While Garda Officer Burke retrieved keys for the container, his partner Sean returned to their car to grab two rolls of plastic crime scene tape to secure the immediate area. As word spread through the facility, a handful of the chemists and technicians gathered outside. Amongst them were Dr. Yang and her assistant Xi Feng.

"This doesn't look good," Yang said.

"I'm all for leaving if you think we should," Xi replied nervously as she noticed several more approaching police vehicles. "We've gotten enough information on their formulas to satisfy Peking, don't we?"

Yang glanced at her associate. Her plan wasn't to return to China when the assignment was complete; she wanted to work without the scrutiny of the government's oversight. "I need to grab my tablet and the flash drive; you meet me at the car," she said as she headed back to the facility.

The two Chinese women were not the only ones interested in the police activity. Michael Connelly was making his way towards the car park when he saw the first police vehicle. "Bloody hell, how did they get here ahead of me?" he remarked, steering the Jaguar away.

Several cars behind him, the two former Legionnaires Clement and Pichon noticed their target passing the facility's entrance and continue down the road. "Where is he going to now, you suppose?" Pichon asked.

"Somewhere the police are not so numerous, I'd say," Clement replied, pointing out the collection of Garda vehicles now occupying an area of the parking. "And it appears they've found something of interest, too."

"What is it?"

"If I had to guess, I'd say they found the container off the *Bonaparte*," he answered, turning his attention back to Connelly and pulling his mobile phone out. "Don't lose sight of him. I'm going to call Gregory and see what he wants to do next."

As he stood next to the shipping container, Inspector Fletcher dialed Sergeant Giles's number. In the rental car, the movie-themed ring tone announced the incoming call.

"Inspector, do you mind answering?" Giles asked, handing the phone over.

Hitting the key, McDermott placed the cell phone to his ear. "Hello?"

"Conor, it's Andrew," the inspector said. "I've found the container from the CCTV images."

"Where is it?"

"Callaghan and Higgins facility in Limerick."

"How did you find that out, Andrew?"

Fletcher hesitated before answering, unsure how his senior partner would react to his presence in Ireland. "I convinced Mister MacCallum having me investigate the facility while you and Giles were in Dublin would be a good idea," he winced.

McDermott sat in silence staring out the window.

"Something wrong?" Giles asked as he followed the Garda sedan off the motorway.

"We've got our hands full, Marcus."

Returning his focus to Fletcher, McDermott directed the young officer into action. "Marcus and I are almost there. Have you contacted the Garda?"

"Yes, it was the second thing Sheila and I did after landing," Andrew answered as he saw Garda Officer Burke approaching. "Do you want me to wait for your arrival?" he asked McDermott as he motioned the Irish policeman closer.

"Aye, I want to see if this has all been worth it," McDermott said.

Within minutes of leaving the motorway, the vehicle carrying Garda Inspector Quinn pulled into the car park followed by Sergeant Giles. As the four men exited the cars, they soon were passing through the crowd and ducking under the police tape.

"Identification, gentlemen," a Garda officer asked as they neared the container.

Each of them produced their credentials. "Who's the senior man?" Quinn asked.

"That be Officer Burke," the officer answered, pointing out the Garda officer standing next to Inspector Fletcher and Gordon. Before he could thank the young man, Quinn saw McDermott striding towards the container and gathered officers.

"Fancy seeing you here," McDermott started, stepping next to his partner. "How's your arm?"

"Sore as you would imagine, but it's still attached and functional," Andrew replied as he flexed his forearm for emphasis. Turning to the Garda officer, he added, "This is Officer Burke of the Limerick station."

Garda Inspector Quinn and his partner had now joined the group. "Officer...?" he began, extending his hand out to the other Garda officer.

"Burke, sir," he returned. "Seems we've stumbled on some evidence Scotland Yard has been pursuing." He nodded to the shipping container.

McDermott walked around to the doors. "You've keys, don't you?" he asked, seeing the brass padlocks hanging from each handle. "A set of bolt-cutters or a torch will dae just as well too."

"The security seal is not the same as the one recorded in Aberdeen," Inspector Gordon explained, leaning over McDermott's shoulder and handing him a pair of latex gloves. "Someone's opened it; I'm just not sure where it was done though."

"Who had access to this?" McDermott asked as he looked at the crowd surrounding him.

"Mister Casey, can you answer Chief Inspector McDermott's question?" Gordon asked, looking at the shipping supervisor.

"The only name listed on the record is Mister Finnegan," Casey replied, holding up a clipboard. "He's been gone all day, but he should be here in the morning."

"Well, I'm nae waiting till the morn' for him to come in," McDermott said. "I'll take the keys," he determined, holding out his hand. Catching the fob holding two keys tossed by Mister Casey, the inspector selected one and slid it into the first lock. Twisting, the key held fast. Glancing up at Casey, McDermott gave the supervisor a quizzical look. "Let's hope this other key works."

"It's the only set for this box," the Irishman said.

Using the second key, the lock sprung open. McDermott pulled it off and yanked up on the handle while pulling it towards him, breaking the seal. "Here, you'll want tae bag this," he said, tossing the plastic tab at Inspector Gordon as he swung the door open to expose the contents.

"Dear God, what's that smell?" Garda Officer Burke exclaimed stepping away from the container.

McDermott took a step back while waving his hand across his face. "Seems a dead rodent found its way inside." He turned to the group behind him and held out his hand. "Who's got a torch?"

"Here you go," Garda Officer Burke replied, placing the half-meter long flashlight in his hands. "Just give it a twist."

Soon the interior was lit up with the piercing beam of light. The group of officers all peered past McDermott, trying to see what they had found. Reaching down, the inspector unlatched the opposite door and swung it open.

"We're missing a couple of boxes," McDermott announced, shining the light on the empty space in the first pallet. Pulling down a box, those closest to the Scotland Yard inspector could hear the rattle of glass bottles.

"Bottles?" Fletcher asked.

"Aye, that's what it sounds like," McDermott said. He tore open the box to expose a dozen bottles. Grabbing one, he pulled it out and shone the light at it. "And they're still full."

"I've not seen anything come into the factory like that." It was Mister Casey making a case for his lack of knowledge on the bottle's contents.

As he stood, McDermott turned to the Garda officer. "Inspector Quinn, can you have a couple of your officers assist Inspector Fletcher and Sergeant Giles? I want to know where the other two boxes are. And if they can't find the boxes, at least the bottles." He flashed the light at the space where they once were. "And we'll also need to hold all the workers until we've questioned them, too."

Garda Inspector Quinn relayed McDermott's request and watched the officers move off towards the facility entrance. Stepping next to

McDermott, the Irish policeman peered down at the open box. "What's in the bottles, anyway?"

The chief inspector glanced around before answering. "We believe a laboratory, possibly in North Africa, altered a form of hashish if it's anything like what we seized in Aberdeen. It's possible something overcomes the users with some psychotic episode depending how strong a dose they've had."

"Not a bad synopsis, Chief Inspector," a woman's voice said from behind the two men. "With your permission, I'd like to work my crime scene," Inspector Gordon announced, holding her digital camera.

McDermott and Quinn stepped aside as Inspector Gordon began her work at the container while Inspector Fletcher and Sergeant Giles led a group of Garda officers into the building. Bypassing the administrative offices, they pushed through a series of double doors that led to a manufacturing center where technicians and specialists stood by their machinery.

The hum of hydraulic pumps and hissing air from pneumatic presses greeted them as they watched batches of powder transform into pills. Off to one side, inspecting stations were in temperature-controlled cubicles next to each machine.

Fletcher divided the officers into pairs. "We're looking for any instance of the bottles or the boxes they came in," he said, grabbing a box of gloves from the wall of an inspection cubicle. "Make sure you wear these before handling them."

Passing through another larger set of swinging doors, Inspector Fletcher and Garda Officer Burke soon found themselves in the open and well-lit warehouse portion of the facility. Highly polished concrete floors with painted lines delineated walking paths showed the way amongst the floor to ceiling shelving.

"We're supposed to be looking for a few jugs of wine in all this?" Burke asked, staring at rows of crates.

"It won't be wine in the bottles if we find any," Fletcher said as he walked down an aisle of pharmaceutical products.

Chapter THIRTY-SIX

As he sped past the production campus along the motorway, the facility growing smaller in his rearview mirror, Michael Connelly cursed at his run of misfortune. "First Gilmore disappears, then the inspectors from Scotland Yard show up," he uttered to the empty passenger seat. "Then Callaghan has the stones to accuse me of problems with the workers he supplied."

As if on cue, the engine of the British sedan sputtered for the moment. "Oh, hell," he exclaimed, looking at the petrol gauge. "I've not considered filling this since I left Belfast." Another shudder shook the car as the engine misfired. Straining to see ahead in the growing darkness, Connelly suddenly felt abandoned.

"Is he slowing down?" Hector Pichon asked his companion.

"A large sedan like that has a big engine which means terrible fuel economy," Louis Clement replied as his cell phone rang. Noticing his partner's number on the screen, he answered, "Hello Gregory, what good news do you have for us?"

"He's getting off the motorway," Pichon interrupted, tapping Clement's arm.

"Follow him," he instructed before returning his attention to the caller.

Connelly nursed the sedan through a roundabout as he left the motorway. A faded sign showed a petrol station a half-kilometer ahead, which provided him a glimmer of hope. "Come on," he exclaimed, urging the Jaguar forward. As he drew nearer, any hope of continuing his escape faded. In the distance, he saw the station under the glow of a single street lamp, fencing set around the perimeter. The two Frenchmen stayed behind and watched the scenario unfold.

"It's bloody abandoned," Connelly said, pulling the car off the road. Setting his head against the steering wheel, he closed his eyes, his mind racing at what his next step should be. The crunching of gravel brought his head up as he saw the lights of a vehicle pull up behind him.

Clement and Pichon both stepped out of their rental and approached the Jaguar. With each of them choosing a side, they could see Connelly

269

was alone. Clement motioned to his partner, providing a silent signal to watch the Irishman for weapons as he noticed the window coming down.

"Did your car break down?" Pichon asked.

Connelly glanced out the window at the man who asked the question. "It sounds silly; I didn't keep an eye on the petrol gauge and I've run out," he explained, waving towards the dashboard while keeping one hand on the steering wheel. "Do you think I can get a lift to an open petrol station?"

"We'd be more than happy to help out a fellow motorist, wouldn't we, Louis?"

By this time, Louis Clement had made his way alongside the Jaguar and could see the Irishman was unarmed. "Of course, what type of comrades would we be," he replied, signaling Pichon to act on their plan.

Pulling open the driver's door, Pichon stepped aside until Connelly was standing next to him. With the glow from the lone streetlight, it subdued the Frenchman's features and did not give the Irishman any sign of who he was dealing with.

"My name is Hector," he said, extending his hand. As the Irishman reached to accept, the Legionnaire slipped his improvised sling over the outstretched hand. In a well-rehearsed move, Pichon yanked Connelly's arm around and upward, slamming the Irishman against the sedan.

After a moment of shock and surprise, Connelly attempted to use his feet and legs to push back against the Frenchman. He kicked against his attacker's legs blindly as he tried to free himself, but the weight and leverage of Pichon was too great.

Hector's partner Clement hurried to his side. Grasping the Irishman's free hand, he drew it back in the same fashion until they placed together Connelly's palms, where Hector secured them. Clement kicked Connelly's legs out from under him, causing the Irishman to fail awkwardly to the ground.

Pulling himself up against the rear door of the Jaguar, Connelly looked at the two men, their faces still obscured as the light shone from behind them. "I wasn't aware there were still highwaymen in the Emerald Isle."

"If we had the means," the Frenchman said, "you'd find yourself heading back to France." Louis Clement leaned closer, giving Connelly a clearer idea who he was dealing with. "You broke ranks, mon ami; that's considered desertion."

Sitting in the sedan's shadow obscured the expression on Connelly's face when he heard the statement and location. It was part of his past that provided him a sense of courage to conduct his business in the manner he did. But he also became disillusioned with the Legionnaire lifestyle and demands. With the help of his friend Kurt VanHoorst, he was able to stage his desertion twenty years ago.

"What do you say, Irishman? You willing to face the tribunal for your cowardly actions in the Congo?" Pichon asked, kicking at the man's legs.

Connelly stared at the men. "You Frenchie's think you're all high and mighty with parades and that silly Kepi Blanc you wear," he said. "I knew right after leaving the Farm I could be much more than what was being offered."

"Your days of prancing around are ending," Clement said. "And we've a message you better consider." He placed the tip of his knife against Connelly's cheek, nicking the flesh just enough to draw blood. "Leave both the lawyers alone, you understand?"

Wincing under the pressure, Connelly turned his face away. "And how do you plan on protecting people you don't even know or where they are? I don't even know where my barrister is, so I know you..."

Connelly never had time to finish his statement. The blow from Louis Clement caught the Irishman against the temple, rendering him unconscious. For the next five minutes, the Frenchmen took turns leveling blows at the prone figure. None by themselves were life-threatening, but the last one from Hector Pichon would cause the Irishman the most pain.

Placing the beaten man into the backseat of the sedan, Louis Clement pulled out Connelly's cell phone and dialed the local Garda station to report the abandoned car. Sliding into the passenger seat next to Hector, he took one final glance at the Jaguar. "Let's see if we can make it back to Dublin before the pubs close," he chuckled.

While Michael Connelly was being confronted by the Frenchmen, Inspector Fletcher was being hailed by one of the Garda officers assisting in the search of the Callaghan and Higgins production facility.

"I think we've got something, Inspector," the officer exclaimed, making his way towards Fletcher.

As they entered the testing area where the drugs were inspected, the officer showed Fletcher to one cubicle near the back of the facility. "One worker we questioned mentioned seeing two technicians handling bottles in this room here."

Inspector Fletcher opened the door and stepped into the space. Two desks and two tables occupied one wall while cabinets filled with equipment beakers, flasks, and petri dishes were situated in the corner. Someone had labeled drawers under the tables for test tube holders, beaker and crucible tongs, clamps, funnels and, thermometers. On each desk were computers for recording the technicians' findings.

"After we entered and began our search, we spotted two glass bottles under the table," the officer said, pointing over Fletcher's shoulder.

The inspector walked over and knelt down to get a better look. Two bottles, their glass reminiscent of pond slime in a country garden, sat against the wall. Fletcher reached under and grasped the first one; it was empty. Reaching back, he held it out for the officer. "Place this on the table," he directed the young man.

Reaching for the second, it surprised him to find this one still contained some liquid hashish. "Be careful with this; there's still something inside." He handed it over to the officer who placed it on the table. Standing up, Fletcher looked over the items left on the tabletop. He brushed aside several papers and noticed the ones below had been written in Chinese.

"Officer, make sure no one enters this room. It's now part of the crime scene. I'll be back shortly." He walked past the Irishman, striding towards the exit to the car park.

While Inspector Fletcher was heading towards his partner McDermott and Garda Inspector Quinn, he was passed by another Garda officer, who trotted straight up to Inspector Quinn.

"There are two chemists missing," he said, addressing Quinn.

"Who are they?" McDermott asked.

The officer pulled a notebook out and flipped to the last page. "One was a doctor, Lei Yang; the other was her associate, Xi Feng. Both had been working here for the last year and a half." Fletcher heard part of the conversation and added his discovery of the bottles and notes in the inspection area.

"We're close enough to Shannon, so it's possible they've made their way out of the country by now," Quinn said, glancing at his watch.

"How do you know?" McDermott asked.

"One of the notices we've had on this firm was for bringing in workers with false documents," Quinn explained. "Our immigration staff were keeping a handful of the permanent workers under surveillance. They'd hope to catch them getting paid off or passing documents."

McDermott thought about the possibility that the stranger mentioned in the reports surrounding his niece's death might be involved. But the description and grain CCTV images didn't lend themselves to the suspect being Asian.

"Inspector Quinn, could one of your men escort me to the inspection area?" Inspector Gordon asked, interrupting the discussion on the Chinese technicians.

"I'll see she's looked after," Officer Burke pronounced, his eagerness for being present in Sheila's company a little too clear as the officer grabbed her forensics kit.

"All right, Burke," Quinn replied, a smirk on his face.

Watching the officers head into the facility, the sudden appearance of Roan Callaghan and his lawyer surprised the group next to the container as they approached with supervisor Casey following close behind.

"Why wasn't I informed about this activity?" Callaghan asked.

"You were informed," McDermott said. "The minute your lawyer reviewed the summons stating we were searching the premises under the Callaghan and Higgins moniker."

"You've no grounds to do so without my lawyer's presence," Callaghan said.

273

"Well, he's here now, so how 'bout we begin with the elements inside this shipping container?" McDermott said with a slap against the metal siding, the thump echoing inside. "What do you know of the contents?"

Callaghan blanched at the idea he would know what was inside the container. "You're a fool for even considering the idea I'd be knowledgeable of everything held in these. That was the responsibility of Mister Connelly; you'll need to ask him."

"We would if he was present," McDermott said, stepping to face the executive. "You've no heard from him since he left your office, have you?"

"No... I have not," the executive replied.

The tension between McDermott and Callaghan was easily felt amongst those standing nearby as the Scotland Yard inspector confronted the heir-apparent to the pharmaceutical firm. Each man stood his ground, confident each was right to be suspicious of the other.

In any other instance, someone could see the two coming to blows as if they were deciding a wager on a football club. But before that could happen, a young Garda officer stepped up to Inspector Quinn. "Sir, we've a message from the Roads Policing office," he said.

The officer's statement was enough to catch everyone's attention and break the tension developing between McDermott and Callaghan.

"What is it?" the Irish officer asked.

"A patrol unit found a motor fitting the description of one leaving Dublin four hours ago," the officer read. "There was one occupant, and they have transported him to University Hospital for treatment."

"Connelly?" McDermott muttered.

"What was the occupant's name?" Quinn asked.

"It wasn't given, and there was no identification on the fella either," the officer said.

"I need to get to that hospital," McDermott said to Quinn. "Sooner is better."

"What about all this?" Quinn asked, nodding his head towards the container.

The Scotland Yard inspector pointed towards his partner. "Inspector Fletcher and Inspector Gordon are in charge of this investigation here.

Your officers can assist them," he directed, pulling the car door open and sliding into the passenger seat. "Sergeant Giles can follow us to the hospital."

Chapter THIRTY-SEVEN

The operating room buzzed with activity for such a late evening. The on-call surgeon looked down at the bruised and swollen face. Shaking his head in disgust, he was amazing at the violent nature of some people. His patient tonight, Michael Connelly, would need months of recovery and several more operations after the beating he took from the parties responsible. The lead nurse continued with her prep work of the patient while a young anesthesiologist prepared to administer a sedative. A tray containing three batches of surgery tools was wheeled next to the doctor.

"Sebastian, how long do you expect getting this fellow stabilized?" the orthodontist surgeon asked as his support staff stood off to one side.

"Mending his compound fracture should take about 90 minutes if we don't find any nerve damage," the surgeon answered. "Your greatest obstacle is x-ray showing multiple fractures to his orbital structure, so I'm thinking you'll need oh, three plus hours."

"Done," the dental surgeon answered before turning to his lead nurse. "Angela, make a note; we've only four hours to reconstruct this poor fella's face. And what's the evening's entertainment going to be?"

"We've prepped a selection of the Cranberries and Corrs for everyone's listening pleasure," the lead nurse answered, turning the MP3 player and speakers on to set the mood. "And a little bit of Van Morrison for the post-op recovery."

A floor below the surgical suite, Chief Inspector McDermott and Garda Inspector Quinn were marching through the doorway of the emergency room. The Scotland Yard inspector wasted no time, heading straight to the nurse's station and cornering the first woman in uniform he saw.

Sitting behind the high counter, a young nurse was engrossed in paperwork. As the two officers approached, the phone buzzed. Grabbing the receiver, the nurse answered. "ER?" As she listened, McDermott leaned over, only to be stopped by her hand being held to his face.

With a deep breath, McDermott took a step back and waited for the call to finish. Before it could happen, another older nurse appeared from behind them and entered the workspace. "Can I help you gentlemen?" she asked.

Each of the officers introduced themselves and showed their identification. "Someone has made us aware of a patient being brought in a short time ago as a possible John Doe," Garda Inspector Quinn said. "Someone severely beat the victim when he was brought in here. And we need to see him so we can verify his identity as soon as possible."

"If you know he's a John Doe, how can you provide his identity?" the nurse asked.

"The victim is a possible suspect in my investigation," McDermott said. "I've had several face-to-face discussions, so I'm certain I'll be able to identify the patient and provide his proper name."

Turning, the nurse grabbed a chart from the table. "After someone saw him, they took the victim straight to surgery," she explained, reading the notes on the clipboard. "Your victim had a broken leg and looked to have been beaten with a hurley."

"How long will he be in surgery?" McDermott asked.

"He was wheeled in an hour ago, but I'm not going to guess how long to fix him up," the nurse answered. "You're more than welcome to wait; the sitting room is on the second floor. Step out of the lift and turn right," she said, sending the officers away from the counter.

"Come on, let's see if the folks upstairs can tell us something," McDermott said with a tug at Inspector Quinn's arm.

In moments, the two officers were standing outside the surgical suite nurse's station. The young man sitting at the counter provided them with an update they didn't want to hear. "They're just dressing his leg wound and will be starting on his face," the nurse said. "They told me the wager is less than four hours once Doctor O'Rourke begins."

"What wager?" McDermott asked. "Are you betting whether the patient survives or dies?"

"Oh..., no I'm sorry. The ER doctor and Dr. O'Rourke always have a friendly wager on the time to perform their procedures," the nurse said. "All the money goes to the Children's Fund collected for holiday parties."

"If that's the case, we've at least four hours until we can see if it's Connelly," McDermott said, collapsing on the hard-plastic chair across from the counter. He rubbed his face, the growing stubble scratching his palm. "Quinn, can you arrange for a lorry and escort to move the container?" he asked, realizing it was now evidence in his investigation.

Before the Irish officer could begin his call, his cell phone buzzed. "Quinn here," he answered. After listening for a few minutes, he passed along McDermott's request for the shipping container loaded with hashish to be moved to a Garda station.

"That was Roads dispatch," Quinn said. "They've picked up the Jaguar and brought it into town. And as you heard, they'll get a lorry to move the container." Taking a seat next to McDermott, he took out a notepad. "What do you fancy for grub? I was going to give a local pub a call for something to eat," Quinn said.

"Aye, I could use a wee bite," McDermott replied. "Can you see if they've a fish and chip platter? Make sure they no forget to add a handful of vinegar packets to the sack too."

Sitting outside the surgery area, McDermott had fallen asleep. Quinn was using his phone to chat with the other officers at Callaghan and Higgins office back in Dublin. With Scotland Yard's summons, the Garda Immigration issued their own request for a search of the premises.

Downstairs, four officers entered the emergency room. Garda Officer Burke walked over to the nurse's station and caught one texting. "Excuse me," he said tapping on the counter. "We're looking for Inspectors Quinn and McDermott."

"I directed them to surgery," the woman replied without slowing her fingers down on the phone's touch pad.

"Thanks," he replied, waving to the other three to follow him.

Entering the hallway on the second floor from the lift, they encountered Inspector Quinn with a cup of tea in each hand. "Mind your back," he said. "Everything buttoned up?"

"Yes, sir," the Garda officer replied. "We've all the interviews done, and they moved the container as you directed." As they turned the corner, they saw McDermott slouched in the chair, his head leaning against a magazine rack. The remnants of his fish and chips were still on the chair next to him.

"How long has he been asleep?" Inspector Gordon asked softly.

"Going on two and a half hours now," Quinn replied. "The nurse said the patient will be moved soon, so I figured he'd like a cup."

"You'd be better off with coffee," Inspector Fletcher said with a yawn. "Thank you for having the container moved. I'll be on the phone with London in..." he glanced at his watch, "say three hours from now to see how they wish to handle the contents." Noting the hour caused him to yawn as he realized how late it had become.

Sergeant Giles sat down across from McDermott. "He does nae sleep well when he's on a case, does he?"

"I think part of it was his time in the RN," Fletcher answered. "You tend to get into a cycle and at times, and you fall back into old habits. I used to have the same issue as a Marine."

"You still do," Inspector Gordon with a nudge to Fletcher.

Just then Doctor O'Rourke emerged from the operating room area. Walking over to where the officers had gathered, he pulled his cap off and swiped it across his brow before speaking. "You don't look like you're the patient's family.... Garda then?"

"Inspector Quinn," the Irish officer said, standing for the surgeon. "This is Officer Burke."

"Who's he?" the doctor asked, motioning to McDermott.

"Chief Inspector Conor McDermott of Scotland Yard," Andrew replied. "I'm his partner, Inspector Fletcher. This is Inspector Gordon and Sergeant Giles of Police-Scotland."

"And the patient?" Quinn asked.

"He's sedated as you can imagine," the doctor said. "He took quite a beating. Just enough damage so he'd need surgery, but not enough for anything permanent. Still, he'll be on a liquid diet for the next few months, I'm afraid."

The conversation was enough to wake McDermott from his slumber. "When can we see him?" he asked groggily, reaching for the tea. "He's a suspect in a major investigation and I need answers."

"You can see him later today, but for now, he's in recovery," O'Rourke said. "Come back in say," he looked looking at the clock, "six hours... nine o'clock should do. Now, if you'll excuse me, I've a wager to pay off."

"We'll need a room for the evening," McDermott said, getting to his feet as the doctor headed back down the hallway.

"You can follow Sheila and I; we're at The Limerick and the police station is right around the corner," Fletcher said.

"Let's go then," McDermott said. "Quinn, are you heading back to Dublin?"

"I'll be staying till after we identify Connelly," the Irish officer said. "And from what I learned while you were sleeping, the Immigration inspectors have detained Roan Callaghan. Seems during their search of the Dublin offices, they found a separate ledger in his safe. It was filled with noted payments to various institutes for staff members to enter the country."

"Not enough chemists in Ireland to go around, I guess," Sergeant Giles said dryly.

"It's what they were being asked to do that could be the issue, Sergeant," Quinn said. "Also, Internal Affairs for Garda is looking into several former officers who assisted him based on a handful of letters they found, as well. I suspect they helped to get documents forged to pass muster at the airports or ferry terminals."

"Seems you'll be having your hands full then," McDermott said, stepping out into the evening air. As the six officers walked out of the hospital, he followed Sergeant Giles to their rental car and slid into the passenger seat. "Officer Burke, we'll be following you back to the hotel."

***

Pacing the hospital corridor, McDermott waited for Dr. O'Rourke to finish his post-recovery check of his patient. Inspector Fletcher and Sergeant Giles sat near the nurse's post and Garda Inspector Quinn was engaged with someone in Dublin talking on his cell phone.

A nurse soon left the room, followed by the surgeon. "You can see the patient, Inspector," O'Rourke said, motioning behind him. "But he won't be making any confessions for the next six weeks, I'm afraid."

"He's already done that for me," McDermott said as he pushed past the doctor.

Lying in bed and propped up with pillows, Michael Connelly's face was still bandaged, but his eyes were exposed enough to see who stood before him. The EKG monitor chirping quickened as the Irishman noticed McDermott enter.

"Seems you've had a nasty fall, Connelly," McDermott said as Fletcher and Quinn entered behind him. "Any chance you can give us a wee idea who did this?"

Connelly looked up, shaking his head slowly from side to side.

"Well then," McDermott began, pulling the chair closer to the bed, "now that I've got you in a position to listen, you'll enjoy this wee bit of news." Connelly turned his head to see the others in the room. By the door, a nurse stood watching.

"You see, Inspector Fletcher there," he continued, pointing to Andrew, "he found your dope; all of it," McDermott said, not hiding his satisfaction for recovering the hashish. "We found out you were trying to be your own drug dealer. Quite noble of you to get young folk hooked on the drugs then producing the anecdote for the hospitals to administer. But you couldn't dae it alone. We know you've had a couple of Asian chemists helping you too."

Connelly pointed to the nurse and waved her over. As she stepped to the opposite side of the bed from McDermott, Connelly motioned he wanted to write something. Giving up her notepad and pen to the Irishman, he slowly scribbled out four words, *Good luck proving that*, and turned it to show McDermott.

"Aye, I'm sure you think we've nae proof," he replied. "You see though, we've got you on telly at the zoo meeting the sea captain. And we've his testimony from the court that you requested he take the dope from the French freighter. And let's not forget your barrister and his notes."

Connelly lay in the bed listening, struggling to control his emotions as the chief inspector described what had happened. He was aware his barrister Gilmore had files, but he never learned of their contents since Blayne Taggert's arrest.

"Aye, and there's more. See, I've saved the best for last," McDermott said. "Your conversation with your friend in South Africa, it was captured and documented. We've passed his information to INTERPOL. I'm sure they'll be interested in his business dealings, too."

As the Scotland Yard inspector described having identified his friend Kurt VanHoorst, Connelly's head sank back in the pillow. He realized his desires to redeem his family's status in Ireland's history had come at a price too great to pay. And his vision of commanding his own armed force to quell any of the Protestant uprisings was fading with each spoken word from McDermott.

"I'm going to leave you in the capable hands of Inspector Quinn here until we can have you presented in court," McDermott said, pushing his chair back. "Not only will you answer for what you've done, but what you had Angus Dunbar do. You'll serve a long stretch of time, and when you're done," the chief inspector said, "I'll see you do another ten years just for good measure."

Chapter THIRTY-EIGHT

Edinburgh, Scotland

The weeks after discovering the container full of drugs and Connelly's arrest went by with little fanfare. However, the last week of the trial was anything but dull. The audience of the courtroom kept their conversations down as members shifted in their seats.

In the front row, Chief Inspector McDermott sat, his gaze fixated on the door behind the judge's bench. Sitting to his left was Priscilla El-Sayed, and to his right, the juror's box was empty for the moment while the court clerk and reporter prepared for the official party to enter.

Separate tables for the plaintiff and the defendant and their legal counsel sat occupied. The barrister for the Crown, George Hamilton was busy jotting down a few notes while the barrister representing Michael Connelly had yet to appear. The murmur of the audience grew as the Irishman's counselor made his appearance.

With the help of his assistant, Desmond McGrew made his way to the table opposite the prosecution team. He eased himself into the chair, and with an audible sigh, he swiped his brow with a handkerchief before opening his briefcase.

Several moments passed before everyone heard a creaking as the door behind the jurors' seats opened. In moments, twelve citizens of Aberdeen and the surrounding community filed in and sat in their respective chairs. While the assembled jurors prepared themselves for the day's proceedings, a constable appeared next to the judge's bench.

The friend and colleague of Sean Gilmore felt uncomfortable sitting behind the railing in the courtroom. "I didn't think this day would ever come about," Priscilla murmured in McDermott's direction.

McDermott patted his hand gently on her knee. "You have tae remember, the doctor said Connelly would need six to seven weeks until his jaw heals," McDermott replied, his gaze unwavering. "Besides, Mister Hamilton told me Lady Callaway wanted nothing mucking up his testimony."

"For all that, he didn't say much yesterday," Priscilla said, pulling a pad onto her lap to take notes. "You would think someone facing the charges brought up would have a stronger argument." McDermott had told her what the Irishman was being arraigned for in court.

"With the evidence we had against him, he'd nae chance to fight against it," the inspector said. "Besides, we've also had the material showing he orchestrated Dunbar's actions." Looking at the notepad on the woman's lap, he added, "Always the barrister?" McDermott asked.

"Always inspector," the Saudi woman answered. She never missed a chance to critique fellow barristers during a trial; she felt it gave her an advantage in winning her cases. In the margin, she placed a few notes down in Farsi while waiting for the judge to appear.

Just before they announced the official party, someone brought in Michael Connelly to the room in a wheelchair, his leg held up while it continued to heal. Clothed in the traditional brown sweatshirt and mottled green pants, he glanced about the audience, noting who was present. Wheeled alongside his barrister, the constable unlocked the handcuffs from his wheelchair, then re-attached them to the table.

"All rise," the constable announced. "The Honourable Lady Theresa Callaway of Her Majesty's Court and, the Honorable Justice John Morris of the Central Criminal Court of Ireland presiding," he introduced each of the judges.

"As heard in previous...." Lady Callaway said, beginning her opening remarks to set in motion the day's session. For the next thirty minutes the judge recapped what had transpired. Recalling testimonies from Sean Gilmore and Captain Clive Duncan to accounts from Chief Inspector McDermott, Inspector Fletcher, and other members of law enforcement.

"Mister Morris, do you wish to add anything before we continue?" she asked her colleague sitting next to her.

"Yes, I do, Lady Callaway," the Irish judge said acknowledging the Scottish member of the High Court. Judge Morris added his observations and opinion on the proceedings before relinquishing the floor. "In closing, it is the position of the Central Criminal Court of Ireland to abstain from imposing any request for extradition for trial of the defendant," he said. "And that any sentencing or imposition of penalties pertaining to drug trafficking charges be retained by Her

Majesty's High Court," he concluded, handing over jurisdiction to Lady Callaway.

Michael Connelly sat stone-faced, listening to what was being said but not hearing the words. Since McDermott's visit to the hospital back in Limerick, he knew his defeat was imminent. The only concern he had now was whether his barrister, Desmond McGrew, could convince the judge to have him serve his time in Northern Ireland.

Lady Callaway motioned to the prosecuting barrister from the Aberdeen Sheriff's Office. "Mister Hamilton, do you have counsel's recommendation for sentencing prepared?" she queried, looking towards to the barrister.

"Yes, we are, Lady Callaway. Based on the evidence presented and the jury's findings of the party being guilty of conspiracy..." he continued. Hamilton spent the next few minutes outlining the charges the jury cast their votes on for sentencing time. "In closing, it is the wish of this court that maximum time be given to the pannel based on the current laws of Her Majesty's Court."

This was a mere formality as the Sheriff's Court members had already prepared their recommendations based on the testimony. Each charge was identified and given a specific time frame which Connelly would serve. The total duration was twenty-eight years for solicitation of drug trafficking and fifteen additional years for soliciting the act of murder by another individual.

Forty-three years, Connelly thought to himself. He knew he'd never see Ireland again if he lived out the sentencing. Turning his head slightly, he glimpsed at McDermott sitting next to Miss El-Sayed, knowing any chance of redemption was now denied.

The slamming of the judge's gavel caused him to jump in the wheelchair as Lady Callaway acknowledged the sentencing recommendation from the prosecution. "Mister Morris, do you have any comments?" she asked.

"Lady Callaway, the Central Criminal Court of Ireland, retains the right to prosecute the defendant on the charge of treason and conducting the recruitment of others for said activities," Morris said, sealing Connelly's judicial fate in Ireland. "However, since the majority of criminal activities undertaken by the pannel took place within the

Crown's jurisdiction, we shall hold our request until said time has been adequately served."

"Let the court proceedings show the Central Criminal Court of Ireland's declaration," Lady Callaway said. "Upon the completion of sentences imposed by this court, the pannel will be transferred to the custody of Garda Síochána for imposition of charges brought forth by the Central Criminal Court, but will not include those charges already served."

Desmond McGrew leaned over and whispered something into the Irishman's ear. Seeing him acknowledge what they said, McGrew backed his chair from the table and pushed himself upright with the help of his associate. "Lady Callaway, on behalf of my client, we wish to acknowledge the jury's decision. I'd like the record to reflect we will submit an appeal forthwith," he said in an attempt to curtail the proceedings.

Steading himself against the table, the portly Irishman continued with his time. "My client also asks Her Ladyship to consider administering sentencing with the greatest possible leniency. According to the doctor's exams, my client requires months of rehabilitation because of ailments incurred through no fault of his own."

"Let the record note Mister McGrew's request," the judge replied. Lady Callaway's assistant took down several notes while the stenographer spoke into her microphone, dictating the statement for the court's record. "Your client will find that the Scottish Prison Service are well staffed with medical professionals and he should be up and walking in no time. Do you have anything else to add?"

Looking down at Connelly, who held his gaze ahead, the barrister responded. "No, Lady Callaway, we do not," he replied, leaning on the table to keep himself upright.

Lady Callaway finished going through the motions of sentencing Michael Connelly. "The defendant will serve the duration of his sentence at Her Majesty's Prison in the village of Glenochil. Time will be served concurrently on all sentences," she added, showing a sense of civility to the Irishman. With a swing of her gavel, the court proceedings ended.

"All rise," the constable declared.

As they led away the official party, the audience filed out. Standing in the hallway, Inspector Fletcher and Sergeant's Giles and Holmes moved off to one side. McDermott spotted his partner and led Priscilla El-Sayed toward the officers.

"Connelly will be old and grey when he gets out, won't he?" Priscilla asked.

"Aye, if he survives his time in prison," McDermott replied. "It's a shame they're giving him his time side-by-side, though. We'd been better off having him serve the time in one long stretch."

"You're not worried about the appeals his lawyer will file?"

McDermott peered over his shoulder at the now empty courtroom. "I'm a firm believer that we've got things well in hand." he said. "Besides, Mister Hamilton and I arranged for the Irishman to remain in custody as a flight risk."

"So, we can close this case?" Fletcher asked as McDermott and Miss El-Sayed joined them.

"Aye, this chapter we can," McDermott said. Loosening his tartan tie and pulling it free, he added, "We've still got a few loose ends in the force to tie off." He looked at Sergeant Holmes, with a nod. "You've something for me?"

"Here you are," Holmes replied, pulling an evidence packet from his bag.

McDermott took it, handing it straight to the Saudi woman. "I keep my word when I can. This belongs to you and Mister Gilmore."

Priscilla took the envelope and pulled the security tape off the flap. Glancing inside, she saw not one, but two folders. "Thank you, Chief Inspector, I'll see they're returned in due time."

"I greatly appreciate your assistance, Sergeant Holmes," McDermott said, extending his hand.

"No worries, Chief Inspector," Holmes replied, shaking hands with McDermott before turning to Inspector Fletcher. "Mister Fletcher, a pleasure," he finished, shaking Andrew's hand.

"Sergeant Giles, it's time to head home," McDermott announced. Turning to Priscilla, he stepped forward and embraced her. "Don't be a stranger; you'll be welcome in Aberdeen anytime," he promised, pulling away.

"Thank you," she replied swiping a tear from her eye. "Thank you all. If you'll excuse me gentlemen, I've a case to prepare for."

Dawdling behind the woman as she made her way to the lift, Inspector Fletcher pondered if now was the proper time to inform McDermott of his decision to leave Scotland Yard and join the Police Scotland office in Aberdeen. The last five months had allowed him to grow close to Sheila, and he didn't want to leave.

McDermott glanced at his partner and could sense something was on his mind. "It'll keep until tomorrow, Andrew," he reassured him, patting him on the shoulder. "Let's catch our breath for one night before diving into something else."

As the officers stepped out of the Sheriff's office, they were greeted with grey skies. A soft mist was falling, and off in the distance below Edinburgh Castle, a host of colorful umbrellas could be seen as visitors strolled through the park.

Pulling up the collar of his field coat, Conor smiled. "Aye, it's bonnie a fine day to see someone put behind a wall," McDermott chuckled as he skipped down the steps toward their car.

Chapter THIRTY-NINE

Aberdeen, Scotland

Chief Inspector McDermott and his partner sat opposite each other in their office, working to complete their respective reports. Fletcher stopped typing and flexed his arm, rubbing the area where Blayne Taggert had caught him with his knife.

"Still bugging you?" McDermott asked.

"This damn scar itches," he explained, rolling his shirt sleeve up to expose the bandage.

"Be glad you've still an arm there," McDermott said before returning to his report. With each laborious stab of his fingers, he filled in the blanks. Documenting the events surrounding their case was a necessary evil in police work, but Conor compounded its difficulty since he hardly took any notes. "You've got those dates from our first trip to Belfast?"

Fletcher glanced over his computer, shaking his head. "Did the seamen on the Edinburgh follow you around jotting down orders?" he asked with a snicker.

"Mind your manners, Left-tenant Fletcher. I still outrank you," McDermott replied, grasping the notepad his partner handed to him. "Besides, didn't you have a corporal do the same for you?" he prodded his fellow inspector.

Before Fletcher could answer, Sergeant McKee stuck her head through the doorway. "Excuse me, sirs, but Mister MacCallum wants you to join him in the conference hall," the woman announced. McDermott and Fletcher both exchanged a look of puzzlement and uncertainty.

"Don't forget to save your file," Fletcher pointed out to his partner. "Or you'll be here all night re-typing it." He pulled his shirt sleeve down before slipping on his sport coat.

"Aye, I'll dictate while you type, too," McDermott replied, selecting the option to save the report. Grabbing his field coat, he was soon catching up with his partner entering the stairwell.

"How do I look?"

"Like a first-year pupil heading to secondary school," McDermott replied.

"After you," Fletcher said, pulling the door open leading to the second-floor hallway.

The officers walked out and strolled the last few meters to the conference room where Sergeant Giles stood waiting with his fellow sergeant, Annie McKee.

"Morning, Marcus," Fletcher said. "Any idea what we're in store for?"

"No clue, Inspector," he replied, pulling open the door. Letting Sergeant McKee enter first, the three others fell in behind to follow. The conference room wasn't empty as Chief Superintendent MacCallum stood at the far end with several other senior officers. McDermott and Fletcher soon noticed one was their supervisor from London, Will Collingsworth.

"McDermott, Fletcher, and Giles, front and center if you please," MacCallum said.

The three officers made their way forward as the invited crowd filed in and gathered behind them. Several of the civilians who were invited took seats to the left while uniformed officers loosely formed ranks to the opposite side.

"Thank you all for accepting the invitation," MacCallum began. Over the next few minutes, the senior officer introduced the dignitaries and recognized the important members of the audience.

"It is my distinct pleasure to officiate this event," he said. "At this time, I'd like to call attention to the following officer, Sergeant Marcus Giles... With the concurrence of the Chief Constable and the board of regents, I hereby designate you for promotion to the rank of Inspector with immediate effect," he announced, stepping forward to present the officer with his certificate. The audience broke out in a raucous applause as Chief Superintendent MacCallum stepped back and saluted the newly promoted member of the force.

Stepping behind the podium, MacCallum calmed the audience then addressed McDermott and Fletcher. "Chief Inspector McDermott and Inspector Fletcher, on behalf of the Chief Constable..." he began, reading the citation for their role in apprehending Michael Connelly and halting a major drug trafficking operation. Once again, the audience showed their appreciation by breaking out in applause. MacCallum turned to his friend and colleague. "Superintendent Collingsworth, I believe you've something to add."

The senior officer with Metropolitan Police stepped forward, beginning his dialogue, which echoed his praise for the accomplishments not only by McDermott and Fletcher, but the officers of Police-Scotland. "So, by direction from the Commissioner of Metropolitan Police and the Chief Constable of Police Scotland, I'm pleased to announce establishment of a permanent office here in Aberdeen."

In the back row of the constables, Inspector Sheila Gordon reached down and squeezed the hand of her friend Annie McKee as a tear rolled down her cheek. Hearing the news gave her hope that Andrew would decide to remain in Aberdeen.

As the applause ended, Collingsworth continued. "Chief Inspector McDermott and Inspector Fletcher will initially man this office until the Commissioner deems their reassignment necessary because of promotion or manning concerns," he explained, setting both into their new roles. "Any objections, gentlemen?"

Both McDermott and Fletcher exchanged glances. "No, sir," they replied in unison.

Collingsworth stepped around from the podium and shook hands with both men. "You've done a fine job on this one. The Commissioner was quite pleased to see your civility with the Garda Síochána, Conor," he added.

"And what about Callaghan?" McDermott asked.

"After the Garda found his hidden files on the payoffs to the immigration folks, Roan Callaghan was arrested with an assortment of charges," Collingsworth said.

"Explains why he wasn't present for Connelly's trial," Fletcher said, shrugging his shoulders.

"But today's news is not all rosy, I'm afraid," Collingsworth said. "Just before leaving London, they informed me Constable Ethan Taylor has gone missing again. Internal Affairs hasn't ruled out someone might have tipped him off somehow. Or Inspector Gordon's call spooked him perhaps."

"So, knowing his uncle is sitting in a cell, we've got to figure out what his next step is?" Fletcher asked.

"Not you," Collingsworth replied. "Even though he's a suspect in your case, you'll both let IA chaps handle things from here. I imagine you'll be busy having an office to prepare and manage."

Approaching the three men, Chief Superintendent MacCallum stood a few paces away until they saw him waiting to speak. "If you'll excuse me gentlemen, the constables have arranged for a wee reception in the break room."

"Safe to say there's no whisky to be had?" McDermott asked with a chuckle.

"No, that'll come later when you buy the first round," MacCallum replied, walking away.

With the pleasantries of the occasion complete, the officers returned to their respective duties, which for McDermott and Fletcher, meant completing their reports. Pulling out his chair, McDermott prepared to open his drawer but stopped. "So, Andrew, when were you planning on telling me you would transfer?" he asked, gazing at his partner.

"I wasn't sure when it would be a good time to be honest," Andrew replied. "How'd you know I was considering a transfer, anyway? I had told no one around here; not even Sheila."

"Just a feeling, I suppose," Conor said. "But it does nae matter now, does it?"

"No… I guess it doesn't," Andrew said with a brief smile on his face.

The sergeant's and inspector's area soon returned to normal as they could hear officers interviewing their suspects, whose handcuffs rattled on steel chairs. While questions were being asked and answers given, the keyboard clicks continued, reports flipped over on their clipboards.

Lost in their own thoughts as they completed their work, McDermott and Fletcher did not notice a constable standing in the doorway to their office. A sudden rap on the jamb caught their attention. "Excuse me, sirs, I've a message from the Sheriff's office for you," the young man said.

"Thank you, Constable Jeffries," Fletcher replied, taking hold of the note.

McDermott was grateful for the brief interruption. "How's the recovery of your back coming along?"

"It's getting better, Inspector, thanks," Jeffries answered. "The physio-types said I'll be able to get back to cycling soon. The lorry company has already made amends for the accident, and they've pulled all stops for replacing my bike too," he added before turning away.

McDermott shook his head. "Who'd thought you'd be laid up just by getting clipped by a bumper?"

Fletcher heard his partner, but didn't acknowledge his comment. He was reading the notice from the officer. "Mister St. James has listed the members of the Standard-Apollo and Nordic Supplier being released," he read, waving the note for a moment. "Seems they couldn't find cause to have them remain in custody for any of the drug trafficking."

McDermott leaned back in his chair, eyes closed. "I'll nae understand the courts, Andrew," shaking his head. We've got the drugs; the crew members were all on the boat; it's pretty simple to me they're involved."

"Looking at this, they're still holding the senior members from the Apollo: captain, first officer, and the engineer," Andrew replied. "I guess we can be thankful for that much, right?"

McDermott ran his hand across his face. "It still bothers me on how they move the drugs though," he said, leaning forward. "It gets shipped in glass bottles, and off-loaded to an oil derrick. Then it's cooked and re-bottled into a cylinder and brought ashore."

"You want to know the next step after the boats?"

"Aye, I do," Conor said. "This drug problem is no going away anytime soon. And we need to get smarter on how the drug types are being fed, and by whom." He let out a dejected sigh. "And I'm afraid this is just one drug in a handful we'll probably encounter, too."

"You don't think the French can give us any help?" Andrew asked. "This current mess began with them, you remember?"

"But they're not the only ones," Conor said. "You've got the dope addicts who want their heroin or cocaine, youngsters wanting to smoke pot at concerts, and worse, the poor folks getting hooked by the chemists and doctors."

"I guess we just take them on one at a time," Andrew said, returning to his report.

Chapter FORTY

Edinburgh, Scotland

After returning to her office in Edinburgh, Priscilla El-Sayed sat in quiet reflection. The events of the last few months reminded her there was evil lurking throughout the world. And try as she might to avoid it, sometimes evilness catches people by surprise.

Slipping her hand into the satchel, she removed the files Chief Inspector McDermott returned to her earlier in the day. The top folder was still in the evidence bag, sealed and safe. The other sat loose, its contents a haunting reminder of one man's dark past. "I'm not sure I want to know how you got this information, Sean," she said to the empty office. "But I hope you destroy this." She took the folder labeled DUNBAR and sliding it into her credenza.

"You on the other hand," she continued, holding the file of Adrian Richelieu. "You seem to be an enigma." She quickly took a letter opener to the seal and broke it. Laying the closed folder on her desk, she picked up her cup and sipped her tea. *What will I find inside?* she contemplated. She waited a little before setting her cup down and flipping it over to open it.

Someone had printed the first three pages from an internet site. Scanning them briefly, Priscilla was surprised to see they were more a history lesson surrounding a French industrialist. The fourth page she saw was a link to another world though.

"You are not who you say you are," she declared, seeing the grainy picture staring back at her. The rugged looks of an archeologist-type man met her gaze. The close-cropped haircut and deep tanned face held no emotion, yet conveyed confidence.

Before she could turn the photo over, Priscilla's assistant Paul knocked on the door, interrupting her examination of the file. Flipping the folder closed, she slid it into her desk drawer as the door opened.

Sticking his head through the doorway, the young man explained his intrusion. "I apologize for interrupting, but you've a visitor, Pri," he started, opening the door for her visitor to enter.

"That's all right, Paul," Priscilla said as she got up from her chair.

Louis Clement waited until the young assistant stepped aside before entering. "Thank you," he spoke, striding past Paul. "I apologize for not making an appointment Miss El-Sayed, but my client wished for me to thank you for your efforts in a recent case."

Priscilla stared over her desk at the Frenchman. "I apologize, but you've got me at a loss. Which client? Was it the McGuire case by chance?" she asked, recalling a nasty tenant-landlord dispute she worked.

"No, mademoiselle," the Frenchman replied. "This was the case against Mister Higgins," Louis said, his expression deadpan as he mentioned the Irishman by his alias. "My client was pleased to see your resilience in facing such a despicable fellow. And he can say with absolute certainty you will have no worries of reprisal... ever."

The last word hung in the air, the tone in the Frenchman's delivery providing a resounding sense of finality to Priscilla's situation. *Is it over?* she contemplated. "I see," she replied. "Am I to assume your client is guaranteeing my safety in this matter?"

Louis stood before answering. "He is a man of his word. The creed he lives by is 'Honneur et Fidélité,' Honor and fidelity," he recited. "If you'll please excuse me now, I've another appointment to keep."

Accepting his outstretched hand, Priscilla shook it briefly. "You've not mentioned your client's name."

Louis Clement paused. "His name is Monsieur Richelieu," he nodded his head slightly. "Have a pleasant day, mademoiselle."

Priscilla watched the mysterious Frenchman exit and then glanced at her desktop, knowing what lay inside. Collapsing in her chair, her hand trembled as she reached for the drawer handle. "I might want to keep a copy of this," she muttered, opening the drawer to reveal the folder compiled by Sean Gilmore.

***

Several days after completing their case files, someone in Metro gave both McDermott and Fletcher a few days' holiday. Relaxing in his friend's fish and chip shop, McDermott sat, finishing his beer. "Sadie, can you add another to me tab?" he shouted above the din.

"This is your second, Conor," the young Jamaican woman said as she set the can down.

"Aye, I know," he replied, opening the lager. Taking a gulp, he was soon attacking the rest of his fish supper. Stabbing the last few chips with a fork, he glanced up to see Malcolm Smythe leaning against the counter.

"You all right, Conor?"

Putting the food down, Conor took another swig of his beer, sending some dribbling down his chin before replying. "Aye, Malcolm, I'm fine," he replied while suppressing a belch. "I've agreed to a wee chat with the family."

Malcolm had seen his friend in this condition before. It was when Conor returned from the Mediterranean deployment while in the Royal Navy, the same one where Malcolm's younger brother died. Conor was full of guilt having not kept his friend's brother safe. But the Smythe family didn't hold Conor responsible for Kyle's death, even though he did.

Finishing the can of beer, Conor stood and emptied everything from the tray into the trash bin just as the newly promoted Inspector Giles entered. "Perfect timing, Marcus," Conor said. "Malcolm, my driver has arrived."

"You'll see he's safe?" Malcolm asked the officer.

"Aye, he's in good hands for the moment," Giles replied, following Conor to the car.

After a short drive, Giles was pulling off the road outside the Newhills Cemetery. Looking at his passenger, the inspector had his concerns for his fellow officer. "Are you going to be okay, Conor?" he asked.

McDermott turned to face Giles. "Aye, I'm fine Marcus. Thank you for doing this for me, by the way," he said as he picked up the bouquet of flowers from the back seat. "I'll be seeing myself back to the town, so you did nae have to wait," he explained before opening the door and stepping onto the gravel parking area.

Closing the door, Conor McDermott slowly sauntered through the wrought-iron gates of the cemetery. Off in the distance, he could see a family gathering near the resting place of a loved one. His chest heaved and he fought back his tears as he drew closer to where a gentleman stood.

Duncan Gallagher watched from his daughter's grave site as his nephew passed through the gates. Conor stopped long enough to dip his hand in the stone font of holy water and bless himself. As he sauntered passed other grave markers, Duncan noticed his nephew keep his head bowed.

As Conor drew close to the gravesite where his niece was laid to rest, he saw his uncle standing to one side. He wound his way up the grassy knoll, reading the names of several headstones, noting the dates and calculating the age when people passed away.

Conor knelt down as he reached the granite marker designating Edna Gallagher's final resting place and placed the bouquet below the stone. "I'm sorry I was nae there for you," he stammered as tears rolled down his cheeks. "I'd try to do the best for you if I could have." Fighting back his tears, Conor patted the gravestone, saying a silent prayer before doing the sign of the cross and getting to his feet.

"You couldn't prevent what happened, Conor," Duncan said, placing his hand on the shoulder of his nephew. "She was growing up and had a mind of her own. I was wrong to accuse you. I was wrong about blaming you for Catherine's death too," he continued, mentioning Conor's mother.

"And the family? What are their thoughts?" Conor asked as he wiped his hand across his face.

"You'll be welcome home when you're ready, son," Duncan said, reaching out to Conor and embracing him. "You'll always be welcome," he whispered shedding his own tears.

*** THE END ***

Thank you for reading my book. If you enjoyed it, won't you please take a moment to leave me a review at your favorite retailer?
Thanks!
Anthony Harrison

Acknowledgements

First and foremost, I'd like to thank my wife, Mary, for letting me scratch this itch called writing and for supporting me with her comments and encouragement, even after I locked myself away for hours at a time.

Next, to my good friend and co-worker, Doretta Burgess, for providing the first level of sanity checks, grammar checks and being that punctuation pundit on all my many pages of random thoughts.

To Cecily of Red Pen Editor who consistently works magic with her reviews, catching my silly mistakes and making my story come to life.

To my friend and fellow motorcyclist, Rob for taking my ideas and descriptions for the cover and getting it right.

About the Author

Anthony Harrison is a first generation American and native Californian, the son of Scottish immigrants, and who's fraternal grandparents hailed from Ireland.

A product of a mixed education (part parochial and part public schools), he developed a thirst for reading early in his childhood, and took to writing fiction as an escape from his work as an Instructional Systems Designer.

When not working on improving his writing, Anthony can be found on the local golf course, honing his game invented by his ancestors.

Other titles by Anthony J. Harrison:

The Irishman's Deception - A Conor McDermott Novel

Betrayed by a Scot – A Conor McDermott Novel

Suspicious by Design – A Geneviève Benoit Novel

Obscure Intentions - A Geneviève Benoit Novel

Provide your comments or feedback at;

mailto:fairwayscribe@gmail.com